Black Treachery

David Wooden

Published; Netwave Publishing

ISBN 978 1 9164728 0 8

Preface

Man is devious. To outwit, deceive, obscure and mislead are inherent traits. Over the centuries, codes, ciphers and secret messages have been employed in many forms.

Consider this ....

..................and how to solve it?

Chapter 1

What was he doing here?

The dining table was a mess. Numerous bottles of wine had taken their toll on both the table and many of the ten guests now currently sprawled around it.

Mrs. Younghusband, the wife of Captain Younghusband of His Majesty's Royal Navy was no exception. Looking across the table Peachey said,

'You are expecting your husband shortly then Mrs. Younghusband?'

Holding his gaze she replied

'a week or so Mr. Peachey I imagine. Much depends on the winds and sea condition as I'm sure you'd appreciate.'

Peachey nodded, keeping his gaze fixed on the woman.

She felt flushed with the wine but more so from the avid attention she was receiving from this newly arrived visitor. She continued

'Thank you for dinning with us tonight Mr. Peachey as I'm sure you are in great demand by London society, especially the ladies'.

'Not at all Maam. I was delighted and honoured to be asked. The company and beauty of the ladies here tonight is second to none. Who would wish to dine elsewhere?'

She smiled at his gracious remark. The eyes that looked back at her across the table were steely blue that twinkled as he verbally jostled with her. Here was a young man of 26 addressing her not as the wife of a Naval Captain and a woman several years his senior, but as one might to a society girl of his own age in London.

She felt very flattered.

He leant back in his chair and sipped his wine, with each movement being slow, deliberate and showing the poise of a gentleman very much at ease with himself and his surroundings. The dark blue of a jacket, of which his tailor would be proud, contrasted with the white breeches and silver buckled black shoes. His attire retained its elegance in spite of a long eventful meal.

Of the five ladies present, Mrs. Younghusband was the second youngest; that attribute belonging to her niece sitting at the far end of the table, looking like a startled rabbit and stunned from boredom from the monotonous ramblings of the besotted retired Admiral to her left. The remaining three ladies were more interested in jostling for supremacy in the female pecking order than courting attention from the remaining far from attentive males.

Mrs Younghusband said

'You are too kind Mr. Peachey I'm sure the honour is ours. Our gatherings must be dull compared with the splendour that society in London must offer you.'

'I can assure you madam that my interests have been fully exercised here'.

He smiled and raised the wine glass in a gentle toast. She dropped her eyes but raised her glass in response.

Studying her again, he felt the lace cap on her black curled hair was in keeping with her fashionable dress offset with a pale blue overskirt. Whilst not being an advocate of fashion, he had been aware that the trend amongst London ladies was for simpler gowns and styles far removed from the elaborate bulbous creations that had been the rage for several years now.

Peachey was feeling decidedly mellow, but his inbuilt sense of duty whispered that now was the time to retreat. It was not that the captain's wife was unattractive or unappealing but his real goal was a closer professional acquaintance with her husband, a Post Captain with high seniority and a forecast of promotion in the wind. Dalliance with his wife was not the best recipe for furthering his contact with this man.

She, however, sensing the mental signals from the other ladies, rose and said

'I think it is time for the ladies to retire gentlemen.'

There was a mixed response from the diners. The ladies rose, some of the men like Peachey readily stood up, others staggered to their feet and the besotted lawyer opposite made a vain effort. More of a gesture actually, with one hand on the table and the other on the back of his chair he mumbled and adopted a slightly raised stance. The ladies led by Mrs. Younghusband weaved their way out.

Regrouping around one end of the table the men refilled their glasses. Peachey eyed them again. There was nobody who appealed to him socially, or could assist him as a useful contact. In fact, time to leave.

The talk was desultory, with two of the gentlemen having lost the battle with numerous bottles of wine consumed before and during the meal, preferring slumber to discourse.

The dinner having started as usual at 3pm had reached 6.30pm, and was now in somewhat of a stalemate position. Peachey had many things to do. His principal goal had been more or less achieved.

Further time was needed to cultivate associations, but time was not a commodity he presently had. The most single factor that governed his stay at Portsmouth was this time factor. Too much had already elapsed for his liking and his task here in Portsmouth was seemingly impossible. He stood and addressed the other diners.

'A thousand apologies gentlemen but I fear I must take my leave of you.'

The recumbent lawyer opposite suddenly appeared awake and said

'We were having such good conversation Peachey.'

Since the man had been comatose from start to finish Peachey felt that this was overstating things somewhat.

Various other mutterings were offered.

Peachey signalled to the hovering manservant to advise that he wanted to take his leave from Mrs. Younghusband. The man disappeared from the room and Peachey bade final farewells. By the time he reached the door, the manservant had returned and indicated that Peachey should follow him.

The room to which the ladies had retired was adjacent, with chairs grouped around two small highly polished walnut tables. There was an air of expectancy as he entered, with an aroma of recent gossip lingering in the air. The topic looked as though it may well have been him.

Reaching out her hand the captain's wife said

'We are sorry you have to leave us Mr. Peachey. It is infrequent that we have guests with current London gossip and fashion here in Portsmouth. No doubt you have other pressing engagements to fulfil.'

'Matters of business I'm afraid dear lady. It had to be to force me to drag myself away from such charming company.'

Looking from one to the other he smiled to each as he gently placed his lips on the proffered hands.

'Perhaps we shall see more of Mr. Peachey as he is staying in Portsmouth' she continued.

'I shall be pleased to call dear lady on as many occasions as I can during my stay. I cannot predict how long that may be though. Much depends on how my business plans develop.'

Peachey was feeling his business plans were vague to say the least, his uncle Sir Richard Peachey only providing scant information about a French plot centred on Portsmouth. Information based solely on incomplete and inconsistent word passed back from France from one of his informants.

The information was clear overall, but totally lacking in detail. So much so, that at London's Court of St. James, it was not taken seriously by King George III who was struggling to contain the problems of rebellion in the thirteen colonies in America.

The other multiplicity of spies and agents in France had produced no word at all to support this plot in Portsmouth. If there were such a plot, it was reasoned that word would be forthcoming from several sources.

With this lack of verification it was considered to be insignificant and lacked tangible support and credence from King George and his advisors.

Sir Richard however, no matter how sceptical the information appeared, was prepared to stake his life on the reliability of his informer. However, he was too wily a character to run the gauntlet against the opinion of the king and his advisors. Any investigation of a plot must be undertaken quietly and by un-attributable men.

One gentleman looking to his future was Sir Richard's nephew, one Henry Peachey. A man of independent means but not wealthy, with a weather eye to the future and in particular to Sir Richard's title and estates.

It was thus that Henry Peachey found himself in the garrison town of Portsmouth, a walled town defending the approach to the Royal Navy's fleet and harbouring shipbuilding and repair activities. If nothing, its geographical location was unique.

The approach to the narrow harbour entrance had to be navigated down a strict approach or be promptly run aground.   The harbour entrance was only a few hundred yards across, defended on one side by the heavily fortified defences of Portsmouth with a corresponding battery of equal firepower across the entrance at Gosport. The whole area was shielded by the Isle of Wight providing a safe haven for His Majesty's ships moored at *St Helens Bay*.

This evening was the first social engagement since his arrival. With credentials and social cards of introduction such as he possessed, an invitation was readily forthcoming, and charming though she may be, it was not the wife but the captain that was the person he needed to see. Captain Younghusband's unavailability was a setback to his plans.

His other main objective was to meet with the Governor of Portsmouth. His introductory letter generally sought assistance for Peachey, at the same time not defining his actual purpose in the town.

Had Sir Richard elected to tell the Governor the truth about Henry Peachey's purpose, life might have been simpler, but *trust no one* had been his watchword. The real reason therefore necessarily complicated matters. The story that Henry Peachey was to proffer implied he was secretly probing into the affairs of certain victualers in the town, suspected of cheating the crown and in particular the Royal Navy.

Henry Peachey suspected the Governor would be singularly unimpressed with this story, as well he should. Victualers had been working in collusion for many years, to the point that it was generally accepted as normal practice. Nevertheless this was his uncle's scheme and one did not question Sir Richard on such matters.

Peachey felt the evening had only been a limited success, however it was a promising start, hopefully the captain would be of assistance once he arrived.

However, if Peachey knew what he was meant to be pursuing, how much easier life would be.

Bidding a final farewell, he left the room and followed the manservant down the stairs to the ground floor. The smell that had haunted him on his arrival still lingered. He now had it - it was beeswax. This had been added to the candles and gave off a pleasant, distinctive and evocative fragrance during burning. It was a demonstration of another interesting and pleasurable effect from the captain's wife. His fascination for her increased with every moment.

The servant gathered Peachey's cloak and hat, and handing it to him said

'Your manservant has been informed that you are leaving sir and awaits you outside.'

Donning the cloak Peachey nodded and stepped out into the early evening air pulling the cloak further round him. His manservant, Tom Fairweather stood at the bottom of the step swinging his arms to keep warm. His short tunic top, knee length breeches and socks had the added adornment of a scarf wrapped twice round his neck producing the appearance of a child's spinning top spiralling down to a point.

'A touch chilly sir.' A greeting accompanied by flayed arm movements.

'A brisk walk Fairweather will soon warm you up.'

Peachey strode ahead into *Penny St.* a long cobbled, fashionable road in the centre of the town. Distinctive houses being located at this end with three breweries at the top end, producing employment for the local workingmen and considerable profit to the owners.

Fairweather readily kept pace with his distinctive gait. His role this evening was not so much domestic assistance to his employer, but more physical protection should the need arise. Portsmouth was notorious for its concoction of elegance, squalor, refinement, debauchery, religious piety, thieves and press gangs. Walking the short distance to *The George Inn* even in daylight, might well present the chance for a footpad of relieving a Gentleman of his valuables.

Fairweather, raised in the back streets of London's Whitechapel, possessed an expert knowledge in the ignoble art of street warfare, utilising slick combinations of kicking, biting, eye poking and head butting. In all he was a very useful person to accompany a gentleman on such an evening.

His employment with Peachey now extended to over a year, yet with all his physical attributes, he nearly failed to meet Peachey's original expectations. This was predominantly due to the fact the where other men could use their fingers and thumbs to count to ten, Fairweather could only manage eight and a half.

His original employment had been working for Bothroyd & Company, high quality furniture makers. An accident in the workshop resulted in his losing his thumb and most of the index finger of his right hand; an event that caused his employment to be immediately terminated by the company. Craftsmen need complete control of their hands and fingers in order to make fine furniture. There was no sentiment in business.

This digit deficiency was not noticed by Peachy at the onset.   A week in his employment had passed before he saw Fairweather's shortcoming.   After Fairweather had respectfully pointed out that he had satisfactorily performed his duties for a week, Peachey agreed a further trial period to determine his suitability. The agreed trial fizzled out; no mention had ever been made about the subject again. Peachey for his part, never really noticed the lack of finger power again.   In fact the dexterity and adaptability of Fairweather's remaining fingers was a wonder to behold.

They continued up *Penny St* and turned left into *Fighting Cocks Lane*.   Never could a street be more aptly named. Money regularly changed hands based on results dictated by the combatant strutting cocks, each being cheered on by their supporters and fanciers.

Peachey was oblivious to the nefarious activities of the area as he headed for the *High St* in which *The George Inn* occupied pride of place.   The inns of the area catered for different clientele and were largely dependant on social standing, rank and money.   Royal Navy Captains lodged at *The George*, First Lieutenants at *The Dolphin* with Midshipman grouped together around the corner in *The Blue Posts*.

The civilian guests tended to group themselves very much in the same strata, a factor of which Peachey had been advised prior to making his own lodging arrangements.

The decision to stay at *The George Inn* was important to his mission. To support his story to the Governor and make contact with some victualers, arrangements had been made for him to pass himself off as an owner of two Privateers about to sail into Portsmouth and needing provisions. Such a person would stay at *The George* in order to make the right acquaintances, hence Peachey's location.

His uncle had carefully studied the information received from his French agent. It was however incomplete, lacking in names and detail, but of a certainty - reliable.   A major spy was living in Portsmouth who was very well connected, had a group of like-minded agents willing to further his aims, as long as it furthered theirs.   These took various forms.   Money was often the principal motivating force but the most deadly of the group were those who possessed the religious goal of Catholic re-instatement.

This was a mission supported and funded by the French despite there being a more tolerant approach being taken towards the active practice of the Roman Catholic faith.   It was only a small step admittedly, as penalties and limitations to Roman Catholics still abounded.

Turning right into *High St.* they headed up towards *The George Inn.*   The biggest pre-occupation that Peachey had was time. Whoever had been sent by the French had to complete his task in a very short time before returning to France. This was bad enough but the most devastating factor of all was that the agent was to put in place a destructive device that would kill or disable half the soldiers forming the defences.

But, and this was where the most staggering aspect confounded Peachey, it was to take effect after the agent had returned to France. What could that possibly be and where on earth should he start looking?

He marched on devoid of one single idea. The spy in Portsmouth who would provide the Frenchman with his local needs must also be found quickly. He was suspected of being of good standing, possibly a merchant or victualer but that was the sum total of his knowledge of the man.

Peachey knew victualers abounded. They were universally acknowledged as being as straight as a corkscrew and to find suspects amongst their number had no start point.

With these troubles still on his mind they reached *The George Inn.* It was a prestigious inn with a large coaching entrance to one side offsetting the grand central entrance. It was towards this that Peachey strode. Fairweather called out

'I will be at the back then sir should you need me.'

Peachey merely nodded and passed through the door.

The place was alive with activity, servants scurrying between rooms carrying drinks, food, cards and comforts for the guests.

To his immediate left was the main room warmed with an enormous fire emitting a fug like an enveloping blanket. Groups sat around talking or playing a hand of cards. With the chill of the evening still about him, Peachey approached the fire to warm. He stooped towards it. Behind him a voice called out

'By the Gods, its Henry Peachey.'

Peachey stood rock still, the voice reverberating in his ears. Not only hearing his name stunned him, but also the voice was immediately recognisable.

He had come to Portsmouth for the first time, on an errand that demanded he assume a different personage and now a man he had not seen for some five years was calling to him.

Hesitatingly he turned round to look towards his caller.

Chapter 2

Rousseliere was a soldier not a sailor. He could endure hardships and deprivations on land, but a sea voyage reduced him to a sick specimen, unable to contribute much to the outside world.

Recovering from the cramped and uncomfortable sea crossing from France, the motions still swirling in his mind he summoned up his reserves and slipped quietly ashore behind the men unloading the cargo so as to be as unobtrusive as possible.

Dover was an active port and as such, had many unseen eyes. Soldiers patrolled the streets but being unaware of this Frenchman's arrival were not actively seeking him, but nevertheless Rousseliere gave them a wide berth.

With an uneasy gait, resulting from the crossing starting in France, he firmly clamped his bag to his side. The contents, if caught, would have him hanged in an instance. The danger was not a new one, he had already undertaken a covert military survey a few years before, but it was not to his liking.

The arrangement to meet his contact was either to wait at midday, or six in the evening outside *The Wayfarers Inn* in the *High St*. As it must be nearing mid-day, he hastened to find the inn that proved to be closer than he had imagined.   It was a squalid looking place, obviously frequented by the lower orders of Dover.

Having quickly peered into its murky interior, he took up position to one side. Waiting for nearly an hour, nobody approached or took the slightest notice of the sailor by the side of a barrel. By early afternoon however it was clear that he had failed to make contact with the agent.

To continue waiting was foolhardy so he decided to stroll around the area until the evening meeting time. Doubts crossed his mind.

What if his man had been taken or had informed on him? He also had little idea how to start his task from here if he were left to his own devices. Finding himself back on the jetty he peered down on a Royal navy vessel moored alongside.

A blue-frocked officer strode to and fro barking orders to a warrant officer, who in turn, had several men scurrying around attending to the orders.   Shortly afterwards he could see a figure on the Quarterdeck standing beside an hourglass. As the last vestige of sand disappeared into the bottom section of the glass, he turned it over to repeat its time span and immediately rang the ship's bell.   He sounded a double ring followed immediately by a single strike - three bells.

Rousseliere knew that the first dogwatch started at four pm and a single ring was always given for each subsequent half hour. Three bells therefore signified an hour and a half had elapsed since four 'o 'clock, making it five thirty.

He turned and retraced his steps to *The Wayfarers Inn*, seeking to be in the vicinity again by six pm. Slowing to a saunter he passed the inn again. There was no contact made and none of the nearby characters paid him any attention. With a level of anxiety now creeping in, he started to retrace his steps when a soft voice behind him said,

'*Bonjour*'

The greeting startled him. A figure was at his side, hat pulled over his face with the collar of his long coat turned up against the evening chill.   The man's head was turned towards him. Rousseliere rapidly glanced about him and replied

'*Bonjour*'.

Was this a trap? Had he been betrayed? This was not how he had imagined the meeting to happen.

'Follow me at a distance' said the man and hurried off. Rousseliere watched him stride further up the street and followed as instructed. They walked until the man turned into a side alley. By the time Rousseliere had reached the small alley the man was gone. Hesitating slightly, he moved cautiously down the alley.   A door opened to one side and he stiffened, bracing himself against the unknown.

'In here' said the voice.

The light was virtually non-existent. He edged himself to the door, which opened wider allowing him to pass. Inside a candle burned on the rough table producing eerie shadowy illumination.

A voice said. 'A cautious man, I'm glad to see sir.' The man was directly behind the door, which quickly closed.   Looking at Rousseliere he queried, 'you have something for me sir?'

Rousseliere put down his bag and after sliding his hand inside produced one of the letters given to him in France. Opening it and holding it at an angle towards the candle the man scanned it contents. Apparently satisfied he said

'Allow me to name myself sir, I am Thomas Courtney. And you sir?'

'I am Major Berthois de la Rousseliere. You are here to meet me as instructed.'

'So it would seem sir.'

Rousseliere could see little of the man and his words were not those he expected, although he was only told that he would be met by a man answering to the name of Thomas Courtney to whom he should give his letter.

'I waited earlier today at the same place' said Rousseliere.

'Yes I saw you' replied Courtney.

Rousseliere frowned 'then why keep me waiting until this evening?'

'I am alive and wish to remain that way sir. I have no desire to dangle at the end of one his majesty's ropes. I needed to ensure that you had no unwelcome company.'

'You were not in view' said Rousseliere.

'Indeed not sir.

Moving into the centre of the room, Courtney removed his hat and Rousseliere studied him as best he could in the dim light. A pock-lined face containing two close-set eyes reminiscent of a weasel faced him. Ignoring the scrutiny, Courtney passed by Rousseliere to a cupboard and produced some bread, meat, glasses and jug of ale.

Rousseliere relaxed slightly. Although irritated that he had had to spend a wasted afternoon, the added precaution of this man increased their chances of survival and a successful mission. The food looked basic but he suddenly realised how hungry he was, particularly as his stomach had stopped turning cartwheels from the seas' motion.

'A welcomed sight Mr. Courtney.'

As they ate and drank Rousseliere look further at his newfound companion. He was not impressed. The shifty eyes over a bleak pointed nose were close-set and devoid of emotion. They looked deeply at him one minute and flashed round the room the next in a state of perpetual movement.

His age appeared to indicate some forty years of wear and his stature was one of medium build. His hands as he cut the meat were not coarse, nor were they smooth as a gentleman's might be. All in all a difficult man to define, which might well be useful if he was to be of use to him and the purpose of France.

As the food and drink began to strengthen and brighten Rousseliere's spirits, he assessed his position. He was now in England and had met the man who was to guide and assist him in his undertaking. Men like Courtney could not be selected as one would a soldier for duty, but had to be someone who had reason to support France or bitter opposition towards the British.

A further motivation may be simply one of greed producing the most dangerous ally of all, for he could desert or betray one for more money elsewhere.

What sort of class did Courtney fall into? Rousseliere's instinct said the latter, which concerned him, although information provided in France indicated that they had used Courtney for several years, but more than that did not specify.

Sitting back in the wooden high backed chair he said,

'You have served the cause of France well Mr. Courtney. You must have reason enough to hate the British.'

'Reason enough Major.'

A pause in the conversation indicated that nothing further was to come from Courtney. He continued

'What are our immediate plans sir?'

Courtney wiped his mouth and drank deeply. His pinpointed eyes looked quickly at Rousseliere.

'We leave for London at first light. We have an appointment there, when I have to collect the special device and some money. We shall then proceed onwards to Portsmouth.'

This special device as Courtney called it engendered considerable unease for the Frenchman. All he had been told was that the device would kill or maimed a large number of British Soldiers, after he had left to return to France. Surely this device would therefore have to be of considerable size to achieve that sort of result.

Passing a hand across his brow, Courtney rubbed his eyes and continued,

'In order for the plan to be effective I must set the device in place shortly to allow time for maximum damage to the troops to coincide with the invasion.'

Rousseliere ran his mind over the military plan that was to strike a devastating blow to the British. Certain aspects were brilliant, but much depended on his surveys and actions with Courtney. Running his mind over the plan for the umpteenth time, its essence was

the French fleet would sail under the direction of the Compte d'Orvilliers to Spain where it would join forces with the Spanish fleet.

Spain was not officially at war with Britain, but would make that declaration shortly. The combined French and Spanish armies would head to northern France and await transportation by ship to the Isle of Wight, the small island opposite Portsmouth, whilst another section would land westwards along the coast where they would storm Portsmouth from the North together with Gosport which lay across the harbour entrance from Portsmouth.

The transportation of the troops however could only be effected once the combined Armada had defeated the British Channel Fleet. A few years ago this would have been unthinkable, but with the current rebellion of the thirteen states in America, a large portion of the British Navy had been deployed by King George III to subdue the troublesome colonials.

This left the Channel Fleet gravely depleted, with less than 35 ships of the line, and totally outnumbered by that of the invading Armada.

The taking of Portsmouth, their premier naval port, was a prize of the highest order, not only territorially but severely wounding their pride, a real point to relish. If the forces could successfully hold Portsmouth and the harbour, it could hold the country to ransom by creating another Gibraltar. The loss of Gibraltar rankled with the Spanish whose delight in the prospect of a quid pro quo *knew no bounds.*

The defeat of the British Channel Fleet would generate prize money and the success of the invasion would replenish the exhausted coffers of both France and Spain.

He looked across at Courtney again. Rousseliere's role was dependant to a high degree by this strange man who sat opposite. The surveys he could readily undertake, but a liaison in Portsmouth with a French Agent depended on Courtney and was totally outside his own control.

Together with his instructions in France, he had been given a snuffbox and introductory letter for the agent. But this was no ordinary agent, he was a fleeting shadow of the past, being a member of le Secret du Roi, a group of men deployed around the world by King Louis XIV to undertake his wishes and foreign policies unknown to his own ministers. The present king was unaware of this disbanded force and their activities, but many were still residing in their locations but predominantly dormant in their activities.

By invoking such an agent was a masterstroke, as he would be elderly, unobtrusive, readily integrated in society but still possessing his allegiance to France, but Rousseliere was entirely dependent on Courtney to lead him to this man.

Of Courtney's own participation, the deployment of a device to maim or kill troops in Gosport was his task although Rousseliere was to assist. The method of delaying such a potent effect weeks after they had left the area was puzzling to say the least. He relished of learning the answer in due course.

The reminder of the required timing, caused a grip in Rousseliere's stomach. His own work, was a precursor to the main combined attack by the French and Spanish. He needed to assess the capability of the defences, and return to France with his valuable information prior to the Armada and invasion to enable the most effective attack on British soil to take place.

He was aware of the timescale but now realised for the first time just how much had to be achieved in such a short period. Looking hard at Courtney he said

'Then we have no time to loose sir. It will take us time to get to London and from there to Portsmouth. I am also charged to survey Gosport before I return.'

Courtney stood and squinted back.

'As I said, we leave tomorrow. I have arrangements in hand. Afterwards we shall go to Portsmouth to meet the man who will arrange for us to be able to complete the tasks and provide finance for local support.'

'A reliable man Mr. Courtney?'

He would probe Courtney to see what he knew of this man.

'Someone in communication with France and also seeking to restore the true faith.'

'I thought that in this enlightened age, the British King and Parliament were more tolerant of the Catholic faith' said Rousseliere.

Courtney's face changed and a small smile could almost be discerned flitting across its rough surface.

'Tolerance is a patronising word Major. Restraint from arrest is not what we call Catholic freedom. The laws still remain the same, we can discreetly practice our faith but careers can be abruptly terminated for those who choose not to shelter their religious views.'

The smile was not one of humour but it gave Rousseliere further insight into the man sat opposite.

'You practice the true faith yourself then Mr. Courtney?'

'Remember my earlier words Major; I am too cautious to be brought to the attention of the authorities.'

Rousseliere nodded. This reticence to answer was perhaps what he should have suspected. However he felt a little better with this news and he considered that Courtney might have other motives other than money. Clearly both men were going to hedge their views at this stage until they had smoked each other out.

Rousseliere felt thankful that France had chosen his aide with care. He had no immediate liking for his companion but the man nevertheless demonstrated caution and aptitude, vital qualities for a successful mission.

Sitting back for a moment he watched as Courtney sliced up some fruit with the strangest knife he had ever seen. Courtney's finger carefully traced the curvature of the blade – a peculiar shape having an unusual sharp and thin curved length. Not a knife used by seafarers or workmen for it lacked practical benefits but possessed sinister, assassin like qualities. A carved ornate handle indicated an Eastern design;

What of this man? They had only just met yet he instinctively had unease about him.

Had Rousseliere possessed even a glimmer of knowledge regarding Courtney's background, the unease would have developed into palpable concern.

Blissfully unaware of his associate's past life, he picked up his bag placing it under his head. No one could tamper with its contents and hidden secrets without disturbing him.

A feeling of cautious optimism began to delicately stir within him. Had he any notions of what was to occur, that feeling would have been stifled at birth.

Chapter 3

If anyone had ever had mixed emotions, Peachey had them now.

Peering through the hazy interior of *The George* he saw the man that had called to him. His mind oscillated between fear of being recognised at the beginning of his task and the pleasure in hearing that familiar voice again after such a period of time.

On a different occasion he would have rejoiced to see Percy Trevelyan. Here was someone on whom he had not clapped eyes for some five years, not since they had parted company at Oxford. At this juncture however his prime interest in Portsmouth was to remain incognito. Being greeted by Trevelyan put that status at risk with one stroke.

Peachey looked around the room to see how many had witnessed the greeting, and from a casual glance - none. Facing Trevelyan, he put his finger quietly to his lips, as might a conspirator, and moved forward to grasp his hand.

'My dear Trevelyan, how delightful to see you and so unexpected.'

Unexpected was a key word. Trevelyan hailed from a West Country family and Portsmouth was many miles away from the seat of his home.

'My God Peachey, time has passed like a trice yet you look unchanged and very well.'

'I hardly expected to see you here of all places.'

Grasping Trevelyan's arm he guided him back into his chair,

'I do not, however, wish it to become common knowledge who I am though.'

'Hardly creditors, it must be a jealous husband or husbands'

Trevelyan's smile remained.

'No nothing so exciting'.

Peering around to reassure himself that they had not become the focus of anyone's attention, he continued 'I am here on private business.'

'Really, life must really have changed for you. Tell me more. But first let us have brandy or a bottle to celebrate our reunion.'

He waved a long slender arm to a servant by the door and signalled for fluid refreshments.

Peachey drew an empty chair around the table to be close to Trevelyan, wondering at the same time how to proceed. The man who had warmly greeted him was as tall and thin as at their last meeting. Not an ounce fatter; the frame still gaunt. His clothes, though elegant, hung on his body devoid of any shape. Dark eyes contrasted sharply with the pale long face, complete with matching nose of proportional length.

Trevelyan was clever, very clever in fact. His academic studies had won approval from their Oxford Tutors, who relished teaching and influencing his bright mind. Paradoxically he could also react with his fellow creatures with incredible stupidity and unworldliness. It was this aspect that had forced Peachey to act as a mediator, negotiator and occasionally protector at Oxford to help smooth Trevelyan's life as an undergraduate.

It was this very characteristic that troubled Peachey now. Perhaps the intervening years had developed Trevelyan's latent diplomacy and social skills but could he rely on that? Now was the time to make decisions. He said

'My dear Trevelyan the passage of time and our social world moulds our purpose in life.'

'Purpose in life? Your singular purpose was to bed as many of the local beauties, and many others that weren't. I can't believe this to be a new profession or business.'

His smile and gentle laughter never wavered. Peachey replied

'That being so at the time possibly, but additional tiresome but necessary occupations have been forced upon me.'

Trevelyan's dark eyes flashed a look at Peachey; one could almost sense his brain being set a task to fathom this new direction for his re-discovered friend. After a short deliberation he replied.

'Your uncle I have a mind is behind all this. The great and good Sir Richard Peachey, manipulator of state, diplomat with the King's ear, weaver of schemes and man of influence and money. Come, tell me I'm not wrong.'

'There is a certain truth in your assessment.'

Peachey knew that too much guile would not pass Trevelyan, but wishing to change the direction of their conversation said

'But you have not told me what on earth you yourself are doing in Portsmouth.'

'Like you Peachey, I am guided by my uncle. You may recall him from his visits and connections in Oxford.'

'By George, not Silas Trevelyan.'

'The very same'. The smile broadened across Trevelyan's face.

'A somewhat eccentric personage' said Peachey.

'Mad as a Hatter' laughed Trevelyan.

This may well have been an understatement. He was undoubtedly peculiar and held fixed, entrenched and strange views on most topics under the sun. As one Oxford Tutor had muttered, *a spirit of madness weaves its way though the lineage of the Trevelyan family and we have witness several of them here, to our cost.*

Peachey probed further, 'But what is he doing here pray?'

'He owns a large stake in one of the breweries just round the corner. Bought on a whim from an unscrupulous fellow who thought the days of profitable brewing were in decline.'

'In decline?'

'Well for many years the brewers here brewed for the Royal Navy, then the navy decided to transfer all the brewing to their own brewery across the water at Gosport. No additional naval supplies have ever been required, as Gosport's Weevil Lane brewery can meet all the Navy's needs. The fellow thought he would get out quickly and sold to my uncle.'

In response to Peachey's raised eyebrow, Trevelyan continued with a smile,

'What has actually happened though, is that the brewery here has been selling more and more elsewhere over the years and now the brewing is as good, if not better, than ever. Luck, mark you, must be the hallmark of this investment rather than my uncle's shrewd judgement.'

'So he resides here?'

'Yes just around the corner in *Penny Street,* not far in fact from the brewery itself. A fact that must irk those who run the brewery.'

Peachey drank from the glass now placed before him. Here was an unexpected source of local information that he had not expected to unearth. He decided to pursue his own purpose a little further.

'I would like to call and pay my respects' he said.

Raising one eyebrow Trevelyan said

'I am sure he would be delighted to receive you - if he can remember who the devil you are. Not that one should take that as a personal affront, as he may well not recognise you a few minutes after having dined with you.'

Studied curiosity lingered in his eyes.

'Now I wonder why you would want to pay your respects?'

'Simply to extend a courtesy.' said Peachey.

'Quite so, quite so'. Trevelyan's eyes returned to reflected humour as he lifted his own glass in a toast,

'To our reunion and future prosperity.'

Peachey acknowledged the gesture.

'Well said, well said. I suppose you are here to visit him yourself then.'

Trevelyan's face suddenly darkened and an expression approaching despair transformed his outlook from humorous to hopelessness.

'Life has dealt me a cruel hand Peachey and reduced me to a position from which I am unable to extricate myself.'

The change in attitude, so rapid and severe was a shock to Peachey. With immediate concern he said

'Pray tell me Trevelyan; it may be that help is available in some form.'

'I am afraid no help can solve this problem Peachey'

'What on earth is it that troubles you so much?'

'I am engaged to be married!'

Being informed that this was a calamitous misfortune was slow to register to Peachey.

'You are engaged to be married and this is the devastating blow that has blighted your life?'

'Quite so, quite so Peachey.' Trevelyan was seemingly unaware of the irony in Peachey's voice.

Peachey continued, 'customarily, one offers hearty congratulations with celebrations all round; publication of the forthcoming event, and feverish preparations being undertaken by all. Somehow this does not seem to foot the bill on this occasion.'

'I see you see the problem sir.'

'Actually sir, I do not seem to be able to grasp the severity of the situation at all.'

Trevelyan concentrated on downing the remainder of his glass and promptly refilling it.

'I was tricked Peachey. A foul trick by a scheming lady.'

'How come?'

'I had visited her and her family on several occasions. A purely social basis you understand. She appeared interested and very attentive, particularly over my relationship with my uncle and the brewery – as I later recalled that is. The prospect of my settling in Portsmouth with the inheritance from my uncle, together with the brewery must have struck a resounding chord with her.'

He drank further from his glass before continuing.

'It was at a dinner at her house, graced with local dignitaries, Admirals and the Governor that I made my mistake. The wine was first class and freely flowing. Having been entertained in this very room to a bottle or two beforehand, I was feeling particularly benevolent to all. During the dinner whilst sitting between her and her mother, she spoke of our mutual love of books and literature wishing that life could be bettered by a joint association in the future.'

Further liquid reinforcement was called for before he continued

'I recall her wishing to be provided for in the future by a gentleman possessing donnish qualities. This is where it becomes slightly fuddled. A request from me was somehow manipulated into being a proposal of marriage by me, offering a prosperous and happy future for her.'

A pause enabled him to examine the contents of his glass whilst recalling the awful moment.

'When I issued the happy and rewarding future comments towards her desire for literature and fine arts, marriage was certainly not contemplated in any way. The situation was transformed as though a Royal Navy ship-of-the-line had been signalled to fire a broadside. Her mother, who had been in cohorts with her, exclaimed her rapture in joyous voice, her father and the men started a shaking hands contest with me, and toasts and congratulations rent the air.'

'But surely sir you could have explained the misunderstanding.'

'It was orchestrated better than Mr. Mozart could have produced in his finest hour. I must confess to not reacting very quickly, thinking misguidedly, that matters could be corrected the following day. But I was tragically wrong.'   Peachey   was mesmerised as Trevelyan relived his ordeal and continued

'Polite society around the world seemed to me to have been poised for this announcement, as the following day plans for the formal engagement and subsequent marriage were fast afoot. Any attempt at retraction was out of the question. Breech of promise, broken word, unspeakable treatment of a lady, future snubbing by all - this hung over me like the sword of Damocles.'

Trevelyan's shoulders had adopted a decidedly drooping posture - that is, if his shoulders could be readily detected. Looking at Peachey he said.

'As you can see my fate is sealed. My future lies in this town with its society and its business. I cannot run foul of the ruling group, particularly with the brewery promising so much. So there you have it sir.'

'The lady must have qualities or you would not have called on her, perhaps she will make a good wife for you sir.'

'You may judge that for yourself sir should you meet her. The problem does not end there, for I love another.'

Only those expert in performing in a Greek tragedy could match the expression of grief that appeared to settle on Trevelyan.

Peachey sensed that his purpose in Portsmouth was already in danger of diversion and only within a few minutes of meeting Trevelyan again. Having his curiosity aroused by Trevelyan he found himself asking the inevitable.

'So who is the fair lady of your heart sir?'

'The Ward of the Governor sir - a Miss Sophia Gifford. A lady to tempt the heart of any man. Beauty to the eye and manna to the soul.'

The Governor's Ward? This was the true Trevelyan. Not only nearly compromising himself with local society, his forlorn love was for the Ward of the most influential man in Portsmouth. Taking in Trevelyan's wistful air he said

'And what of her love for you? Particularly as you are now betrothed to another.'

'She now has nothing to do with me. An attitude I, for one, do not blame her.'

'Does the Governor, know of this situation between his Ward and you?'

'Good heavens no. Sophia and I have much in common but I was biding my time with her. I saw no need to rush things.'

'You implied that your new fiancée also had a love of books and literature. Perhaps she is better suited to you than you think.'

'A sham Peachey. A sham to ingratiate herself to me and to put me at my ease. She has no knowledge of the works of great authors and playwrights and her appreciation of music is limited to simple works.'

'Not an inspiring start then sir. What is the lady in question's name?'

'Miss Elizabeth Attwick. She looks like a horse, drinks like a fish, with the social graces of a whore.'

Trevelyan appeared to have little enthusiasm for the future lady of his household.

The name meant nothing to Peachey for which he could thank the good lord. Having Trevelyan causing difficulties that encroached on Peachey's own business would be a poor start.

Another gulp from his glass left the world to disappear down Trevelyan's throat, meeting little resistance en route.

The scope of this topic seemed terminated, as Peachey could see no avenue of hope. If marriage were a must, as it indeed appeared, Trevelyan would have to honour his commitment, and demonstrate a respectable face to society.

A curious thought struck Peachey. *Why was Trevelyan in The George Inn and not in his uncle's house?* He said.

'You appear to be a frequent visitor to this establishment sir.'

'I have been staying here of late. My uncle has a full house and I need some respite from his company. They treat me well here and I am in no hurry to seek a house of my own. No doubt my fiancée and her mother have plans already well advanced in that direction, a final approval being all they will seek from me.'

Peachey needed time to digest this information. The clever move was perhaps to use Trevelyan to take the focus away from himself. In any event Trevelyan already appeared to have made many acquaintances that might prove useful to him. Currently Peachey had only the briefest of notions of how to start his quest.

Looking at Trevelyan he said

'There is always hope sir, we should not dwell on an event that has yet to happen.'

'Were that to be true Peachey, I would be a much relieved man.'

'In the meantime I required some assistance from yourself, for which I should be most indebted.'

This request had a surprising result. Trevelyan's appearance transformed itself back to almost its earlier state. He looked at Peachey.

'I should be honoured and delighted to be able to provide some small service to you sir; as history will show that it is I who have always been in need of your help. Pray let me know of your wants.'

The germ of an idea which had been given birth in the depths of Peachey's thoughts, now matured and blossomed at a prodigious rate. The strands congealed into a decision, a decision that was to affect Peachey's life over the ensuing days to an unbelievable degree.

Looking around the room, Peachey said.

'Let us retire somewhere where we can speak undisturbed or overheard.'

Putting down his glass Trevelyan stood up.

'My room is suitable. It is up the stairs and at the end of the inn.'

On reaching his room, Trevelyan led the way into a spacious area equipped with a small marble topped table with stylish gilt chairs in addition to expected bedroom accoutrements. A chess set occupied the centre of the table with pieces remaining in the state of play. Peachey said.

'I see your love of chess remains undimmed in spite of your predicaments.'

Trevelyan glanced across at the board.

'If time permits we can resume where we left off years ago. Opponents are hard to find who are as devious and callous a player as you sir.'

Peachey gave a thin smile,

'As I recall Trevelyan, you were the winner on most occasions and as for devious play, none could touch you.'

Drawing up the chairs to the table Peachey moved the chess pieces to one side, reached into his inner pocket and produced a letter. The remnants of a large wax seal hung at the base and the document looked well used. He spread it out on the table.

'Trevelyan, I asked for your services downstairs. I also mentioned that I was here on business but hesitated to say that it was on the King's business.'

Looking for a reaction from Trevelyan he found none other than a look of curiosity. He continued.

'What I have to say is for your ears only my friend. I seek your word that you will keep all that I have to say to yourself and pass to no other without my approval.'

'You have it freely Peachey you must know that.'

'My task is difficult. When I say I am on the King's business that is true but there are difficulties. The Kings advisors are not at one over this. My uncle has word from France that someone is to be in Portsmouth on a serious mission and will contact a traitorous spy here for assistance. The other King's advisors have heard nothing from their own informers. They are envious of my uncle and hasten to cast doubt of the correctness of the information.'

'But of the King?'

'The King has much on his mind. He flits from one subject to another and, with no other advisor willing to give credence to the information, he has left my uncle to deal with it. In any event too much evidence of the King's men and soldiers in Portsmouth may well send the Frenchman and his spies to earth.'

'So what is your plan? Have you information on this Frenchie, his purpose or role?'

'What I have is a letter from my uncle to the Governor for assistance should I be in need of it. However, the local spy is known to be well placed and I am to make my own enquiries. I must only seek assistance should the need arise.'

'I, of course know the Governor.'

'And wish him for a father-in-law.'

'A spiked gun there. My future does not lead in that direction although I wish to God that it did'

'The information that I have is of a threefold nature. Firstly the man the French have sent is a military man. Secondly he can access money for local supporters to aid his cause. And thirdly, the task giving the greatest concern, is that he is to inflict serious damage to our defences.'

'What possible damage can one man cause to the defences?'

'This is the strangest part of the whole story. His task is to kill or injure a whole section of the men guarding the defences. That would be dozens of men, but this is the real puzzle Trevelyan, it must be done *after he has left*!'

'Is the man a phantom or a demon? He must surely get the local traitors to do it for him after he's gone.'

Peachey shook his head and said

'This is the mystery and point that we cannot fathom, he is to bring a device to Portsmouth that will do it for him.'

Trevelyan stared at him. 'How big a device? It cannot be of any great size if they have to transport it here.'

'We are given to believe it is quite small and easily carried. It cannot contain gunpowder for that would have no real effect.'

'But what if he were to plant the device within the powder store. If that were to be ignited it would have precisely the effect you mentioned.'

'There are many difficulties with that. The powder is now stored across the water in Gosport, away from the main defences and troops. That was moved from Portsmouth three years ago in 1776 because the townsfolk feared for their lives if the powder exploded. He would also have to get passed the guards and have a key just to get inside. Once in how does he arrange for a delay and remain unnoticed?'

'Perhaps the Frenchies are unaware that the powder store has been moved.'

Peachey stood up and paced the floor. 'That has been considered, but the other points still remain. We have spoken to the Royal Armouries and they are quite clear that no slow burning device, particularly for such a time, can possibly exist.'

'Perhaps he has solved the problem that eluded Guy Fawkes and will start a fire under or near the powder room that will in turn cause it to explode.'

'That is a possibility sir, but the time delay?'

'He must have an accomplice to start it at the time; the mysterious device is simply an aid for the fire to be set off at the time.'

Peachey turned from his pacing to face Trevelyan.

'Reasoned thinking I grant you sir, but why bring it here? There are many simple ways to start fires.'

Trevelyan rubbed the side of his nose with the fingers of his left hand. Looking back towards Peachey he said

'I shall need to dwell on that particular problem sir. I'm dashed if I can plumb that one. Are there no further indications of the man who is to assist him in Portsmouth or the target?'

'We know the man is well connected and the only information we have regarding the target are the words, *black house.*'

Trevelyan's nose rubbing continued apace. He said

'I must say your information is singularly unhelpful sir. No wonder the King's men were sceptical of the plot. Do we look for a black house in Portsmouth? I for one have no knowledge of any such house.'

He looked down at the chessmen as though for inspiration and said

'Someone who may know is my opponent in my current chess game. A clergyman by the name of the Reverend Stephen Weston who officiates at *St Thomas' Church* just down the High St. from us here.'

Peachey looking from the chessmen back to Trevelyan said

'We must be careful with whom we share our knowledge, is he a suitable person to entrust with our information concerning the *black house.*

Trevelyan looked a little startled.

'He is a man of the cloth, he must be trustworthy.'

'My dear Trevelyan, I did not for one minute doubt the sincerity and honesty of your clergyman, but they lack a little in worldly affairs. This may occasion him to make an indiscrete remark and inadvertently disclose our interest.'

Trevelyan quickly thought for a moment then said,

'If we tell him our enquiries are of a delicate nature and we do not wish to sully a ladies name, I am sure he will behave with the utmost decorum.'

Peachey tired of pacing the small room returned to his seat.

'Has he resided here for many years and does he know his flock, their generations and more importantly the dwellings? Would he know where we might locate a *black house?*'

'He is a young gentleman, younger than I, and has only been in this living for some six months. However he has already established himself and has reopened a school for the poor, where he himself teaches. This fact and his duties in the church must bring him in contact with much of the town. I have no doubts about the man.'

Peachey sat back in the chair.

'Then that's agreed, we will proceed on that basis.'

Trevelyan's frown developed again.

'Did you say that the target actually was a *black house?*'

'My uncle's informant could not overhear a particular conversation too distinctly. Apart from the information I have already given you the remainder consisted of words here and there – *black house* being one such phrase, but it is considered to be important.'

'Then that's something we need to resolve then. It will at least take my mind off my fiancé for a spell. In all seriousness Peachey, what you have told me this evening is quite disconcerting. Do you propose to tell the Governor?'

'No, not just at present. As far as anyone else is concerned I am quietly investigating the business activities of some victualers.'

'The only time you will find a straight victualer is when he is flat out in his coffin, and the only time you will find an honest one as well.'

'Not telling the Governor is a dilemma for me as well Trevelyan, but it is my uncle's wish at this stage. If needs be I can call on his support when the time arises. For the present, taking you into my confidence is more than enough.'

These words were a truism that he failed to appreciate at that precise moment. Who could have predicted the events that would occur within the next twenty-four hours?

Chapter 4

London looks and smells like Paris thought Rousseliere, but here there were more people from all walks of life going about their business. Others were sprawled in alleyways and doorways more reminiscent of Paris.

Here, Gentlemen and their ladies passed oblivious to these creatures, being transported at a trot by sedan chairs or carriage. The movement by carriages resembled a battle with each carriage struggling to fight their way towards their destination at the expense of others. Sedan chairs however could move rapidly along footpaths, the bearers trotting at a steady pace calling *'by your leave'* to any pedestrian presenting an obstruction. Collision with a sedan chair moving at a pace was not to be recommended.

To Rousseliere, the lot of the common people in France - the *Third Estate* or peasant working class, appeared far more downtrodden and taxed than the daily throng here filling the streets. The London men appeared able to provide for their families with no onerous taxes such as existed in Paris.

Better than most in France he thought.

He and Courtney were on foot moving down on the northern side of the river Thames. Proceeding from the docks they were now approaching *Threadneedle St.* Courtney had lived up to Rousseliere's initial expectations and had not made a good travelling companion. He said very little and provided no further insight into his motivation for betraying his country and providing his services for France.

Rousseliere had assumed Courtney was British and nothing he had said made him think otherwise. Although the reason for Courtney's treachery had no bearing on his own task, Rousseliere still had an urge to discover the reason. In any situation the fact of not knowing was itself a little unnerving. Courtney, who was half a pace ahead suddenly stopped and walked round the back of one of the houses fronting the road. The fact that he did not climb the short flight of steps to the front entrance was curious but he must have his reasons.

Loud voices from a kitchen reverberated in the narrow alleyway in which they now found themselves.   Reaching a side door Courtney banged on it.

After a brief interval it was opened by a footman who was looking over his shoulder continuing his conversation with a member of the kitchen staff.   Courtney's voice was harsh, interrupting the footman's dialogue.

'Tell your master that two visitors have arrived, that are expected - and be quick about it.'

The footman's head swivelled to the front and he hesitated for just a second, but on looking at Courtney and the figure behind him, left the door ajar and disappeared off with low mutterings.

Returning moments later he opened the door fully saying

'You are to wait in here.'

Courtney barged straight in with Rousseliere following at a gentler pace. They were shown into a small quiet room adjacent the kitchen where they remained for some five minutes before a bustling outside signalled the arrival of the owner.

Entering and closing the door behind him his eyes darted rapidly between the two men.

'I have been expecting you. Why are you late?'

Rousseliere expecting a warmer reception, or at least a greeting, was taken aback. He said

' We have travelled here at the utmost speed sir, and none could have arrived quicker.'

The man studied Rousseliere carefully but the vision did not mellow his approach. He continued

'Time is a matter that we have little of. It is crucial to the total success. My own security is also threatened if we do not carry out our plan and I do not have a mind to be dependant on others for that.'

Walking further into the room he turned and looking directly at Rousseliere said

'I need to know that you are the man I am to expect. You have a proof for me?'

Rousseliere returned the gaze. Taking in the man's appearance, he sensed that he was not a natural gentleman but had acquired status and position by wealth.   He was possibly of the merchant class. He was portly with a matching red complexion housing two popping eyes swivelling rapidly in their sockets.   His clothes were of good quality but his bearing did them no justice since he lacked the grace and style of a true gentleman.   There was however a certain earnestness that one couldn't fail to miss in his looks and approach.   Rousseliere was given to believe that these merchants were now prospering in England, but not readily accepted in society.

Rousseliere withdrew a small white rod with carvings on the side from inside his bag.   It was the object given to him by the count.

'This is my proof sir.'

The man looked at the rod and from the inside of his jacket took out a similar sized one. His was much smoother and polished, as though designed for a gentleman.   Both were curved and made of bone and had been carved as scrimshaw - the practice of carving bone, adopted by seamen on board ship to wile away the tedious hours.

Taking Rousseliere's from him the man quickly placed the two together. They fitted exactly.

He grunted and returned the bone to Rousseliere. The method of identification was simple and effective.   Had Rousseliere's bone ever been discovered it represented nothing more than a carving made by a seaman in His Majesty's Royal Navy. The man 's was a piece of artwork worthy of a gentleman. Placing them together however, they fitted exactly as a tally stick should and provided instant verification.

'You are the one expected' muttered the man. 'Wait here.'

He eventually reappeared carrying a cloth with an object wrapped inside.

Turning to Courtney he unwrapped the cloth exposing a package wrapped in sailcloth. It was about nine inches in length, cylindrical with a diameter of six inches and made from dark grained hardwood. He said

'You are the one assigned to plant this. It is now in your care, together with this.'

From the cloth he took a second small container, sealed with wax and cord.

Courtney looked at both, nodded and re-wrapped them in the cloth.

The man drew out a small bag and said

'Your payment is in ready money, as agreed.   You have no need to examine it now.   You will have many opportunities to do so at a later date.   Our plans are not to be jeopardised by short changing you.'

Courtney's weasel eyes peered at the man for a brief moment, nodded, pocketed the money and said

'I shall complete my tasks, to time and unobserved. On that you can be assured.'

The man returning a hostile gaze said

'Your own life depends on it. We shall hunt you down like a jack rabbit should you fail us, be very sure of that.'

Rousseliere was still puzzled by the two men. They were both engaged on the same goal but were antagonistic to one another, the man almost scornful of Courtney as though he were nothing more than a paid servant or tradesman. There was obviously a difference in approach to the task.

Rousseliere's eyes wandered round the room seeking further details. He was unaccustomed to being treated as a subordinate; he was after all a major in the French army. He musings stopped with a start. Although the room was sparsely furnished, the furniture was a good quality with one piece - a cabinet, catching his eye. It wasn't the cabinet so much as what it held. One of its doors was slightly ajar and he could see items inside that were instantly recognisable to him. There was a rosary and cross together with other items lying on a red satin cloth.

That was the man's secret. *He was a practising Catholic.* A visiting priest for mass probably used this room. The man looked towards France for his religion whilst Courtney for gold, albeit that he may also have Catholic sympathies. This would account for the poor relationship between the two.

Were they both trustworthy? Rousseliere felt that unless the British captured them, they probably were, both having their own reasons for their treachery.

Courtney speaking to the man again interrupted his analysis.

'I have also much to loose sir; I am the one who is taking the most risks. My courage is not to be challenged on that score.'

The man nodded and breathed deeply. It was as though having given Courtney the items; a weight had been lifted from his shoulders. He said

'Indeed sir, no slur was intended on your character. It is trying time and this time we must not be defeated. It could change much for us all.'

Turning abruptly Courtney said

'We shall away now.'

The man moved towards the door

'Have a care with your entrustment sir; no harm will come providing you keep them separate until the time arises.

'I shall have a care, of that you can be sure.'

Courtney followed the man from the room. The servant hovering in the background in the hallway, moved forward to escort them from the house.

The man's voice behind them quietly said

'God speed.'

No other farewells or contact was made. In a brief moment they found themselves back in the alleyway and heading towards the road.

Each was absorbed with his own thoughts as they walked along the bottom of *Threadneedle St.* Courtney led the way through the maze of coaches and pedestrians, kicking out at any child or drunk who happened in his path. Darting down an alleyway he turned sharply left bringing them to a door half hidden in the decaying wall.

Looking both left and right he knocked twice on the door, it swung slowly open to reveal – nothing at all. As Rousseliere peered into the interior there was nothing but blackness. A figure emerged from the gloom. She was a hag. Strands of wispy hair hung down either side of one of the most leathery and wrinkled faces he had ever encountered.

She clearly recognised Courtney as she stepped aside and he disappeared into the blackness. Rousseliere followed suit and on passing the old woman was almost overcome with her smell and revulsion.

Rousseliere stood still for a moment to assess his position, his eyes slowly becoming accustomed to the gloom. Courtney knowing his whereabouts had walked straight ahead through a far door, which Rousseliere could now just make out as his eyes became adjusted to the inky interior.

A shaft of light suddenly appeared as Courtney opened a further door and passed into the room ahead. Following this beacon of light, Rousseliere found himself in a warmer room that lacked the pungent odour of the access route to it. Courtney placed his package on a rough-hewn table situated to one side. Turning, he said

'We shall be safe here until tomorrow. No one will venture passed the harridan at the door.'

He smiled thinly at Rousseliere's obvious distaste for the place.

'You are thinking this is no place for an officer and a gentleman I fear. It is not the most choicest of locations I grant you, but one can be totally lost in London in hovels such as these and it also enables me to examine more fully this deadly device.'

Placing the cloth containing the units carefully on the table, he unwrapped it and scrutinised the two items.

'I cannot afford to fail with this; it must be working perfectly in order to wreck the havoc that is expected of it. I have not seen one like it before but I am given to understand that it has been well tried and tested ensuring it will function very accurately. The time factor is of the essence.'

He carefully put them into another bag. The bag contained clothes, so that when the units were inserted they were both hidden and effectively cushioned from knocks.

Courtney studied the bag as though visualising the lethal combination he had just hidden there. Clearly musing over the unfamiliarity of it's operation and still focusing on the bag he said

'That little lady will reek a swift and painful end to many.'

Rousseliere not understanding if Courtney was addressing him or not countered

'Little lady?'

Courtney glanced up at him.

'The deadliest items in history have always been named after women.   The Iron maiden was a medieval cage that had internal spikes such that when it was closed with the victim, inside they pierced his body. The Spanish ones had a woman's cap and wig affixed at the head for good measure.'

Rousseliere nodded but said nothing. Indicating the bag, Courtney's theme ran on.

'This is a *Mistress Misery* and no mistake; a typical mistress that appears docile but causes pain and misery. It's a hundred times deadlier than an Iron Maiden.'

'Your views of the fair sex is somewhat unusual.'

Courtney glanced back at him

'An accurate assessment sir, be sure of it: deadlier than the bravest soldier and no mistake. This *Mistress* will come to be known as a mass slayer, those who are not killed outright will wish to god they had been.'

'*Mistress*' echoed Rousseliere quietly to himself. *A peculiar name given by a peculiar man to a peculiar device and that's for sure.*

Courtney then seemed to break free from his thoughts. Removing the money he had received earlier, he counted it, being carefully to shield the view from Rousseliere. Rousseliere gauged that it was a considerable sum, but if the outcome was to be achieved, it was good value to France.

Rousseliere looking at Courtney's back said

'That should compensate you somewhat sir for your troubles.'

Courtney spun round,

'Not for my troubles sir no, it will assist us to complete our tasks with payment left for me, but as for my troubles, this will in no way recompense me.'

'You have been mistreated sir I take it.'

'More than you can imagine sir. My repayment will arrive when France has its grip on English soil.'

With no further comment he put the money back in his jacket pocket.

'We journey to Portsmouth tomorrow. It will be an uncomfortable trip as two sailors would not be expected to travel in style and we need no questions to be asked either during the trip or as we arrive.'

Rousseliere simply nodded. His destiny was now in the hands of this man, who was an unfathomable creature, having a love of money but none for his country.

Would he prove trustworthy, and more to the point, would he ensure that the mission was successful? It was almost unbelievable that the future of France hinged to a large degree on the future actions of this strange complex individual.

Chapter 5

The wind buffeted the sea around the entrance to Portsmouth harbour, producing pitching choppy waves; a cutter's oarsmen skilfully countered this effect with the appearance of effortlessly rowing their captain ashore.

Captain Younghusband's ship was moored at St. Helens Bay, off the Isle of Wight. It was now moored alongside the other British warships operating out of Portsmouth harbour and forming the Channel Fleet.

St. Helens Bay proved to be a safe enough distance from Portsmouth harbour to contain the ship's crew, many of whom were pressed men with an eye to escape if the right opportunity presented itself. It presented a short sail or hard row for the oarsmen ferrying their captain.

Having entered the harbour entrance, they rowed towards the Sally Ports. These consisted of two small openings in the ramparts defending the town, with a short pier jutting into the water from each. One was for the exclusive use of officers and the other for men and provisions.

Generally known singularly as Sally Port, it was located between the Round Tower and Square Tower, forming part of the formidable sea defences of Portsmouth. These were strengthened by Sir Bernard de Gomme's excellent design after King Charles II commissioned him, and never breached.

The Round Tower was originally used to collect dues from incoming ships, whilst Square Tower, up to three years ago, housed gunpowder and munitions. It was not until 1776 that King George finally granted permission for this potentially lethal content to be moved to a more remote site across the harbour.

The townsfolk were now able to sleep a little more easily in their beds at night, knowing that the prospect of being blown sky high had been removed from their doorsteps.

The coxswain expertly brought the cutter round to the leeward side of the officer's pier and the crew shipped oars. This action took place under the watchful eye of the captain who made no comment, but was satisfied that his arrival indicated a well-managed ship and crew.

The marine sentry standing guard at the end of the jetty promptly stood to attention as Captain Younghusband, followed closely by his manservant, strode though the opening of the ramparts and into the town.

Passing through the gate in the wall they found themselves at the bottom of *High Street* and close to the main Guardhouse.   The Governor's residence lay to their right beyond the Guardhouse abutting the Garrison Church.

Looking to the left one could see the towering King James' Gate, one of the main entrances fortifying the walled town, which, when leaving *Broad Street* in which they were standing, led to the infamous area known as *Spice Island;* its curious name claiming different origins.

One derivation centred around the fact that ships brought spices in to its Camber Docks, whilst another centred on its colourful reputation for spiciness. Although small in area its dark universal reputation abounded as it teemed with inns, drunks, villains and whores. It specialised in illegal and nefarious pastimes.

It was little wonder the respectable townsfolk of Portsmouth were relieved when the soldiers closed the gates at sunset each day.

Being familiar sights to Younghusband he turned instinctively to the right then up *High Street*, before bearing to the right to enter *Penny Street* and head towards his house.

*

Whilst Captain Younghusband strode up *Penny Street*, Henry Peachey was finishing his breakfast at *The George*.   A certain anxiousness had set in since last night. His desire to make progress into determining potential agents and locating the *black house* was uppermost in his mind.

Surely a black house, or a house that resemble such a dwelling shouldn't be hard to find in the town?

Certainly with the help of the clergyman Trevelyan had spoken about, its location ought to be fairly easily determined.

Many of the houses were dark and drab, but none he had seen since his arrival could actually be described as a black house.

Trevelyan seemed confident that his clergyman would have the necessary detailed knowledge of the town to recognise it immediately. He needed a start point for at the back of his mind a nagging doubt suggested that the critics at court might well be right, and that this could turn out to be a wild goose chase.

Fairweather re-entered the room and pausing to glance at the furniture said

'There are some good pieces in here sir.'

Peachey broke from his thoughts and remembered that Fairweather's work origins were in making fine furniture. Although now unable to pursue that skill, his thoughts apparently continued to gravitate to his craft, with an inherent appreciation of others still able to finely fashion wood.

'No doubt Fairweather' he said 'they also have craftsmen in Portsmouth I believe.'

'As you say sir, but with respect, I imagine they are more skilled at warship building. These pieces came from London.'

Peachey's curiosity was slightly aroused,

'How do you know that Fairweather?'

'Its not only style but markings sir. It's something like the stonemasons. On the back of each stone in a cathedral or major building, the stone has the mason's own individual mark, these have telltale marks so it's easy to find out who built a particular section.'

'Only if you pull the building down I fear' mused Peachey. He pointed to two chairs.

'How about these chairs; they're Chippendale aren't they? Come from London as well then?'

'No sir, the designs are Chippendale but any craftsman working to his design can make them. These were probable made in these parts.'

'There is more to this business than one imagines. It seems it is only worth transporting good pieces from London then.'

Standing and walking towards the window Peachey continued,

'On other matters, I need to explore the town. Remember my true interests are not to be broadcast to anyone. I must appear to be solely investigating replenishing of ships in Portsmouth. I have however, other matters that I wish you to enquire about.'

'Absolute discretion sir' said Fairweather tapping the side of his nose with his forefinger.

'Go and find Mr Trevelyan, and with my compliments, see if he has a mind yet for me to meet his clergyman.'

Fairweather replying 'at once sir' departed to complete his errand.

Peachey returned his gaze to the view from his window. There was much activity below, as only to be expected from such a town as Portsmouth.   Its trade links, army and navy presence, and immediate proximity to the Dockyard ensured there was much work for the local merchants, tradesmen and workmen.

With so much movement, it was almost impossible to detect any action by an individual that might provide a clue towards his quarry. Men acting furtively may be doing no more than avoiding the attention of the press gangs, who continually sought new occupants for His Majesty's warships. With nine out of ten men being pressed, the work of the press gangs was constant, although nowadays, many men having originally been pressed were staying on in the service.

Conditions were harsh but there was discipline, routine, beer, rum and regular food to temper the desire to return to the drudgery of life many had previously undertaken.

Almost immediately Fairweather reappeared,

'Compliments from Mr. Trevelyan sir, if you find it convenient, would you care to visit him in his rooms. The clergyman has arrived.'

Peachey swept form the room relieved at last to start his quest. Entering Trevelyan's rooms he saw an intense young looking man wearing the collar of his calling, sitting beside Trevelyan at the small table holding the chess board.

The man was undoubtedly young, probably only in his mid twenties, dark hair drawn to the back of his head and a seriousness normally seen on a much older head. On seeing Peachey, he rose to his feet and looked across at Trevelyan who said

'Mr. Peachey allow me to introduce the Reverend Weston who is in holy orders at *St. Thomas'* church across the road.'

Peachey said

'I am delighted to meet you sir. A tireless worker in the parish I am given to understand.'

The Rev. Weston produced a small self conscious smile and replied

'I do what I can to carry out God's work in this town, which heaven knows is in dire need of such help.'

'Also an avid chess player' said Trevelyan, producing a slight smile on the clergyman's face.

'Enthusiastic but lacking the cunning and guile of some of my opponents' replied Rev. Weston.

'Much can be learnt and related to real life from chess, but that's not to say your regular opponent here utilises those skills in everyday use' hastened Peachey.

'Indeed sir, I find Mr. Trevelyan an honest god fearing man.'

Not necessarily the man I know thought Peachey but let any further extension to the introductory pleasantries terminate. He continued,

'I hope that with our acquaintance I may be permitted to learn more of Portsmouth. I understand that you also run a school?'

'A small venture' said Rev Weston. ' Nothing to compete with the Grammar School just up the road and hardly an academic institution, but we try to teach some local boys to read and write together with some basic mathematics as there is no formal education available for them.'

Peachey nodded approvingly. Weston continued

'They are then able to find employment as apprentices and tradesmen such as shipwrights. They can thus support families and so, in a way, they repay their education indirectly. Once working, they contribute to the school coffers, so it has an element of being self supporting.'

'Admirable, admirable' said Peachey.

Weston smiled modestly and Peachey furthered

'I imagine then that you are fully acquainted with all aspects of the town. As such, I have a strange request. I was asked to visit a house that was described to me as *the black house,* but foolishly I do not have an address or directions. Perhaps you are familiar with such a property?'

A thoughtful expression accompanied by a short pause occurred as the young man deliberated on the question. There was no immediate response and finally he said

'A strange request indeed sir. There are many dwellings that could be described in such a manner but none to which I would subscribe the definite article. Have you no further clarification?'

Peachey shook his head.

'I admit sir that I feel rather foolish in this, but it is of some importance for me to visit to a gentleman.'

'A gentleman sir? Then I expect a more superior residence than those I have been considering.'

A further pause whilst a review of his parish occurred, then he said

'I am at a loss sir and regret that I am unable to be of assistance. I shall make enquiries to see what I might establish….'

'Pray do not trouble yourself sir on my account' interjected Peachey. 'A trifling matter and one that has no importance warranting serious deliberation.'

Under no circumstances did he want this clergyman to alert anyone to the fact that such a search was underway. If the man could not recall any house with his knowledge, such enquiries would immediately stand out. He sought to deflect the Rev. Weston's attention with some haste.

'Your interest in chess has been long sir?'

Rev. Weston appeared slightly taken aback by the change of tack, but as it was to a subject close to his heart he readily responded.

'From my school days. Although one would imagine I would have progressed further than I have. As you are aware sir, ones progress is dictated by ones opponents. I have had little opportunity of expanding my horizons of late, as my opponents have tended to be older members of the cloth whose moves have been established over the years and are totally predictable. You yourself play sir I take it?'

Peachey, glad to have moved onto a safer topic replied

'A little sir, a little.'

Trevelyan, now sitting quietly behind them broke in

'If you are looking for originality, a fox's cunning, bravado, apparent recklessness, then Mr. Peachey is your man sir.'

Rev. Weston's eyes moved from Trevelyan back to Peachey.

'I fear I am outclassed again sir, but if you could summon enough patience to play with a lower quality player, I would be honoured if you found time at your disposal for a short game during your sojourn here.'

Although disappointed that he was no nearer to locating the *black house* Peachey sensed that this unassuming clergyman had both personal appeal and the advantage of local knowledge. In spite of the failure to make direct progress, making a closer acquaintance to this man may well prove helpful. He replied

'Indeed it would be my honour to pass some of my time engaged in the noble game.'

'I thank you sir' said Rev. Weston with a polite nod of his head, continuing

'I'm afraid that I shall have to make my apologies and leave gentlemen as I have the school to attend to.'

'Indeed sir, indeed'

Peachey raised an arm to wave generally in the direction of the door

'We shall be delighted to see you again when circumstances permit.'

As the door closed on the retreating clergyman, Peachey sat down and looked at Trevelyan.

'Not a roaring success in the location of the *black house* was he?'

'Give him time sir. He is an industrious man and will apply himself to the task. However it does raise the question of the visibility of the house. If the name is given to be a landmark or as a locator, then its suitability is open to debate.'

Peachey replied,

'you are right sir. I placed too much hope on a quick result.'

Rising he walked across to Trevelyan's window.

'Its just that I have a difficult task and a limited time to determine its validity. I am no nearer the start point. That is the main disappointment.'

'Shall we walk around ourselves so that you may gain a first hand impression?' said Trevelyan. 'This may provide you with some thoughts as to how to proceed.'

' I need to do something. I feel the time marching on with the deadline approaching by the minute, yet I appear to be standing still'.

Peachey's view from this window proved to be no more helpful than his own.

Where was this Frenchman? Was he even in the town? The questions seemed endless.

Trevelyan sensing some action was required said

'Then let us go. Your man will have to pay a call on the spy who is to help him. He will therefore most certainly be a man of some means. Our route seems to lie on the more affluent side of the town and perhaps some of the other inns which are frequented by gentlemen, businessmen and merchants.'

Peachey looked back

'I thought most gentlemen were patrons of this establishment?'

'So they are, so they are, but others prefer to conduct their meetings in different establishments. We can also pay our respects to my uncle while we are passing.'

Peachey recalled previous meetings with Trevelyan's uncle. Whilst being of considerable financial means he lived in a world devoid of much opulence. He had scant regard for the trappings which polite society regarded as essential and engrossed himself in books and personal interests leaving the running of the house to his sister and staff.

A visit to him seemed as unrewarding as the clergyman had been this morning. However he had resided in Portsmouth for most of his life and undoubtedly knew anyone of importance. Obtaining information from him might produce dividends, as no explanation would be needed as to the reason for enquiries. He said

'An admirable idea. A trifle quaint and unpredictable but he's a good potential for information.'

'Precisely' replied Trevelyan.

Turning right on leaving the inn Peachey and Trevelyan made their way up *High Street*, followed a short distance behind by Fairweather. The wind swirled up the street causing Peachey to wrap his cloak further around his body. The cloak was a particular favourite of his, made by his London tailor with distinctive curved metalled fastenings. A very suitable garment for today.

Trevelyan's uncle's house was only a short distance away. The fact that Trevelyan chose to stay at *the George Inn* indicated as much about his uncle's household than anything else. A few minutes walk saw them outside the house that fronted onto the street and was accessed by a short flight of steps. Trevelyan led the way up the steps and banged on the front door.

An aging butler, on answering it and seeing Trevelyan on the steps, promptly opened it wide allowing him and his fellow visitor immediate access.

Fairweather waiting outside noted their entrance and then stared fascinated at the two pillars either side of the entrance door – they were totally *black*.

Peachey blinked his eyes as they entered Silas Trevelyan's house, not because of any blinding light but exactly the opposite. The interior was dark and cluttered with a miscellany of furniture and other items. Following Percy Trevelyan, they passed into a ground floor room where Silas Trevelyan was seated by the window.

'Good morning uncle' rendered Percy Trevelyan 'I am accompanied by Mr Henry Peachey. I am sure you remember him from your visits to Oxford.'

Silas Trevelyan looked up. Peachey remembered him vividly. He was a walking paradox and could be described as a young man looking old for his years or an old man looking younger. He had the enduring feature of the Trevelyans, that of being tall and thin.

His face had two creases either side of his mouth extending down from just below his eye sockets producing the effect of an independent jaw moving up and down on his face when talking. But the most captive feature was the watery eyes.

Peachey had learned that eyes showed the true feelings of a man rather than any expression he was exhibiting. They could be critical, evaluative, mocking, sympathetic, baleful or bland.

With Silas Trevelyan, he often gazed at a person leaving them unsure if they had been heard correctly. A similar look meant he just wasn't paying any attention. Most of the time the eyes were bland.

Silas Trevelyan made a gesture as if to rise.

'Pray remain seated sir' said Peachey, moving forward to greet the man. 'I am delighted to find you looking so well.'

Silas Trevelyan peered up at Peachey through watery eyes.

'How are you young man. How are the studies going at Oxford?'

Nonplussed, Peachey casually replied

'I have finished there now sir, in fact for some years now.'

'Is Beaufort still there? Give him my compliments. He was my tutor you know.'

'So I believe sir.'

A perennial question Peachey always received from him. The fact that Beaufort was at a very advanced age when Silas Trevelyan was himself at Oxford never appeared to register with him and that the man would have been long since departed this earth. It was as though time was stationary in Silas Trevelyan's world on occasions.

Percy Trevelyan moved across to take his uncle's hand.

'It is pleasing to see you again uncle and how is my aunt?'

'She's fidgety you know, never settles. All set to go to the American colonies you know but all that nonsense in Boston and reports of uprising with the thirteen states has rather dampened matters for her.'

'Good heavens, who would accompany her? No you uncle surely?'

Silas Trevelyan showed no sign of surprise at the question but carried on as though discussing some mild local issue.

'She has a new lady companion. Young woman, too intelligent by far for a woman, even has her own ideas. She travels everywhere with your aunt but appears to keep her in a good frame of mind so I don't interfere.'

Peachey looking a little apprehensive said

'I am informed sir one shouldn't underestimate the problems with the thirteen American states. The rebellion is occupying much of our foreign policy and much of our military strength. Anyone should be advised to remain in England until quashed.'

Silas Trevelyan's eyes slowly focussed on Peachey.

'Anyone who thinks this is going to finish shortly sir is mistaken. The Frenchies will see to that.'

'The French sir?'

'Its what the French were put on this earth for – someone for us to battle with - and then defeat. They were trounced recently in the seven years war and have been like a dog with it's tail between its legs ever since. They have now sided with the colonies and attempt to take us on indirectly.'

Peachey was taken aback that a man such as Silas Trevelyan who appeared to sit in his rooms in his own world should have such a grasp of matters taking place so far away and posses such knowledge of French intentions. It all seemed too accurate. He continued

'You have the advantage over me sir with your perception of these events. It would appear that you are favoured with reports from knowledgeable sources.'

Peachey watched for a reaction to his question. His own information tallied exactly with that of Silas Trevelyan's, but whereas his information came from his uncle and originally from the King's Counsel; where could Silas Trevelyan obtain such awareness?

Silas Trevelyan failed to notice any inquisitiveness in Peachey's comment and glassy eyed said

'Title tattle from sailors and soldiers tell one much and the amount of ale and beer Weevil Lane produces indicate how many ships are in the home waters.'

'You appear to have little time for the French. I was not aware at previous discussions of such a vigorous feeling.' said Peachey.

'I spent some time in France many years ago and my opinion and views of them were formed at that time.' Silas Trevelyan replied.

What exactly his opinions and views were was left to conjecture, Peachey noted. The assumption was that they were of distaste and hateful but a small lingering thought suggested that they could be exactly the opposite.

Strange but he had never thought of Silas Trevelyan as anything other than an eccentric. Perhaps a clever man might use that ruse as a cover for other activities. A second thought was that this was all nonsense and his task had distorted his perspective on anyone in Portsmouth with the remotest association with the French and local information – however.

Percy Trevelyan broke into Peachey's reverie and said

'Uncle have you ever heard of somewhere called the black house in the town?'

Peachey could have slain him on the spot.

Far from being helpful he had asked the very question that could alert a spy or someone in the pay of the French. Peachey spun his head to gauge the reaction from Silas Trevelyan. The eyes were bland, no discernable trace of anything unusual in the request that would provoke a different response. Silas Trevelyan replied

'We have bawdy houses galore, badly built houses, two inns with the colour blue in their names but of a black house or *maison noir*, none of which I am aware. Why do you ask?'

Peachey interjected before Percy Trevelyan had chance to reply.

'It was a wager I had; I had to find a house the same colour as my cloak. It is of trifling importance.'

'We have several houses that are grubby sir, would that suit your wager?' The eyes were now alive again with a mischievous twinkle.

The moment had passed and Peachey laughed at the man's prompt repartee. However it had not escaped his notice that Silas Trevelyan had used the French word for black house just a moment ago. Was he toying with him?

A discrete knock heralded the arrival of the butler with an ornate tray holding a finely cut decanter and three sparkling glasses. Silas Trevelyan nodded and said

'Gentlemen let us refresh ourselves after all this talk of French and coloured houses. Pray be seated and partake of a glass or two of this fine brandy.'

Looking directly at Peachey he continued with a slightly brighter than usual eye

'I've had it shipped all the way from France.'

Chapter 6

Fresh salt laden air told Rousseliere's senses they were approaching Portsmouth. It was refreshing.

Portsmouth actually lay on an Island. A fact not widely appreciated. The water to the north, separating the island from the mainland of England was however confined to a narrow strip. It was an island nevertheless.

The analogy to Gibraltar was obvious. Apart from Portsmouth being on flat land as opposed to the dominating rock overshadowing Gibraltar, they had many similar properties.

Capture of this piece of land would be of staggering strategic value.

Rousseliere was aware of the sea to his right immediately after crossing the *Hilsea Lines* which formed the northernmost defence, some five miles from the actual walled town of Portsmouth.

In addition to forming the first line of defence against invading armies it also provided protection to the farming activities within, absolutely vital to providing supplies to the town and surrounding area.

It was at the *Hilsea Lines* that he fully regained his composure as an army officer. They had purposefully broken their journey to enable him to spend a short period examining these defences. He felt that he was now looking to his duties and not simply conducting the charade of masquerading as a seaman and enduring the unsavoury company of Thomas Courtney.

On examining this defence position he was immediately downhearted and dejected. They were sound, well constructed and in excellent condition, proving to be a very formidable obstacle to a foot army devoid of heavy artillery.

These first reactions led him to believe that with the defences as secure as this, the plan would fail. British forces could readily hold the area until their reinforcements could be mustered from the mainland. These would immediately ensnare the invading forces in a pincer device, trapping them between the impasse of the *Hilsea Lines* and the northern relieving troops.

With a sinking heart he had climbed to vantage points to identify troop numbers. If he were to report back that the lines were impenetrable, then he would need to present the very fullest detail. The thought of being the bringer of bad news was unpalatable. An enthusiastic king with ardent supporters of the plan would hardly welcome such news.

Rousseliere would receive no thanks for undermining the military strategy of the main army force landing along the coast and attacking Portsmouth from the rear. To overrun such defences was unthinkable.

However, when studying the movements of the soldiers manning the Hilsea Lines' ramparts, a strangely curious pattern suddenly quickened his pulse; so much so that he could hardly believe what he saw.

The cramp that was beginning to deaden his legs disappeared in his excitement, and he willed himself to stay for a longer period. Time was critical to his task but so was obtaining the correct information, information that was so vital to the thousands of French and Spanish soldiers being assembled for this attack.

The guard changed again and - yes, it was repeated. The number and, more importantly, the fitness of the soldiers remained as before. The staggering fact was that the lines *were insufficiently manned and the soldiers that were there were mainly invalids or barely trained youngsters.*

He looked again not daring himself to believe it. The conclusion was stupendous. The invalids, although trained men were not fit for frontline engagement and limited in their effectiveness.

The youngsters would have no knowledge of actual warfare and apart from making up the numbers, would again be ineffective. A surprise attack would quickly overcome this force, and once having secured it with fit, able and trained French or Spanish soldiers would be easily able to hold off any British reinforcements sent to relieve the lines.

The earlier depression was replaced by total elation. Previously, and secretly at the back of his mind, was the thought that it may have been an over ambitious plan, but this changed it all. He now knew the plan would be successful and that he would be part of it.

Writing his findings of numbers, positions military strengths and weaknesses in his book, the then carefully tucked it back into the secret lining of his bag and resealed it.

Returning to a very impatient Courtney, he gave no indication of his discovery.   With such a lightened heart, he would have loved to share the news with a companion, but Courtney was not such a companion for this knowledge. Rousseliere was unsure exactly why, but inane caution dictated prudence.

The sea air thence seemed fresh and bracing. The memories of his sea crossing from France were eradicated from his mind and replaced with the feelings of a huntsman with the scent of the quarry in his nostrils.

Travelling the remaining distance to Portsmouth itself, he could see no further military defences on the way from the *Hilsea Lines* to *Landport Gate*.

Landport Gate was one of the solid stone built structures housing the gates providing entrance to the town. It was wider than the *King James Gate* near *Spice Island*, and was the main exit from the town to the North.

At the gate, the duty soldiers, preoccupied with their own affairs took no notice of two humble seamen returning to their ship.

For the first time since the *Hilsea Lines*, Rousseliere spoke to Courtney.

'Where do we stay now that we have reached Portsmouth?'

Courtney still rankled by Rousseliere's independence replied

'We are not. We shall stay at *Spice Island*.'

'How far away is Spice Island?' queried Rousseliere 'is it not part of the town then?'

Courtney looked at him with a scornful smile and said

'*Spice Island* is the lawless hellhole at the tip outside the wall of the town. We shall not draw attention to ourselves there. Two sailors with little money is a common enough sight and an expected one.'

You seem to have a penchant for lowly stinking places thought Rousseliere. He could appreciate the need for secrecy and not being observed, but Courtney seemed drawn to squalor. However from the splendid findings at the *Hilsea Lines*, Rousseliere could readily endure further discomfort. He now felt secure in the knowledge that he was discovering the Achilles heel of his hated enemy.

Side by side they walked down *Warblington Street* from *Landport Gate.* Rousseliere had gained in confidence every day since his arrival at Dover. Not once had anyone looked twice, let alone challenge him. The idea of disguise as a sailor from the Channel Isles was perfect. His view of the scheme and the planning improved as each day passed.

The old spy from *Le Secret du Roi* that they were to meet would prove interesting. He would be well established in the town and perhaps could provide better shelter and company than Courtney did. On the other hand he would be regarded as a gentleman or person of similar standing and would not be expected to deal with sailors, especially from the Channel Isles.

Rousseliere instinctively felt the side of his bag for the snuffbox. Passing that over to the spy would be another part of his task completed, and a further relief. The snuffbox was an interesting piece of work with a peculiar decoration on the lid. He had examined it carefully on several occasions and found it fascinating.

Trudging southwards the scene was multi faceted - similar in many respects to London, but with a different flavour. It was the proximity of the sea and the Royal Navy that caused the difference. There were street traders, peddlers, drunks, Naval Officers, Midshipmen, washerwomen, and merchants all going about their business with complete disregard for those in a different social order.

The disconcerting feature was that the sailors looked healthy, the civilians well kempt, and the merchant traders reasonably prosperous, how different from the France he had left, where starvation of many was the norm and others left to die in the streets.

They reached *Golden Lion Lane.* Rousseliere looked carefully, relating and maintaining his bearings at all times. This particular lane or street was an apparent dividing line between social strata, with poor, narrow hovels on one side and more prosperous dwellings away to the left.

They reached the crossroad with *St. Thomas' Street,* with the eponymous church to the right. It was a large building, which, according to Courtney, had its origins with Richard the Lion Heart.

This point rankled with Rousseliere, as Richard1 had apparently been revered by the British, but was in fact French speaking, and apart from six months or so in England, had spent all his time in France. Even when fighting in the crusades against the Muslims he returned to France.

The British always seemed to manipulate events to the detriment of France he thought.

A sobering thought flashed across his mind. If he were ever required to enter the church whilst he was here, he must remember not to cross himself. He must keep firmly in his mind that they did not practice the true faith openly. A slip such as that could bring much attention. He resolved to keep his wits about him; it was remarkably easy to give himself away.

Moving past the dominant presence of the church, his heart beat faster. There were rows of red-coated soldiers moving in line along by the sea wall ramparts, moving down to what was obviously the Guard House.

Looking to see where he now was, the sign said *Battery Row*. This was mentally noted to add to his mental map of the town.

The soldiers on view were a mixed bunch with hardly a sound or able man amongst them. The elation of his original discovery was kept on the boil.

Courtney was oblivious to Rousseliere's inner consternation on the proximity of so many solders and turning right again, walked past the retreating soldiers.

Ahead was the gate leading to *Spice Island*. It bore an inscription in its stone façade - *King James Gate*. This was erected for King James II who was King of England for such a short period following the colourful reign of the lusty King Charles II.

With the arrival of William of Orange, the Protestant claimant, James II retreated from London to France and Italy, being driven out by his faith. Rousseliere thought *the British have much to account for*.

The gates were open and no attention was given to them as they passed through the gates and over the drawbridge. Courtney being more ready with conversation said

'You are now leaving civilisation as you know it – we are entering *Spice Island*.'

Rousseliere recalled the small area on his map. It was like a toe at the end of Portsmouth; adjacent the small docks and teeming with low life, cut throats, villains, fugitives, whores and poor families.

Every other building appeared to be an inn, often with their patrons slumped at tables. The rooms upstairs were constantly vibrating with the exertions of the whores attempting to jettison the built up passion of their clients, in the shortest possible time.

All in all, not exactly the place for any god fearing novice.

Rousseliere was not exactly a novice but he had not been required to reside in such area before. Courtney was right however; the place was ideal to hide from the military. Any known informers were probably dispatched to their maker by means of a severed throat or drowning in the dock.

Here, he was effectively invisible in the midst of his enemy's stronghold. From his encouraging start that morning he was now anxious to continue his survey of the harbour.

They walked down *The Broad*, the main street leading down to the tip of Spice Island, known as *The Point*. The object was to find somewhere to stay in one of the unappealing inns that fronted the thoroughfare.

The words that Rousseliere would hear next would mark the start of a most dramatic chain of events.

'Hallo darling, have you got something to give me? You're a big strong fella ain't you, come on inside and let me soothe your troubles away.'

The siren voice, slightly more mellow than the raucous callings of the other whores made him turn his head.

She was young, dark haired, dressed in a simple blouse and long skirt that appeared unable to ward off the chill afternoon air – she looked perished. He hesitated for a brief moment and then the weaselled grinning features of Courtney said to him

'We have to stay somewhere, if you fancy her this is probably as good as any.'

Sleeping with whores on Spice Island was not Rousseliere's idea of doing his duty, but Courtney continued

'We can take a room upstairs, pay for the girl and have the room to ourselves all night. I don't want to share a room with any others.'

Again Courtney's reasoning was bizarre but practical. It had been a constant concern to Rousseliere that the security of his belongings would be a problem in this area. Sailors would not normally pay for a room for their own but would share one, which heightened the problem.

At least they could pay the girl off, get some food and drink and keep all intruders at bay. He looked again at Courtney who sensed his tacit agreement turned to the girl and said

'We will share the room with you'

'That will cost double and not half each' she promptly replied.

'You will get what you're worth. There's plenty more who will welcome us if you wont'

Courtney's response was a veiled ultimatum.

She looked from one to the other. They both appeared healthy and possessing the money. She was very cold, hungry and in need of money; money she couldn't afford to pass up from two sailors.

'Come sirs let's go inside'

They followed her through a low doorway to find themselves being scrutinised by a pock faced older man standing behind a crude bar.

'What'll you be drinking you fine gentlemen?' he said reaching for two small glasses.

'None of your fake gin at scandalous prices' replied Courtney, 'we'll have ale and it'd better be your best or we're not stopping.'

The man looked them up and down. Sensing that they weren't drunks or simpletons ready to be overcharged, and might cause trouble if angered, promptly complied with their request without a murmur.

Two other men of similar age to the innkeeper, sat huddled round a low fire. They dropped their eyes as Courtney looked round the room. They were aware that it was better not to be too curious if one wanted a longer life on *Spice Island*.

The landlord pouring the second drink looked at the sailors, then to the girl waiting at the bottom of the narrow stirs said

'By selecting our Kitty, you have chosen the best girl in these parts, clearly discerning gentlemen I'll be bound.'

He gave a coarse little laugh and looked at his colleagues for an audience. They smirked but said nothing only glancing up furtively at Courtney and Rousseliere.

Courtney focussed his attention back to the innkeeper.

'What meats that are fit to eat have you? Only good wholesome fare will do.'

The barkeeper was becoming uneasy with the smaller of the two sailors with those narrow piercing eyes. He was if anything sinister and he told himself to humour this one.

'Good cold meat sirs, fresh from the docks, tasty for two fine sailormen such as you. I'll have it carved and sent up to you. Do you want it before or after?'

He was about to smirk again but suddenly thought better of it.

Meat from the docks, true, with the owners still looking for it thought Rousseliere. Looking at the girl waiting somewhat dejectedly he motioned to Courtney with his fingers for three portions. Courtney glanced at the girl and was about to reply but suddenly closed his mouth again. Turning to the innkeeper he said

'We'll have three portions and now, and now means now!'

The innkeeper nodded as Courtney barked the order and said

'Right away gentlemen with no delay. Kitty will bring it up.'

Signalling to the girl, she disappeared out to the room beyond and the innkeeper came round from behind rubbing his hands on a grubby cloth.

'Come my fine lads, let me show you to the room.'

Leading the way he climbed the stairs with no great agility. Courtney and Rousseliere followed in his wake. They went up two flights to the top of the building where he opened the door to a small room housing a bed, a chair and very little else.

'Our best room gentlemen as you can see' he said waving his hand expansively around the room. Now if I can trouble you for payment I will leave you to your pleasures.'

Rousseliere walked into the room over to the small window while Courtney settled the payment.

Rousseliere, in keeping with his military training, hung his had out of the narrow window to check what means of entry or escape this afforded. There was a shear drop down the back of the house to a very narrow alley. No one was able to enter by that route. Walking across the room he sat on the solitary chair.

Courtney sat on the edge of the bed.

'This is our refuge for the night. The innkeeper thinks he has a couple of rampant sailors upstairs, but he's been well paid and content to let us remain in peace.'

A knock on the door precipitated its opening, and Kitty carrying a tray with the food and drink entered. Placing it on the floor, she handed a plate of meat and bread each to Rousseliere and Courtney. Rousseliere signalled to her for her to take the remaining plate. She looked at Rousseliere saying

'Thank you sir, you are very kind.'

Rousseliere nodded and replied

'You are in need of it I sense.'

She looked up sharply.

'You speak funny sir. You'll not be from these parts that's for sure.'

'I am from some way away but I serve on a British ship-of-the-line.'

Rousseliere normally always allowed Courtney to do the talking to avoid standing out. His English was good enough to pass for a sailor but the accent was unmistakeable.

'Many different folk pass this way from the docks.' She said.

She was now sitting cross-legged on the floor relishing the food that had unexpectedly been provided. Her colouring was returning and she became more animated as the food restored her spirits.

Rousseliere thought grimly, *there will be a great many more different folk passing this way in the not too distant future; French and Spanish will be the languages you will hear then.*

A period of silence followed as they eat in silence. Rousseliere sensed that she kept glancing at him from time to time. Once they had finished, Courtney wiped his lips and leant back.

'Sustain the inner man, that the first priority.'

Supported by his arms he half lay on the bed and looked from one to the other.

'We have time on our hands till the morning. Let us see how we are going to be entertained.'

Looking at the girl Kitty he said

'We shall have to agree who is to be first.'

Kitty looked from Courtney to Rousseliere. Her preference was clear. Rousseliere replied

'I am tired from my travels and am in need of air. I shall leave you both for a while and take a turn outside.'

The words were almost a slap in the face to Kitty. Her face fell as she looked back at Courtney to gauge how she would fair next. Without waiting for a response, Rousseliere rose from the chair and made for the door.

'I will warm her up for you,' were the words ringing in his ears as Rousseliere opened the door and started down the stairs.

At the bottom, the three men still in the bar area looked up.

'Taking it in turns are we?' said the innkeeper

'Perhaps some more ale will revive flagging spirits.'

The smirking recommenced but Rousseliere simply shook his head, said nothing and walked outside.

The air felt better to Rousseliere once he was outside. He took note of his bearings, and headed towards the water at the harbour entrance. He reflected on Courtney.

He had never warmed to him; but there again why should he? They were compatriots in arms only. He was keen to examine the defences at Portsmouth. He turned and looked back at *King James Gate*. It was integrated into the ramparts and walled defences of the town - *all these defences were in pristine condition.*

Reaching the water's edge he looked directly across the harbour. On the far side was Gosport with its own battery defences. One could almost touch the other side it appeared so close. It was not until actually seeing it, that the narrowness of the harbour opening could be appreciated.

Any ships attacking from the East would have to sail along the coast past Fort Cumberland, Frazer Battery and then past Henry VIII's well-constructed and positioned Southsea Castle. Ships that survived that barrage, then had to round the approach to Portsmouth Harbour. They then faced the seaward defences from Portsmouth and the Battery at Gosport. Under normal circumstances it was a suicidal approach.

Looking across to the 16 heavy gun Gosport Battery, the military skill and brilliance of the plan could now be fully appreciated. It was essential to take both sides of the harbour. With both Portsmouth and Gosport silenced; ships would be allowed a free passage into the harbour.

It was a bold plan, and taken unawares, Portsmouth was theirs for the asking. A quiet satisfaction settled on Rousseliere. It only remained for the troop positions and deployments to be recorded before planting *The Mistress*.

They were on time for that. The only other remaining task was to liase with the spy from *Le Secret du Roi*, brief his confederates, arrange to locate the money, and then set up Portsmouth ready for the invasion.

Military life can sometimes be very rewarding.

Rousseliere decided to walk a little further then return to the inn; Courtney should have exhausted himself by then.

Chapter 7

Nathan Oates was eleven and hungry. Last year he was ten and hungry. The prospects for next year failed to indicate much improvement in the way of nourishment.

His widowed mother was resigned to living her life on Spice Island with himself and his ten-year-old sister. Her prospects of finding another man who would be prepared to support her and two children were so slim as to be non-existent. Nathan was therefore destined to be an early breadwinner.

He was thin but wiry with a torso that could twist and bend and coupled with good arm strength, was capable of supporting his weight from slim ledges and bars. He needed to do this because Nathan climbed, and scaled apparently un-climbable structures, where his grip on the smallest of projections would allow him to pull himself ever upward.

This was of particular benefit to him, because Nathan was a thief.

It was not necessarily a chosen profession, but one foisted upon him by the absence of father and money. He had promised his mother that he would contribute to their income, and apart from running errands and other miscellaneous tasks producing next to nothing, this was the only occupation he had stumbled on to achieve that goal.

His mother took in washing which his sister collected, and any menial task that she could find.

To date his thieving results had not been an overwhelming success. The hauls had generated only meagre sums for stolen items exchanged for ready money from a local innkeeper – one that cast a greedy eye on his illegal acquisitions.

One thing he knew for certain, the penalties were harsh if caught. That was another reason he kept his newly developed skill from his mother, reasoning that she had enough troubles without her worrying about her offspring's activities.

He had set off that day to seek new pastures for his nefarious skills, but had found none suitable. On walking back to *Broad Street* the thought occurred to him, *why not rob the very man who has been robbing you.* There appeared a perverse logic to this idea that appealed to him no end.

Arriving outside the inn and looking through the window, he could see the innkeeper standing by the bar with two others sitting over their ale. They were sharing a jest about something and appeared settled in the room for a while. Skirting around the back he looked down a very small alley. A rat scurrying past made him jump and he kicked out at it, but it was long since gone.

Looking up, he could see a small unfastened window right at the top of the building. There were no projections for either hand or foot holds but with the gap between the two walls being small, he placed his back on one wall and stretched out his legs to touch the opposite one. Pushing back, and putting one foot above the other, he was soon suspended above the ground between the two walls, and moving upwards. Providing he maintained the pressure he could easily move up the wall. He commenced the slow upward journey towards the window.

This was to be the most dramatic and far reaching action he would ever take in his life. Its outcome would produce a staggering turn of events.

Chapter 8

Peachey descended the steps from Silas Trevelyan's house in contemplative mood. Percy Trevelyan had elected to remain with his uncle as he wished to speak with his aunt on her return.

He on the other hand, having determined that his quest for information had run dry from Silas Trevelyan, decided that a more direct approach must be taken. To date he had failed to locate the *black house*, that, according to his uncle's informant, was to feature so prominently in the unknown attack.

He had assumed that the person living there would be the instigator of the activities. The fact that no house or building answering that description was to be found, was a major setback.

He had confidently expected it to be pointed out to him, enabling watch and further discreet probing to lead him to the plotters. The fact being that the *black house* was not a local landmark and totally unknown.

His uncle would be waiting for news that would allow him to convince the king and other counsellors to send some form of presence to take over the task from him. A nagging sensation failed to leave his thoughts – his uncle's information might be false.

His own purported purpose regarding his presence in Portsmouth was investigating the activities of some victualers. He now had urgent need of help from the Governor to make any start at all. He must therefore make some contact with the victualers and go though the motions of dealing with them, enough at least, to convince the Governor that his forthcoming request was of a secondary nature.

Rapid footsteps sounded behind him, turning slightly Fairweather appeared at his shoulder from the direction of the rear of the house.

'Back to the inn sir?'

'No not yet awhile' replied Peachey, eying the manservant who miraculously and regularly appeared without summons,

'What have you learned from the servants?' - for that was where the man had obviously been.

Fairweather gave a wry smile.

'A strange house, if I may say so sir. Mr. Percy Trevelyan's aunt is the lady of the house but the cook seems to run most of the activities, his aunt not being there for most of the time.'

'Of Mr. Silas Trevelyan?'

'Begging your pardon sir, but they expressed a certain sense of eccentricity.'

'You mean they think he's mad.'

'Them was the words they used sir, but I am only repeating them to you.'

'Have no fear Fairweather, that is the considered opinion of most. What were your impressions of the house?'

'A strange collection of furniture in there and no mistake sir. Some I wouldn't give houseroom, but also some very good pieces, - one or two well made French items...........'

'French?' Peachey interjected.

'Yes sir, a fine inlaid table and two very good chairs, gilt legs with splendid coverings.'

Peachey mused over this fact. Silas Trevelyan was an enigma and no mistake. Was he mad by design? What were his beliefs, patriotism and motives? More to the point was his eccentricity genuine?

Every time he had met him in the past, he had endured him without paying much attention. If he did harbour feelings for the French, they had been safely concealed for many years.

Sir Richard Peachey's words kept repeating themselves in his ears – *this spy serving the old Le Secret Roi has been undetected for years and is likely to be well placed. Be wary of placing too much trust in anyone, lest he hears directly, or by chance, that we seek him. He will then hide behind his façade or go to ground.*

This was the major problem – *if he hears directly or by chance. An overheard innocuous remark would alert him. Had Silas Trevelyan been alerted? If the Governor was informed of his own true purpose, could he inadvertently warn the spy?*

Sometimes too much caution leads nowhere, and that was exactly where he was at this moment – nowhere.

Wrapping his cloak tighter around himself he turned back to Fairweather.

'Did they inform you much of interest regarding Mr. Silas Trevelyan?'

'Nothing much other than his habits sir. They say that he takes little interest in the brewery or his business affairs. There is a lawyer who attends to these for him and his nephew, Mr. Percy sir, comes frequently to keep an eye on matters.'

Fairweather pulled his own thin coat across his chest to keep the chilly wind blowing up from the sea at bay.

'Oh, and they say that Mr. Silas has strange visitors at peculiar times.'

'What visitors and what do they call peculiar times?'

'I'm afraid I'm not aware who the visitors are, but they say he has visits after the staff have been dismissed and gone to bed sir. More than that I cannot say. I have made my acquaintance with the cook who seems to have taken a shine to me,' he added with a tinkling eye.

Peachey being aware of Fairweather's exploits with the ladies and the euphemisms used, smiled inwardly at his man's rapid progress. At least Fairweather was making some headway in his dealings, - which was more than he could claim.

'Keep a weather eye on that area and report anything else of consequence. Bear in mind though, Mr. Silas Trevelyan regards his cook as much of a housekeeper as a cook, so don't create problems for the household with your interests, - if you've a mind for what I say.'

'Perfectly understood sir,' replied Fairweather, the twinkle still undimmed.

Further food for thought mused Peachey, Silas Trevelyan appeared to have greater depths to plumb than one imagined. He turned his attention to the matter of the Governor and how he was to handle his approach to him. Looking back at Fairweather he said

'Are you yet familiar with an inn called the *Golden Lion*?'

'Indeed sir, it is around the corner from *The George* in *Golden Lion Lane*. It faces the church.'

'Then we proceed there now' dictated Peachey. 'My understanding is that several of the merchants and victualers meet there to discuss business and affairs of the town. When we arrive I want you to find them, say that I am interested in victualing my privateer ships and seek worthy suppliers with whom I may conduct business.'

'Where shall you be sir?' enquired Fairweather.

'I shall also be in the inn. You will come and fetch me if they agree to meet with me.'

'As you say sir.'

The Golden Lion was another coaching inn, located, as Fairweather had said within a short distance from *The George*. Many said that it attracted a similar class to *The George*, but that less senior naval officers frequented it.

It may have been the factor that if business was to be done, then it was not the senior officers who performed it, but those below them. Those men together with those civilians in the pay of the Admiralty.

Peachey strode through the door and after carefully looking about him through the smoky interior, took a seat at a table near the window. This allowed him to survey the occupants of the room with ease. There were three groups sat round tables, talking and drinking, with one group playing a hand of cards. Each group appeared prosperous and too interested in their own affairs to pay him much attention.

Fairweather had parted company from him on entering and could now be seen in discussion with the innkeeper who pointed to the far group. This comprised two older men and one much about Peachey's age. Fairweather approached them, touched his forehead and spoke.

They listened for a moment then obviously enquired where his master was. Fairweather pointed towards Peachey who promptly looked out of the window to avoid having to meet their gaze. From the corner of his eye he saw the younger man rise and make his way across to him.

'Begging your pardon sir, may I name myself. I am Jeremiah Porter. I carry on the honourable business of a victualler, being trusted with contracts from many ship owners such as your good self. Your manservant advises that you have ships requiring victualing when they arrive in Portsmouth. Would you care to honour my colleagues and I at our table where we can offer you some refreshment and discuss your plans.'

Peachey spent a moment or two in looking at the man. He did not wish to appear too eager to discuss business with them and needed to assess the situation. Finally he said

'Thank you for your offer sir'.

He followed the man across the room, who, from the rear view, was of similar height to himself, wearing a well-cut light coloured jacket, doublet and hose – *hallmarks of a good tailor* thought Peachey – the shiny black buckled shoes completed his appearance.

Money to afford to dress well was clearly visible. As they neared the table, one of the older men stood but the other remained seated. The young man who had introduced himself as Jeremiah Porter said

'May I introduce my colleagues. This is Mr. Erasmus Faulkner – and may we seek your forgiveness if Mr. Faulkner does not rise, as he is smitten with a malady that produces shortness of breath with physical movements.'

They nodded to each other.

'Your servant sir' said the elderly man.

The three looked expectantly at Peachey.

'I am Mr. Henry Peachey - Gentleman.'

'This is Mr. John Gunn' said Porter indicating the third man who had already risen.

They exchanged greetings and Peachey looked at this man who was in his mid fifties, possessing a hard face, unaccustomed to smiling; of stocky build, medium height and clothes that, although of good quality, lacked the panache of his younger companion. An accent was apparent in his speech.

After offering a chair to Peachey, they all regrouped around the table.

'A glass of port or brandy sir?'

Porter enquired proffering a glass and two bottles residing on the polished table.

'Brandy thank you.'

Porter poured a glass and handed it to Peachey. Sipping the brandy, he immediately discovered its taste was inferior to the good version that Silas Trevelyan had produced earlier in the day - g*ood French brandy Silas had boasted with a smile.*

John Gunn stared hard at Peachey.

'You have ships you say sir, and you have not brought them here before.'

The tone was mildly accusing.

Peachey was careful with his reply. These men knew ships, their owners, and exactly what was required for each type of vessel. They knew how much to charge and would arrange side transactions if required. It was second nature to them.

'I have just acquired two Privateers gentlemen. They are not from these parts as you can imagine.'

He left it at that. They would immediately surmise that they were probably acquired as prize ships from somewhere like the West Indies. If they wanted business, they would not enquire too deeply and cause offence to a potential new purchaser of their services.

'Quite so, quite so sir,' continued Gunn, ' I myself am the owner of much property in the town and have extensive business dealings. I am not engaged in the business of being a victualer, that being the prerogative of Mr. Faulkner and Mr. Porter.'

He gestured as he spoke to the old seated man and the young well dressed man. He continued

'I may however be able to assist you in other matters, - perhaps you require premises for your business interests, - a dwelling maybe. If so, I am at your command sir.'

Peachey nodded his head in acknowledgement. Now that Gunn had spoken for longer, he now knew the accent, – he was a Scot. The unmistakeable lilt was clearly discernable.

The old man, Erasmus Faulkner, now quietly said.

'There is a shortage of ships sir, if you have recently acquired them, then you have chosen a very opportune moment.'

Peachey surveyed the man who communicated in slow ponderous speech. Again, there was a distinct accent, not so readily definable as Gunn's, but still discernable.

Slow and ponderous appeared to be the hallmarks of this man. His features were broad with a flattened nose central to a lined face. His lips had a distinctive bluish hue to them, and with red veined cheeks gave him an unwarranted bright complexion. Animated hands accompanied his speech as if to add emphasis to each word. The hands with age-lined folded mottled skin, bore witness to his age, which Peachey gauged at late sixties.

Looking into remarkable bright eyes, Peachey replied

'I have been informed that the investment that my friends and I completed would reap a good harvest.'

'Good indeed' added Porter enviously. The younger mans eyes were never still, darting from one to the other as though not wishing to miss anything, -or perhaps any opportunity. He said

'I myself run a modest victualing enterprise and also look after Mr. Faulkner's interests in this matter.'

His eyes glanced at Faulkner with these words. Peachey was astounded to see that the bright eyes of Faulkner responded with malevolence. Not what he expected at all – *something to bear in mind*?

Porter didn't notice or didn't care as he continued

'We can take care of your entire requirements sir. I take it you will not handle the day to day affairs but will have your own pursers?'

'After I have established the business arrangements, of course I will do just that' Peachey replied. He had no intention however of becoming embroiled in any negotiation, only to sow the seeds of his apparent venture.

Having now met Porter, Faulkner and Gunn he felt that he had three names with which to bandy with the Governor. This should make his role look more convincing. He continued,

'I would naturally wish to compare prices and costs with other suppliers.'

'Unnecessary sir, if I may make so bold' said Porter hastily, 'we can arrange for the best prices and for any arrangement you may wish to make.'

Porter gave a knowing look at the last remark, leaving Peachey in no doubt that some manipulation with the figures or payments, presented no difficulties.

Porter continued,

'How would you propose to make payment sir?'

'In ready money' replied Peachey.

The effect was a rapier thrust. All three moved in their seats in unison. The thought of ready money for payment instead of credit notes, barter or exchange was like manna from heaven to them.

Faulkner's sonorous voice said

'You can rest assured sir that, if you do us the honour of your business, none shall better our proposals. I have lived long enough and in many places to know that the service you will receive shall be never equalled.'

Curiosity motivated Peachey; he asked,

'I detect from your speech Mr. Faulkner sir that you have resided out of this country for some spell.'

'Italy sir' was the prompt response from the old man.

Italy was not the origin of his accent, - of that Peachey was sure. The Italians tended to bounce their words along in distinct syllables unlike the British or French that placed stress on groupings of a word. However Peachey had no desire to dwell on the old man's history but nevertheless it was still slightly puzzling.

Peachey nodded however and said,

'it would appear gentlemen that I may well have my wants satisfied here. If so, I shall be indebted to you.'

Turning to Gunn he said

'I have a mind to have a house here Mr. Gunn and perhaps somewhere ashore for my fittings. Regarding a house, where would a gentleman live in order to be a party to polite society?'

Gunn although still stone faced, exhibited a thawing warmness from his eye and said

'You seem to have an uncanny knack of selecting the right time for your ventures. I have such a dwelling in *St. Thomas' Street* ideal for a gentleman, and suitable for entertaining and all other social engagements. You must permit me to show it to you.'

'It sounds very suitable for my purposes Mr. Gunn. I was told that there were various houses here, and a dashed peculiar feature was that some of them were black.'

Peachey had decided that this was a moment to play to a chance, and watched all three men closely for their reactions. If they were aware of any significance, they all disguised it to perfection. All three looked perplexed. It was Gunn who replied.

'That is a most strange statement sir. I have no knowledge of any dwellings even remotely answering that description Is your informant familiar with the town sir?'

'No, it was merely a passing comment made whilst in London. Obviously a error by the person who made it.'

Seeking to move on Peachey said

'I hope to establish my plans in more detail soon, and would then be obliged Mr. Gunn, if we can make arrangements to visit your property.'

So there it was – another barren enquiry. If these men today had no knowledge of a *black house*, what reliability could be placed on his uncle's informant?

Their conversation was interrupted by the approach of a youngish woman clutching the hand of a boy aged around eight years old. She hesitatingly approached their table and on reaching them addressed Porter, - holding the boy in front of her almost as a shield.

'Mr. Porter sir, I am very sorry indeed sir to approach you whilst with your friends and acquaintances, but I have not been permitted to speak with you at your place of business. I have matters that are extremely pressing sir, and seek leave to address you.'

Porter swung round with a furious look; in fact Peachey had seldom seen someone so instantly angered to such a degree. He raised his voice to the timid woman,

'How dare you speak to me, particularly when I am talking business. I have nothing to say to you. If you are enquiring about the barrels your late husband made, you are lucky that I don't have you thrown in prison.'

'Those barrels were of the highest craftsmanship sir. My late husband – God rest his sole, was a first class cooper, and his barrels are widely used. I desperately need the payment for them sir, as my family is not provided for otherwise. I know not what will become of us if we are not paid soon. Fifty barrels are now owed for sir.'

'You will end up in the Debtors Prison if I have anything to do with it' blazed Porter. 'That your husband did not provide for you is none of my doing. If he had been alive I would have had him imprisoned for deceit and fraud. I have had to replace all those useless barrels that he supplied me with.'

'But I have seen them being used ....'

'Are you calling me a liar madam!' Porters voice now reached crescendo pitch. 'Not another word will I say on the matter unless you want me to have you arrested.'

The woman, looking from one man to the other, blinking back tears and holding on to the petrified boy backed away, and deciding that further appeals were useless, rushed from the room firmly grasping her son.

Porter's rage damped rapidly as he saw her retire. The red blotches that were visible either side of his neck paled, and he turned around and faced the table again. He regained his composure with remarkable speed, and a rising smirk replaced the thunderous outlook previously ruling his features.

'Apologies gentlemen for that unwelcome intrusion into our discussions.'

'You appeared to have been singularly unlucky with your barrels then sir' said Gunn looking intently at Porter.

'A question of business sir, as I'm sure you will appreciate. That cooper was unskilled in his business affairs, he deserved his rewards.'

'So the barrels were useless then?' said Gunn.

'On the contrary sir, the workmanship was first class, those fifty barrels will last me for many a year. He failed to obtain his payments and allowed the debt to increase to fifty barrels, so he's only himself to blame for his widow's predicament. As I say, good business for me don't you know.'

There was no immediate endorsement of his actions from those assembled. Gunn remained staring with his customary stony look, Faulkner examined his aging hands and Peachey sipped his drink, looking around the room purposefully avoiding anyone's gaze.

Anyone's that is, other than Fairweather's, who was standing quietly at the back of the room adjacent the door.

Peachey looked at him and nodded almost imperceptibly towards the receding woman. A very brief acknowledgement, - finger against the side of his nose, signalled Fairweather's understanding. He slid unnoticed from the room.

It was Faulkner who broke the silent impasse.

'Mr. Peachey you implied you were from London.'

The focus of attention at once changed from Porter to the newly announced ship owner.

'I, like your good self sir have lived in various places. London is my principal home.'

'Have you resided abroad then sir?' furthered Faulkner.

'Indeed sir, I have stayed in France when our country's relationship permitted.'

Faulkner's eyes looked straight into Peachey's, but it was Gunn who continued.

'And how did you enjoy the experience sir.'

'It is an uncommonly large country sir, and for the brief period I was there, I found the people with whom I met agreeable and pleasant. It is country against country rather than people against people that causes much of the friction.'

Both Gunn and Faulkner nodded in agreement. A fact that Peachey found somewhat surprising. He had, on impulse, decided that he would float the notion that he was not totally opposed to the French, with the hope that this may attract any French sympathiser who was to hear of it; not that he expected any such leanings from the three grabbing rouges that surrounded him.

'You have the language then sir?' enquired Faulkner.

'I have a gentleman's education sir. Knowledge of French and Latin being customary of course.'

Taking a decorated watch from his inside pocket, Peachey studied the dial.

'But I must not take up anymore of your valuable time gentlemen, and I have another appointment, - unrelated to our business,' he added for their ease of mind.

He rose, signalling his departure that triggered a similar response from two of his three companions. Faulkner remaining seated, nevertheless performing polite gestures to excuse himself from his restricting impediment.

'May we enquire where you are staying sir' added Gunn.

'I am at *The George Inn.*'

Approving nods indicated that this was in accordance with his role as ship owner.

Peachey reached across to where his cloak was draped over the chair and swept it around his shoulders.

A gentle cough, 'mine I believe sir'. Porter indicated the cloak.

Peachey looked at the garment, it was remarkably similar to his own, black with almost identical metal fastenings.

'Abject apologies sir, they are surprisingly the same.'

Peachey returned the garment to the chair and retrieved his own adjacent to it continuing

'Another tailor with fashion in mind, I have a care.'

Porter produced a small smile from nowhere.

'Mine does his best, but is not to the level of London style I'll be bound.'

Peachey was unsure; Porter clearly was conscious of his dress and had paid well for that cloak. His attention to sartorial elegance was both costly and surprising for such a man.

'Till we meet again' concluded Peachey.

'Your servant sir.'

Similar rejoins were given by the others.

Peachey threaded his way through the tables to the door, conscious of a trio of eyes watching his departure.

A mixed bunch, unlikely companions at any time, no doubt drawn together by business, although the episode with the cooper's widow brought no unison to them.

Back outside there was a bite in the air contrasting with the snug warmth of the inn. Of Fairweather there was no sign. He had obviously attended to his task of following and making contact with the widow. A fool's errand? - perhaps so. Nevertheless the more relevant information he could discover regarding local personages, the better; a fact that might prove useful in discussions with the Governor, and who knows? It may even help his cause – heaven knows it was needed.

Retracing his steps back to the *High Street* he turned right at the junction and headed down towards the water, away from *The George Inn*. His destination was the Governor's residence where General Robert Monkton conducted his duties.

He was bracing himself to take the Governor into his confidence, a matter not lightly undertaken as Peachey's uncle had strongly advised against any such confidences, unless it was utterly imperative to do so. Peachey had already breached that instruction by the inclusion of Percy Trevelyan and now was intending to do likewise with the Governor.

With every minute the adversary moved closer to his goal, totally unopposed by Peachey who had no awareness of him or his contacts. He had to beard the lion in his den with the Governor, and alleviate the growing desperation of his plight.

Turning left at the bottom of the street into *The Battery* he passed the Guardhouse en route to the Garrison Church lying behind its stalwart protection.

The Garrison Church provided the entire spiritual needs of the soldiers plus church parades with military precision. To one side but part of the same large building including the church, was the Governor's residence, a stone construction improved architecturally over the years by incumbents who refused to accept the military bleakness foisted upon them with the house.

On reaching the entrance, a red fronted soldier stood on guard. He made no effort to confront Peachey, having obviously ascertained that no threat was to be encountered by the Governor.

Passing through an open porch door he pulled the bell rope to summon attention. A wizened soldier opened it. He was, no doubt ending his fighting service to the nation by answering doors and similar tasks. Without waiting, Peachey walked on through and found himself face to face with an army captain, seated at a highly polished desk in the expansive hallway.

The captain looked the most unlikely candidate to lead troops from the front into a bloody battle. He was fat with swollen flabby red cheeks indicating the taking of more bottles of wine than prisoners. To emphasise the conflicting image further, he was probably no more than mid-thirties in age. He looked somewhat disdainfully at Peachey,

'Good afternoon sir, how may I be of assistance?'

The speech had an element of a slur to it and was unwelcoming in its texture.

'I wish to speak with the Governor'

The surprise of such a statement registered in the captain's response. It was as though an unknown visitor passing through the door had never had the temerity to request such a meeting before.

'May I ask the purpose of such a meeting?'

Peachey faced him down.

'I have private business to discuss with him.'

'Does the Governor know of your visit?'

'He is unaware of my arrival.'

'Then I must ask you again sir, as to the purpose of your request.'

Peachey felt his anger rising. The captain was utilising his post to be obstructive but under the pretext of performing his duty.

'The business is mine alone, and pray who am I addressing sir.'

The veiled threat of asking his name cut no ice with the captain, who was warming to his task.

'I am Captain Gadfew, head of the Governor's staff. It is through me that visitors meet with the Governor. 'This was issued as a form of bait.

Peachey restated his position

'I am not at liberty to disclose my purpose sir.'

'Then I am not at liberty to permit a meeting with him, - I feel we are at a stalemate sir.'

The captain was relishing this encounter - no doubt buoyed up from a wine sodden luncheon. He then purposely appeared to busy himself with some papers on his sparsely covered desk.

Peachey knew he was being goaded, but also knew that it was futile to attempt to argue it out with Gadfew. The captain was exactly the type of person that should not be entrusted with any form of information about his visit to Portsmouth. However he had no real story that he could readily give, to circumnavigate this obstacle before him.

He decided to change tack.

'I think that the Governor will subsequently confirm that what I have to say is of a very private nature.' he said carefully.

'Then I must ask you to name yourself sir.' Gadfew suddenly realised that he was unaware of whom he was addressing.

'Mr name sir, is Henry Peachey - Gentleman, - and I am on a visit to Portsmouth.'

'So I gather sir, as you are not known here.' He shuffled more papers then looking up as though tiring of the game said

'The Governor is not here, he has travelled to Winchester but is expected back tomorrow. Come again at eleven in the morning and I will see if I can arrange a meeting. Private business you say – and he does not know you?'

It was as though he was weighing up a mighty problem and was delivering his decision.

Peachey, fuming internally, could see that nothing was to be gained by further dialogue. The man had the whip hand – for the moment. *Here was a man that needed taking down a peg or two but that will have to wait. Regrettably no mention of the king or his uncle must used to make this wine sodden idiot show due respect and mind his manners. Time will come though.*

'I am indebted to you' replied Peachey. 'I shall return at eleven as you suggest' and before Gadfew could respond, he gave a short bow and took his leave.

Tuning on his heel he passed the spellbound old soldier and headed for the door, not stopping in his stride until he was well in the way towards the Garrison Church again.

The vigorous steps dissipated some of his anger, and on reflection he congratulated himself that he had not be drawn too much by the bad mannered captain. The Governor wasn't there so he couldn't have seen him in any case.

Tomorrow he would prepare himself before facing Gadfew again. Preserving an oriental calm, as his tutor had always remarked, was the best interim strategy.

As Peachey paced back towards the George, passing the Garrison Church, two ladies headed towards him. The younger of the two was dark, with attractive pert features. Her youthful looks were accentuated by her close fitting dress covered by a stylish blue full-length coat.

Her older companion was in smart but less flamboyantly tailored apparel. To an experienced eye, this second woman was the companion to the younger lady, well attired but showing due deference to her mistress.

Peachey sensed that this young lady was the love of Percy Trevelyan. She was indeed pretty and had the gaiety about her that youthful spirits and pleasantness of character transmitted.

The two paid passing glances at Peachey as they continued their way towards the Governors residence, and then resumed their animated conversation.

Peachey had never meet Miss Sophie Gifford, but recognised her attributes from Trevelyan's detailed description; a description that had not failed to miss one single point.

If this were his true love, the comparison with his actual fiancé would be fascinating. Trevelyan was certainly sorrowful enough, and from the appearance of Sophie Gifford he was beginning to understand why.

But striding ahead Peachey had little care for Trevelyan's problems. He had enough of his own to contend with. Rounding the corner of *The Battery* and heading back up High Street he saw the stocky figure of Fairweather approaching. Fairweather slowed slightly as Peachey approached him.

'I hoped to catch you sir. I thought you might still be at the Governor's residence.'

'He's not there. I spoke to a very disagreeable captain, a man whose head needs to be shoved up his arse and no mistake. He informs me the Governor may be back tomorrow or the day after.'

Looking at Fairweather who had glanced back to the house in anticipation of sorting out the Captain, Peachey said

'What of the widow then Fairweather?'

'She is the widow of a cooper who supplied barrels to Mr. Porter sir. She was reluctant to speak to me as she thought I might be in the pay of Mr. Porter and was trying to trick her.'

'I trust you reassured her?'

'She was reassured after I purchased her and her son some thick soup and ale' smiled Fairweather.

'And did the soup loosen her tongue? And was it worth while?'

'All I can do is to repeat it sir. She says that Mr. Porter is a thief, a scoundrel and a charlatan.'

'He is a victualer, so that appears to be one of the qualifications for the trade. Did she say more?'

'His rise to eminence has been rapid to say the least. As little as a year ago he was no more than a lowly employee for Mr. Erasmus Faulkner, but then all that changed and since then he has become prosperous. So much so that many think that Mr. Faulkner is an employee of his.'

'He told me he handled the affairs on behalf of Faulkner.'

'He has total control and undertakes many transactions on his own behalf. It was the purchase of the barrels that brought Porter into contact with her late husband. He refuses to pay for them although she says they have been in use since they were first delivered.'

'Does this widow have a name?'

'She is called Mary Burgess and her late husband was a Benjamin Burgess. She thinks that Mr. Porter has some hold over Mr. Faulkner, for, although he is of advanced age, he is still seems quite capable of controlling his own affairs.'

'And of the other man?'

'A Mr. John Gunn. He is a man who keeps himself to himself. He owns much land and property in the area, which he has acquired over the years. No one is sure how extensive his business affairs are. He is unmarried, the same as Mr. Faulkner, and has a house in the town and another large one outside, going Eastwards to a place called *Southsea.*'

'They appear to be who they are and what they are. What Mr. Porter's hold over Mr. Faulkner is I know not and cannot see what interest it may prove to be. Apart from strengthening my knowledge, it provides nothing that I need. What of the widow Burgess?'

'I said I would see what transpired while we were still in Portsmouth, but could give no undertaking.'

Fairweather seemed sympathetic to her cause.

'Quite so. It is not of our business to trifle in the local affairs of Porter and this widow.'

Fairweather fell into step with Peachey as they walked up the darkening High Street towards *The George Inn*. Peachey was in low spirits and mentally composing the letter that he would write to his uncle when they reached *The George*, - a letter that had absolutely nothing to advance to the supposed plot destined to take place within the area, in an increasing short space of time.

A depressing thought indeed, only brightened by the mental prospect of revenge in various forms over this surly Captain Gadfew lifted him somewhat.

Chapter 9

Rousseliere entered the inn to the sound of shouting and raised voices. Stooping as he passed through the door he saw Kitty, the young whore, at the foot of the stairs clutching her dress about her and Courtney at the top shouting down.

God what was going on. The whole purpose of staying in this place was not to draw attention to themselves. Courtney the fool was doing exactly the opposite.

Courtney's face was flushed and his normal caution had deserted him. Kitty was cowering somewhat and refusing to move but was shouting back

'He's an animal and I'm not going back up there.'

Courtney remained glowering down at her and the innkeeper seemed unsure quite what to do next. Rousseliere decided to act. He walked across to where Kitty was crouched and, looking up to Courtney said

'Sir, retire at once.'

Courtney, raised to such an emotional state was initially having none of it thinking *I will not be ordered about by this Frenchman.* However on seeing Rousseliere's intense determined look, he hesitated. Rousseliere's insistent voice said

'Retire sir, so this matter can be quickly settled.'

Courtney recovered himself somewhat, turned on his heel and disappear back into their room slamming the door shut.

Looking at Kitty Rousseliere said quietly

'I fear there has been some unpleasantness.'

'He's an animal' she repeated.

He noticed her arms were bruised; marks that were definitely not there before. He knew he must quickly resolve the issue.

'Whatever the problem, take this and leave.'

He pressed some coins into her hand. She glanced down at the money and looked back at him.

78

'I am happy to go with you sir, I have nothing against yourself, only that other beast.'

A small encouraging smile appeared on her whitened face.

'Some other time perhaps but you are to forget the whole incident.'

'Sir I............'

'There's nothing more to be said. Leave us.'

Rousseliere's tone was sharp and had the desired effect.

She gathered up her dress and disappeared out the back leaving Rousseliere facing the three men in the downstairs room.

'I think the matter is closed' he said simply.

The innkeeper appeared greatly relieved that the incident was at an end and that the men had not asked for the return of any money, nodded.

'Perhaps you would care for some ale sir, to settle the matter.'

'No.' replied Rousseliere glancing back up the stairs. 'I will return to our room. See that we are not disturbed.'

'Of course, of course.' Responded the relieved man.

Rousseliere quickly mounted the stairs and entered the room. What he was to encounter he would never have anticipated in a million years.

Courtney was by the open window looking down to the ground below. On hearing Rousseliere enter he turned and cried

'We've just been robbed!'

Rousseliere's heart jolted.

'How can we have been robbed? You have been here all the time.'

'He came in through the open window while I was outside – that whore must be connected with this.'

Whether the whore was involved or not was not the immediate problem - Rousseliere saw his bag with the slackened retaining cord lying half open on its side.

'What's gone? - My bag's been opened.'

'I don't know, I've only just come back. Check your bag, - mine's not been touched. He's probably not taken much – he's taken the food that was left on the plates though!'

Rousseliere wished with all his heart that was all that he had taken. His shaking fingers grouped inside his bag. Feeling for the secret lining he could feel his notes on the defences still resting inside. A wave of relief surged through him and he looked for other items. Relief turned to new fears as his probing failed to reveal the small package containing the snuffbox and the letter of introduction wrapped around it.

'We have been betrayed' breathed Rousseliere.

His racing mind now tried to determine how events had turned the way they had. He looked to Courtney and said,

'What have you lost?'

'Nothing' replied Courtney 'look my bag's not been touched.'

It was still as he had left it. Looking around the room revealed little else. Apart from the sparse furniture and their own shoulder bags, there was little to take. Courtney continued

'He can't have had much time as the room wasn't empty for long, just for the time I chased after that bitch of a whore, just before you arrived back.'

He came over to Rousseliere 'have you lost your plans of the defences?'

'No, that is the good part, but I've had the snuffbox taken.'

Courtney digested that information then said

'The loss of the snuffbox will not jeopardise our work; you still have your plans, and I still have *the Mistress*.'

'There was a letter with the snuffbox; a letter of introduction to give to the agent. It was written in French and carried a seal' whispered Rousseliere.

'The snuffbox can wait, when we contact him we shall make ourselves known and he can be sent another snuffbox after you return. The letter names you?'

'No,' said Rousseliere,' it says the bearer of the letter must be accepted as an agent of France. But the snuffbox holds the key to the money. The thief must have known what to take.'

'If he knew what to take and had to work very quickly, why did he take the food?'

Rousseliere had to admit that this was a valid point.

'A mystery indeed, but that doesn't alter the fact that the snuffbox and letter are the only things taken. These give us away.'

'If we were betrayed, we should have been arrested and the snuffbox, letter, plans and device would have had us swinging by the neck by now.' Courtney's narrow eyes squinted even further.

There was much truth in that statement. Furthermore unless the thief knew to whom to give the snuffbox, there was no gain other than

the value of the snuffbox itself; which, whilst a valuable item, would realise little ready money when sold in the back streets.

The letter? Again, it would have no use to a thief as it was intended solely for introduction to a local agent. Who then knew they were there and what to take? And then, why not the plans? Thoughts raced through his mind.

These were far more of a traitorous nature than the snuffbox and letter; and why not, as Courtney had said, just arrest them with all the proof of their treachery?

Courtney started gathering his discarded clothes up.

'One thing is for certain we cannot stay here. We must leave at once. I cannot plumb the problem but I am not waiting to be caught like a rat in a barrel.'

'Where do we go?'

'There is only one place left to go. We must get back to the town quickly before they close the gates. We must seek out the French Agent.'

'But he doesn't expect us and we have no letter or snuffbox to give him.'

'As I said, he will have to accept our word for who we are. We can have another snuffbox sent. As for the time, we shall wait inside the town until it's late enough and then call on him when it's dark. '

Doing what any military officer would do, Rousseliere rapidly assessed his position. They needed to leave the inn with all speed. The thief's motives were far from clear, but he and Courtney were at risk. The plan of the defences was still safe – vital information to the invasion: the spy and his accomplices were unknown factors,

Courtney appeared set on leaving. Rousseliere's mind ran on

Was the snuffbox really necessary to establish ones credentials and retrieve the money? If the agent had access to the money surely the snuffbox could not be of such value for its release?

Pulling the cord to tighten up his bag, he headed for the door closely followed by Courtney. On reaching the bottom of the stairs Courtney stood immediately in front of the innkeeper and in a voice dripping with menace said

'I shall return later to deal with you and that thieving whore of yours. I know you are at the bottom of this somehow and I will have my dues.'

'As God is my witness sir, I have done nothing to you. We have spoken to no-one regarding your stay here.'

At this point he looked at the two men seated at his right, who nodded their heads rapidly in agreement. Courtney looked from one to one and then with no further word moved quickly from the inn.

Chapter 10

Nathan Oates stopped to catch his breath. His young legs had carried him from the inn at high speed without him looking behind once.

Pausing for a moment, he reviewed the hair-raising events. After scaling the inn wall and looking through the window he has seen the man chase after the young girl. Thinking they would be gone some while, he had clambered through the window when he smelt the aroma of the remaining food on the tray.

Gulping it down, it produced a sickly sensation, but was none the less nourishing. Being both frightened and anxious he had spotted a bag by the side of the bed. Bags were easy and he quickly undid its tie cord.

Outside the door the shouting never ceased. Suddenly he realised the man wasn't going downstairs. Having feverishly sought for money or food inside the bag his fingers had closed over a solid object wrapped in a cloth.

Wrapping something implied care and probably something of value. On lifting it out he had stuffed it inside his shirt, prior to plunging his hands back for more booty. The shouting outside suddenly ceased - a danger signal!

Instinct and self-preservation had told him to flee. The risk for meagre pickings such as these wasn't worth it by any manner of means. He had just made the window and forced his way back through the narrow aperture before the door flew open.

Pushing his feet against opposite walls again he had supported his body and worked himself down, only this time his descent was speeded by the fear of being apprehended. Dropping the last ten feet, he landed awkwardly, but fear had had him running once back on his feet.

My foot hurts but I'm clear.

He continued fleeing until well clear of the inn. Apart from one or two glances at the running boy, no alarm had been raised. He reached inside for his trophy. It was wrapped in a cloth.

Quickly shredding this outer layer he was surprised to find a document providing a second layer over the item. The document appeared to be a letter but more importantly a large wax seal was affixed to the back. Letters being of little interest, he held that to one side to reveal a small coloured ornamental box – but this was not an ordinary box. It was a snuffbox with a picture outlined on top.

No one he knew would deal in pieces like this on *Spice Island*. The only person he could bring to mind was his cousin, working as an under footman at an inn in Portsmouth. His cousin had contacts with various dealers in the town, but would any be interested? However it was his only possible outlet. He must get to the town before the gates shut for the night.

Hugging the shadows leading to *Broad Street* and the entrance to the town, he cautiously moved with as much speed as he could safely muster. He hoped his cousin would be around to examine this strange but exquisite box.

As to the letter? - Probably worthless, but the big wax seal was interesting.

Chapter 11

Henry Peachey juggled with the words, but skilled as he was, one can only disguise a disaster not hide one. A disaster was what he had on his hands, no matter what he wrote in the letter to his uncle. There was a total lack of success or progress in his report.

Of the location of the *black house* there was - nothing: of the Frenchman sent to survey Portsmouth – not a trace: the identity of the old agent of *Le Secret du Roi* – faceless; and as for the source of the money to fund the local support – it could be fools gold.

An onlooker might say that none of this was Henry Peachey's fault, but failure was failure no matter whose fault it was - the information in the letter was a reflection on him. This lack of progress would be ammunition for his uncle's detractors.

Heavy of heart he put down his pen and sealed the letter. Summoning Fairweather he said

'See that this letter is on the two o'clock coach to London tomorrow afternoon.'

Rising from his chair he stretched himself and added

'What have you discovered in your travels amongst the good folk of Portsmouth? I am desirous of good news Fairweather, something to lighten my heart, something to provide me with a course to set, to seek French dealings in the town.'

'Very little sir I'm afraid. No more information on Mr. Silas Trevelyan's habits and no one I have encountered is aware of a *black house*, although many have fanciful ideas as to its location, many based on the activities of the devil. None worthy of consideration though sir. To know what to search for would be a blessing.'

Peachey was aware that Fairweather was not in total possession of the facts of his quest. There was only so much that he would impart to his manservant, as reliable as he was. A general interest in French activities or victualing misdeeds was about the limit of Fairweather's information.

One point of which Peachey was acutely aware, centred on Fairweather's nose for information. This was a distinct asset but on the other hand, perhaps Fairweather's insight into what Peachey was about was more than he cared to admit.

He walked to the window,

'We seek a will-o'-the-wisp Fairweather, a phantom, a faceless enemy, - I wish to God we knew what we actually seek myself. We look for something that we shall only know – if and when we find it!'

Fairweather interrupted Peachey's wanderings

'Ah I was forgetting sir, Mr. Percy Trevelyan's compliments and would you care to join him downstairs for refreshment. He is entertaining his fiancé in the Smoking Room.'

'His fiancé Fairweather? Have you seen the lady in question?'

Fairweather coughed and dropped his eyes.

'A lady perhaps not to your taste sir. If I may make so bold, looks like a horses' arse, but I'm sure she's many qualities suitable for Mr. Trevelyan.'

Peachey smiled 'you mean hidden qualities Fairweather.'

Fairweather returned the smile,

'Carefully hidden and unassailable to most, if you follow me sir.'

Peachey turned towards the door,

'Then I mustn't keep this lady waiting then Fairweather. I must say that my curiosity has been awakened as to Mr. Trevelyan's plighted love.'

Descending *The George Inn's* stairs, Peachey made for the Smoking Room at the end of the narrow corridor. On entering, he saw the betrothed couple sitting directly opposite. Fairweather had acute observation – the lady's qualities were hidden with a vengeance.

She was around the same age as Trevelyan, sitting bolt upright in her chair, lips pursed with an almost hostile expression. Darting eyes topped a long straight nose on a waxed white face that, although it was the fashion, had had the wax rather liberally applied, producing a somewhat eerie complexion.

A close fitting bonnet framed her head with wisps of mousy coloured hair protruding at irregular intervals around the edge. Her black velvet dress contained no ornamentation save a small crucifix held by a gold chain at her neck. Hands clasped before her she appeared ready for battle.

How she had snared Trevelyan could only be laid at the doorstep of the wine and spirit producers – a sober man would never have walked into that matrimonial trap. Accepting that beauty is not all, the surface character of this woman implied that no sharp intelligence, wit or feminine comfort was to be found within to be a counterpoint to physical attraction.

If Trevelyan had been a condemned man awaiting execution, his dejection couldn't have been improved upon. On the table before them was a bottle of wine, which was receiving attention. On seeing Peachey enter the room a weak smile flashed fleetingly across his face. He rose

'My dear Peachey, good evening. Pray allow me to introduce Miss Elizabeth Attwick.'

Miss Elizabeth Attwick appraised Peachey as he politely said

'An honour to meet you Miss Attwick. Allow me to congratulate you and Mr. Trevelyan on your engagement to be married.'

'Thank you sir.'

She glanced at Trevelyan who managed a very thin smile.

'I have heard much about you sir.'

Her expression indicated that this was probably not a glowing testimonial, more an indictment.

'I understand that you and Mr. Trevelyan were at Oxford together.'

'We were indeed madam, Mr. Trevelyan of course achieving many scholastic honours against my humble endeavours.'

She nodded as though this were only to be expected. A fact that rankled Peachey a trice. However he was pacified by the persistent doleful expression on Trevelyan's face. In fact, in a perverse way, this mightily cheered him. It is said that no matter how bad things are, there is always someone in a worse position than you.

Peachey's depression after his letter writing was brought into perspective by Trevelyan's own predicament. After all Peachey's own troubles wouldn't stay with him for a lifetime, unlike Trevelyan who was saddled with her for the duration of their marriage.

A slight pang of remorse overtook him, for Trevelyan had been a good friend and companion – too good for such a destiny.

Peachey was however brought rapidly to his senses when Trevelyan said

'I have a request Peachey. Would you do me the honour of entertaining Miss Attwick for a while? I had given my word that I would play a hand or two at cards with gentlemen I met from a previous evening? An undertaking that I feel unable to break.'

He moved from his standing position to manoeuvre himself away from the table.

'I am sure that you both have much in common.'

Without waiting for a reply he said 'Thank you' and headed to the far side of the room where three men already sat at a table awaiting his arrival.

Peachey smiled graciously at Elizabeth Attwick whilst mentally devising the most ghastly torture possible for Trevelyan. The solution, would be to leave things as they were - his forthcoming marriage couldn't be bettered as an excruciating penalty.

His musings were abruptly terminated when he realised he knew one of Trevelyan's card playing companions – it was the Governor's belligerent administrative captain – Captain Gadfew. He was both easily seen and heard. His red cheeks and neck radiated an outward encircling glow and his voice continuously sounded above those adjacent and even further a-field.

Being conscious of Elizabeth Attwick speaking from his left, he turned his attention to her questions.

'You are a member of polite society in London then Mr. Peachey?'

'I do have the honour of being invited to certain social gatherings madam, yes.'

She appeared to be continually assessing people and levels; she continued

'Our social world is tame, I imagine, to that of London.'

For a moment his mind flashed back to the coquettish glances of Mrs. Younghusband, the Naval Captain's alluring wife.

'Hardly tame I would have thought madam.'

Signalling for a glass from the servant, he continued,

'The London society is very mixed you know, much of the money being in the hands of families that barely existed as an entity a few years ago, but are now increasingly prominent due to their wealth.'

'Upstarts!' she exclaimed. 'Breeding and position is the over riding factor. Don't you agree?'

A matter near and dear to her heart, he thought. *No wonder Trevelyan was her target to achieve and improve her social position in Portsmouth. Not an ounce of affection seemed to be forthcoming for Trevelyan however from her tight lips.*

'The world is a changing dear lady, one never knows who is arriving and even with whom we shall next be at war.'

Somewhat puzzled by his reply she vainly attempted to put the social position back in the centre of conversation; when suddenly without warning, a shout filled the room and Gadfew staggered to his feet. His red bulging neck throbbed over his collar and he shouted directly at Trevelyan

'You are a cheat and a scoundrel sir! You have deliberated cheated my colleagues and me by your manipulation of the cards! I demand return of my monies or satisfaction!'

Trevelyan was clearly at a loss. He remained seated under the baleful gaze of Gadfew who was now virtually leaning over him. Being taken aback and surprised, he took a few moments to phrase a reply

'You are mistaken sir, the cards are have been fairly dealt, you are unfortunate to have had a run of bad luck and………..'

'Run of bad luck - run of bad luck! You have cheated me out of my money,' shouted Gadfew, looking round to gauge how many were a witness to this accusation, and hopefully to engender some support. Now getting into his stride with his theme he continued

'I demand satisfaction and return of my money!'

Trevelyan's resolve suddenly seemed to stiffen.

'I repeat you are mistaken sir; the cards have all been fairly played. I reject absolutely the charge of cheating.'

'I demand satisfaction, I will have satisfaction, or are you a coward in addition to a cheat?' bellowed Gadfew, who now had the attention of everyone in the room and a few crowding the door from the adjacent ones. He continued

'You appeared to have uncanny luck to start with the other evening but now I have plumbed your deviousness.'

'Nothing seems to pacify you sir. I am no cheat but I will give you satisfaction' Trevelyan's quiet voice was hardly audible after the ravings of Gadfew.

'I will have my seconds call on yours' continued Gadfew in a raised voice and rocking unsteadily on his feet, 'you are not fit to be in this establishment with fine gentlemen.'

He grabbed his coat and started to leave the room, talking and complaining to every table as he passed about unfitting behaviour for a gentleman.

Stunned, Trevelyan sat alone at the table, having the image of a pariah and ostracised by the surrounding groups. Elizabeth Attwick looked around at the assembled faces; some muttering about cheats being hung, others bemoaning the demise of gentlemen at cards; and in general all derisory comments to the character of one Percy Trevelyan.

A mature lady being escorted from the room stopped and looked down to Peachey's table. Addressing her remarks to Elizabeth Attwick she said

'I am afraid after this unpleasantness with your fiancé, I do not think it fitting for me to receive you for tea tomorrow afternoon Miss Attwick. Good day to you.'

She continued on her way after issuing this chilling rebuff.

This portent of social isolation produced an impression on Miss Attwick of a fish gasping for breath. Peachey watched her eyes flash around the room. The eyes slightly widened from usual, exhibited apprehension and fear.

Fear, not from concern for her fiancé, but for her and exclusion from the social strata of the town, he thought. With a set look on her sallow face she stood, and with no comment to Peachey walked purposefully over to the immobile Trevelyan.

Raising her voice to obtain maximum attention she exclaimed.

'Mr. Trevelyan, you have brought shame to yourself and have acted disgracefully, I cannot be expected to marry a man unworthy of the dignity and respect that I and my family warrant. Be advised sir that our engagement is at an end.'

With this outburst she slammed her hand down upon the table, on removing it again, a glistening engagement ring remained - a stark indicator of the finality of the engagement.

Surveying the assembly, she mentally acknowledged how public the act had been, witnessed by so many of the townsfolk and important members of the community.

Trevelyan for his part remained curiously expressionless. He stared down at the solitary ring but made no move to respond. Elizabeth Attwick on the other hand completed a dramatic exit, failing to acknowledge Peachey, let alone present her farewells.

This snub was the cue for Peachey to react. His instinct was to keep his distance from this fiasco. His prime aim in Portsmouth was to remain out of the public eye. But a regard for his friend gained predominance however, and he rose and walked across to the recumbent Trevelyan.

Without a word he pulled up a chair and sat down. Trevelyan's trance was broken.

'Ah Peachey. A spot of local difficulty has arisen I fear.'

'You may well say that my friend. You cannot of course go through with this and provide him with satisfaction.'

Trevelyan turned weary eyes to Peachey.

'You and I both know sir that refusal is out of the question. My reputation, social standing and future business dealings would all be jeopardised by such a refusal. I would also be branded a coward to boot, a thought that I could not stand.'

A very real fear struck Peachey in the pit of his stomach.

'Fine words sir, but ones likely to be short lived. This so called satisfaction will be a duel by pistols.'

He lent over the table to cross-examine Trevelyan further.

'Have you ever used pistols in your life?

Trevelyan gave a small shrug of his shoulders. Peachey went on

'I imagined as such. You are from a family with country estates, yet to my knowledge you have never hunted with the gun or ridden with hounds. How can you be prepared to take up pistols and face Gadfew? He is a trained soldier. He may not be the fittest or bravest but he's familiar with pistols and will shoot you dead!'

Looking back to the table, Trevelyan said

'I have used pistols a couple of times before.'

He turned to Peachey continuing,

'Their function is quite simple; you point them at an object and pull the trigger. It requires no undue force or detailed explanation of the principles.'

Leaning back in his chair, Peachey paused for a moment then said

'You will remember you trigonometry sir, - a subject in which you excelled, together with many others with monotonous regularity. Any small deviation in an angle at source produces a significant deviation the further away one travels.'

Peachey moved his hand to emphasise the point.

'In short, if your aim is slightly off when you fire, it will eventually miss the target by a very wide margin. Gadfew will be trained to offer a firm steady hand when firing, resulting in striking the target as required. The target is, in this instance, you my dear Trevelyan.'

Re-consideration was clearly not an option Trevelyan was prepared to consider. In his own heart Peachey knew that his friend's career, social position, business dealings and shame being brought to his family precluded any real option of refusal.

Discussions and revaluations were immediately terminated by the arrival of another officer – a very young fresh-faced Second Lieutenant in shiny red uniform, displaying dubious confidence; although standing ramrod backed. He addressed Trevelyan.

'Sir I have been sent - err, requested to attend to consult with your seconds.'

That he had been sent or ordered to was plain. Obviously ill at ease and never before having had to perform such a task, he kept his eyes on Trevelyan alone, not wishing to involve Peachey in any way, being unsure who he was.

Trevelyan was flummoxed.

'Seconds? I have………'

'I have the honour to be one of Mr. Trevelyan's seconds sir,' Peachey interjected without hesitation. 'Perhaps I can be of assistance to you.'

For the first time the young officer looked at Peachey. It was a relief for him to be able to discharge this unsavoury duty, having been ordered to do so by a triumphant Gadfew - a man he was unable to stomach as an individual but obliged to obey in deference to his rank.

'I thank you sir' he said, 'I would be obliged if you would attend with your Principal at Governor's Green tomorrow at sunrise. The choice of weapons is yours of course.'

Peachey rose to his feet.

'Thank you sir. We shall be in attendance and we select pistols. I take it you will provide the same.'

The young officer nodded.

'Thank you. I will make all arrangements accordingly.'

'A further issue if I may,' continued Peachey carefully, 'your Principal was mistaken this evening, maybe by a combination of poor light and over generous wine hospitality. I would be grateful if you would request him to reconsider his action for satisfaction and perhaps we can arrive at some amicable solution.'

'I will certainly ask him sir.'

The doubt in the officer's voice was plain to all. Gadfew had much to gain. His losses could be declared negated, and his upholding of a gentleman's code of conduct stored for future credit. The dispute was totally one sided, the likelihood of a wound being sustained by Gadfew was slight, whilst the potential for serious wounding to Trevelyan, high.

With a polite, slight bow to the head, the officer remarked

'Thank you gentlemen; until tomorrow morning then,' and turning on his heel, retreated from the room.

Reaching out and picking up the ring, Trevelyan said

'I am indebted to you sir.' Toying with the ring in his hand he continued,

'At least I can enter the contest with no fear of leaving a widow or grieving fiancé behind. I suppose I can count my blessings on being a free man again – even if not for long.'

'Gallows humour sir' murmured Peachey. ' Efforts must still be made to avert this action. The other gentlemen at your table were not a party to the accusation I note. It's only Gadfew that has raised the issue – the very man who had sustained heavy losses by his own ineptitude.'

'Agreed,' sighed Trevelyan 'but they will not face Gadfew. He will intimidate all who are weaker than he, and he has a powerful position in the service of the Governor. Most men cannot afford to run foul of Gadfew, and I am of little consequence to those others in the game I fear.'

A wave of intense weariness suddenly overcame Peachey. He had been low of spirits on his own account earlier in the evening, now that position had been worsened ten-fold with the addition of these developments.

Glancing round the room that had lost interest in Gadfew's challenge, he felt of heavy heart – a generated loathing for Portsmouth, the French and in particular Gadfew. Until the loss of someone or something confronts one in the face, the absence is never really envisaged. Looking at Trevelyan he realised that he didn't want to lose this friend or see him wounded – he may be exasperating on occasions, but in is own way loyal, dependable, good hearted with a latent humour that could be brought to bear even in the bleakest of situations.

He perked himself up and said

'If you have had sufficient of the company here, let us retire to my rooms and discuss tactics and more pleasant subjects.'

Trevelyan pocketed the ring that he was still fingering.

'I think my entertainment and sport for those here has finished for one evening. Let one unencumbered from future matrimonial containment accompany another so likened. We can review the prospects as you say. Perhaps a good brandy or two will alleviate the situation and lead to more convivial thoughts.'

In the quieter surroundings of Peachey's rooms, Fairweather poured two generous measures of brandy for his master and his friend. Brandy that had been obtained by Fairweather from the landlord by special inducement – sometimes described as intimidation.

Retreating to the rear of the room, Fairweather noticed that both men were subdued, even the fine brandy escaping comment. He had been summoned by Peachey and told of the impending duel and to stand by for unspecified duties. He now awaited clarification.

Trevelyan was lost in his own thoughts – not an unusual action for someone prior to an uneven duel perhaps. Peachey was deliberating on the best method to limit the damage and possible fatal outcome to his friend.

Looking at Trevelyan, a germ of an idea slowly nurtured into a possible prospect for a solution. He said

'Perhaps you would care to stand for a moment Trevelyan. I need to run through your stance should this wretched duel go ahead.'

A puzzled Trevelyan climbed to his feet and stood facing Peachey who said

'Face me, that's right, but not square on. Turn your body sideways.'

Trevelyan followed the directions and tuned sideways. Peachey continued

'Now the object is to present the smallest possible target to Gadfew, a fact particularly easily accomplished by a Trevelyan, since sideways on you are almost invisible!'

A slight raising of one eyebrow was Trevelyan's only response. Warming to his topic Peachey said

'Your slightness of frame is your biggest asset in this venture. In poor light, chill of the morning, and raised emotional state your opponent will not be delivering his keenest shot in any case. Your presented target is a fraction of his and a challenge at the best of times.'

Making adjustment to his friend's stance, Peachey had him hold out his right arm as though pointing the pistol. Keeping the remainder of his body tucked in tightly, Trevelyan practiced this position until Peachey was satisfied that it was readily achieved from a normal standing position.

Nodding his approval, he indicated that the impending duellist could now resume his seat and drink his comforting brandy. That was as much as he could do for Trevelyan at this point - the remainder of the plan rested with himself.

After a short interval he said

'I suggest you rest now sir, as best you can. Fairweather and I have additional matters to discuss.'

Peachey gently raised his friend from his chair and with the assistance of Fairweather guided him towards his own room.

On their return, Fairweather looked expectantly towards his master, who turned and said,

'In any combat, it is essential to have an edge or advantage over ones opponent. We cannot fight the duel for Mr. Trevelyan but perhaps we can level the odds slightly. This is what I want you to do.'

Chapter 12

Portsmouth appeared to continue with as much of its activities at night, as by day. It could never be described as being asleep; traders, beggars, drunks, thieves, ship loaders, innkeepers, could all be observed going about their lawful or nefarious dealings around the clock.

An exception was with the various servants who tended the houses crammed into the town, and sheltering behind it's walls and ramparts. Servants worked from dawn to dusk.

Scullery maids lit kitchen fires, cleaned pots with sand and lime, and completed other tasks of pure drudgery from the dim early morning light; to repeat similar tasks at the final hours of the day. They then slept, exhausted on the floor where they toiled.

Even rising up the strict hierarchy to the butler, didn't reduce the hours of attendance. These hours might not be spent in actual work but involved the more mind numbing and boring duty of being in attendance awaiting a summons.

Without exception, the advent of nightfall came as a welcome relief and respite to household staff once their employers had dismissed them for the day.

This day was no exception. The staff of one Portsmouth house, grateful for the break between duties, settled down to rest. Although late, candlelight still shone through the downstairs window where the master was at his desk.

It was this quietude and light that signalled Courtney and Rousseliere to move from their cramped position in the darkened corner of the small garden. Courtney crept to the window and peered in. Satisfied all was well, he rapped on the small panes of the glass window, loud enough for the occupant to hear but insufficient to arouse the staff.

Rousseliere could see a shadow in front of the window where the man had come to investigate. A pause followed whist he spoke in whispered terms to Courtney through the narrow gap he had made by opening the window slightly. The window closed again and Courtney motioned to Rousseliere to follow him.

Walking as quietly as possible, their footsteps seemed to echo on the stone slabs forming the base around the edge of the house. On reaching the front door, it opened with no further command and they were quickly hustled inside.

They moved forward to where the candlelight cast a beacon to the man's room. The hallway appeared to be cluttered with oddments of furniture, set out with no apparent order.

The man closed the door behind them, having glanced along the corridor and up the stairs to ensure no enquiring eyes had observed them.

Resuming his seat he looked briefly at Rousseliere but then addressed his remarks to Courtney.

'You say you have business from France?'

'We have sir. I am Thomas Courtney and this is Major de la Rousseliere. The major has been sent to survey the town and to liase with yourself regarding support and money for the cause in Portsmouth.'

The man said nothing, but simply gently nodded politely to Rousseliere and returned his attention to Courtney.'

'So you say sir, but I need some reassurance that you are who you say you are.'

He lapsed into silence and looked expectantly at both men.

Rousseliere knew what was expected but now had the difficulty of convincing the man. He said

'I was given a letter and item before I left France to present to you on my arrival.'

The man nodded and held out his hand.

'It is to our regret that both were stolen from us this very evening' an embarrassed Rousseliere added.

Dropping his hand abruptly, his aged face darkening into a scowl he looked from one to the other.

'So, two men appear at my door claiming to be emissaries from France and seeking my help. Help, which you have noticed I have not acknowledged or agreed to. To support this story they claim to have had a letter and an item - which is unspecified, - that has just been stolen from them this evening.'

He sat back looking at them again, having completed his views. There was a moment or two's silence again, and then Rousseliere continued,

'I am aware of your caution sir, it was a most unfortunate occurrence, and one that never should have happened. Those were the only items that were taken however.'

The old man snarled

'How very fortunate for you sir. The only two items that you claim you wished to present to me were these very two. You appear very able bodied men' and looking particularly at Rousseliere said,

'And you sir are a soldier, trained in military skills, defence, weaponry, a safe-guarder of secrets and yet you had items stolen from you.'

Before any answer was forthcoming he quickly said

'Were you overpowered and who robbed you?'

A sheepish Rousseliere replied

'It was while we were resting, and then only for a brief period that the thief entered the room. We didn't get a glimpse of him and were certainly not overpowered.'

A look of alarm spread across the lined face of the man.

'You have no idea who robbed you; and that was all that was taken, taken whilst you posted no guard to your belongings. Did you leave them on the table for all to see?'

The sarcasm was heavy in the man's voice causing great discomfort to Rousseliere. The man was clearly worried however, which showed in the biting remarks.

Courtney who had been looking from one to the other broke in and said

'What does it matter? That's all he took. You appear to doubt our word sir, but apart from the contents of the letter, we can at least tell you what the item was.'

The man changed his focus to Courtney but said nothing but raised his eyebrows.

'It was a snuffbox' said Courtney triumphantly.

Dropping his head and shaking it at the same time, the man pondered on his reply then said

'A letter I can read sir. The item may be anything. I think you might be the men I expect and will tell you this, the actual item, snuffbox or otherwise means nothing to me. Whatever the item is, it contains a key, without it you are of no use to me. At least with the letter I could have peace of mind as to your credentials.'

His face contorting with rage, Courtney sprang forward to confront the seated man

'You are taking this loss as an opportunity of keeping the money for yourself. The fact that we haven't the item in our possession is of no consequence for you know how to access the money.'

The man was taken aback by this sudden verbal attack. Courtney continued his onslaught,

'You know we are here as expected and we have risked our lives in doing so. The letter would simply be a letter of introduction for the major and myself and informing you to offer assistance. Assistance that, for reasons beneficial to yourself you are not proposing to provide.'

The man suddenly looked very old and frail. He shrunk back from Courtney and appeared to attempt to catch his breath; Courtney failed to notice since he continued with his tirade

'I am not going to be fobbed off. The money is not yours. It is for the cause!'

Struggling to overcome his difficulties the old man gasped

'I told you before you fool, I cannot locate the money without the key, the key which through your incompetence and neglect you have failed to produce. For blame, look no further than yourself and your accomplice.'

Courtney was now incensed, he reached down and grasped the collar of the man's coat and shook him

'You are a liar sir. I have seen liars before and they all look like you. Having sent us away empty handed you intend to retrieve the money at your leisure.'

Each phrase was accompanied by a severe shake.

Rousseliere had witnessed Courtney's lack of control earlier in the evening. The man may or may not be telling the truth but nothing would be gained this way. He moved forward, grabbed Courtney's arm and wrenched him away from the gasping man.

Spinning around to face Rousseliere, Courtney started to remonstrate but on seeing the expression on Rousseliere's face staring past him, he quickly turned back to the old man.

He was sitting back, mouth open, eyes glassy with a distinct blue colouring around his mouth and cheeks.

They both bent over him. Rousseliere waved a hand over his eyes – nothing. Courtney held him by the shoulders and gently shook him – nothing.

'My God Courtney, you've killed him.'

Rousseliere immediately crossed himself.

Courtney shook him further,

'I didn't kill him, I was only getting him to own up to his deeds'

Courtney then also crossed himself.

Rousseliere bending over the slumped body checked the eyes and body for any remote signs of life. But he had seen too many dead men on the field of battle to have any serious doubts – the spy from *le Secret du Roi* who was to have provided so much – was dead.

Stepping back he surveyed the scene. It was an ordinary room for a gentleman; the desk was the main feature. Odd papers were scattered on it with a book or two but absolutely no indication of his earlier role in *le Secret du Roi*.

Whatever the rights or wrongs, this death, together with the theft of the letter and snuffbox, had shattered the all the previous success.

He went to the door and carefully opened it, listening for any sign indicating that they had been heard. The house was as dead as the old man.

Closing it quietly behind him he spoke in whispered tones to Courtney

'We have to leave, but we must leave no trace of our visit. Here, help me.'

'Not so fast' replied Courtney 'if he has the money as I suspect, he must keep it hidden somewhere.'

With that, he reached beyond the expired body of the man and began rifling the desk, working through the compartments looking for some sort of money or valuables. His frustration was rising all the time as he wrenched open the last drawer.

'Bah' he expelled the sound through gritted teeth 'it must be hidden'.

Rousseliere watched as Courtney ran his fingers around the top and sides of the desk.

'These things always have hidden compartments' muttered Courtney tapping the panels seeking a hollow sound.

Rousseliere glanced around. This was another disaster. Courtney was proving to be more of a liability that an asset. Given time he felt he could have persuaded the man to accept their story, but the hot headedness of Courtney had again been their undoing.

What they could not afford to do was to be caught red handed in this man's house. He looked back to the searching Courtney whose actions were becoming increasingly frantic – and noisy

'Courtney we must be away. We have too much to lose and a noose awaits us if we are caught.'

Courtney, ignoring Rousseliere, carried on with his search. Finally, having failed to locate any compartments or hidden wealth, looked around the room.

Rousseliere was now becoming concerned

'We must leave now. Come help me move him. Put the papers back in the desk, we don't want anyone to know we were here.'

Courtney glancing around the room for a final time, reluctantly did as he was bid. He then stood by Rousseliere.

Reaching under the dead man's arms, they manoeuvred him until he was slumped over his desk. Head resting on his folded arms, and carefully arranged to look as though he had died in his sleep or had had a spasm.

Courtney reaching from the bookshelf placed a bible under the man's hands.

A touch macabre - typical of Courtney thought Rousseliere.

Courtney made as if to extinguish the candles. Rousseliere whispered sharply

'No leave them, if he died whilst reading he would never have extinguished them himself would he?'

Courtney nodded his acknowledgment and jerked his head, signalling towards the door. They both looked around once more, and then carefully retraced their steps to the front door. A barely audible click as it closed behind them, signified their escape from the doom-laden house.

A short distance away, the agile thief Nathan Oates was warm, comfortable and sleeping peacefully. The occasional snorting or gentle stamping of horses hooves in the stable did nothing to disturb his slumbers.

His cousin had managed to procure some leftovers from the Inn's kitchen, which, when washed down with some ale produced a satisfying end to the day. A day that ended on a high for Nathan, since his cousin seemed confident that he could dispose of the snuffbox and probably the letter to the same buyer.

They may be lucky in getting a shilling or two for the loot. Not a King's ransom but good money for an evenings work. His leg was feeling better and apart from the scare at the inn on the Point, was unscathed from his exploits.

All in all, a good day. He was certainly unable to visualise the impact his day would have on the fortunes of others.

Chapter 13

The trio of reluctant duellists made their way in silence to *The Green.*

This was probably the worst possible location for a duel, as *The Green,* or to give it its full title - *The Governor's Green,* was set in an area behind the Garrison Church and just out of sight of the Governor's Residence itself.

Conversation was non-existent. Peachey had attempted to put some cheer into his friend's demeanour but had long since abandoned that as a fruitless task. His own spirits were in a poor condition in any case.

He and Fairweather had collected Trevelyan from his bedroom before daybreak. It was apparent that he hadn't slept much, if at all. An ominous hand written envelope bearing his uncle's name, was propped up on the table - to be delivered should the worst possible outcome occur.

Visibility was limited as daylight was only just emerging. Grass and gravel crunched underfoot as they rounded the corner of the church. A carriage was parked beneath the large chestnut tree bordering the far side of the green. A small group of men were talking in hushed tones.

Their roles were self-evident. The young officer acting as Gadfew's Second, held a flat pistol case, while the bag of the person next to him signified a physician. Gadfew stood with the other second and the erect figure of the referee - the man to officiate the duel.

To their right a small group of onlookers looked expectantly across as Trevelyan, Peachey and Fairweather approached. Fairweather, unusually attired in a full cloak and wide hat, adopted the role of Trevelyan's other second.

They stopped a few yards from Gadfew's group and the young officer promptly moved towards them holding the pistol case before him. It was an elaborate leather bound case with a green soft lining containing two superbly crafted matching pistols. The craftsmanship of polished light wood and gleaming barrels could be discerned even in this breaking light of the morning.

The officer, having obviously rehearsed his duties said

'Good morning sirs' and then remained standing to one side.

The referee walked slowly up to stand facing Trevelyan and Peachey. He spoke in a slow measured manner.

'Good morning gentlemen. Captain Gadfew has demanded satisfaction from Mr. Trevelyan whom he accuses of cheating. This is to settle his grievance over cards for which he has received no apology or admission.'

He glanced from one to the other as he spoke but didn't pause in his delivery.

'In accordance with established practise I offer you the chance to reconsider your position and the opportunity of correcting that again.'

Trevelyan looked at him but simply shook his head. Peachey however spoke,

'I speak on behalf of Mr. Trevelyan sir. He himself is an honourable man and this affair is no more than a misunderstanding. As such he clearly cannot be expected to apologise for matters that are not correct.'

The Referee looked back at Trevelyan who remained silent. Peachey continued

'It is our express desire that this duel should not continue and would ask that an opportunity be presented to Captain Gadfew to reflect and withdraw his challenge.'

The young officer looking puzzled said

'I am certain that Captain Gadfew is under no mind to withdraw sir.'

Peachey looked straight at the officer and replied

'We acknowledge that the captain has placed himself in a precarious position. He has been extremely brave to challenge Mr. Trevelyan, but there is no certainty that Mr. Trevelyan will be able to limit his shot to a simple wound.'

Astonishment appeared on the officer's face. Peachey continued

'I repeat that the captain should be afforded the same opportunity as Mr. Trevelyan.'

The young captains face changed from puzzlement to incredulity.

'I do not understand your remarks sir, the captain has been brave to challenge Mr. Trevelyan?'

Peachey stepped back a pace and looked hard at the young man.

'I cannot believe you are in ignorance sir.'

He turned to the referee

'With your approval sir I would like to speak to this officer in private for a moment. It may help to settle this affair.'

The referee looked from one to the other. This time it was his turn to look perplexed.

'I suppose it is my duty to settle this affair if at all possible' he replied, 'a moment's private discussion is acceptable if there's the possibility of a favourable outcome.'

Peachey moved forward, gently took hold of the officer's arm and led him a few paces away from the others. Peachey spoke in an urgent whisper.

'I cannot believe that the captain has entered into this unaware of the capabilities of Mr. Trevelyan.'

'Again I am at a loss sir. I understand the captain has knowledge of the gentleman but – special capabilities?'

Peachey frowned,

'I was beginning to fear that might be the case sir. You and the captain are clearly unaware. It would be a travesty if this were to be allowed to continue without the captain being in full possession of the facts.'

Looking round, bending closer to the officer and appearing to share a confidence, continued

'Mr. Trevelyan is one of the finest shots in the country!'

This revelation caused the officer to instinctively turn his head round to reappraise Trevelyan. He then turned his amazed face back to Peachey who continued with his confidence

'He is even known to the king in this respect. There is a group of similar fine shots who shoot in the country and have entertained his majesty at county houses with incredible performances.'

The officer looked back once again at the motionless Trevelyan. Peachey spoke again in the officer's ear,

'To illustrate my point sir, they shoot at live chickens from a distance of twenty-five yards at least. The object is to cleanly shoot the birds, but only by shooting their heads off.'

Now it was the officer's turn to step back. He looked astounded.

'Moving chickens at that distance is challenge enough, but to have to kill them by shooting off their heads is almost unbelievable.'

Moving forward to renew his intimate discussion with the officer, Peachey said in low tones,

'You can see sir why I was alarmed at this challenge by your captain. It is a totally unfair contest. Mr. Trevelyan will do his utmost to limit the damage, but I'm afraid that, in the heat of the moment, he may cause a fatality.'

The officer's composure was now shattered. He glanced from Peachey to Gadfew who was now staring intently at the two men in conversation. The young man's face looked bewildered and he swallowed hard.

'I beg leave to acquaint the captain of this information sir, for I believe it to be important.'

Responding with a short nod, Peachey returned to the referee and the other two. Turning to the referee he said

'The second is referring back to the captain sir. We await a reply.'

Across the way the discussions were not proceeding without drama. Gadfew's voice could be heard but not the words, the young officer was apparently explaining the shooting accomplishments for his arms were indicating moving targets and distance. The discussion was not short lived but involved questions and answers accompanied by further arm gestures.

It was Fairweather who made the next move. Wrapping his cloak around him he walked over and beckoned the physician. The physician, pleased to be able to do something rather than stand around, moved across to Fairweather.

They in turn had a short discussion and Fairweather pointed to Gadfew and where he would be positioned in the contest. From inside his cloak he withdrew a dish and white cloth. It became abundantly clear that they were discussing treatment to Gadfew after the duel, staunching the loss of blood, and using the carriage to transport him from the scene.

Gadfew was now knocked completely out of his stride by this unexpected turn of events. He looked wildly round at Trevelyan, Fairweather, the physician and the group of onlookers now silently watching the saga before them.

His eyes finally rested on the carriage, before returning to talking earnestly with the young officer. Gadfew's consultation was now taking longer than the referee anticipated for he walked over to seek a decision. Gadfew could be seen talking to the referee and gesticulating to the onlookers and shaking his head.

The referee returned with the officer to Trevelyan's group watching the proceedings with anxious eyes. He spoke to Peachey and Trevelyan as one

'The captain has considered your proposal but under the circumstances feels that he is now unable to accept. The duel will therefore continue as arranged.'

Peachey's heart sank for they had been close to preventing the duel. However, secretly, he had felt that Gadfew would not have been able to face a climb-down at this stage. He was too far committed and the onlookers would not condone such an action particularly as he was supposed to be fighting the cause for honest men against cheats and un-gentlemanly behaviour.

Nevertheless the second ploy in his scheme, which was to un-nerve Gadfew, had been successfully accomplished. Even from here, Gadfew now appeared flustered exhibiting a somewhat frantic look, contrasting dramatically with the smug self-assured image he was projecting on their arrival.

The officer opened the pistol case again, offering it to Trevelyan, he selected one pistol, examined and casually checked it. Holding it upwards at arms length, he looked down the length of the barrel as though he was the expert Peachey had described.

From the corner of his eye Peachey could see Gadfew watching spellbound as this performance was conducted.

Retreating to Gadfew, his young second offered him the remaining pistol. The referee called the two men and Gadfew reluctantly extracted his weapon from the case and walked to where the referee stood.

Looking solemnly at both men while the pistols were being loaded and checked, the referee issued his instructions.

'You will stand back to back; then each pace out ten steps; turn; aim, and after my count of three - fire. Is that understood gentlemen?'

Both men nodded their assent.

'Stand back to back.'

The referee paused to ensure to ensure both men were ready.

'Take ten paces.'

On completion both men turned to face each other and raised their weapons. The referee's commands rang out

'Take aim. One; two; th.....'

A shot rang out! - shattering the still morning calm.

Eyes darted from one contestant to the other. A telltale wisp of smoke curled upwards from Gadfew's pistol as he stood, wild eyes staring, and his body clearly sweating in the chill morning air.

Eyes focussed back to Trevelyan who was leaning forward, still standing, white featured with a widening red stain running along his side and back.

The initial surprise over, howls of anger and discord rang out in unison from all quarters. The referee moved rapidly over to the bending Trevelyan who perceptively straightened up as he approached.

'Are you badly hurt sir? Your opponent fired before the count was finished!'

Trevelyan wiped his mouth and looked down at the red stain.

'I believe I am still alive sir.'

The referee was now a little unsure of the procedure to take but said

'If you have a mind and can carry on sir, it is your turn to fire.'

Trevelyan stood up as best he could and faced the red faced perspiring Gadfew.

He slowly raised the pistol and pointed it directly at him. The pistol didn't waver one iota. Trevelyan's voice calm and still echoed around the green.

'Captain Gadfew - you were as mistaken in your demands last night as you were with the count just now. You are however from a fine regiment. If its officers must die then let it be with their customary glory and not like this, – God Save the King!'

Turning the pistol upwards and to the right, he fired directly into the broad Chestnut tree.

The tension evaporated immediately, but was suddenly re-imposed when a rustling, bumping, and thudding sound drew everyone's gaze to the tree.

After what seemed an eternity, something fell heavily from the tree and landed on the grass. All eyes were drawn to the object. It was a dead pigeon.

It had been shot, but most startling of all – its head had been completely shot away from its body.

Gadfew collapsed.

Back in The George, the physician tending Trevelyan began replacing items back in his bag.

'There is no serious wound. It looked worse as the shot traced a path along the surface of the body. Wounds near the surface produce more blood, which the shirt readily absorbed making it look as if he were bleeding profusely. We have no need of a surgeon.'

Peachey discreetly paid the man for his services.

Thank God he was not required for a more serious injury he thought *we were lucky to have escaped as we did.*

Fairweather had removed the bloodstained garments and had taken them downstairs. Having completed his treatment the physician gathering up his cloak and bag bade them farewell.

Trevelyan was lying on the bed with a bandage around his midriff. Peachey offered him a clean shirt that he slowly stood to put on. Looking at Peachey he said

'Your advice as to standing sideways on, paid good dividends sir. He almost missed me.'

'Or almost killed you' said Peachey. 'A few inches the other way may have proved fatal. However his aim was far from perfect.'

'Thanks to you. Had you not shattered Gadfew's composure, he would have been far more competent and I would not be discussing the situation with you now with just a minor scratch.'

Cautiously walking over to the table, Trevelyan picked up the letter he had written to his uncle the previous evening. Glancing again at the scrawled handwriting he tore it up into several pieces before throwing it on the fire.

'That will not be required to be delivered which is good – I was not happy with the contents anyhow, and my uncle would have been less so I think. Not a man of great emotion – probable as well.'

Not indeed mused Peachey *there is much to smoke out from that gentleman.*

Watching Trevelyan attend to his appearance he said

'Your performance indicates to me that you've missed you calling.'

Trevelyan frowned. Peachey continued

'A position in the travelling theatre group appearing down the road is made for you. You adopted the role of renown marksman with consummate ease – worthy of any thespian.'

'I was beyond caring at that stage I fear. Surprisingly, by imagining you are the person you are playing, it is far easier than putting on a brave front yourself. I must adopt that style more often.'

Trevelyan permitted himself a small smile. Sitting down in front of the fire he continued,

'Your plan Peachey was first class and I thank you for that. Gadfew would have been a major threat had you not done what you did; and Fairweather, when he had the physician, complete with blood container, stand where Gadfew would have fallen, was a masterstroke.'

Peachey shaking his head a little said

'Your stance at the end was amazing. Your aim was steady and I thought for one moment you were about to shoot him.'

Trevelyan grimaced

'I couldn't have hit him had he been only half the distance away. As it was I was fortunate in hitting the tree. How that poor bird was hit, let alone shooting it's head off I will never ever know.'

Peachey smiled,

'The tree was laden with pigeons. If you hit one, the force of the shot will often have a devastating effect, so removing what appeared to be it's head is not so amazing as you might think.'

'Perhaps not, but the effect was almost to kill Gadfew with a spasm.'

Trevelyan's smile grew with the recollection.

With his position by the window, Peachey glanced down below and frowned,

'Our smiles may be a little short lived I fear sir. Three determined officers are, as we speak, marching into this establishment – not intent on ale or pleasure from their appearance I'll be bound.'

'A little more hostility from the natives then?'

'It would appear so.'

They both remained silent and their ears simultaneously heard the clamping of boots on the stairs, which continued until reaching the door.   Three raps on the door, confirmed their suspicions that they were the intended recipients of the visit.

Peachey walked over to the door and slowly opened it. Two unfamiliar uniformed officers confronted him, with the recognisable young second standing behind them.

The senior of them said,

'Good morning sir, allow me to name myself. I am Major Salter. We request that we may speak with Mr. Trevelyan if he is able to see us at present.'

Peachey opened the door wide,

'Come in gentlemen. As you can see Mr. Trevelyan is resting but happy enough to receive visits from His Majesty's men of arms.'

The officers bowed their heads in acknowledgement and followed Peachey into the room. Peachey continued,

'Pray be seated gentlemen'

'What we have to say is best said whilst standing thank you sir.'

Trevelyan and Peachey exchanged quick glances. Their assessment of the visit was appearing to prove accurate. The major continued.

'Mr. Trevelyan sir, I speak not only for the officers here now, but on behalf of the regiment. It concerns your conduct this morning.'

Trevelyan shifted a little uncomfortably in his seat. The officer continued

'We refer of course to the behaviour towards one of our officers. It cannot be said that this is a pleasant duty to perform but it has to be done.'

Further looks were exchanged between Peachey and Trevelyan.

Looking behind him to the young second lieutenant he continued,

'My brother officer here has informed me of a conversation he had before this morning's event took place, which I must say we find most disturbing. Had we been aware of this fact we would have most certainly interjected.'

'Ah' murmured Trevelyan, feeling that he ought to comment but unsure of any appropriate words.

The officer held up his hand as if to silence Trevelyan before saying

'Captain Gadfew as much as admitted to him that he had fabricated the whole episode concerning last night's unfortunate affair.'

Trevelyan looked hard at the major as though unable to believe his ears. His expression didn't alter, but should have done, as this was unexpected.

The major cleared his throat with a nervous cough.

'Matters were magnified when he acted in the manner he did and attempted to take advantage of the count.'

His embarrassment was clear as he continued

'Your conduct sir, was exemplary, in that you failed to follow up your subsequent position and even more so, were still gracious enough to pass the fine remarks you did regarding the regiment.'

Trevelyan felt that a slight wave of he hand was probably the best reaction to give under the circumstances. He was particularly careful to avoid the eye of Peachey standing in stunned silence by the window.

Shifting slightly onto the other foot the major said

'We would like to apologise unreservedly to you sir on behalf of the regiment and ourselves, for the unjust and totally false allegations levelled against you by one of our officers.'

Trevelyan nodded graciously and the major said

'Matters cannot be undone, but we shall use our best endeavours to ensure that your reputation is untarnished in any way. We would be grateful of you could advise us if you would like us to make representations to any other quarter.'

Trevelyan wanted to relieve the major from having to continue with the apology that was not of his making. Furthermore he still retained a guilty feeling regarding the tactics they employed that almost certainly caused Gadfew to fire early. He said

'Major I am indebted to you for your apology which I readily accept and would hasten to say that I am desirous of establishing good relationships with yourselves and your regiment.'

A sense of relief passed across the major's face. He looked briefly to his companions and said pleasantly

'Thank you sir, your manner is very agreeable. If you are happy to allow us to make amends, may we invite you and your colleague to dine with us in the officer's mess as a beginning? We can thus decide on how to best to then remedy the situation.'

Trevelyan simply looked across at the major who said

'The regiment's honour has been jeopardized, in marked contrast to your own sir, and we are anxious to demonstrate our thanks for your words and actions.'

Trevelyan finally brought himself to look at Peachey then said to the major,

'We would be delighted to accept your hospitality sir.'

'Champion sir, champion.'

The major was clearly delighted that the situation had been so readily resolved.

'If you feel able sir, we should be delighted to see you today at say three-thirty.'

'We shall be there major and thank you.'

Peachey joined the conversation for the first time.

'I was to visit the Governor today or tomorrow when he returns. Captain Gadfew was to arrange the meeting. I now wonder if the captain will ensure that meeting is fulfilled.'

With a darkening face Major Salter replied

'Captain Gadfew will no longer be holding that position sir. In fact we expect him to resign his commission immediately. Regrettably this is not the first occasion of some unpleasantness with him.'

Trevelyan raised his eyebrow slightly. The major continued

'He also has major outstanding debts that we trust will be settled by his family. I will deem it an honour to make your arrangement for you, and provide any facility within my power which you might require in Portsmouth.'

It was Peachey's turn to look pleased.

'Thank you sir, I will take you up on your very kind offer.'

'I will send someone to escort you this afternoon then gentlemen.'

With that, the major and his colleagues took their leave of them.

Peachey closed the door after them and looked at Trevelyan.

'I think we can safely say that we have a very satisfactory conclusion to that affair.'

Trevelyan nodded and smiled,

'My wounds are all the better for that. You also have your problem solved at the Governor's residence to boot Peachey.'

'I have indeed. I need some good news and that's a fact' he replied.

The colour began to reappear on Trevelyan's face and his easy smile gradually emerged from behind the previous mask of strain.

'Time for some sustenance Peachey' he said while waving his hand at the brandy bottle.

Peachey moved forward from his customary window seat to accept a glass from him.

'I need some fortification; the past few hours have been somewhat of a strain. At least your problems have taken a shine for the better Trevelyan, more than can be said for mine I fear'.

Peachey was about to speak when there was a gentle rap on the door. Raising one eyebrow at Trevelyan indicating puzzlement, Peachey again opened the door.

The Reverend Weston complete with a serious ecumenical look attempted to peer past Peachey as he said

'Forgive me sir, word reached me that Mr. Trevelyan had been severely wounded this morning. I came immediately I heard.'

Peachey smiled a welcoming smile and on opening the door said

'It is true that he has sustained something of a wound, but fortunately he is not in need of your spiritual services as he is, as you can see, alive and well and making remarkable progress.'

Relief and a small smile changed the expression of the Rev'd Weston. He moved forward into the room and whilst still casting an examining eye over Trevelyan said

'I am much relieved sir. A very unpleasant and distasteful situation that has now been resolved I hear.'

Moving over to where Trevelyan was reclining in his chair, glass to his lips, he furthered quietly

'Are you sure that your wound will readily heal Mr. Trevelyan?'

'Thank you for your interest sir, I am appreciative of your enquiries and concern. The physician informs me that the wound is superficial and will rapidly heal. He assures me that my chess playing will not be impaired but might in fact be improved by the incident.'

The twinkle that had been absent from Trevelyan's eyes was beginning to return, heralding his rapid return to his usual self.

After a slight moments hesitation the Rev'd Weston acknowledged the good-natured humour that Trevelyan was making at Weston's expense was an expression of friendship. Weston felt himself smiling in spite of his concerns and replied

'Then I shall require ten times the number of duels to raise my standard to win a match I fear.'

Trevelyan laughed and picked up the decanter again.

'Perhaps you would care for a glass to celebrate my survival, unscathed to any great extent in the land of the living?'

The Rev'd. Weston again hesitated then said

'A small one under the circumstances and to rejoice that the good lord has established an amiable solution.'

The glass that Trevelyan handed Weston could, under no stretch of the imagination, be considered small, but Weston made no comment or objected in any way.

'To your recovery and continued good health' proposed Weston.

They all three raised their glasses and sipped the brandy. There was silence for a few moments, each man with his own thoughts. This silence was cut short by a further knock on the door. Peachey now produced a somewhat exasperated face and said

'It seems that the whole world wishes to call and pay their respects to you Trevelyan.'

'Come!'

Three pairs of eyes focussed on the door. It opened and the head of Fairweather appeared around the edge.

'Excuse me for intruding sirs but Miss Attwick is downstairs and wishes to speak with Mr. Trevelyan. She cannot call on him in his rooms and has asked me to request him to oblige her by coming downstairs. I have already informed her that Mr. Trevelyan is wounded but is able to move about.'

All three looked at each other, attempting to understand why the lady who had severed the engagement last night was now seeking a meeting.

Trevelyan leaned to one side and pushing up on the table made to his feet.

'I suppose I should not keep the lady waiting. I must confess I had hardly expected a courtesy visit from her of all people.'

A thoughtful Peachey said

'It may not be a courtesy call sir, pray be on your guard.'

Trevelyan looking at the other two said

'Perhaps you will provide me with some assistance in going downstairs.'

Returning Peachey's look he said

'I had considered that possibility myself. Wretched woman, she still torments me.'

The Rev. Weston felt that this was a matter best left to the principals. He said

'I think it best that I take my leave sir. I am delighted to see you far from being mortally wounded. We shall I hope resume our chess at an appropriate time.'

'Indeed sir. I thank you for your interest in my well-being.'

The clergyman headed off down the stairs and, supported by Peachey with Fairweather standing by for additional help if required, Trevelyan followed at a slower pace, heading to the room at the front.

Elizabeth Attwick was accompanied by her mother. A mother looking annoyed, bewildered, vexed and apprehensive – in fact an amalgam of emotions which took turns at taking stage on her face for short periods at a time. For her part, Elizabeth Attwick looked a trifle uncomfortable but determination was never far from the foremost of her appearance.

She rose as soon as they entered the room and half ran forward to greet Trevelyan.

'O sir, I heard you were injured this morning by that ghastly man Gadfew but that you overcame him and are now the toast of the officers. I feared for you when I first heard and we had to visit straight away.'

Glancing briefly at her mother for confirmation of her statement and without waiting for verbal comment continued

'Mr. Peachey's manservant said that you were wounded but were recovering. Is it too bad? Does the wound trouble you?'

Trevelyan looked at her and said

'Good morrow Miss Attwick' and nodded his head in greeting, then turning to her mother said

'Good morning to you also madam.'

Looking back to Elizabeth Attwick said

'Thank you for your concern madam, but the wound is relatively slight and will soon heal I am told.'

Elizabeth Attwick half reached out a hand but was unsure quite how to continue.

'I thought for a moment that your injuries might delay our forthcoming marriage.'

Trevelyan took a pace back as though he had been struck in the face.

Recovering slightly he said

'I have given much thought to your words last night Miss Attwick and have come to the decision that you were correct in every detail. I am not worthy of your hand and give thanks to the good lord that our paths were severed before I might inflict untold damage to you and your family.'

The effect was predictable but he continued

'You were right to take your stand on this point and I respect you even more, but sadly marriage is out of the question for us.'

Elizabeth Attwick's mother was on her feet in a trice. A small dumpish person, being of opposite build to that of her daughter, she appeared as one who was witnessing the disappearance of her daughter's secured future as wine flowing to waste from a ruptured barrel.

It was as if the thought of her daughter remaining unmarried in her house was a disaster with only the great fire of London or the Black Death having more disastrous consequences.

'Sir you must forgive the outburst of an emotional overwrought girl who has spoken out of turn.'

She eyed her daughter as she spoke with her own venomous eyes.

'Her words terminating the engagement were never meant to be taken seriously.'

Trevelyan having had a moment to compose himself now adopted a more composed stance,

'On the contrary madam, many true things are spoken straight from the heart on such occasions, and it would be foolish to ignore them. I have thought deeply about the subject and apologise for any scandal that may have affected you, but my mind is now clear and I will trouble you no longer, even though it will cause me much grief.'

He stopped and Peachey was almost afraid that Trevelyan would wipe an imaginary tear from his eye; such was his second major theatrical performance of the day.

Elizabeth Attwick was furious with both Trevelyan and herself. She knew that she had terminated the engagement in the most public of ways, - this being her intention at the time, and that Trevelyan had taken back the ring with no protestations whatsoever.

His claim of grief and sacrificing himself for her greater good, approached martyrdom, and was one for which she had no answer.

Her anger boiled over

'You are simply using this as a ploy to escape from your obligations sir, you have dallied with me and I intend to seek restitution for the suffering you have caused us.'

Her mother seeing this latest outburst as one of total futility spun round and hissed at her daughter

'Be quiet! You have already said too much in front of too many people and are only making matters worse by your ill termed comments.'

'I will not be quiet!'. Elizabeth Attwick's response was uttered through clenched teeth in a matched snakelike hiss. She stamped her foot to give further emphasis to her words

'I have been humiliated in front of society.'

'All of which was all of your own stupidity.'

The finality of the situation was crystal clear to the mother - her careful manoeuvrings perfect in the run up to the engagement now lay in tattered ruins with no hope of salvage. She grabbed her daughter's hand

'We shall leave immediately Elizabeth.'

The abruptness of their retreat took everyone by surprise and Trevelyan found himself saying

'Good day ladies' to the back of the two departing figures.

Peachey turned to Trevelyan.

'Another fine performance sir as the heart-rent depressed suitor of unrequited love. Othello would have much to learn from your emotionally packed delivery.'

A mischievous grin balanced the twinkling eyes.

'I believe I have found my calling after all sir. But of seriousness, I thank you again Peachey for this resolution as much as any other.'

Turning to take Trevelyan's arm Peachey said

'Let us return to your rooms. You shall rest for a while and then we dine with the officers. That will be an interesting meeting, and hopefully a rewarding one.

Chapter 14

Rousseliere thought *a doorway in St. Thomas's church was not the choicest of locations to spend much of the night.*

He faced Courtney.

'We mustn't remain here, we are now in an exposed position.'

Courtney's red and bloodshot eyes glared back at the Frenchman.

'We are in no danger. No one saw us enter or leave his house and no one has ever seen us there. I used no real force on him and he appeared to die of a seizure in any event.'

Rousseliere scoffed,

'With elderly men such as him, little force is required. Had you not manhandled him we could have persuaded him to at least give us the names of his accomplices.'

Courtney saying nothing maintained his glare. Rousseliere wasn't finished,

'As for the money, what he said may be true – that wherever it's hidden, it can only be located by means of the snuffbox.'

Lowering his own voice he continued

'We must take stock of our position. Staying in the town now that we haven't the money or the names of our local supporters has no benefit. Our plans must be updated to reflect the current situation.'

'Spoken like a military strategist and commander.'

Sarcasm hung heavy on Courtney's words, then he said

'Our position is simple. We have no money to pay for the local men or for me. Your masters in France, ever cautious, provided me with two paymasters - one in London and the other here. Who is going to pay the piper now I ask?'

That was it. With a cold look Rousseliere said

'I will ensure that you are paid fully for your services. We cannot afford to fail at this point.'

'Can I trust you on that?'

Courtney looked thoughtful as he stared at Rousseliere, his mind clearly assessing the chance of receiving his payment via him. To have an option was a luxury – at present he had none.

His mind made up and continued

'I will accept your word on that but don't try and cross me.'

Although they were thrown into this uneasy alliance, both had a grudging respect for each other's role. Their personal mutual dislike was of no consequence to the plan that was of paramount importance.

Courtney continued

'I still feel that landlord at *Spice Island* knows more than he lets on. If he and that whore of a girl were not a party to the theft, I'll wager he knows or suspects the identity of the thief and where he might be found.'

Turning his head in the direction of *Spice Island*, he muttered

'I've not finished in that quarter by any manner of means.'

Rousseliere stretched his aching body, cramped from the confined space that had hidden them.

'If you return you may well be placing yourself in a trap.'

Courtney looked up sharply,

'What trap?'

Rousseliere had just begun to realise the full implication of the theft.

'The letter – that's the problem. The snuffbox itself leads nowhere but the letter was a form of introduction and will certainly cause problems if it fell into the wrong hands.'

Courtney looked unconvinced. Rousseliere continued

'The first place anyone in authority would visit, would be the place where it was stolen.'

'The thief would hardly be likely to impart sort of information.'

'He would if he were paid for his trouble or offered a pardon if caught. Led to the inn, the innkeeper would tell them of that two sailors and provide descriptions.'

'That would lead them nowhere.'

'No but if you returned to cause trouble, you may well walk straight into their waiting arms, or the innkeeper would quickly inform on you.'

Courtney had bent to massage his stiff leg but he looked up promptly.

'If, if, if….. The thief won't be able to read and will probably throw the letter away.'

Pausing to resume easing his aching leg Courtney returned to his theme,

'However, one cannot discount your reasoning. That being the case, we have to take further precautions. Two sailors on their own will be easy to spot – we shall have to split up.'

'Split up?'

Rousseliere was trying to assess its full meaning; he anxiously protested

'I shall stand out far more than you.'

'Not necessarily, it depends on where you are. In any event, without knowing who was to shelter us we now have nowhere to stay in safety. If you leave the town and cross to Gosport you will not be so obvious.'

'And you, what will you do?'

'I will obtain some other clothes. I can pass as a local and will find some other lodgings.'

Courtney paused

'There is a problem though, until *The Mistress* is required it needs to be hidden. You will have to take it and hide it in Gosport. It will be much easier over there.'

'How long for? I don't need days to survey the defences at Gosport.'

Rousseliere acknowledged that Gosport was far more safer than Portsmouth, but once he had seen the strength of the Gosport Lines his work was finished there.

Courtney's view became stronger as he spoke

'You will be far better there than here, although it's by no means certain that we shall be sought. But by your own reckoning, it's possible the letter may lead them in our direction. Would you have been named in it?'

'No it would be a letter saying the holder of the letter was to be afforded every assistance and possibly mention something about the snuffbox, but certainly no names.'

'Much as I expected, then we proceed with the survey and then the attack. I shall take more soundings around the inn, you never know I may find out more than we expect. Rest assured, I shall not be taken.'

Rousseliere decided. Picking up his bag he said

'Give me *The Mistress* and take me to get a boat across to Gosport. I also need to know when and where to meet you again.'

Courtney didn't hesitate,

'Five days time outside *The India Arms*, that's the large inn in the main street in Gosport. Be around on the hour every hour from ten in the morning until I make contact - amble past and don't stop, just as you did in Dover.'

'Don't keep me waiting this time' warned Rousseliere.

'I shall be there have no fear. Hide *The* Mistress and be on your guard.'

'I need no guidance from you on being on my guard, I am a Frenchman in a major British naval port, surrounded by soldiers, marines, sailors and civilians who would betray for a reward with no second thought. I have thought of nothing else since my arrival.'

Gathering up his own bags he watched as Courtney slipped from their shadowy refuge. Rousseliere followed some hundred yards or so behind. His mouth was dry, and lack of nourishment vibrated in his stomach. Summoning up his reserves he steadfastly strode into *King Charles Stre*et and followed the route take by Courtney.

Passing through the *Landport Gate* was no obstacle at that time of day. Although there was much activity, their progress was not difficult.

Once outside, Rousseliere turned left, following Courtney across the millpond – a large shallow waterway that extended northwards. They walked south of the millpond, the way the locals followed to reach the dockyard.

A steady pace for ten minutes brought them to within a short distance of the dockyard gate, set in a tall retaining wall – *a wall constructed by captured French prisoners* Rousseliere remembered ruefully.

The Hard was, as its name implied, a stone hard standing where a miscellany of small boats plied for the business of ferrying passengers to Gosport across the harbour.

Other longer trips were undertaken to moored ships, the Isle of Wight and occasionally to Cams Hall, at the top of the harbour.

As Rousseliere approached he could see Courtney moving between the boats apparently negotiating a crossing. Courtney turned and beckoned Rousseliere to a small boat moored by the small wooden landing stage.

He placed the bag containing *The Mistress* on the stones and turning so that his mouth was close to Rousseliere's ear said

'He is crossing; I have paid him for you and told him you are sick. He is already taking that woman. I shall see you in five days time as arranged.'

With that he turned his back and retraced his steps towards the town. Rousseliere casually picked up the bag Courtney had left.

It's quite heavy for two small items. Hiding it in Gosport is a sound idea. Carrying it around in Portsmouth is dangerous and impracticable.

The boatman held the boat while the young woman climbed in, indicating Rousseliere to do the same. Both passengers were seated in the rear, she with her back to the oarsman facing Rousseliere. Looking at him she said

'You're going to Haslar then?'

Seeing his puzzled look added

'Your companion said that you were sick, I assumed you were going to the hospital.'

Haslar Hospital! The name suddenly made sense to him. On his plans the Naval Hospital was clearly marked, being located away from Gosport town, but accessible by both foot and boat via *Haslar Creek*.

A section of the *Gosport Lines* - the defence system guarding land based attack from the West, lay just beyond the hospital. His attention had never focussed on the hospital but he knew it was a large site containing many buildings and curiously enough, surrounded by high walls manned by armed marines.

Back in France, having queried these high walls, he had been told that as most of the sailors were pressed men, the hospital had to be guarded to prevent escape, which was also the reason for its location away from Gosport.

He met her gaze

'I may well be going there.'

Pointing to his stomach he indicated that there was a wound or problem there that was not immediately obvious.

Nodding she said

'I have a position there; I will show you the way if you are unfamiliar with the route. Following the main road is far longer than cutting through over the flats.'

Rousseliere hesitated. His first response was to say he was not going there yet, but a saying flashed through his mind, *the best place to hide a book is in a library*

There were five days until he met with Courtney again. *Where else in heaven's name was a sailor to hide for that period?*

He replied,

'If I go straight there I may not get out again in a hurry, I think it is more a prison than a hospital'

Shrugging his shoulders and giving a mock grimace made her laugh.

She replied

'Aye, it is that for some' she laughed, 'but not for others.'

Seeing that she hadn't made much sense to him she said

'The sentries guard the gates and boundaries but those that know, come and go almost as they please.'

Puzzlement showed on Rousseliere's face. She continued

'There is a very large drain that goes from the centre of the hospital out to sea. It floods twice a day. As the tide comes up it floods and keeps the drain clear. But at low tide you can walk out through the drain to the seashore with no problem.'

The benefit of this was quickly obvious to Rousseliere. *If I can get in and out of the hospital easily it would provide a perfect hiding place for a few days.*

'I think I need to see the drain' laughed Rousseliere.

'Maybe that could be arranged. In our block we have a removable grill that leads into the drain – providing its not flooded of course.'

'That sounds magnificent, that would be better than being caged up.'

'If I show you, you'll have to carry this for me. It gets heavy after a while.'

He glanced down at her burden, with his own bags and *The Mistress*, it would be a fair load. The labour however was nothing compared to his good fortune at meeting the girl. He said

'What's your name?'

'Nell'

'A nice name for a nice girl'

She was never fond of it before but his quick charming reply gave her second thoughts about it.

'More than my husband thinks' she replied.

'Not that he's had any opportunity to use it this past two and a half years.'

In answer to Rousseliere's enquiring look, she continued

'He was pressed. All I know is that his ship went to the West Indies and I've been left here to fend for myself. We'd only been married for a month when he was taken.'

'To be pressed is bad enough, but to leave a wife behind him is double damnation.'

'And what is your name if I may enquire?'

'Berthois.' Rousseliere had spoken before thinking,

She looked sharply at him.

'That's a peculiar name for a sailor and no mistake.'

'I come from the Channel Isles. It's a common enough name there'

'I thought you weren't from these parts, not that I know exactly where the Channel Isles are either though.'

She laughed again with an easy manner. Rousseliere replied

'Do you live in the hospital then?'

'Yes, I work and live there. There's nothing else for me. When my husband returns he knows where to find me. At least I can get food from the galleys.'

She took on a wistful air for just a moment as though having memories of her missing husband, then continued

'Food is allocated to the sick sailors by name, but many are too ill to eat so their rations can be had by us. Not that good but it keeps me going.'

'No check on the names then?'

'Not where we are,' she laughed again, 'we're in the area that's quarantined. They pass the food through a hole in the wall that keeps us from the rest.'

Rousseliere's face looked horrified as she went on

'It's not as bad as you think. We stay down one end away from the sick ones. We leave them their food but many don't want to eat. They drink mostly and lie around. That's why non-one checks what we do — they're too dammed scared.'

Rousseliere had seen sick men in quarantine before — they were listless, perpetually sick, couldn't eat and cared nothing for their surroundings. They were totally unable to fight, that was for sure. Many died but others recovered.

The British treated their men, France tended to rely on the Gods.

She laughed again at the serious expression dominating his face

'You could stay there if you don't want to be locked up each night' she ventured.

'The very last thing I want is to be locked up' he replied with total honesty.

'Alright I'll show you'.

The conversation was interrupted by a lurch as the boat swung round to face the jetty on the Gosport side.

A similar scene was also to be found at this side of the water. People busying themselves earning their livelihoods; plying their trade as water boatmen, transporting provisions and wares across the busy stretch of water.

The boatman shipped the oars and hopped up to the jetty in one practised movement. Holding the boat steady he indicated for Rousseliere and the girl Nell to do the same..

Gathering up all the bags Rousseliere did as instructed. Nell followed.

An incline led up to meet the road. On reaching the top she said

'This way' and made off up the road.

Rousseliere looked about him familiarising himself with the layout. Gosport was nowhere near as busy as Portsmouth, a fact quite obvious as they walked up the street.

Ahead he could see the swinging sign of *The India Arms Inn* – the rendezvous for five days hence.

He could see why Courtney had said to walk by rather than wait, as anyone would be easily noticed remaining there for any length of time.

Nell however turned abruptly left before they reached the inn and followed a narrow alley between two houses. At the end, it opened out with Haslar Creek before them.

Cutting down to the shoreline again they walked alongside until they reached a small bridge. In the distance, he could see a large building peeking over a high continuous wall around its perimeter.

Seeing him looking she said

'That's the hospital. We're over the far side.'

Once across the bridge she kept to the shoreline again until they reached a small jetty. A naval cutter was unloading several men, some able to walk, others being laid onto trolleys that ran on rails leading up towards the main gate of the hospital.

A marine in striking red uniform strolled around watching the proceedings.

'Come' said Nell.

They walked up just as the first trolley was set in motion towards the entrance gate.

Following on behind, they passed through the gate, turning left down a small path away from the trolley.

No one had paid any attention to the girl or her companion. The fact that they knew where they were going and were carrying bags dispelled any queries.

Turning to Rousseliere, Nell said

'I don't know who you were meant to report to but we can get you seen to without getting logged into the books here. If you report officially they will lock you up most of the time, and any one who can, will be set to work. We go this way.'

The path fronted between two imposing houses,

'The Superintendent's house' Nell said nodding towards the one facing them on the left.

Imposing residence and buildings - the British care well for their sailors, and that's a fact.

Rousseliere was impressed with the size of this hospital dedicated solely to the Royal Navy.

Reaching a stout wall within the grounds she followed it until reaching a small door set into the wall. Looking further along the wall, a small opening was visible. Nell said

'That's where they pass the food and provisions through. You can see that, unless absolutely necessary, no one comes in here.'

The door shut firmly behind them. Rousseliere felt a slight shiver run down his spine. This was a danger that he had not prepared himself for, however Nell seemed oblivious to any risks and walked on ahead.

The first thing that struck him was the lack of activity. He had expected to be confronted with sick sailors and signs of plague or some devastating maladies, but all was quiet. The buildings facing them showed little signs of life, a scullery maid or servant went in a door further down the building carrying a large pot but otherwise no one was to be seen.

Nell continued to the end of the building and then turned the corner. The sight caught Rousseliere by surprise – it was the sea. The hospital at this end directly faced the Isle of Wight and slightly to the left, the Battery at Gosport stood sentinel to the harbour entrance.

The Battery faced the open sea. The ramparts could be seen with their menacing firepower awaiting any ship foolish enough to attempt to force their way into the harbour.

Rousseliere felt a distinct wave of alarm. From this position, he could see that the Portsmouth fortifications across the water counterbalanced the devastating armament of the Gosport Battery.

It was no wonder that the British felt little threat at Portsmouth. It appeared to be total madness for invading ships to attempt to approach head on – they would be blasted out of the water.

The plan was correct, without pre-planning and surveys in Portsmouth, the attack stood absolutely no chance of success.

Should the plan not go as planned, death and carnage awaited his invading countrymen. The potential danger of being in the compound with quarantined sick men was nothing compared to that.

He looked to Nell. She crossed to the building and opened a solid door presenting a long dark corridor.

An immediate smell of death almost overcame him. It hung like a dense vapour, almost like a blanket. He swallowed hard, Nell continued on her way down the passage with no regard to the cloud of mortality that was sucked in with every breath.

Having lived there for over two years she must have become used to the everyday smells and odours.

Rousseliere followed past several closed doors to the far end of the brick lined corridor. Entering a small room and taking her bundle from him she said

'Wait her while I give these back. I'll find out if you can stay here.'

His impression of the room was that it was a store room of some sort. There was little air and what little there was had a somewhat stifling effect. However it appeared very quiet outside and that had a calming effect on him.

She suddenly reappeared.

'It's alright to stay here for a while. You can slip back across to the main hospital to be attended to. They won't know that you haven't been booked in at the main gate and allocated a berth.'

Opening the door she indicated

'To the right here is where the food is distributed to the sick. Just take what you want as there's always some left over and they won't stomach it back over the main site because it's come from here.'

Putting his head around the door he could see where she was pointing. She continued

'Just a little further on you can see the grill that leads down to the drain in case you've a notion of getting some fresh air by the shore.'

Nodding he quickly assessed the layout.

This is surely a stroke of fortune if what she says is correct. Not only is there a place to stay but I can slip out to survey the defences when the tide allows.

'I'm indebted to you for your help.'

She looked up at him,

'I only hope someone is also helping my husband, wherever he is. I'm only down the far ward and might see you from time to time.'

With that she closed the door and was gone.

The storeroom only had a small aperture at the top to let in both light and air, but Rousseliere counted his blessings. *Being holed up amongst the enemy's is a curious experience, perilous and secure at the same time.*

As his eyes became accustomed to the dim light, his first thought was for hiding *The Mistress*. A small pile of wood platters looked as though they hadn't been moved for a long time. Gently lifting the top ones away from the wall revealed an opening just wide enough to secrete the device.

On replacing the platters nothing looked amiss. There was also no telltale sign of rats. No food in here and nothing to entice them in. *Ensure it is kept that way.*

Moving some canvas covers to one side provided a reasonable bed. Not realising how tired he was he laid down drifting into sleep punctuated with thoughts of Courtney, sick men, France and unknown demons merging into an uncoordinated theme.

This coordination was to become real in quicker time than he realised.

Chapter 15

Fairweather, having escorted Peachey and Trevelyan to the Officers Mess, eventually made his way back to *The George Inn* after having been given a sustaining meal with the non-commissioned officers. They then returned to their duties whilst the officers continued their wining and dinning of the two gentlemen guests.

This had been an interesting occasion. He had been treated as "Mr. Peachey's man" and not just his manservant.

The first fact he'd established was just how hated Capt. Gadfew had been. He bullied and ill treated the troops; was vindictive, and took a delight in persecuting the junior men. Being an officer, everyone needed to obey him, but none mourned his departure – in fact they rejoiced at their good fortune – another factor that made Fairweather and his master most welcomed.

He parted on good terms with all assembled, with offers of help ringing in his ears, should he ever require it.

Striding back to the inn he was buoyant. Apart from the almost hero's welcome he'd received, his income had been enhanced by a generous donation given by Mr. Trevelyan on the way to the mess.

Fairweather had much respect for him. He was a brave moral man.

On reaching *The George Inn* and through the coaching entrance, he headed to the back room. The sounds of voices and activity filtered through the door where menservants and working travellers gathered.

Entering the smoke filled room, he saw two of those who were sharing the same room as him. They sat at the far table, engrossed in deep discussions with one of the young stable lads. Calling for some ale he sat alongside them.

The stable lad had something wrapped in a cloth.

'I don't know what it says, but it must prove that it's worth far more.'

On seeing Fairweather one of his roommates said

'You can read and have some foreign knowledge – what's this all about?'

He beckoned to the lad to open the cloth. Something he did with great reluctance, being uncertain of Fairweather. Slowly pulling back the cloth, he exposed a shiny coloured box and a document of some description.

The man said

'What's this paper say then?'

Lifting up the object he retrieved the paper lying underneath and passed it over.

Fairweather saw that it was in fact a document folded in the form of a letter with writing on the front. The writing however, was none too clear.

'Let's see it in better light' Fairweather said.

The lad made as to restrain him from taking the paper away but Fairweather was already heading over to the candle stand near the fire. Turning over the document as he went, he noted a large wax seal over the join.

Something about the seal grabbed his attention. He didn't actually recognise it, but had seen similar before. Much of the furniture they used to make had crafted family crests.

This crest was different. It had flowing feather-like shapes adorning a large central design. Not only was it different it was much larger than normal, a point he found curious.

Looking at the writing - it wasn't English. Knowing a few words of foreign languages from furniture designs and styles, it came to him in a flash – it was French and that must be a French seal on the reverse!

Returning to the table, all eyes focussed on him. He looked at the lad.

'Where'd you get this?'

The lad looked startled and looking rapidly round the table said

'It was given to me. I'm trying to find the owner so that I can claim a reward.'

It was a common enough reply when a thief was found with something that didn't belong to him.

Fairweather looked at the lad and the object in the cloth.

'Let's have a look at that.' Without further ado Fairweather promptly picked up the box snuggling in the cloth.

It was a snuffbox with a distinctive picture painted on the top. The lad made to snatch it back, but Fairweather, clutching it in his deformed hand moved back out of reach. Looking between the lad and the box he said

'I don't know exactly what is says on the letter as it's in French. This however, as you can see, is a snuffbox belonging to a gentleman, and not for the likes of us. Now where'd you get it?'

The lad sensed that he could be in serious trouble if he didn't keep his wits about him. He certainly had no liking for this manservant. He seemed to know too much. He said

'It was passed to me by a lad who lives on *Spice Island.*'

'*Spice Island*?' queried one of the other men.

'What's something like this doing down *Spice Island* then?'

The lad was finding himself beset from all sides now. He mumbled

'Perhaps someone dropped it, he didn't say that he got it on *Spice Island.*'

Fairweather, not wanting the matter to get out of hand calmly said to the lad

'I'll get you the reward. My master will almost certainly know how to locate the gentleman. He can read French and will know whom to contact.'

'How much is the reward?' The lad looked cunningly at Fairweather.

'A reward? I would think half a crown.'

'Its worth more, look at the workmanship' exclaimed the lad.

'It's a reward. If someone paid you more for its value and it were stolen, then they would be hanging at the end of a rope as well as you.'

The mention of hanging had an immediate sobering effect on the lad. He knew he was out manoeuvred, *but the money was good. If they called it a reward he couldn't be guilty of theft could he?*

'I'll not hand it over until I see the ready money' cautioned the lad.

Fairweather mentally thanked Trevelyan again for his generous payment – some of that could be used.

'I'll give it you now' said Fairweather to the astonishment of those around the table.

'I have funds for my master, so you can have that.'

The immediate prospect of half a crown brought a smile to the lads face, and he hastily pocketed the money before there was any chance of a change of mind. Touching his forehead in mock acknowledgement, he was gone.

The others looked at Fairweather. One queried

'Does your master know who that belongs to then?'

'More than likely, and the document will help' replied Fairweather carefully secreting the cloth into his pocket. 'I must be away, I'll see you later.'

Making his way through the room Fairweather hoped his gamble would be successful. Peachey was looking for anything relating to the French and would be prepared to reimburse him even if the transaction was of no use.

In fact Mr. Peachey was appearing to become quite desperate for any information relating to the French in Portsmouth. They had come from London without much warning and Mr. Peachey kept on asking him if he had heard anything relating to french activities of any sort and to 'keep his ear to the ground'. Well here was something relating to the French – it was all he'd been able to locate at present. Hope I've made the right decision.

Peachey and Trevelyan were in a mellow mood. They were so mellow that Trevelyan required assistance in walking the short distance back to *The George Inn* because of his mellowness.

The dinner with the officers had been an overwhelming success. Both sides had been anxious to offer the hand of friendship and offers of assistance of any description were ringing in their ears as they made their way slowly up the High Street.

A familiar figure approached them.

'Ah Fairweather' said Peachey 'lend a hand and assist Mr. Trevelyan back to the inn, his wound is playing him up and walking is somewhat arduous for him at present.'

Fairweather promptly assessed the arduousness of Mr. Trevelyan's condition and laid the blame at the door of several bottles of full-bodied red wine rather than the wound that must have become oblivious in the process.

'Certainly sir. Come take my arm Mr. Trevelyan if you would sir, its not far to the inn.'

Trevelyan peered at the voice and recognised Fairweather.

'To help again already Fairweather.'

Looking generally in the direction of Peachey he mumbled 'Dependable man this Peachey, knows his furniture too.'

Peachey nodded but made no comment. The officer's offers of help and the promise to arrange a meeting with the Governor at the earliest opportunity was all very useful indeed.

He felt however like an archer who had been given a superb bow and a quiver full of first class arrows, but not the target.

Digesting his thoughts and following behind the duo of Fairweather and Trevelyan, Fairweather turning said over his shoulder

'I have acquired a document written in French and a snuffbox – certainly French. It came from a stable lad who got it from someone on *Spice Island.*'

Peachey thoughts suddenly became focused on what had been said.

'You have what Fairweather?'

'Its certainly French but I don't know where it came from. The document is addressed in French. I paid a reward of half a crown to secure it from the lad to stop him disposing it to others.'

'Well done Fairweather. It may be nothing of course but it's the first sign of the Frenchies we've had since we arrived. Where is it now?'

'In my pocket sir.'

'Let us look at it as soon as we get to the inn.'

Well now. Peachey's mind thought around the development. *Who had got it and why? It may be that it belongs to a family who is lawfully entitled to it. There are a lot of items in London of French origin that have been held by family for years. This could be an instance like that.*

It seemed a lifetime for Peachey before they reached the inn. Fairweather struggled manfully to help Trevelyan along but progress was slow. Nevertheless they duly staggered up the stairs to Trevelyan's room where he was placed on the bed and promptly fell asleep.

Much of what Peachey had said was true. Trevelyan had not slept a jot last night; he had received a wound that drained his energy. The officers had enthusiastically entertained them, where Trevelyan was the guest of honour. No wonder the poor man was exhausted.

Back in his own room Peachey waited while Fairweather drew out the cloth containing the snuffbox and document. Gently taking it from him and lightly fingering it, it was undoubtedly a very fine piece. The picture on the lid was curious. He reached for the document. Feeling the texture of the paper he looked closely at the writing on the top.

The translation was straightforward it was simply addressed to *"The Deliverer."*

Deliverer – deliverer of what and to whom? There was no sense to that. Where did it come from?

Turning the paper over he looked at the large intricate seal. The sight produced a shiver down his back and a curious feeling of hairs standing up on his neck.

It was regal and he couldn't decide if he'd seen this before, but whoever it belonged to – it was French and no mistake.

Could it be that Fairweather had unearthed tangible proof that there really was something afoot here?

Turning it back over, he had to decide now what to do with it. Had there been the name of an individual on the front, he would have made contact with him.

At least then he could satisfy his curiosity as to who *"The Deliverer"* was. Now, there was no way of tracing the rightful owner. Therefore he had a duty and some form of dubious rights tp open it.

Fingers slightly trembling he carefully broke the seal.

The document unfolded easily. It was short in length but was easily translated –

"To Our Honourable Patriot

Let it be known that the bearer of this letter is, by the grace of God and our Sovereign King Louis XVI of France, a true representative of his Imperial Majesty and an accredited Agent of France.

He should be afforded the fullest assistance to enable him to perform his duties.

He bears with him an object with holds the key to release the long held monies to pay those loyal to his majesty.

May God speed you and aid the cause of righteousness, for the return of the true faith and governance."

There was a scrawled signature and another wax seal – which again looked vaguely familiar.

Peachey re-read it several times. He looked to Fairweather,

'This is evidence that we have been seeking Fairweather. It is essential we act at once. We need to find this stable lad and locate the person that gave him the items.'

Fairweather could readily sense the urgency from the serious expression that transfixed his employer's face. However he was uncertain how they would find the person who passed the items to the stable lad.

He was certain the lad would prove very reluctant to name anyone, even if he actually knew their identity. Reprisals were short and savage for any betrayal. He rubbed his nose and said

'Getting the person may well be difficult. He will refuse to say, even if he knows.'

'He will when threatened with a noose. It loosens most men's tongues and will certainly do so for a stable lad I'll be bound.'

Peachey saw Fairweather's continued doubt but continued

'I will write a note to the Army Major seeking assistance. I can now play my hand more fully than before. He has promised to assist me should I need help. I shall be requiring it though much earlier than either of us envisaged!'

Walking over to the table he selected a pen and quickly wrote a note to the Major. Looking up to Fairweather he said

'Take this with all speed to the officers quarters and let no one impede you from your task. Escort the Major and his soldiers here and we will then questioned the stable lad once you have identified him to us.'

Fairweather took the note and said

'Begging your pardon sir. I know these type of men. If we pay for information, even from those who took the things, it will speed matters and also, if men see that we pay well for information will prompt others to do likewise.'

Peachey dwelt carefully on this for a moment or two, then said

'You are right in your thinking Fairweather. The correct way may not be the right way. I was beginning to despair at not having anything to report back. Right, - pay, threaten, cajole, or whatever but trace the person who had this in their possession with no delay whatsoever.'

He set off at a fast pace for the officer's quarters.

Peachey re-examined the snuffbox, turning it over, it readily opened to reveal - an empty interior.

There were no sub-divisions and close examination showed that on the white pearl-lined inner surfaces, no marks or scratches indicated that a key or anything metallic had ever been housed there.

If this held the key to what was sought, it certainly didn't now and if it had, it had probably been carefully wrapped in something. The key would have had to be quite small, and as such what could it possibly fit?

Picking up the letter again he looked at the seal. There was something about it that irked him. But whatever conclusions he might arrive at, nothing would be achieved until they had traced the whereabouts of the two men and le *Secret du Roi* Agent. The time was ticking and it was against him.

Fairweather would not be back for some while yet and Trevelyan was oblivious to the outside world. Peachey picked up his pen again and started another letter to his uncle.

Chapter 16

Spice Island was never quiet. It never slept. One day was never the same as the proceeding one. With its renown reputation, Courtney easily blended into this scene of life.

Making his way down *Broad Street* he headed for the small inn where they had stayed. It seemed every other dwelling was an inn, existing to fuel the drunken state that perpetuated throughout the whole of *Spice Island*. No notice was taken of the apparently drunken man in front of the inn and casually peered inside.

The same two men who had been there the other evening were the sole occupants. These men either stayed there or carried out their activities from the inn. Courtney knew that there were many villainous deeds performed on *Spice Island*. Illegal dealings from the docks were a profitable underground source of ill-gotten gains.

Moving round he peered down the side alley – the side alley that Nathan Oates had used to access the back of the building and scale the wall up to the bedroom. It was deserted. A small window opened into the alley. Drawing a long bladed knife from inside his coat, he forced the window with one sharp movement. The slight crack of the action was inaudible.

Access through the window was difficult, but he finally squeezed through. He was now in a small passage. Voices of men talking in the bar filtered through a closed door. Peering round the end of the passage there was another entrance to the bar area. Opposite was obviously the kitchen and scullery area. No sound emerged from that area as he crept along towards the far door.

The door abruptly opened. The figure of the innkeeper was framed in the doorway by the bar's candlelight. He was looking over his shoulder as he passed through, completing a conversation with his cronies. On closing the door behind him to cross to the kitchen he felt the cold steel of Courtney's knife pressed sharply against his throat whilst his arm was pinioned to his side. The shock of the quick action momentarily immobilised him. A quiet voice whispered in his ear

'One sound and you're a dead man my friend.'

A series of small nods from the innkeeper signified his understanding of the sinister warning.

The voice continued

'Now my friend it is a little matter of the items that you stole from my friend and I.'

The identity of the speaker and also of his fellow visitor flashed to the innkeeper's mind. This was the thin-faced man with the evil eyes – the one who had sworn vengeance. He gave an involuntary shiver.

That he had nothing to do with their theft didn't help matters in the slightest, for this man had that cold and unbelieving look of someone to be feared and no mistake. He spoke with difficulty as the knife was pressing hard into his windpipe

'Believe me sir I had nothing to do with your loss, I neither planned or had anything to do with it.'

'Not only are you ugly but you lie as well' came the reply.

'On God's word sir I had nothing to do with it.'

'God's word…….. God's word – it's blasphemy as well is it?'

'Please believe me sir I…….'

'I want our things back' interrupted the voice 'give them to me now or take me to whoever you passed them to.'

'I don't know, for I had no part of this, but I suspect someone who might have been involved. It's a young boy who occasionally brings me unwanted trinkets to buy that have come his way.'

'Trinkets that he has stolen and you buy, for next to nothing no doubt. I have no interest in your dealings my friend. He either has our items or he hasn't. Where do we find this young gentleman?'

'He hasn't been around for a little while….' - the knife pressed further into his throat 'that's why I think it's him and the fact that he can climb up anything that's got walls.'

Courtney sensed that the last piece of blabbering from the innkeeper might have sense to it. The wall was at first sight impossible to climb, and now the innkeeper had offered a solution to how the thief had got into the room and escaped so nimbly – a boy.

Courtney moved the man around slightly and said

'I repeat for the last time where is this boy?'

'I don't know for sure but I can find him, I know that.'

'Do you indeed? So shall I let you go, and then you fetch him here to me?'

'Indeed sir, I will do just that'

'You must take me for a fool my friend' whispered Courtney 'I wait, while you gather some cut-throat acquaintances and return you mean.'

The trapped head shook negatively.

Courtney, for all his whip hand advantage at the moment, knew that it was almost a stalemate. To regain the snuffbox and letter would be a masterstroke. He would love to see that Frenchman's face if he produced them in front of him, but to do so he had to give this wretch of a man some leeway to trace this boy.

'I will tell you what we will do my friend. You will walk ahead of me very slowly to where this boy is. When you find him you will regain our items, or your life will be worthless. Should I think you are trying to cross me I will disappear and will return at some future time to kill you – very slowly. Do I make myself clear?'

'Very much so sir. I will do my best.'

'No, you will *not* my friend - you will succeed. I will have our things back or you will serve no more bad ale – or good for that matter.'

Courtney gradually released the man from his grip but kept the knife in readiness against any foolhardy response the innkeeper might make. The innkeeper, relieved at his release, felt no inclination to do such a thing. It was the solution that troubled him. It was no foregone conclusion, only a feeling that he had, that it was the boy.

Certainly the ability to climb as the boy could, gave credence to the idea and the more he thought about it the more feasible it became. How to reach the boy and retrieve the stolen items with this dangerous man in tow was another matter.

The fact was, he was released, which at least gave him more breathing space. He was not confident in overpowering the man but he had lived on *Spice Island* for many long years, and knew many people and routes that gave him a hidden advantage. If he were able to signal or get word…..

'Start moving my friend!' Courtney's harsh whisper broke the innkeeper's deliberations, and then continued

'Open the door and tell those two to leave as you are shutting up. I shall be watching you from the side; any attempt to give a warning will mean you have signed your own death warrant. Understand me my friend?'

The innkeeper nodded and did precisely as instructed.

Outside in the street with the door bolted behind him, the innkeeper now had to decide which direction to take. He turned right having felt that going to the very tip or Point and working round to the docks would give him a better chance of locating the boy in one of his regular haunts.

Courtney allowed him to move fifty yards or so ahead, a distance that would enable him to maintain a clear view of the innkeeper but far enough away to affect an escape should the situation turn against him. The innkeeper knew that should he try to give Courtney the slip, it was only a matter of time before Courtney would return and kill him – of that he was certain.

Not more than a few hundred yards away from where Courtney was observing his man, another strange procession filed its way across the millpond bridge from Portsmouth towards the Point. It comprised an officer and a file of soldiers holding the frantic looking stable lad from *The George Inn,* with Peachey and Fairweather bringing up the rear.

Samuel Cooper, the officer, was the young man who had been required to act as Gadfew's second in his duel with Trevelyan. His duty on this occasion was to lead the search for Nathan Oates.

This activity had started after Fairweather's return with the officer and soldiers detailed off by the Major Salter. Fairweather led the party to the stable lad, who, under quick fire questioning by the young officer, promptly told them that Nathan Oates had been the one who had brought the snuffbox and document to him.

Before the lad knew what was happening, he was being escorted to *Spice Island* to find Nathan Oates without delay. The lad had never known anything to happen so quickly. From what was initially easy money for the items, it had now developed into a nightmare. The importance of these items was unbelievable and all the forces in Portsmouth now seemed united to track down the source. Peachey called a halt once they were down *Broad Street* and spoke to the officer.

'The stable lad says that if we march in as we are, we will have little chance in catching this Oates. We shall have to free the stable lad to find and point out Oates to us. We can then apprehend them both. It is vital we find this Oates lad; much depends on it.'

Nodding his head in agreement, the officer instructed the soldiers to free the lad. Turning to him he said

'One false move and we shall shoot you. You will not evade us. Do I make myself clear?'

'Yes sir, very good sir.'

The stable lad's mouth felt dry, with his legs beginning to tremble with the thought of the muskets blasting into his back.

The soldiers stepped back and assumed a less obvious role as the lad moved forward towards the rooms where Nathan Oates might be. He went inside and called out......

It was at this moment that the innkeeper turned the corner, intent on an identical task, with Courtney a little way behind. As he approached the building he saw to his relief Nathan Oates coming out with another lad. He moved rapidly forward only to find himself bustled out of the way by six burly soldiers and two other figures and found himself entrapped in the middle of this group with one of the men speaking to Oates.

Courtney, turning the corner, now witnessed the innkeeper in the middle of armed soldiers talking with them and some others. There were two young lads there in conversation with the men and, lo and behold, the innkeeper was brought into the discussion.

Suddenly someone turned and pointed in Courtney's direction!

He instinctively pulled back. The group turned and started off towards him.

Courtney wasted no time he slipped back around the corner and headed for a dark narrow alley directly across the road. Experience had taught him that to run was what was expected; to remain in the same location but out of sight was a far better ploy. It took courage, but for all his faults Courtney possessed nerve, knowing it paid dividends in the long run.

Pressing himself up against the wall he witnessed the men, lads and the innkeeper all being ferried along by a line of soldiers. They passed without a glance in his direction and carried on in the direction of the inn, where he and Rousseliere had stayed. Pausing for only a few moments, he peered around the corner. The group were pushing their way through any pedestrians who paused to look at the commotion.

Courtney thought quickly. Without hesitation he followed the departing soldiers. He was right in his thinking, they continued until they reached the inn where the innkeeper opened the door. He, the officer and the two men went straight in. The soldiers remained on guard outside.

Courtney made for the shadows again, question upon question galloped through his mind.

How did the innkeeper contact the soldiers so quickly and betray him? How could the innkeeper betray him if he himself was involved? How did those two lads feature in it? One of them must be the climber and thief, but which one?

The more he thought about what he had seen, the more complex the issue became. One point remained constant in all of this – he could not recover the snuffbox and document now, with the place crawling with soldiers.

The whole of *Spice Island* now seemed to be one big question.

An inescapable fact was that he and Rousseliere had been discovered by the snuffbox and document – just as Rousseliere had predicted – *dam him.*

What he certainly didn't know was that Nathan Oates had drawn the innkeeper into the conversation and the pointing of fingers was not towards Courtney, but the inn itself.

As far as Courtney was concerned, what he was sure about was that the innkeeper would regret he had ever been born.

Within the inn, Peachey scrutinised the innkeeper. Having examined the room where the two men had stayed, the man was facing hard questioning from him.

'And there were two men you say.'

'Yes sir – sailors'

'How do you know they were sailors?'

The innkeeper hesitated, *what a question. How did someone on Spice Island recognise sailors?* But he answered nevertheless

'Why they had the tunics, bags, hats that reeked of tar and said they were.'

'Did they speak like sailors?'

The innkeeper thought for a moment. *Curious but this gentleman's questions brought some doubt to his mind.* He said

'Well now you come to mention it sir, one of them said very little and my girl told me later that he came from some foreign place.'

'From France?'

A tinge of excitement echoed in Peachey's voice.

'Definitely not sir, we wouldn't have no Frenchies in here.'

Peachey sat back and thought. *This man was used to lying and was a definite stranger to the truth, but somehow what he said seemed to sound correct.*

The innkeeper continued

'Now that you mention it, the dark one had very smooth hands, like a cook or surgeon's mate might have; I didn't notice the other one.'

'Have you seen either of them since?'

The question was certain to come up sooner or later but the innkeeper hadn't really thought how he would reply to it. Now it was presented, he thought to himself

If I tell them and they capture him he will be gone for good. If I tell them and they don't find him he will be back to kill me. On the other hand he may well be back in any case looking to kill me. It was settled then.

'I saw one of them this evening'

The words produced a start. Peachey sat bolt upright in his chair.

'Where was this man, why didn't you tell us before?'

'I didn't really have a chance sir, and I wasn't too sure what you were looking for'

'Never mind that, where was he? Was he alone or was the other one there as well?'

The questions were fired rapidly at the innkeeper who almost shrank from the ferociousness of the questioning.

'He was on his own sir, just down the road apace. I wouldn't...'

'Come at once!' Peachey voice rang loud and clear and turning to the officer said

'Please fetch your men immediately sir.'

Turning back to the innkeeper he said

'Come. You lead us to where he was and keep your eyes peeled for the other one as well. There will be a handsome reward for those helping capture these two.'

The innkeeper licked his lips. Not only might he escape the threats of the mean featured man with the knife, but he also might be very well rewarded in the process. The way the gentlemen spoke, the reward could be handsome indeed. He turned to the gentleman

'This way sir, I'll show you where I saw him last.'

They rose as one and followed him back out through the door into the street. The troops were summoned to follow.

Marching back down the road, the innkeeper's eyes darted from one side to the other hoping to get a glimpse of the squinty-eyed sailor.

Following them back up the road, Courtney, his narrow eyes blazing in hatred, watched the group whom he was now sure was looking for him. They were looking ahead, totally oblivious of him being directly behind them. The most unlikely position a fugitive would take.

Some two hours later Samuel Cooper took Peachey by the arm and said,

'I am afraid sir that I must take my men back. They have other duties and we are short staffed. I fear we are not going to sight them now. Word will have spread like a forest blaze that we are about, and all will have gone to ground by now.'

Peachey nodded and said

'I thank you sir. I am disappointed that we have not captured those we seek but am re-assured that we have them on the run. I will keep the innkeeper to his mettle and get him to report as soon as he sees either of them again.'

Peachey and Fairweather began their return to *The George Inn*, and Samuel Cooper marched his men back to the Guardroom.

Neither group had reached their destination when the innkeeper joined the heavenly host of innkeepers – his body slumped in the side alley of the inn. A ragged and painful wound to the stomach had been followed some while after by a slithering knife slit across his throat. A painful exit to life.

Courtney had wiped his long knife clean on the innkeeper's shirt, fingered it sensuously for a moment and then slid it back lovingly into his waistband. On walking away, his evil face was decorated with a sneer, which if anything, increased the foulness of his appearance.

Chapter 17

Trevelyan sat facing the Revd. Weston as Peachey came into his room. Looking from one to the other Peachey said

'I sense an air of misfortune.'

Trevelyan replied

'Indeed you do sir. Our man of the cloth here is in trouble and his Queen is now in jeopardy.'

If it's chess then hardly a national calamity Peachey thought.

With a dramatic flourish Trevelyan knocked the chess piece gently with his Rook and looked about him triumphantly.

The Revd Weston leaned back in his chair and said

'I concede sir – again. It is only a matter of time before I am in checkmate and I have a school to run. I think I will never be able to master your cunning moves, which appear from nowhere.'

Trevelyan faced Peachey and enquired

'And how for you sir? How goes the hunt?'

Sitting down, Peachey's frown clouded his face again.

'We have found where two French Agents have been, one of which is almost certainly the man we have been seeking.'

'Great news sir.'

'Not so good I'm afraid. We searched for them last night, aided by an innkeeper who could identify them, but he was found murdered this morning.'

Looking down at his hands he continued

'We have found where our elusive prey have been, but now have no means now of identifying them.'

'Is there no–one else at the inn who has seen them?'

'There was a girl there, but she has disappeared. If there was anybody else, they've gone to ground and are staying well clear of us.'

Trevelyan's manner changed to a more sympathetic frame

'Are you able to continue the search with what you have?'

'The soldiers are in short supply. If we have a positive sighting they will aid us, but they cannot be spared to traipse around *Spice Island.*'

He signed and continued

'Furthermore, when the soldiers are seen, the word moves faster than a gale force wind and everyone scatters so fast, that any other fugitive will simply follow suit. I have sent Fairweather to poke around. He is armed with some money. That simple expedient will bring results from any quarter, if any is to be had.'

The Revd Weston who had been watching but saying nothing, now broke in.

' If I am able to assist in any way please call upon my help.'

Peachey thought for a moment before answering.

'Thank you sir. You may be able to help in a slightly different way. In addition to seeking the men, we are anxious to spike their guns in their activities.'

The clergyman leaned forward with interest as Peachey continued

'We are informed that they are seeking to reclaim something to pay for local support. To do which they have brought a key with them. The key was in a snuffbox, which we have recovered, but found to be empty.'

'It must be a small key' observed Revd Weston.

'Indeed' replied Peachey. 'That is why I mention it. The snuffbox has a painting of a crown and shield on its face which include the words *Domus Dei.*'

'God's House' Weston murmured.

'Precisely. As it is God's House, and you are officiating at the very same here in Portsmouth, I pose the question. Have you knowledge of anything that springs to mind in the church that relates to money or that might require a small key to open it.'

The Revd Weston slowly shook his head as he mentally ran through coffers, nooks and crannies or any other depository for such items.

'I have only been here a short while, but absolutely nothing comes to mind I'm afraid.'

A short period of silence followed, then Weston said

'The snuffbox had a painting on it you said. What did that show?'

'Well, other than the words *Domus Die*, the shield has what looks to be a bible and some keys' Peachey replied.

'Too much I trust for it to be the crest of a family, or other lead' Weston ventured. 'Nothing seems to sit well together.'

'Nothing sits well with each other in any respect.' grumbled Peachey.

One. We have located our French spy and another man – and lost the only person we know of who can identify them.

Two. We have a snuffbox that purports to hold a key to money to fund local support for their cause – a key that is missing.

Three – we are to look for a black house - which is a complete mystery to all who have lived here all their lives; and finally

Four – there is a resident French Agent here of whom we know absolutely nothing. As I said, nothing sits well together.'

Each dwelt with their own thoughts for a moment, then Trevelyan continued

'The picture on the snuffbox seems unusual. I have only seen a few decorated ones, and each time they have been elaborate designs or portraits of ladies. A scene like this must surely be unique?'

Peachey thought about the question.

'I suppose now that you mention it, you are right. Are you suggesting the painting may be more than just a decoration?'

'Well, maybe we need to examine it again that's all.'

Peachey, reaching inside his jacket, extracted the snuffbox. Its colour and shape had a curious attraction. He moved the chess pieces to one side and they gathered round as he laid it on the table. The only significant feature was the book, obviously a bible, and *Domus Dei* written on the top. The keys were identical. A period of scrutiny followed before Weston said

'Certainly *Domus Dei* means God's House and the book is clearly meant to represent the Good Book or Bible. The keys perhaps signified that a key of the same shape was originally contained inside it.'

The picture's subject matter gave rise to many interpretations but nothing with a central theme or enlightenment. Trevelyan who had remained quiet for the duration said to Peachey

'What if there was no key?'

'No key? But the letter said as much.'

'The letter said that it contained a key, not that it held one. We have started looking at the picture, and I think we are correct. I think the snuffbox *is* the key.'

Weston and Peachey both looked at him in slight puzzlement but nodded just the same.

'It would give a certain impetus to our examination of the box' said Weston 'but we are floundering a little already are we not?'

'One thing has occurred to me' continued Trevelyan 'it may be a coincidence of course but whoever painted that picture has shown keys and we think we are looking for a key.'

Peachey looked hard at the painting. 'The keys are identical and there are six of them.'

Still looking at the scene Weston continued 'but the number six may be related to the Bible that is in the painting – not a common number though. There were twelve disciples, five loaves, two fishes – the list is endless but six does not appear readily amongst them.'

'Ah, but maybe that's exactly the point' said Trevelyan.

'If there were countless references then one would become confused, but if we located a single occurrence, that maybe that's what we're looking for.'

Weston shook his head.

'A tall order I think sir, but I will apply myself to the problem when I return to the church. I must take my leave however as I have to visit the school and I am late already.'

He stood, nodded to both men and took his leave.

'The bible!' Trevelyan suddenly exclaimed. We have identified the book with *Domus Dei* as the bible and it also meaning God's House but what if it were the bible *in* God's House?'

'You mean in the church itself?'

'Precisely.'

Trevelyan looked somewhat triumphantly at Peachey at his reasoning. It seemed a logical thought to Peachey

'Then the Revd. Weston is our man after all. He can show us the actual bible and we can see what we can make of it in the church itself. He should be back there later, we can arrange to gain access at that time.'

Their deliberations were broken by two short sharp knocks at the door. Trevelyan answered

'Come' and Fairweather's head poked around the door.

'Begging pardon sir' he said looking at Peachey 'but a letter has been brought round for you.'

Peachey paced over to the door and took the letter from Fairweather.

'Its origin?' he said enquiringly to Fairweather.

'From the household of Captain Younghusband' he replied, then added 'I believe it was the lady of the house who sent it.'

Peachey noted that there was the slightest hint of a smile at the corners of Fairweather's mouth and that the man didn't look him fully in the face. He suspected that he kept his eyes downcast for fear of showing his ill-disguised humour. Casually opening it Peachey noted it was, as Fairweather had surmised, from the Captain's lady with an invitation to call again.

Time to reflect he thought. To divert the topic he said

'Fairweather what of other matters? Is there any word from *Spice Island*? Does the stable lad or this Oates boy recall anymore than they did yesterday, particularly with a refreshing shilling or two to ease their memories?'

'All avenues I explore lead to nowhere at present sir and I'll not be handing out money of the realm for worthless information. If they have something then I'll pay – they know that, but I'm not a muggings for false payments.'

'Quite so, quite so Fairweather. Then I shall pay my visit as requested here later' he said tapping the letter.

'In the meantime keep your ear to the ground.'

'Very good sir'.

With a touch of his finger to his forehead Fairweather was gone - the door closing quietly behind him. Turning to Trevelyan and reverting to their earlier discussions, Peachey said,

'My uncle has dire need of something of substance in his quest. I sent him the letter, both as proof that someone has arrived in Portsmouth and to see if he could recognise the seal. It will be three days before I get a reply, that's assuming he gets it and replies at once. Meanwhile I shall do what I can and explore any avenue open to me.'

'I am sure you will use your best endeavours Peachey. I myself will attempt to see my elusive uncle. I called earlier but was told that he had not been seen today. Apparently he had late night visitors and hasn't be seen since.'

Later that afternoon, Peachey swung his black cloak round his shoulders with one expert move, before heading to the door of his room *en route* to the house of Captain Younghusband.

He was a little unsure of the way but Fairweather had provided guidance, which he hoped he could follow.

Outside *The George,* the light was failing fast and the landmarks of the town faded from view. Crossing *High Street* he took the turning into *St Thomas' Street* and followed the road. To access the more fashionable area he needed to pass behind the blocks of the dwellings before him, that were closer to the docks. Fairweather had identified a short cut to save him some legwork, that necessitated turning left down a narrow cut that he could now see to his left. Although nearly dark, there was light at the end of the cut where it widened out to the street beyond.

Gathering his cloak around him he swept down into the cut. Ten strides later he was aware of rapid movement from the corner of his eye. A black outline of a man wielding a knife was bearing down on him.

Instinct prevailed – he stepped to one side and put up his hand to parry the blow. A searing sensation ran down his arm through his cloak and he heard the knife clutter to the floor just before hitting the ground himself. Shouts came from behind him. He tried to roll over to avoid a second attack and could see the man hesitating before running away. A second figure emerged from the gloom running at full pelt. Peachey put up his arm again to ward off a blow but heard a voice say

'Are you alright sir - Mr. Peachey sir?' The familiar figure of Fairweather loomed over him and he felt his strong arms gently holding his shoulders.

'Fairweather who was that? What are you doing here?' Confused questions rolled off Peachey's lips. Fairweather was more concerned with the wound.

'Your arm sir? You've been hurt.'

Peachey tried to move his arm but it felt numb. He said

'His knife struck my arm but missed my body. I can't tell how deep it is.' Fairweather cautiously cleared the cloak away from the wound and gingerly ran his fingers along the incision.

'Not too bad sir by the looks of things. You protected yourself well.' Peachey felt for the damage himself and gradually flexed his arm, which responded although made him wince.

'He dropped the knife' said Fairweather stooping to pick it up. It had a very distinctive blade with a shaped handle angled away from the cutting edge. Looking again at his master Fairweather said

'Can you stand sir?'

'Yes I think so.'

With the support of Fairweather, he clambered to his feet. His arm was sticky where the knife had severed the flesh and he felt shaken, but otherwise could stand on his own. Fairweather looked closely at him and said

'I'd just got back from the *Spice Island* and found you'd already left sir, and knowing the rogues, footpads and lowly life that set out on foot in the darkness here, hurried after you. Good job too.'

'Indeed it was Fairweather. For that I thank you. If you had not come along I fear he would have had me.'

Fairweather looked in the direction the would-be assassin had gone and said

'No sense in trying to chase him, he will have disappeared amongst the alleyways and cuts in no time.'

'I need you here Fairweather,' Peachey said with some concern. 'He may have an accomplice or may still be lying in wait.'

Standing upright, Peachey looked about him and mused

Why me though? Was it simply for money or was it perhaps to do with our Frenchie?

'Strange knife' said Fairweather holding the knife and turning it over in his hands.

'Good enough to do this' said Peachey looking down at his blood stained frocked coat which now had an extra vent down the arm, not originally envisaged by his tailor.'

Fairweather looked at the result of the wound and said

'We should not linger sir and should return to *The George.*'

'Quite so, quite so Fairweather, then afterwards go and present my apologies to Captain Younghusband and say I have been unavoidably detained.'

If this does have anything to do with our Frenchie, then we must be closer than we thought - now that's interesting.

Chapter 18

Rousseliere swallowed hard at the unappealing sight. A smell was wafting up as he peered down through the iron grill into the total blackness of the drain. A lantern borrowed from Nell dangled from his wrist but produced no discernible light into where he had to go.

Placing the lantern on the stone floor and lifting at the grill, it came up easily.

No sense in wondering about it, he thought. *Just do it. It's the only alternative to attempting to climb the wall or risking trying to get past the guards at the gates.*

Lowering the lantern by its cord he could now see that it was only a short drop to the bottom. Once down, he gauged it to be some six-foot in diameter, enough to almost stand upright. Holding the lantern him he looked towards the sea end, and sure enough, daylight showed at the end. Looking back up the drain towards the main hospital buildings, it simply disappeared into total blackness.

Another advantage in being located away from the main buildings was that they were close to the sea. Having to go all the way up to the main part of the hospital in the drain would be far from easy.

The biggest surprise was how relatively clean it was, but two tides a day pushed their way to the top end and washed away the debris as it ebbed.

Whilst not being able to walk freely and upright, when it was empty was fairly straightforward. The slippery green lined surface was a perpetual hazard, but knowing that, careful placing of the feet either side kept one clear of the bottom and surefooted. The tide was low but as it rose, the water level would rise quickly as the gradient was gentle.

On reaching the outlet, the entrance to the sea housed another grill, but again was easily removable. Extinguishing the lantern he tied it around the top of the grill. Moving the grill back he squeezed past.

Once clear he gingerly put his head round the outlet. The shingled shore rose away from the outlet enabling him to move unobserved up to the shoreline. The outlet was several yards out to enable the drain to be flooded whatever the height of tide. The surrounding area was deserted. Unless someone had a reason, they wouldn't come that way. Sitting on the shingle he removed his bag from around his neck.

Looking back at the hospital, he could see its three-sided construction. He thought *this British Sailor's hospital was larger than his regiment's barracks in France*. The task this morning was to survey the defences protecting attacks from the West.

Heading off, he kept the sea to his left and preserved a safe distance from the hospital. A few minute's walk brought him to within sight of the high-banked defences. Extreme care was needed here. Close proximity was required to assess the defensive strengths, but not close enough to arouse anyone's suspicions.

The hospital was now behind him. The open area just outside the wall must be *The Paddock* that Nell had told him about – the area where they buried the dead. It wasn't laid out like a cemetery and burials were like those at sea where the corpses were sewn up in hammocks and committed with no precise location.

Again it was deserted. A small clump of trees provided protection and by climbing a tree produced a splendid vantage point. His heart rejoiced.

As before, the defences were good but the manning almost non-existent.

Dropping to the floor he extracted the map from his bag and wrote up his findings. He mused

The survey will be a brilliant success. I shall personally benefit from this and no mistake.

Replacing the plan in the bag's hidden lining, he headed up towards the town. Passing the almost deserted Guardhouse he followed the remainder of the fortifications until satisfied he had seen all that was needed.

Feeling smugness with his findings he headed back. Reaching the entrance to the drain again, the surprise was that the water level had risen sharply. He hadn't been away more than an hour. *Something to bear in mind for the future.*

Retrieving the lantern, and pushing past the grill, its comforting light weakly illuminated his return route. He thought *heading back up a drain to the security of the infectious diseases wards – might to many seem a surprising place for sanctuary.*

The drain system was very efficient. He smiled to himself as he thought of the armed marines sentries stationed to retain sailors within the hospital grounds. To escape by using this tunnel was so easy - easy that is, if you knew of its existence and find an way of getting in.

The resulting shaft of lantern light outlined the odd slithering rat as they continued their never-ending scavenging but he found the grill for the storeroom readily enough.

Now was not the time to be caught coming out of there. Listening carefully there were men's voices intermingled with those from one or two women. Bending down he removed his wet shoes. Rubbing the soles of his feet on his trousers he dried them the best he could. The last thing he wanted was a to leave a telltale set of footprints leading from the grill to his hiding place.

Once inside the storeroom he relaxed, not realising how tense he'd become. Carefully extracting the plans from his bag, he re-read the notes made this morning. Afterwards a satisfied smile spread across his face.

The defences are sound, but the manning almost non-existent. Once overrun by French and Spanish troops, the defences could readily be held by them against a much superior force. The British were such fools!

Chapter 19

Unfamiliar features gradually focussed before Peachey's eyes. His throat was parched, vision blurred, head thumping and all accompanied by a throbbing and pulsating arm, a stark reminder of last night's attack.

Flexing the arm, wincing as he did so, he was relieved that it responded to his command. The wound should heal quickly and the aches and pains would gradually disperse.

Things could have been mightily worse. The mental image of the swinging arm with a glinting knife descending towards him was imprinted in his mind. Without his quick reaction, he could well have been dead. Fairweather appearing from nowhere prevented a second chance for the knifeman. That would certainly have proved fatal.

The point was – who the hell was the attacker?

Through this misery he heard a knock on the door.

'Come'.

His voice was more of a croak than a firm command, but resulted in the door opening and Fairweather's head appearing.

'I have your clothes here sir. How are you feeling?'

'Better than I would be had you not appeared last night Fairweather. He would have finished me I fear without your help. Who he was I have no idea.'

'I now know exactly who it was sir'.

Peachey instantly looked up, pain from head and arm temporarily disappearing with this revelation.

You know who he is?'

'You can see for yourself sir. I have him downstairs in the back room.'

Peachey looked in amazement.

'How on earth did you find him so quickly?'

Fairweather moved over to the bed, laying the clothes out beside Peachey.

'That knife sir, I said it was distinctive, that is what led me to him.'

Before Peachey could ask more, the door knocked yet again and Fairweather went over to answer it. A hurried, inaudible conversation was quickly followed. Fairweather turned and said,

'They want to know what to do as they can't keep him held there indefinitely.'

'Inform the authorities of course' said Peachey, but on noticing Fairweather's hesitant look continued 'have you not said anything to anyone?'

'No sir, I thought best not at this stage as you would want to question him yourself before handing him over.'

Peachey nodded. Fairweather was right. It was important to know who he was, who sent him and perhaps to get to the bottom of this before making matters official.

'I certainly do Fairweather.'

'Then I will go down sir and get matters under control again. Perhaps you could follow at your convenience sir.'

'Very good Fairweather. See to it at once.'

Fairweather touched his forehead and was gone before Peachey realised he still had no knowledge of his attacker.

How had Fairweather traced him by that knife?

He hurriedly dressed to see just who this man was.

The sight of the man set to kill him last night took him aback. He had to look around to make sure that he was looking at the right man. Fairweather and another man unknown to Peachey stood menacingly over the slumped figure seated at the solitary rough-hewn table in the centre of the room.

Peachey had steeled himself to face the man who was intent on killing him, having had mental visions of a vicious killer flashing across his mind all night. If this was a paid assassin with no care for his victims, the presented image bore no relation to expectations.

He was in his forties, of moderate build, hair pulled back and tied behind his head that exposed an ugly red swelling at his temple.

Obviously Fairweather had been persuading again. The man's clothes were those reminiscent of a local workman and when he glanced up at Peachey's entrance, he showed no sign of recognition and looked behind Peachey as if to see who else was entering. Seeing no one he dropped his head again and continued looking dejectedly at the surface of the table.

Peachey looked at Fairweather.

'Who is this wretch and who sent him?'

'His name is William Bishop and he says that it was his vengeance.'

'Vengeance? What the devil does he mean?'

'He says that you would know.'

At this the man looked up.

'Not this gentleman, the one that I attacked' he said.

Fairweather's hand slapped him across the head.

'Talk sense man. This is the gentleman you attacked and we want to know why and who paid you.'

The man, William Bishop, looked again at Peachey,

'I said the man that I attacked. I have never seen this gentleman before in my life.'

A thud as Fairweather cuffed him around the head again.

'Look again friend, this is the gentleman alright and you have exactly 10 seconds to tell us the truth.'

Bishop looked from one to the other.

'I don't know what you mean sir, I have never seen this gentleman before and I made no attack on him.'

Peachey stepped forward as Fairweather prepared to repeat the inducement and said,

'How did you trace him?'

'It was the knife sir. As soon as I saw it I knew it was a working knife. It had a special shaped blade for cutting and a serrated reverse edge. Not one used in joinery or butchery but I fancied it belonged to a sailmaker – and I was right. It had the initials *WB* carved on the handle and it was easy to find a WB who was a sail maker.'

Peachey nodded. He had come with vengeance on his mind and a strong desire to confront his attacker. Something was wrong here and he couldn't fathom out what. The man had confessed to the attack, but why not admit to attacking him? Looking again at Bishop he said

'You say that you had not seen me before, that could well be correct, but the person who paid you certainly could.'

Bishop looked up

'No one was paying me sir, I attacked what I thought was my target and cannot for the life of me see how it was your good self sir.'

'Who was the man you thought you had attacked and why.'

Bishop looked down again and gently shook his head from side to side.

'It was on account of my little Polly, my little girl that that swine killed.' He shook his head again and remained silent. Walking over to the table, Peachey pulled up a chair and sat near the table. He wanted this charade finished.

'Speak up man or I shall be gone and hand you over to the authorities.'

'I'm truly sorry sir for any hurt and inconvenience I have caused, but I needed to avenge my Polly. I thought you were the man who had taken our little girl from us and he was on his way to see that other old devil.'

Fairweather shouted at him

'What other old devil, you speak in riddles my friend. Talk with a plain tongue or you'll have me to answer to.'

'The man who killed Polly always visits him this time each week, I think he gets money from him for he has become exceedingly prosperous this last year. That old man is probably just as bad, what with his leanings towards the French.'

Exasperation began to overcome Peachey but he looked at Bishop. His last remark about the French was a peculiar one to make. He turned to Fairweather.

'Fetch some water for him.'

He nodded towards Bishop. Fairweather did so and returned with a pot of water and a mug. He set it down before Bishop who poured the mug full and gulped it down, wiping his mouth with the back of his hand on completion. Peachey leaned forward,

'Now let us assemble the story together, piece-by-piece. Who was the man you wanted to attack?'

Bishop looked at Peachey and studied him for the first time.

'He is a local man who works in the shipping business.'

'His name?'

'Jeremiah Porter sir.'

Peachey lent back.

'I know this man. I met him recently. He is a victualer.'

Bishop dropped his head again. This was not what he wanted to hear. Peachey continued

'Why should you seek this man? You say he killed you daughter. How come?'

'I'm sorry to have spoken of one of your acquaintances sir.'

With that he reverted to staring at he table.

'An acquaintance is correct, I hardly know the man in question. I repeat how do you say he killed you daughter?'

Bishop looked again at Peachey. As he began to speak about Porter, a grim determination lined his face with hatred brimming in his eyes.

'He started to stop and talk to my Polly when he passed by. He gave her a sixpence and some sweet things and told her he liked her smile. My dear wife was pleased and felt that he had seen the bright spirit that lived inside Polly.'

Bishop paused and shook his head from side to side before continuing

'He took her to the old man's house and gave her a little more money and some ribbons. But after a few times she changed, her smile left her, she used to sit in the corner, rocking gently and saying nothing.'

Neither my wife nor I could understand it or get her to say what was troubling her. She appeared to retreat into another world and never smiled.'

Bishop paused again, poured himself some more water and looked as though he was collecting his thoughts and summoning up his courage. He said

'One day my wife saw Porter at the end of the alley, he had called for Polly, had her little hand in his and was walking away with her.'

Bishop temporarily lapsed into silence again. He sipped the water and stared into the mug before continuing,

'They found her dead that afternoon, down by the docks. Porter said that she had died after a seizure or apoplexy in the street and he had attempted to bring her back to life but she was gone.'

He shuddered.

'What he should have said was that he had attempted to make her to do what he wanted, and when she refused, he forced her and killed her in the process when she struggled.'

'Were there witnesses to this?'

'None that would speak. Tongues seized, eyes were looking elsewhere, others had been about their business, none stepped forward to admit what they had seen.'

He shook his head again.

'It must be remembered that he's a prosperous man in the town with many friends and much influence. My little Polly was a sailmaker's daughter – of no consequence, certainly not to cause a scandal amongst society.'   Bishop looking up at Peachey again said

'I'm sorry sir I was not meaning to be disrespectful about members of society, it was just that that was how it was covered up.'

Leaning forward again Peachey said 'you have absolutely no evidence for this, certainly not for attempting to kill a man.'

'With respect sir, I said none that would give evidence. Many spoke quietly to me about how he was seen to shake and throttle her after she had run out from the house. That was when she died; she never had any fit or nothing. He killed her'

No one said anything for a moment or two. Peachey remained looking at Bishop, then said

'You say you didn't mean to attack me. How come you did so? Why did I resemble Porter?'

'It was the cloak sir.'

'The cloak?'

'Yes sir, you were wearing it last night. Mr. Porter has a cloak exactly the same with a shiny silver clasp shaped something like a dagger. When I saw that, even though you had your head bent under a hat, I was convinced it was Porter coming – same as he always does that evening each week.'

Peachey slowly slid back in the chair.

The recollection of the inn where he had met Porter and when taking his leave being called back by him remained crystal clear. His insidious smile informing him he had picked up the wrong cloak still rankled. Bishop was telling the truth. He couldn't have known about that fact and lacked ability to concoct a plausible and convincing story about mistaking Peachey for Porter.

Now, where did one go from here?

A knock on the door broke the tension. The man who had been standing outside cautiously peering round it saying

'Excuse me sir, a gentleman, a Mr. Trevelyan is here enquiring if he may enter.' Peachey glanced round and replied

'Please ask him to come in.' Peachey realised that he had not seen Trevelyan since the affray but somehow the man appeared to have picked up the news with little delay. With that Trevelyan stepped in, looked around the room, glanced at Bishop who was still with a hangdog expression and finally at Peachey with a frown.

'How are you Peachey?'

Without waiting for a reply continued 'I came as soon as I heard. I am relieved to see you appearing none too ill from your attack.'

Peachey replied

'I am fine apart from a scratch or two'

Trevelyan continued

'I would have attended sooner but I have been attempting to see my uncle. He's not been seen for a couple of days now. I know he is an unpredictable man but no one seems to know where he is.'

He looked across the table,

'This is the man who attacked you I take it .'

Peachey only nodded, his mind was troubled by something and he couldn't quite put his finger on it.

He stood up and putting his arm around Trevelyan walked to the back of the room, outlining in quiet terms what had been said by Bishop. Trevelyan paused then said

'Firstly I think you are a lucky man, your injuries are similar to mine and will heal in no time. Secondly, your assailant appears to be one of the least likely killers I have ever seen.'

Peachey nodded as Trevelyan said

'But on the other hand a vengeful attacker is fired with much passion and will stop at nothing. A strange tale about this man Porter though and the mistaken attack because of the cloak – no doubt about that I take it?'

'None at all. He had no means of knowing about the cloak. If I could make a mistake in picking up the wrong one, then I suppose he could just have easily made a similar error.'

'One thing I'm not quite clear about. You say Porter should have been on his way to see this old man…….'

'Ah!' Peachey broke in, 'he also said he was a French liker, I haven't asked him about that.'

Turning on his heel Peachey walked back to the table and leant over Bishop.

'What did you mean when you said that the old man Porter was to visit had French sympathies?'

Bishops watery eyes finally looked up into Peachey's.

'I followed Porter to this man's house one evening, and after they had gone indoors, looked through the window. The old man was talking to another man I had never seen before, well dressed and younger than the old man. He had some papers and they were talking in French.'

'You speak French?'

'No sir but I know the tongue when I hears it. There's been French prisoners in Portsmouth on and off for many years, building the dockyard walls and being held on prison ships. I can recognise their speech.'

'Go on what happened then?'

'After he had gone, Porter came in before the old man was ready for him I think, for he spun round and spoke angrily to Porter. Porter on the other hand was all smiles and seemed completely unruffled at the old man's outburst, in fact it seemed to please him.'

'Were they speaking in French?'

'Oh no sir, it was English, quite loudly in fact as I could make out what the said, Porter was saying something about the old man's French connections and how he could end up at the end of a rope.'

'What was this old man's reactions to all this?'

'He didn't say too much after that. He just sat and looked at Porter, but you could see that he was not pleased by his visit.'

'So what did you do then?'

'I went back home sir.'

'And who did you tell about what you saw?'

'No one sir, I was only worried about my Polly. Who the old man saw and what he and Porter discussed weren't no interest to me. I needed to find out what was going on there.'

'It looked to me as though you saw exactly what was happening.'

'Yes I could see, but it twasn't what I was looking for sir'.

Peachey moved to the side with Trevelyan and said,

'Who says they're French plotters? Because a man speaks French to someone doesn't necessarily mean that they are the enemy.'

'Don't you think that may mean something then?'

Peachey shook his head from side to side and pursed his lips.

'It may well have a connection, but I'm not clear where we are on this.' Trevelyan remained silent for a moment, carefully deliberating on what Peachey had said. Looking at the dejected Bishop and then back to Peachey he ventured

'It's a rum affair all right, but my money is on the fact that these incidents are connected. Not directly I grant you, but you need to follow it up.'

Peachey leant over Bishop.

'Your story makes some sense but is incomplete. I want to know who this old man is and where he lives'.

Bishop looked straight at Peachey.

'I can show you where he lives.'

Standing upright Peachey signalled to Fairweather to get Bishop on his feet. Fairweather tied Bishop's hands behind his back and lashed another rope to the bindings so he couldn't escape. The group then made their way into the High St. where Bishop signalled left down towards *Sally Port*.

He gestured left however at the next junction, down into *Fighting Cocks Lane*. Remaining a pace or so behind Fairweather, Peachey and Trevelyan walked in silence, each churning over the possibilities as they walked. Peachey knew this route; turning to Trevelyan said

'This is the way to your uncle's is it not?' Trevelyan nodded. The thought had crossed his mind, along with several other snippets that Bishop had mentioned. There was an frisson of peculiar anticipation *impossible* he thought, *the fact his uncle's age, ability to converse in French and living in this direction, surely these couldn't possible link him to these strange happenings could they?*

Turning the corner into Penny Street did nothing to dispel these thoughts. As they approached Trevelyan's uncle's house a carriage that had been moving up the street towards stopped in front of the house. Peachey looked enquiringly at Trevelyan who shrugged his shoulders, for he had no idea who the carriage belonged to.

A middle-aged man with a long flowing cloak alighted and looked back into the carriage. With that another figure emerged and the first man reached across to provide assistance.

As the second man came into view, the face turned towards the approaching group - the quizzical features of Silas Trevelyan faced them.

Peachey saw Percy Trevelyan give an audible sigh of relief. He hastened forward and gently grabbed his uncle's arm.

'My dear uncle, it's good to see you. I was wondering where you had got to.'

Silas Trevelyan turned his head and watery eyes looked over the face of his nephew.

'I have been in good hands.'

He motioned to the middle-aged man at his side,

'Allow me to introduce Mr. George d'Arcy, an exponent of the noble science of astronomy.'

'A pleasure to make your acquaintance sir: I was not aware my uncle had leanings in that direction.'

Putting his arm around Percy Trevelyan's shoulders Silas Trevelyan moved towards the front door.

'A new interest for me my boy. Strange hours I must confess, but Mr. D'Arcy has a fine telescope in his house in Southsea and one can only study the celestial sights at night.'

Turning from one to the other Silas Trevelyan continued

'I have had a *situs invertus* and have slept during the day and peered relentlessly during the nights. Fascinating, endless, looking into the future and past at the same time you know.'

Mr. D'Arcy spoke for the first time.

'The pleasure is all mine sir' he said acknowledging Percy Trevelyan's greeting. 'Your uncle is a fine convert. He has a flair for it you know, picks up the names and positions of the planets and stars with ease, a delight to host him at my house'.

Percy Trevelyan looked sideways at his uncle who had a smile playing at the corner of his mouth. His uncle said

'And were you coming to see me or are you on your way to a more exciting venue?'

He eyed Peachey, Fairweather and the hapless Bishop who were waiting.

'We were being taken to visit someone who may have a bearing on Mr. Peachey's task here'

Trevelyan replied rather slowly, adding 'I had hoped to find you in when I returned.'

Silas Trevelyan paused on reaching the short flight of steps and released his arm from Percy Trevelyan's shoulders.

'A capital plan; I need to rest for a while and then I will tell you all about astronomy when you call.'

He looked at Peachey.

'Good day to sir, you appear to been in the wars.'

He eyes studied Peachey's bandaged arm still visible beneath his cloak.

'A small scratch sir, nothing that a little rest won't cure' replied Peachey.

Silas Trevelyan nodded and a brief smile flittered across his face, with such speed that one had to be quick to spot it.

'Until later gentlemen ' he said. Mr. D'Arcy replacing Percy Trevelyan's arm with his own guided Silas Trevelyan up the steps into the house.

Bishop had remained quiet and stationary, A prod from Fairweather goaded him to continue, and a thankful Trevelyan breathed more easily as the group made off further down *Penny St.* towards *The Parade*. Towards the end Bishop paused and nodded with his head towards the first house.

'That's the one sir. You can see the passageway to the side'.

Indeed what Bishop had said was borne out by the layout.

Trevelyan looked at Peachey.

'Well this appears to be the house, what now?'

Peachey studied the apparently lifeless house. Looking at Fairweather he continued

'Mr. Trevelyan and I will call. Should we be permitted entrance, try and slip up that passageway and get a view through that downstairs window that Bishop said he looked through.'

'Come' said Peachey to Trevelyan 'let us pay our respects.'

They followed the path leading to a short flight of steps accessing the front door.

'By no stretch of the imagination could this be termed a black house' quietly murmured Trevelyan.

On reaching the top step, Peachey pulled the doorbell. The immediate response was – nothing. No sound, no footsteps, no voices. The two men exchanged glances.

'We are not to be in luck then' said Trevelyan.

Peachey looked over the front of the house and pulled the doorbell again.

'Such a house should not be unoccupied. There must be a servant or housekeeper in attendance somewhere.'

Peachey's surmising was correct. A few moments later the door swung open to reveal an old stooping man.

'I am Mr. Henry Peachey and this Mr. Percy Trevelyan. I have an appointment but am uncertain if I have called at the correct house. What is the name of your employer sir?'

'My master's name is Mr. Erasmus Faulkner sir.'

Peachey reacted with surprise that he quickly disguised.

'Mr Faulkner who carries on the business as a victualer if I am not mistaken.'

'That's correct sir, but he rarely sees gentlemen on business nowadays.'

Unless they might be French - Peachey thought.

'The very gentleman I wish to see' continued Peachey

'I am not sure if Mr. Faulkner is at home gentlemen, he has long retired to his study and always insists on being undisturbed when that occurs.'

'I am sure he will wish to see me' said Peachey, with an edge in his voice.

The old man hesitated again. He was in somewhat of a quandary, but before he could make a decision Peachey moved towards him

'We shall wait inside. Inform your master of our presence.'

With that the two men stepped straight past the old retainer into the hall. Peachey intent on maintaining the advantage said

'I also have had business with a colleague of Mr. Faulkner's, a Mr. Jeremiah Porter.'

He watched the old man gauging his reaction, but he simply replied

'Mr. Porter comes here regularly, but very seldom during the day sir.'

Trevelyan who had adopted a docile role up to that point enquired

'When did Mr. Porter last visit?'

The old man shook his head

'Mr Porter usually comes late in the day sir, in fact Mr. Faulkner seldom has day visitors, that is why I was surprised when you said you were calling on business at this time.'

'So has he been late in the day recently?' pressed Trevelyan.

'Mr. Porter would have been here last night sir, he regularly comes once a week to see Mr. Faulkner.'

'You say would have been - did you not let admit him?' The old man shook his head,

'Apparently Mr. Porter insisted that he have his own key sir. Mr. Faulkner let him have one eventually'.

'A little unusual is it not?' continued Trevelyan.

'Because of Mr. Faulkner's and my own health. I am not able to get about quickly in the evenings sir' he added looking at both men,

'What would happen if someone called at night who didn't have a key then?'

The old man was clearly uneasy at the line of questioning, but could find no way of heading off the questions that the two gentlemen raised. He kept his head down as he replied

'Mr. Faulkner would admit them himself'.

It was as though this was a heinous crime. The servant was unable to perform his duties fully and he appeared ashamed of that fact.

Trevelyan appeared interested in a hanging picture and spoke as though an after thought had struck him,

'I was under the impression that Mr. Porter was coming last night'.

'I am uncertain sir who has called these last few evenings; I have been struck with a fever and have not been in attendance.'

Trevelyan waved his arm as if to dismiss the problem as being of no consequence.

'Perhaps you could announce us to your master and see if he is able to see us' said Peachey.

'Very good sir' said the old servant and hastened – if hobbling slowly down the passageway could be so described, towards a room further on down. When he was out of earshot Trevelyan said to Peachey

'If Porter came last night he was a fortunate man in escaping the attentions of Bishop.'

Peachey surveyed the interior and replied

'I think Porter is of secondary importance. I have met the man and consider him dubious but of limited ability. I would be happier to know about this French-speaking visitor that called on Faulkner that evening Bishop saw them through the window.'

'Indeed' replied Trevelyan 'there is much to establish. Your meeting with Faulkner will hopefully lead to greater clarification.'

'He will need to be carefully played' murmured Peachey 'he is of higher calibre than Porter and will not give anything away I fear. If he is an agent he has survived many a long year and will know how to cover his tracks.'

Trevelyan nodded in agreement. Peachey said

'Our discussions will be circumspect and I mustn't put him on his guard. The business aspect may soften the approach. Most men are more forthcoming with the prospect of earning god money in their business transactions.'

Trevelyan nodded.

'A peculiar taste in house furnishings' he said looking around the cluttered hall, 'a miscellany collection of items, I for one cannot see much obviously of French origin.'

'He is hardly likely to display such wares and advertise his allegiance, should that prove to be the case.'

Trevelyan placed a finger on his lips to caution silence as the old man shuffled back down into the hall.

'Gentlemen, I'm afraid I cannot get a response from Mr. Faulkner.'

The announcement was broken by heavy thudding of the door, clearly startling the old man. He broke off and opened the door; a look of amazement transformed his resident mournful expression. The two gentlemen heard Fairweather's voice say

'I need to see my master Mr Peachey as a matter of some urgency'

Without waiting for the old man to respond Peachey strode to the door and peered around it.

No wonder the old man had looked startled, for on the threshold stood Fairweather with the bedraggled Bishop held close to him.

Fairweather looked at his master.

'Sir I need to have a private word.'

Fairweather's urgent tone was coupled with a knowing look.

'Very well' said Peachey and stepped outside as Fairweather crooked his head so as to speak discretely into his master's ear.

'Sir, I looked through the window at the side. It looks into a library or study. There is a figure slumped over on a desk. From its position it looks like he's dead.'

Peachey turned speaking directly to the old man.

'Is your master in the habit of sleeping in his study?'

The old man lifted his head again as though bewildered at the question.

'I am afraid I don't understand your question sir' he replied.

'My man happened to glance through a downstairs window whilst seeking to find me and he has seen someone lying slumped over a desk.'

Peachey watched for the old man's response – it was complete bafflement. He continued

'The room that has a window facing the side, what room is that?'

'It is the master's library sir, I am not permitted to enter there unless he is there.'

'I think that it may well be your master in there and may need some assistance.'

The old man looked around as though seeking some guidance before looking back to Peachey.

Peachey moved down to the far door and turned the handle. It readily twisted and with a gentle push he stepped inside. The room was stuffy with a distinctive smell pervading the air. Looking firstly to the window then glancing across to the desk, the slumped figure was immediately recognisable as Erasmus Faulkner.

Staring sightlessly ahead, the face was strangely coloured – it was bloodshot red with a strange hue about the nose and lips. Peachey sensed Trevelyan immediately behind him.

'Good Lord Peachey, the man's been poisoned, look, his lips are blue'.

It was an accurate observation. The lips were definitely bluish, the colour spreading outwards on his face to merge with the bloodshot effects on his cheeks. Erasmus Faulkner had seen better days. Turning to the old man he said

'Is this your master?'

The old man nodded with his eyes still fixed on the body of his late employer. Peachey realised that Trevelyan had not met Faulkner and was confirming who the dead person was as he looked around the room. The candles by the desk had burnt away until they became extinguished.

He noted the room had the same cluttered style as the hall. Turning to Peachey he said

'If Bishop knew of this he certainly wouldn't have brought us here'.

Peachey called Fairweather

'It's Mr. Erasmus Faulkner, and, as you thought, he's dead.'

'Yes sir' replied Fairweather.

Entering his eyes scanned the room and stopped when he looked at the body again and said

'There's your French connection sir'.

Peachey followed his gaze and said
'What do you see Fairweather?'
'That desk sir'
'Well what about it Fairweather?'
'It's French.'
 Peachey looked at the desk then back to Fairweather
'You sure?'
'Plain as a pikestaff sir'
'Take a closer look then.'
Peachey turned to Trevelyan
'What do you make of this?'

'A trifle fortunate I must admit Peachey, although I'm not sure what exactly having a French made desk does to move us forward.'

Moving around to the side of the desk he continued

'Unlike the innkeeper at the Point however, he doesn't appeared to have been murdered, unless he were poisoned – his face is certainly a peculiar colour.'

'It looks more likely that he has had a spasm of some kind' admitted Peachey 'but where does Porter fit into all this?'

'Perhaps he has no direct connection with his death. What they were up to in this house is still a mystery.'

Flipping his hand casually through the papers on the desk Peachey said

'Not the most tidiest of desks but there appears nothing stolen or ransacked.'

Looking again at Fairweather he said

'Anything of value you can contribute regarding this desk then Fairweather?'

'Possibly sir' said Fairweather.

Bending on one knee ran his hands over the side of the desk and the underside, being careful to avoid the body that was slumped across the top surface. It was a beautifully crafted piece of furniture, polished walnut with small ornate handles on the numerous compartments to the rear and matching handles on the drawers

'How can you tell this piece of furniture is French – they all look similar to me.'

Fairweather looked up and removing his hands from the underside indicated the curved top and the rear legs directly beneath it.

'Just like an ewe knows its lambs from all the others in the flock sir, the style tells one from another.'

He continued running his hands over the surfaces.

'See the shape of the top as it joins with the rear legs, this is different from English desks, also the inlaid work, It has the marks'

Trevelyan ran his hand over the surface close to the dead man's arm.

'A magnificent piece of craftsmanship Fairweather, but aren't these things made with secret drawers?'

'They are indeed sir' smiled Fairweather, 'this type has two and so secret that everybody knows of their existence.'

Trevelyan shrugged his shoulders

'Can you locate them?'

'Oh yes sir, but we shall have to move the gentleman first. There's one each side of the back. But what most people don't know is that when these are made they often have an additional one that can be located in different places.'

Peachey moved forward ' does this have them?'

'Almost certainly sir, that's also what I was feeling for. They are not meant to be used very often, unlike the ones at the top and are also difficult to open.'

They watched as Fairweather continued his exploration. Finally he said

'This one has a compartment right underneath, but…'

He looked from one to the other

'It may never have been opened since it was made – that I can't tell.'

Peachey and Trevelyan peered down at Fairweather like hounds with the scent of a fox in their nostrils. Fairweather nodded and they watched as he grasped the beading surrounding the underside and gently applied pressure in a leverage motion.

With a slow movement the beading appeared to bend and move then – snap!

A thin drawer slowly slid out, powered by a spring mechanism.

'By all the saints' said a startled Trevelyan.

All eyes focussed on the drawer, which was far from empty. Peachey looked in amazement. Of all of them, he was the one who was the most taken aback by what he saw.

Chapter 20

Although it was warm, the air in the washroom was heavy with steam. A suffocating blanket enveloped Kitty carrying the washed clothes into the drying room. The work was laborious, hours long, wages abysmal but at least she felt safe. Her Aunt had performed this daily grind for years and had used her influence to gain the position for Kitty.

Having fled the Point in fear of her life, Kitty's mental image of Courtney still haunted her. The gruesome tale of the murder of the innkeeper had left her shaking and in a constant state of alarm.

Every dark corner or sudden noise appeared to announce his imminent presence. She shuddered as she recalled him in the upstairs room of the inn. If that other sailor hadn't returned, anything might have happened.

'Don't be all day'.

The summons from the back room brought her back to reality.

'I'm here' Kitty replied, picking up a bag of clothes, 'do you want me to deliver these?'

Emerging out of the hazy mist of washing fumes her aunt said

'Those must be there this afternoon or else there'll be the devil to pay.'

The chance to escape from the toil of the washroom was a welcomed relief. Gathering up the clothes she threw a shawl over her shoulders and peered cautiously around the door. Her fear of Courtney never left her. All seemed clear.

The route to her destination took her first to the *High Street*, then up past the church towards the *Landport Gate*. Away from the washroom, the air gradually chilled her as her body heat evaporated. She increased her pace. Pulling the shawl tighter around her body with one hand she held the bundle of clothes firmly with the other. The *High Street* was busy with its usual activity.

Counting the houses she arrived at the fifth one. A well built dwelling but in some need of repair. The path to the side tradesmen's entrance was overgrown with weeds and on reaching the door saw the paint was peeling, although the door itself appeared sound.

In response to her knocking it was opened by a gaunt man who peered firstly at her then to the bundle she was carrying.

'I was beginning to fear you would be late girl'.

That said, he appeared relieved that she had finally come and reached for the bundle. As he did so a window further along the side of the house opened and a rasping voice cried

'Only just in time lassie. I was going to send round for you. I said this afternoon and this afternoon I meant. I pay good coin for the service and I'll no be cheated, I say I'll no be cheated.'

The Scottish accent in his voice was clearly distinguishable. The message it carried was plain. The man who had answered the door put his head out and replied to the speaker at the window

'No difficulty Mr. Gunn sir, I'll see that the clothes are aired this minute.'

Kitty looked again at the window and the Scot still glaring from inside. So this was the Mr. Gunn that all were in fear and trembling over. Her aunt had described him as a fearful man, and she seemed correct in her assessment.

He was apparently a self made man who had started selling farm produce from a cart that he brought into town at first light. *Not that you would know it,* said her aunt disapprovingly, - *he's mean and a stickler for payments and value for money.*

Gunn continued,

'Nah, bring them inside. I want to see how well they've been done and that they have returned every garment.'

Gunn eyed Kitty as he spoke. *He hadn't seen her before. It certainly wasn't the usual hag that came.*

Kitty gathered the bundle and followed the other man into the house. Gunn's seated figure studied both of them. With no more than a second glance to his servant he concentrated on Kitty.

'Aye, it seems in order' he said gruffly.

'Thank you kindly sir' Kitty responded with deliberate servility. Gunn huffed to himself and settled back in his chair.

'I've no seen you before lassie'

'I've just begun sir - with my aunt' she added, 'she stressed how important it was to be on time with your items.'

'Never failed me yet' he mumbled, which Kitty felt was as near a compliment as one could expect from this dour Scotsman. He continued in a quiet voice to himself

'That's more than can be said for some I fear.'

'Begging your pardon sir?' said Kitty.

'Nay matter lass. It's not for you. But I'm a simple man and a time's a time, a contract a contract. In business, payment must be sharp and on time for me. Its how I've always been and I'll no be cheated.'

Breaking his reverie he said

'Now away with you lassie and back to your work. It'll be no good for you to idle away your time chatting to an old man like me when there's work to be done.'

Kitty gave a slight bow and made for the door. She was slightly puzzled; if ever there was a case of a bark being worse than his bite, it was probably him. She felt he was covering it all with an aggressive veneer.

However woe betide anyone falling on the wrong side of him she thought. On her way out she glanced round at the furnishings. There was a distinct lack of a woman's hand, no lady of the house, no organisation of the arrangements. There only appeared to be this enigmatic manservant of his. On the way out she said to the manservant

'Does the gentleman not have a lady of the house?'

'Died of consumption several years ago' he replied, but quickly added 'but that's not your place to ask.'

'Blackmoor!'

Gunn's rasping voice reverberated down the corridor. She watched as the man shuffled to answer the call. *Should she carry on and leave or was there something else to collect?* Deciding that waiting was the better option, she remained in the hallway as the retreating man disappeared back into the room. Gunn's voice was plain

'Tell the Reverend Weston that he had to noon today to pay his rent for the schoolhouse. This has not happened and from tomorrow morning the school is now shut.'

There was no mistaking the finality in his voice. It left no room for doubt.

'Begging your pardon sir, but he is awaiting the money from some source I believe.'

The manservant's voice couldn't be more different – quiet, persuasive, a request buried in its content.

'A time is a time. I said noon and noon it is. He knows my terms. As for you, deliver my message at once and then you are dismissed. I will not have my orders questioned.'

'Very good sir, I will go at once'.

The slightly stooping figure of Blackmoor reappeared. Kitty was shocked. *That poor old man, he had tried to intercede on behalf of the Rev. Weston and had now been dismissed.* Blackmoor appeared somewhat startled to find Kitty still standing there. Kitty blurted out

'I'm very sorry that you have been dismissed and lost your position. You were right to speak up for the Reverend but no one should be dismissed for that.'

Blackmoor shrugged his shoulders.

'Very kind words girl, but the loss is not serious at it might first seem.'

'But you have lost your position.'

'Have no fear. This is the third time this week he's dismissed me, or it might even be the fourth I can't remember.'

He moved towards the front door.

'Come with me, you must leave now. I must get to the Rev. Weston or I really will be dismissed.'

Kitty was totally taken aback. Gunn's reputation preceded him. He had just said that he was closing down the school and everyone knows he means what he says; yet the apparent dismissal of his man Blackmoor was a sham. Mr. John Gunn was a mystery and no mistake. The strident voice of Gunn sounded again.

'Lassie, you still here? Come here a wee minute.'

Kitty hesitated, Blackmoor was now gone on his errand and she was a little unsure. The episode with Courtney had shaken her confidence. But nevertheless she did as she was commanded and returned to the room. Gunn had not changed position. He still lodged in the same chair. As she entered he glanced up and looked straight into her eyes.

'I have a mind you canny do something for me lassie. It'll be worth a shilling.'

Kitty left the house in a puzzled state of mind, but also at the back of it was the thought of seeing Courtney again. Fear, not just of seeing him but of not being able to escape was reminiscent a bad nightmare when frantic running still kept you rooted in the same spot.

Heading towards the church she pulled her tattered shawl about her to ease the chill. Smoothing down her hair, she attempted to regain a little composure as she reached the church house. The Rev. Weston lived in the smaller part and was attended by the same housekeeper that cared for the whole household. Avoiding the main door she skirted round the feeble shrubs and knocked on the rear one.

It was dark. The towering presence of the church kept the light for itself, depriving the nearby dwellings of God's rays. In any event it was already dark and the internal flickering candles cast haunting images on the thick bulls-eye glass windows. The black heavy knocker thudded down on the door.

Enough to waken the dead she thought. Her wait was short, the door opening to reveal the housekeeper, arms covered in flour.

'Be quick girl, I'm behind and very busy.'

Kitty lifting her chin to show she would not be talked down to said

'I have an important message for Reverend Weston.'

'Then it will have to wait' the housekeeper replied.

'But it's important'

'Who's it from then pray?'

'It's from Mr. Gunn.' Kitty replied somewhat triumphantly.

The housekeeper looked hard at Kitty,

'I think the Reverend has had enough messages from Mr. Gunn. Anyways he's out.'

'Did he say where he was going?' Kitty queried.

'That's not for you to ask'

'But it's important '

'Where the Reverend goes is the Reverend's business and his alone. The housekeeper who was becoming impatient with Kitty's persistence said

'You will have to come back later, I must get on with my work'.

With that the door slammed shut in Kitty's face.

Walking dejectedly back to the front of the house she knew she couldn't return to her aunt with the message undelivered, especially as Mr. Gunn had given her a shilling to do just that. Turning right at the gate she saw the departing figure of Reverend Weston entering *The George*.

Thank the Lord she breathed.

Trevelyan, Peachey and the Reverend Weston were musing over Gunn's message regarding the shutting of the school. It was interrupted by a sharp knock on the door.

'Come' said Trevelyan. Fairweather's head came into view.

'Begging your pardon gentlemen but I thought I should interrupt your discussions. I have a young lady here who has an important message for Rev. Weston.' All eyes turned to Weston who looked perplexed.

'Can it not wait Fairweather?'

'Begging your pardon sir but she says the message is from Mr. Gunn.'

Nothing was said. Weston looked dismayed. They could see that he was deliberating whether to take this message that was certain to be further unpleasant news. It was Trevelyan who spoke.

'I suggest sir that you confront the issue at once. A problem will not vanish or lessen by procrastination.'

Weston looked at Fairweather.

'How did she know where to find me?'

'She spotted your arrival sir.'

Weston sighed.

'Very well then. Bring her in and let us hear what other misfortune Mr. Gunn wishes to inflict upon me.'

Fairweather half closed the door and an air of expectancy descended upon the three men, who remained silent awaiting the entry of this mysterious messenger. When he reappeared it was with Kitty. She glanced hesitantly about her as she entered the room, not expecting to be brought into a room full of gentlemen who examined her at close quarters, but without further ado Rev. Weston said,

'What is this message that was so urgent – be out with it!'

Licking her lips, Kitty was uncertain why she felt ill at ease when it was only a message to bring. She looked at all three then back to Rev. Weston. Summoning up her courage she said,

'Sir Mr. Gunn had paid me to bring a message to you.' Weston interrupted,

'I have already had one from his man, I need no other if it is about the school.' Kitty hesitated again

'Sir I was at Mr. Gunn's when he dispatched his man to tell you that he would be closing the school tomorrow. He gave me this message after his man had left.'

'Get on with it then' Weston said sitting back preparing himself for further bad news.

'Mr. Gunn said that the rent money for the school has now been paid by a benefactor and the school can remain open as usual.'

Weston said

'Was that all?'

'Yes sir.' Peachey stepped forward and motioned to Weston

'Providence seems to be in abundance tonight sir.'

Before Weston could reply, Trevelyan said to Kitty,

'You implied that you were there when Mr. Gunn gave his original instruction to his manservant about closing the school.'

'Yes sir I was in the hall.'

How long did you have to wait before he gave you your message to deliver?'

'Almost straightaway sir.'

Trevelyan looked at Peachey,

'Dashed curious do you not think sir? These messages seem peculiarly close together do they not.'

Looking back to Kitty he said,

'Did you see any gentleman likely to be a benefactor before he gave you the message?'

Kitty knew exactly what was troubling Mr. Trevelyan, but was uncertain how to answer.

She recalled the conversation she had with Mr. Gunn on entering his room.

'A shilling for delivering a message lassie. It must be done at once. I'll warrant no delay.'

'Who is it for sir?'

'It's the same man as Blackmoor has gone to see – the Rev. Weston'

Kitty was puzzled. Why couldn't Blackmoor have done that at the same time, he had barely left the house?

Gunn had studied her expression.

'A wee bit perplexing is it lassie?' Kitty had nodded.

'Begging your pardon sir but I thought Blackmoor would have taken both messages – and saved you a shilling' she added. Gunn's facial muscles either side of his mouth twitched and for a brief instant it looked as though he was about to give a semblance of a smile.

He had taken an instant shine to this wee girl from the washroom that had the nerve to taunt him about his money.

'This message is not one to be delivered at the same time Lassie. You are to wait a few minutes before telling Rev. Weston that I have just had the money for the school rent paid from a nameless benefactor.'

Noting Kitty's continuing uncertainty, he continued

'I'll no be cheated lassie. He needs to be clear that if he defaults on his payment time, then I will close the school. Blackmoor will teach him that I mean business to be conducted properly and that people should not enter into financial arrangements with me if they cannot abide by them. '

'You mean to scare the poor man then?'

'I mean to teach a lesson, the same way as he teaches lessons in that school. I have always had to pay my way, received no favours from any man and never asked for any. If that scares him, then so be it. Anyhow your shilling is for delivering the message not to question my motives lassie.'

Kitty now had to reply to Trevelyan's question. She simply said
'No sir.' Trevelyan studied her for a moment then said
'it would appear he knew all about this benefactor and the payment before sending his man to the Rev. Weston.'
Kitty shrugged her shoulders
'I'm sure I don't know sir.'

'Hmm.' Trevelyan said to himself then turning to Rev. Weston said

'I must say though that I think our man Gunn has been playing demons with you. Have you had other mysterious donations for the school?'

Weston nodded.

'Quite a few'

'And these have always come via Mr. Gunn?'

Weston nodded again.

'I sense that our Mr. Gunn himself is your benefactor. He maintains a tough unwavering business approach to protect his image, but has a regard and admiration for the good work you do in the school for the more unfortunate of the area.'

Weston looked a little dejected.

'It seems that I was perhaps being tested as my thoughts of Gunn were less than benevolent.'

'Our Mr. Gunn is not one to change. I suggest you ask Gunn to pass on your thanks and indebtedness to the benefactor and say how much this means to the boys of the school, without indicating that you think it was him.'

'God moves in a mysterious way' murmured Weston. 'I shall certainly do as you suggest sir. Thank you for smoking him out.'

Peachey in the meanwhile had returned to his seat. This was a useful accomplishment but as far as resolving his own problems, it was of no value.

The fact of finding a letter in the hidden drawer of Faulkner's desk confirming that Faulkner was an agent of *Le Secret du Roi* had been welcomed, but since the man was now dead, another avenue for information had also been closed.

Every time progress was being made something arose to defeat the outcome. Even with the Rev. Weston a mysterious benefactor had appeared at the last moment to stave off the closing of the school. Always a mystery, nothing straightforward.

He looked at the girl again. She appeared to be simply bringing a message, but what else did she know? He recalled Gunn being present with Faulkner and Porter, what was the connection between them. He said

'And what other messages have you run for Mr. Gunn my girl. How many more shillings have you earned? I am willing to pay more than a shilling for information that assists me. Have you for example delivered messages to the black house?'

He cursed inwardly as Kitty looked genuinely puzzled. She replied

'I have only delivered this one message sir and as for the *black house* I've never heard of it here or on *Spice Island.*'

'*Spice Island*? You are familiar with that area?'

'Sir I have lived there for many years and have only just come to stay with my aunt here in the town to escape from a man who wants to kill me.'

'What man would want to kill someone like you? Have you cheated him?'

'Oh no sir, he killed an innkeeper and knows that I can recognise him and wants to silence me. I have………'

Her voice trailed off. She was immediately aware of all eyes being turned on her.

'You have seen the man that killed the innkeeper the other night?'

Peachey had leaped out of his chair and advanced towards Kitty who cringed back. She felt Fairweather's hand on her arm, not apprehending, but giving a reassuring pat. Peachey checked his stride. Frightening the girl would serve no purpose and needing to extract the maximum amount of information from her said,

'I said that I would pay for information and more than a shilling for your trouble. This man I need to find. It would help you too if I can remove this threat to your life.'

Kitty, confidence still in short supply, was still trying to recover from this sudden and almost violent interest from her innocent remark.

'There's not much I can say sir, he was with another man. They ate and stayed a short time at the inn. The dark haired one, the one who said little and was not from these parts, went out for a short time. When he returned the other one threatened the innkeeper and told him to keep his mouth shut.' Trevelyan butted in

'Had they just been robbed?'

Kitty was astounded. She looked blankly from one to the other. *How did these gentlemen know so much about what had happened that night?*

She had omitted her part in the story but that appeared to be of little consequence to them. It was tracing the killer that fired them, much more so than a casual killing at the Point would normally cause. She licked her lips. Fairweather's hand squeezed some further reassurance into her.

'They had sir, but it wasn't anything to do with me' she added.

'We know that' replied Trevelyan.

How did they know that? The depth of their knowledge was disturbing. What else did they know? Peachey continued

'So you can recognise the other man as well. You say he was not from these parts, how do you know that?'

'His accent was strange sir. He spoke the King's English but in a strange way – that's when he spoke at all.'

She felt a little guilty at betraying this man. She had no fight with him and was, if anything, indebted to him for keeping the other man at bay from her.

'Where are they now lass?' said Peachey, trying to sound calm but with the hunting scent of blood in his nostrils.

'I have not seen either of them since that night sir'.

Peachey knew in his heart that this would be the answer.

Damnation - he was getting closer all the time but was always kept a frustratingly elusive distance away.

He forced himself to try and think out the position.

These must be two of the men his uncle had been told about. Locating Faulkner as an agent was positive proof; knowing that two men were at Spice Island was additional knowledge.

What was the connection between these two and Faulkner? It made the demise of Faulkner more intriguing than a natural death. He recalled the face slumped over the desk, lips a strong bluish colour, was he poisoned? If so why? He still had much to piece together.

He knew his only chance of success was to wait for a breakthrough. He had no way of knowing that this would come from a totally unexpected quarter.

Chapter 21

Sophia Gifford was ecstatic. She beamed rather than smiled, skipped rather than walked, gushed rather than spoke and radiated her happiness to all within range.

'Louise dear, isn't he the most charming, witty, handsome and intelligent person you have ever met?'

Louise Farthing was, as usual, held in two minds.

Although companion to Sophia Gifford, she was actually employed by the Governor to watch over his Ward.

She was therefore torn between friendship for Sophia and to performing her duty as prescribed by her employer. The Governor paid her to guide his Ward and steer her well clear of difficulties.

Although classed as his Ward, it was widely acknowledge that the unmarried Governor had two sons and a daughter and that the precise arrangement was unclear.

She replied,

'A few weeks ago you were insistent that you never wanted to lay your eyes again on that – what was the expression? Mean, two faced, double dealing, unreliable scoundrel Percy Trevelyan, as long as you shall live.'

'Oh how I misjudged the poor man. He was manipulated by that terrible hag Elizabeth Attwick, performing his duty but all the while maintaining his fondness for me.'

'You mustn't use that word Sophia – it's not proper for a lady.'

'A hag is what she is and what she should be known as. As for tricking Mr. Trevelyan as she did – well! No wonder though, her looks would sour wine and her personality curdle milk.'

She appeared to not be an avid supporter of Elizabeth Attwick. Ignoring her companion's frown she continued

'To capture a man and one as charming as Mr. Percy Trevelyan would be out of the question by normal methods for the likes of her.'

Attempting to subdue a bubbling Sophia Gifford was a task beyond the capabilities of Louise Farthing. She nevertheless made valiant attempts to restrain Sophia's enthusiasm and act the lady.

'I met him again this morning.' Sophia sighed.

'Really, you know that's improper and what would the Governor say?'

'Have no worries dear Louise, he was with the Rev. Weston and they were on their way to St. Thomas' Church.'

The bright morning air, warmed a little by the watery sun struggling through the casement window, aided Sophia's bright cheeks, already glowing with the thought of the prodigal Percy Trevelyan – now returned to the fold.

Louise moved across the drawing room of Governor's House and straightened a lace tablecloth knocked askew by the effervescent Sophia. She said

'The Governor returns this morning and what he will say to me for letting you have discussions with the very man you said you despised, I don't know.'

'The Governor is a fair man as you well know. I will speak to him and he'll see how matters have changed. He'll say nothing ill of the meeting.'

Of this Louise was sure. First impressions were that a harder, stricter man would be difficult to find. The Governor was a renowned military man, a leader bound for the history books. Fearless, ruthless with no time for fools. With Sophia the opposite actually occurred, he found it increasingly difficult to understand, let alone guide his Ward in her future womanly duties. Her pleas and beseeching always appeared to fall on fertile ears and the Governor found it nigh on impossible to refuse the desires that always emanated from her heart – or so it seemed.

That was the reason for employing Louise Farthing. The manipulation of her Guardian and twisting him round her little finger, had reached a level in which Sophia was unsurpassed. His desire for her happiness trumped all other considerations and he wallowed in the change she brought into his otherwise rigid life.

However, Sophia was no one's fool. She could accurately assess the dividing line and never overplayed her hand. If pushed beyond it he would become intractable and unshakeable. It was not for nothing that he had risen to high command in the army, an MP and Governor of Portsmouth. He had been Governor for around a year now and had a warranted reputation. Louise shook her head in mild reproof.

'You must be ready to receive him as the lady of the house when he returns from Winchester this morning. Dignity and decorum must be seen before you cast your spells over his view of Mr. Trevelyan.'

'I shall I shall'

'After all you said about him, I imagine the Governor will take some convincing that acceptance rather than horse whipping is now the social order of things.'

'Fear not Louise I will wear the blue gown with matching ribbon that never fails to please him. I have a mind though that he will be surprised that Capt. Gadfew is not here to attend to his appointments. Major Salter will have to find a replacement in quick time, but anyone other than Gadfew will receive a warm welcome and that's a fact.'

Louise shuddered at the thought of the repulsive Capt. Gadfew who attempted to force his affections on her. He had threatened to use his influence with the Governor if she failed to succumb.

The memory of the gross man fumbling with her dress, breathing stale beer fumes and perspiring like an overworked dray horse still left her shaken. The return of the Governor himself on that occasion provided a fortuitous escape for her. She had afterwards gone to great lengths to avoid Gadfew.

Her rejoicing at his departure was as enthusiastic as anyone's. Beneath her disapproving veneer, Louise Farthing was secretly pleased for Sophia who had always shown a marked affection for Percy Trevelyan.

'Now Miss Sophia, away and put on the blue. The Governor will be tired after his journey and you must brighten his day on his return.'

Sophia, still radiating an aurora, tripped from the room to make ready for the Governor's return.

The Guardhouse in *The Parade* was the last landmark before the carriage turned to the front of the Garrison Church and around to the entrance of Governor' House.

Lieutenant General the Hon. Robert Monckton, Governor of Portsmouth stretched himself. His leg was stiff, throat parched, temper short and was lacking in sleep. He thought, *that fool of a Bishop in Winchester had delayed him unnecessarily again this morning. Last night's dinner and discussions were unsatisfactory on both counts, but now sensing the crisp sea air it lifted his spirits somewhat even if it did nothing for his leg.*

Throwing the covers aside he eased his aching limbs into an upright position as the carriage door was opened and the steps dropped into place.

Once down on *terra firma* he looked up and was surprised to see Major Salter waiting to greet him. *A good officer, that one. Expert at disguising his wound and as smart an officer as one would likely to get.*

Salter stepped forward

'Good morning Governor. A pleasant trip I hope?'

'Winchester is an irritating distance away. Too far to be a short trip and too near to be a long one. Dammed leg seized up again. How you manage with yours beats me.'

The Governor banging his leg went on

'Still I'm back again now. What brings you here Major? Where is the rotund Captain Gadfew?'

'Captain Gadfew has resigned his commission sir. I am arranging for a replacement as soon as possible. In the meantime I put myself at your disposal.'

The Governor limped towards the front door, talking as he attempted to rejuvenate his reluctant leg.

'Resigned his commission? What on earth is the man going to do? This position was almost beyond his capabilities. Has he inherited money?'

'No sir. I'm afraid there was some disagreement at cards and he, against all King's Regulations took part in a duel.'

'He's injured?' The Governor's voice expressed disbelief.

'No sir, but I'm afraid he forfeited his honour and besmirched that of the regiments.'

'He duelled with a fellow officer?'

'No sir, a gentleman. A Mr. Percy Trevelyan.'

'Trevelyan!' The Governor stopped and looked in amazement at the Major, 'that man deserves to be shot on sight.'

'Sir on this occasion he acted most honourably and the regiment is indebted to his actions.'

The Governor shuffled on again

'Well you will need to give me the fullest details inside. This is not a topic for discussion for all to hear.'

His face showed anger at the news but suddenly gave way to an increasing smile as he saw Sophia standing awaiting him just inside the pillared doorway. She said

'Sir, what would happen if the wind changed and you were stuck with that expression?'

The Governor's face relaxed as his Ward moved forward and kissed his cheek. He broke into a natural smile

'I prefer unexpected news when I am comfortable and can hear the fullest details. Salter began to tell me about that fellow Trevelyan and..... '

'Oh sir he was wonderful; he's the talk of the regiment. He wants to call on me and I'm so pleased.'

The Governor stopped in his tracks and looked in total bewilderment at his Ward. 'But I thought you despised him and......'

'Oh that was before. Now matters are fine again. Tell me you agree to his calling, please?'

'Let me settle down and refresh myself. I have been bombarded with news and views the moment I arrived, I need to catch my breath first.'

'Of course you must. I have had coffee, brandy and some of those delightful little cakes that you like prepared. I intended to tell you all after you had had your refreshments.'

'A ladies trick, no less. Get a man in a mellow mood before making demands.'

His smile dispelled any rebuke and he headed for the sanctity of the drawing room.

Peachey and Trevelyan strolled slowly back from St. Thomas' Church towards *The George* at the time the Governor was being manipulated by his Ward. They had left Rev. Weston behind in the vestry and both possessed a sense of failure.

'Whatever the snuffbox picture conveys, I cannot for the life of me see the solution being in the church' said Trevelyan.

'*Domus Dei* means Gods House and the book clearly denotes a bible. There is something we're missing, some missing link between those two references.'

A thoughtful Peachey felt vexed at the almost simplest of pointers that failed to produce any solution.

'Weston has used his best endeavours I'm sure' replied Trevelyan 'but nothing fits. He even checked that the bible has been used for years so we are not looking in the wrong book.'

'However' Peachey said, 'that's only the secondary issue. Locating those two men is the priority. Remember they intend to attack their target very shortly. I can see no link between the snuffbox and a *black house* either. Whatever way we look only a dead end is in sight.'

Looking upwards almost seeking guidance from above, Trevelyan mused

'Finding the letter in Faulkner's secret drawer establishes once and for all he was the French Agent, so who has been working with him?'

Peachey shook his head. Trevelyan continued

'Did the two Frenchies from *Spice Island* make contact with him?'

'Impossible to tell'

'Another point you seemed to have overlooked, was he the only French Agent or are there more than one? A major town with its military strengths is a certain target, it may be that Faulkner was not alone.'

'Firstly, we don't know that those two were Frenchies. According to that girl, only one was from foreign parts, but you are right, did they contact him before he died? And if there is another agent, have they gone to see him and are now under his protection.'

They walked on in silence for a few paces, and then Peachey said

'Again the same problem. Help is desperately needed to find these men but in so doing, will a warning that we are actively seeking them keep them hidden? Whatever way is turned, it could be the wrong way.'

Turning his head to look at Peachey, Trevelyan said

'Also, what of this Porter, the young girl molester and killer? Where does he fit into the overall scheme of things?'

'I have sent Fairweather out to talk and sound around. The sooner I know about that man the better.'

Trevelyan nodded at the thought as Peachey continued

'I have given Fairweather ready money to help loosen a few tongues if he has to.'

Pacing a few more steps, Trevelyan said

'You seem to have come to terms with your attacker - Bishop then?'

'He has about as much assassin about him as a dead sheep. The poor wretch grieves for his daughter and mistaking me for Porter I now accept.'

'Which takes us back to Porter then. He was Faulkner's partner or assistant or had some working connection.'

'I've got Fairweather probing that conundrum as well. A year ago he was apparently almost penniless yet now he is of good standing – and can afford to buy cloaks from a well established tailor to boot' he added ruefully.

Trevelyan's frown re-appeared,

'It could well be that he was an accomplice of Faulkner, hence gaining in wealth.'

Peachey shook his head.

'Much of the work is for a religious cause. Acquiring that sort of money within that time would not come from spying or being an informer. No, Porter is an ill defined problem at the moment.'

They reached the junction with *High Street*. Peachey looking down towards Sallyport said

'I shall go and see if Salter has made an appointment for me to see the Governor. He should be back from Winchester now. I will see you later at *The George*, if you have a mind.'

Trevelyan gave a small wave.

'I shall do that my dear sir. I too need to arrange to visit the Governor, but I fear my request is more delicate than your own.'

Looking in the direction of Governor's House he appeared thoughtful, then continued

'I hope I will be able to call again on Miss Sophia.'

'And I hope you are not going to exchange one binding engagement for another.'

'If only I could, I should be a happy man. You should consider matrimony yourself sir. Meanwhile a little planning and subterfuge might not come amiss.'

Peachey gave him a knowing look and said

'Until we meet later.'

They went their separate ways, each lost in their own thoughts, Peachey's on treachery and treason, Trevelyan on love and female beauty.

A beautiful smiling face; blue dress with matching ribbons; coffee; brandy; delicate biscuits; soft chair and warm fire, worked in unison to produce a more conducive Governor. He listened carefully to his Ward's story about the once errant Mr. Percy Trevelyan. Trevelyan now seemed to be the local hero, regarded in high esteem by his troops, held in awe for his shooting prowess and was the delight and centre of attraction to his Ward.

Captain Salter's whispered account of the duel and its background didn't come as too much of a surprise. He had always regarded Gadfew as obsequious, too willing to want to please but then speaking in deprecating terms behind his back.

Of course he hadn't been officially informed of any such duel. As far as Major Salter and he were concerned, their discussion never took place.

The desire of Mr. Henry Peachey to meet with him was more intriguing. He was fully aware of his uncle – Sir Richard Peachey; a powerful man providing constant advice to King George III. His thoughts were cloudy on this visit. *It may well be that Sir Robert's nephew wanted nothing more than a personal favour over some trivial issue. On the other hand a word or information passed from someone so near to the king should not be taken lightly.*

He had agreed to see the man at the earliest possibility. He was now conscious of Sophia, maintaining an unusual silence, waiting for his reply. He said

'It may be that circumstances have changed for Mr. Trevelyan. I shall deliberate the point and give you my decision shortly.'

'Thank you sir. I know you won't regret it'

Sophia jumped up and bounced out of the room. Her gait signified that as far as she was concerned, permission had already been given. Governor Monckton shook his head. He returned to his thoughts.

The sudden death and exposure of Erasmus Faulkner as a traitor was more serious. Not only did he himself know Faulkner but also the man was an attendee at The Garrison Church. In fact he had paid for some of the officer's pews and other decorations.

Standing he paced up and down easing his leg as he did so.

The outlandish and embarrassing situation was that a traitor and French Agent of Le Secret du Roi had attended the Garrison Church amongst soldiers of the country he was betraying. Whether Peachey was aware of that was unclear, but he resolved that he wouldn't raise the matter first.

Peachey quickened his pace on leaving Trevelyan, heading across *High Street* towards *The Parade*. Glancing up at the towering fortifications, he noted the colourful bust of King Charles I, embedded in the walls overlooking the town. This had been erected as a thanksgiving for his safe return by sea to Portsmouth. The Jacobites had many secrets, some still undisturbed, others festering but waning in influence. *What secrets and influence still remained?*

Territory or religion was the cause of many of Britain's problems. It was one or both of these issues that was dictating his visit to the Governor. He was still unsure which. Curious that religious problems should still be dominant. Tolerance was now seeping through the fabric of society. That said, worshiping was one thing, but holding office and influence as a Catholic was another. What was known, was that time was not on his side. The clock ticked relentlessly on. The odds of tracking down and thwarting the enemies in Portsmouth's midst seemed stacked against him.

Could the Governor provide a lead to assist him?

The suggestion posed by Trevelyan that there could well be another agent was not original. It had crossed his mind on several occasions of late, but the reluctance to mention it further hinged around the fact that Silas Trevelyan featured prominently as a suspect. The man was undoubtedly clever. Was he introducing innuendo and conflict into a conversation under the guise of innocence or eccentricity?

Crunching gravel beneath his feet signified that he was approaching the Governor's house. It was a somewhat peculiar setting for house as it abutted the Garrison Church to form one large building. The Governor could pass through a door in the house directly into a gallery in the church itself. He could thus survey the congregation from a single vantage point.

As Peachey approached the main door a solitary sentry was on duty. What purpose the soldier did, was open to question. His ill fitting uniform fitted an ill shaped body. A fact that probably improve the fit; but instilled little confidence that military defence was being offered to the Governor. An active day's duty looked well beyond this man. Similar to his first visit, when he encountered the acidic Gadfew, the soldier made no movement as Peachey passed into the doorway. Once inside a welcoming greeting came for Major Salter. Peachey noted that he rose awkwardly from his chair, but once erect maintained a good posture.

'My dear sir, good morning. Welcome to the Governor's residence. I trust you are well?'

'Good morning to you sir. I am as well as can be expected thank you kindly. I am hopeful that you have been able to arrange for me to see the Governor.'

'Indeed sir. He arrived back this morning and is looking forward to making your acquaintance.'

'I am delighted to hear it' replied Peachey.

'Pray be seated, and I will announce that you have arrived' said Salter.

Turning he made his way down the passage to his left. The wait was short. Salter re-appeared and beckoned for Peachey to follow, leading him into a more homely room, but one that still possessed the influence of state.

The Governor stood before him. A man in his fifties Peachey imagined, upright, tending to portliness around the middle but in most respects well preserved. His face adopting a serious governing image was lined, but strong in character. His reputation preceded him. He moved forward.

'My dear sir, I am delighted to make your acquaintance. I have heard of your uncle of course. How may I be of assistance?' He signalled for Peachey to sit and a servant appeared with a tray. He continued

'May I offer you some refreshment. The brandy is passable but the little cakes are a real delicacy.'

'Thank you sir, you are most hospitable. Perhaps you would care to view this letter of introduction from my uncle that will confirm my credentials.'

Handing him the letter, sealed with the distinctive stamp from St James' Court, he accepted the proffered seat.

'Thank you sir.' The Governor broke the heavy red wax seal with a silver knife and read it contents without a word. On conclusion he repeated 'thank you sir.'

The opening polite exchange having been dispensed with, both men were assessing each other. Peachey was deciding how much to disclose and the amount of help to seek. The Governor deliberated on the real reason for the visit, particularly from such a well-connected person. Peachey accepted the filled glass and nibbled on the proffered cake. He deliberately took his time before coming to the point of his visit.

'The cake is really delicious' he added 'you have a good cook by all appearances.'

'They are supervised in their making by my Ward' replied the Governor.

'Ah yes, Miss Sophia isn't it?'

A slight start from the Governor

'You are acquainted with my Ward sir?'

'I have not yet had the pleasure sir, but I have heard glowing attributes from my friend Mr. Percy Trevelyan.'

If Peachey had said that the King was a Catholic, it couldn't have brought a greater shocked response from the Governor. He looked incredulously at Peachey,

'You are a friend of Mr. Trevelyan sir. I find that a trifle surprising.'

Colour had tinged the lined face and the expression made Peachey regret he had raised the matter so soon. Nevertheless the man was entitled to an explanation.

'We knew one another at Oxford. I came across him again when I arrived a few days ago.' This seemed to mollify the Governor somewhat, who appeared to have discovered he had invited a viper into the nest. The Governor responded.

'Mr. Trevelyan is a man of many parts sir. I am not sure of the extent of your friendship but I must say he bemuses me. When I left for Winchester, boiling in oil was too good a fate for him - according to my Ward.'

Governor Monckton then waved his hands about and said

'On my return he has transformed himself from villain to hero in her eyes, has won the ultimate regard from the regiment here and is regarded as a man not to be trifled with.'

The Governor, now seated in a gilt chair, refrained from asking a question, but simply raised a quizzical eyebrow as though seeking a reply from his guest. Peachey said

'I believe an unsuitable matrimonial prospect was entered into under a contrived misunderstanding - which he felt obliged to honour. That being terminated he has now regained his freedom. The events that you mention, have I believe, demonstrated that he may have been misjudged in the past.'

A small smile flitted across the Governor's face that he attempted to conceal by sipping his brandy. He raised his glass in a toast towards Peachey

'Your health sir. If I may say so, your eloquence indicates an education and perhaps influence of court diplomacy'

'Your health and that of the King' replied Peachey.

'Amen to that for the King' said the Governor.

Peachey tended to be guided by his instincts. He had taken an immediate liking to this man, who spoke quite openly concerning his original misgivings about Trevelyan. There was also honesty about the Governor, appearing ready to lay his cards on the table than engage in a verbal duel of obscuring words. Peachey decided that an open game plan would be his strategy.

'As you have surmised sir, I am my uncle's man and my reason to visit Portsmouth is one that demands the utmost secrecy and diplomacy.'

The Governor said nothing but the seriousness of his expression spoke volumes. Peachey continued

'There are hostile and envious forces at work, even within our own ranks, that add to the discretion sought.'

'Serious accusations sir.'

The Governors face was quite steely.

'Alas sir, events appear to bear out the charges.'

Peachey aware that he was talking to a decorated senior army officer steeped in honour and dedication added

'It was the seriousness of the situation that prompted me to contact you immediately on your return.'

The Governor was still wary but replied

'I am completely at your disposal sir. Pray tell me what is the problem and what part I can play in the solution.'

Peachey then related how the information had arrived with his uncle and the resulting situation that had developed in Portsmouth. He left nothing out. It was too late for foiling with the Governor; he had to be brought totally into his confidence. The Governor sat absolutely still, hands held together as if in prayer over his lips. On conclusion, he slowly looked up and held Peachey firmly in the eye.

Chapter 22

It was still there, secure and undisturbed.

A relief nevertheless that *The Mistress* or *piece de resistance* of the mission was still intact and nurturing its deadly potential contents. Removing it from its hiding place in the storeroom, Rousseliere checked both packages. Satisfied, he swung the bag gently over his shoulder, slipped through the storeroom door and crept past the quarters where the infected men were kept. Few ventured near, as fear cloaked the area as though some magical shield was thrown around it.

The ward doors were locked or bolted, but not many of the men felt the urge to leave. Scurrying around the final bend he made for the drain.

The water was cold, very cold, but it was only trickling around his ankles in the main drain. Progressing towards the exit he was thankful that it wasn't too high; he would be clear before the route became impassable. The initial coldness had subsided due to a certain numbness creeping up his legs. He was now semi-wading and the power of the tide's force opposed him.

Reaching the mouth he clambered up to the shore. Sitting on the deserted bank he attempted to remove as much water as possible from his shoes and clothes. Stamping his feet to regain feelings and warmth he set off to his rendezvous with Courtney. A nagging doubt remained that the man wouldn't be there, either through choice or by having done something rash and been caught.

If that were the case, he himself might be betrayed. After several minutes of walk, he crouched down by a tree and watched the movements over the small bridge. Having time to spare, it provided him with an observation position to ensure there was no unexpected activity.

Most of the traffic to the hospital took place by boat so the small bridge mainly catered for local movements. Climbing down and rejoining the path, he started across the bridge. The rising tide swirled beneath him as it made its unrelenting way up the creek. He was just a few yards from the end when he saw them. His heart jumped into his mouth and he felt exposed. A single line of red-coated soldiers were a few yards away. Their pace was regular, their mood silent and depicting a sense of determination. There was no escape he couldn't retrace his steps across the bridge and ahead offered no opportunity for avoidance.

The steady thud of their footsteps was their only sound as they approached him. Visions of Courtney, betrayal, capture, defeated mission, failure for France, certain death, all in jumbled form flashed through his mind.

Could he throw the device into the water? No, insufficient time to do anything in fact.

His mind whirled - soldiers at this time and in this location couldn't signify anything other than he was discovered. At the end of the bridge they were now only a few paces away. The soldier in charge barked a command and they halted in front of Rousseliere.

Breaking rank they moved towards him. The first soldier to arrive looked him firmly in the eye. The look spelled hostility. The weather-beaten skinned face was lacking any form of emotion or expression. Rousseliere stood back with the end pillar of the bridge bearing into his shoulders. No retreat was possible.

Over the soldier's shoulder other men bunched behind him. An impulsive urge made him lick his lips; he straightened his shoulders and stood erect. He would not be taken as anything other than a French officer, albeit that his apparel did not warrant such grandeur.

He steeled himself. The soldier had lowered his weapon from his shoulder and was holding it with one hand as he came up to Rousseliere, then with a grunt – he walked straight past him.

The second soldier came abreast and carried on following the first. Slowly it dawned on Rousseliere that they had not come for him, and that they had only broken rank to pass over the bridge. The last man was the corporal in charge who only gave him a cursory glance.

It then dawned on him that they were not soldiers – they were Marines; the armed soldiers who were the soldiers in the Royal Navy. They were ferocious at close quarters and equally unhesitant when firing upon any of their naval shipmates attempting to flee a British warship or in revolt against the Captain.

He had heard about them, men who had taken the King's shilling and lived in a no-mans area on board ship; friendly with their own but distant from the companionship of the remaining ship's company. That's why they were there - because of the Royal Navy and the Haslar Hospital. As the corporal passed by, Rousseliere strode on. His face felt flushed but a cold shaft hung down his spine in contrast.

The moment had been real enough, the danger imminent, the fear absolute, and courage not lacking. His strides felt as though there was now unseen energy aiding every step. A certain exhilaration now replaced the dread that had just occupied his heart.

Forcing himself not to look back he continued until he gauged he was well clear of them. Turning his head he could see that they had crossed the bridge, reformed their rank, and were now marching on to allotted duties at the hospital no doubt.

Where he had become accustomed to moving freely in an enemy country, it was a salutary lesson that this was still a military area and danger lurked for the unsuspecting or unwary. Moving towards the centre of Gosport he resolved to keep this episode to himself. The mocking squinting eyes of Courtney if told of his near confrontation, was an event he could afford to do without. Strange though it was, it would be a relief to see this man at their rendezvous, even though his companionship was not to his liking.

For his part, Courtney was *en route* to the rendezvous. Looking up the harbour, the number of ships of any size lying in the trot were few. They were either being rigged or de-rigged for repairs in the dockyard. Two more were taking on stores and preparing for sea, swinging barrels, crates and spars with consummate ease from the dockside to the bowels of the ship.

The agile movements of the top men, and hands coiling ropes in precise formation on the decks, showed the Royal Navy at its daily duties in readiness for its forthcoming duty – whatever that may entail. These duties ranged from defence of the shores, chasing slave ships, sugar control in the West Indies, laying siege, delivering soldiers to the thirteen rebellious colonies in America, or boarding foreign vessels on demand.

These sights brought no sense of patriotism, honour or pride to Courtney. They were daily actions having no relevance to him. His particular world revolved around him.

Money brought advantages, honour bought nothing; his father had been honoured yet died poor. Courtney had had to struggle through life establishing his own rules and nurturing hatred and contempt for anything he regarded as a weakness.

A few swift strokes of the boatman's oars brought the boat around to the pontoon jutting out from the shore at Gosport. No sooner had they stopped, Courtney rose, gathered his things and stepped out, dropping payment into the boatman's outstretched hand.

The boatmen, having been paid, lost all interest in Courtney, busying himself with the task of finding a return fare. Making his way along and off the pontoon he passed through the collection of boats dragged up on the hard.

Up the short slope to the bottom of *South Street,* left him only a short distance away from the *India Arms* and his scheduled appointment with Rousseliere.

Scanning the street and people, he looked for any telltale sign of danger. After a few paces he darted behind the houses and made his way up the back parallel to the street, until he was opposite the *India Arms*. With the minimum of movement he casually inched his way until he had another clear view of the street. No troops in waiting, no-one watching from the outside judging by the actions of passers-by. All in all a typical routine scene.

Remaining where he was he watched the locals at their work.

With a quiet movement he was gone, slipping across the street and disappearing behind the *India Arms*. The smell of a well-used alehouse wafted from an open door. Barrels stacked in regimented lines provided ample cover as he moved to the rear window and peered in. The interior was dark, but no troops or King's men – the Frenchman was not apparently taken or had not been forced to betray him. Retracing his steps to the front of the building the narrow eyes watched for his accomplice.

From the corner of his eye a sailor appeared walking up the street carrying two bags, one casually slung over his shoulder. It was Rousseliere. Rousseliere looked around as he drew level with the India Arms, but Courtney made no move. He allowed Rousseliere to carry on up the street and looked carefully to see if his man was being followed.

He cursed himself for not telling Rousseliere to carry his hat if he had been taken and was being followed. This simple ruse would be all an accomplice would need to be warned off.

Slipping from his secluded viewing position he walked after the Frenchman. On drawing alongside, Rousseliere saw him for the first time. He opened his mouth to speak but Courtney frowned, said nothing and walked on. Turning the next corner he waited for the trailing Rousseliere to arrive.

'You have *The Mistress*?' Courtney dispensed with any formal greeting, being intent on learning of their position.

'Of course'

Courtney nodded and gestured for them to continue away from the South Street. They now walked side by side, Courtney said,

'We have several hours to kill before we strike. We must find somewhere to lay up before setting off.'

'There is a barn further down just before the creek.'

Courtney looked at Rousseliere. The Frenchman had obviously kept his eyes open and had noted the terrain that was useful. He nodded

'We'll go there and wait.'

The barn was only secured by a bar. It easily came away to allow ready access.

Neither man felt inclined to speak, Rousseliere grateful for the respite, and Courtney reviewed the details of the task that lay ahead. Rousseliere was awake but resting, conscious of a stillness of movement from Courtney. It was still and quiet in the gloom of the barn with a few everyday noises drifting in from outside.

He could hear a slight rustling away to his left. He stayed motionless. A rat twitched and probed forward until it was outlined.

Whoosh - it was pinioned to the wooden floor with a long curved knife. It wasn't dead although the blade had travelled through the main body. It twitched and wriggled in a useless struggle to free itself. Without a word, Courtney raised himself, trapped the rat's head with his boot and slowly slid the knife backwards splitting the animal's body with a deliberate slow movement.

Rousseliere was no lover of rats, but the cruel deliberate slicing rather than a quick killing caused him to look up at Courtney's face. It had a glazed look with a slight smile or sneer playing around the mouth. It implied enjoyment rather than satisfaction of the rat's termination. On completion he wiped the blade on the back of the rat, and resumed his silent position.

Once again Rousseliere looked forward to the completion of their mission when he would see the last of this strange man. He also made a mental note to watch for that knife should he and Courtney have any reason to argue or seriously disagree.

No other inquisitive rat ventured out, leaving Courtney devoid of further sport. Rousseliere settled back to while away the time until they would leave to plant the device that would kill far more British soldiers than Courtney could ever match with his rats.

As Rousseliere lay back and closed his eyes, so Trevelyan in *The George* opened his. What had caused him to break from his nap? A tap on the door provided the answer. The door opened and Peachey peered round the edge.

''Ah, Trevelyan, I 'm not disturbing you am I?'

'Not at all sir. I was just having a short rest. My wound has decided to make itself known to me again. Nothing serious though.'

He stood up to demonstrate the fact. Peachey entered and walked over to a vacant chair. Sitting down he appeared to gather his wits as Trevelyan paced to and fro to flex his limbs. Peachey said

'I had an interesting meeting with the Governor. I took a liking to the man. He has shared his thoughts with me about the likelihood of agents in Portsmouth and has indicated that he has more to reveal on that and broader issues if I care to return late this afternoon.'

'A man of honour and principal ' replied Trevelyan. 'I was sure that he would be of assistance if he could.'

Pacing a few more steps he turned and enquired

'Did the subject of his Ward and myself become raised at any point?'

'Boiling in oil seems a phrase that sticks in my mind ' Peachey remarked in a casual manner.

Trevelyan looked crestfallen.

'I was hoping events may have taken a turn for the better in that respect.'

'He did go on to say that he was bemused but that he had been impressed with what Major Salter and his Ward had said.'

Trevelyan brightened a little,

'Really?'

Peachey paused a little for effect before continuing

'He also said that with his compliments, if you would wish to call on him and his Ward this afternoon, they would be pleased to receive you.'

Picking up a discarded chess piece, Trevelyan threw it at the reclining Peachey.

'You are a tormentor of spirits sir.'

His broad smile couldn't disguise his obvious delight at the news.

'Did you see Miss Sophia Gifford whilst there?'

'No, but I understand that she is anxious for you to call again.'

'Peachey this is splendid news, my aches and pains are vanishing as we speak.'

Trevelyan moved to and fro as though having downed an elixir of life to rejuvenate him. He continued

'Then we shall return together this afternoon, you to further your quest and I mine.'

'Yours is of the easier solution I fear' Peachey said. 'The Governor was somewhat vague, implying no specific knowledge, but he is considering and consulting before my return. He did know Faulkner though, but not as well as I had hoped, for he had little to say about the man.'

Trevelyan, having completed his rejoicing, resumed his own seat.

'By the way, has Fairweather unearthed anything of use with his probing?'

'I have left word for him to join me as soon as he sets foot here. If there are skeletons in cupboards, Fairweather is one to set them rattling.'

In response to a single knock, Trevelyan's voice sang out

'Come.'

Fairweather appeared, almost on cue.

'Begging your pardon sirs, I received instructions to come at best speed.'

Peachey called over

'Indeed Fairweather, we are agog to know if you have unearthed news to help us.'

Fairweather stood erect.

'Firstly I have been making discreet enquiries about Mr. Porter sir, as requested. My best source was the late Mr. Faulkner's man. He has now lost his position and was appreciative of some money to ease his plight.'

'Was it good and trustworthy though?' enquired Peachey.

'Indeed sir. He spoke with a certain amount of vengeance about Mr. Porter which tallies with what other people have told me, but now we now why.'

Peachey and Trevelyan both looked eagerly for enlightenment. Fairweather continued

'It would seem that Mr. Porter was blackmailing Mr. Faulkner, for at least a year. The reason, I think we know sir, and his manservant doesn't, is that Mr. Faulkner was a French Agent.'

'Sounds most probable' murmured Peachey.

'He used to call on the same evening each week and our man believes money changed hands.'

Trevelyan said 'what of Porter's penchant for little girls?'

'The man knew nothing of such happenings. My guess is that that was Mr. Porter's own activity.'

Trevelyan nodded his head

'That matches what that wretch Bishop said about his daughter. Porter has all the qualities of the devil himself – blackmail, molester of little girls, killer and a bad taste in tailors.'

Other than a vexed look, Peachey let the comment pass but said

'Suspicion is one thing but the application of justice is another. I am convinced that servant is correct, as is Bishop. The loss of his daughter weighs heavily on his soul, not just the loss but in the manner of her death.'

Putting a hand to his head he continued

'The fact that Faulkner was being blackmailed is useful information, but I seek knowledge as to where the *black house* is, and what is being planned regarding this attack. I have nothing that helps me with my own problem. Let us deal with that first before we trouble ourselves about these other happenings.'

Looking from one to the other he continued

'The Governor himself is alarmed at the thought of an attack and will double the guards and put all on alert. But alert against what and where? He seems to believe in my warning but we're all chasing an unknown target or a will-o-the-wisp.'

Unbeknown to Peachey, the will-o-the-wisp pair were at that very moment across the short distance of water to Gosport, gathering their resources to start a devilish and debilitating attack.

Chapter 23

'Louise this dress makes me look hideous. He'll not call again if he sees me like this.'

'That's the third dress you've put on, and on each occasion you've felt that your appearance will dismay Mr, Trevelyan. I'm sure that he will be delighted to see you and will scarcely notice which dress you are wearing.'

Louise Farthing walked round to view from the rear adding

'That dress makes you look perfectly charming. It is fashionable, highlights your natural colouring and tends to enchant.'

Sophia looked at Louise,

'Do you really think so? I am so undecided and flustered I'm sure I will show it.'

'You have known Mr. Trevelyan for some time. He makes you feel at ease immediately.'

'That's true, but this time I feel uncertain.'

'The dress is fine. Here hold this fan, by holding something it will enable you to put your hands to good effect and not have them waving all over the place as they are now.'

'Louise you are a great comfort. You look so calm and poised, I wish I could mimic your actions.'

'Nonsense Sophia, as soon as he arrives and you two begin talking I shall become invisible.'

Louise knew that for a certainty. When he arrived, her role was simply to have a presence in the room and to discreetly busy herself with needlework whilst they talked. Social etiquette needed to be observed - otherwise she was not needed.

'I shall do as you advise Louise and wear this dress. The fan matches the sash doesn't it? I must appear at ease and not too interested.'

'Just enough to give him some encouragement though.'

A smiling Louise was aware that when the meeting was over, Sophia would regain all her usual poise and their relationship would return to normal. But for now it was support that was required.

Picking up the fan and practising a few deft sweeps Sophia moved to the window in anticipation of Mr. Percy Trevelyan's impending visit.

'They're coming' squealed Sophia.

'Whose they?' queried Louise joining Louise at the window to peer cautiously from behind the drapes at the visitors.

'The other gentleman is Mr. Peachey - the man who called on father this morning. I wonder what he wants? Since he left, father has been summoning people left, right and centre, and Major Salter has been running to and fro as though the devil himself has been let loose.'

'Right, come away from the window; I'm sure you'll find out soon enough what its all about. Now just come to the drawing room and let us await Mr. Trevelyan.'

Peachey and Trevelyan were in deep conversation regarding the scope of a likely attack in Portsmouth. After endless discussions and speculations, the question still remained, what could be set be set in train for a major blow to the defences of Portsmouth, something to occur at a later date? How could an explosion, for that was all one could think of, cause such injury to the troops?

The main powder and arms storage was across the water - had been for years. If that were blown up, it would cause a shortage of powder, certainly, but would not kill many troops. The method of delay was the real puzzle; a few hours would be one thing but a matter of weeks something else again.

The conversation had returned to its start point before they realised that the Governor's House was before them.

They passed into the hallway. Major Salter was in earnest discussion with a sergeant and indicating on a map some form of deployment. On seeing Peachey he broke off and came across.

'Ah Mr. Peachey' then greeted Trevelyan, 'Mr. Trevelyan sir'

He ushered Peachey to one side.

'If you would care to wait a moment sir I will have Mr. Trevelyan announced by the servant and then we shall see the Governor.'

He looked about him and quietly added

'The Governor has raised bedlam since your visit, the whole regiment is mobilised for action, although the enemy is undefined at present.'

Peachey watched as a servant appeared and led Trevelyan off for his meeting with Miss Sophia.

'We shall meet in the Governor's Reception Room' Salter said, leading the way in the opposite direction.

A gentle tap on the door preceded their entry into a book-lined room. Maps on the wall, a large globe of the world suspended in a walnut frame and a highly polished table took Peachey's eye immediately on entry.

'Mr Peachey sir.'

The Governor was seated at the desk, a large map spread before him. A Royal Navy Captain stood at his shoulder, the blue and white of his uniform in stark contrast to the sombre attire of the Governor.

'Allow me to name Captain Younghusband'

The Governor indicated the solid figure with whom he had obviously been in deep discussion.

'Your servant sir, an honour to meet you at last. I called to see you but you were still at sea. I was advised by the Lords of the Admiralty in London that you were to be contacted and am pleased to finally make your acquaintance.'

The mention of the Lords of the Admiralty had its intended effect on Captain Younghusband. All senior officers required influence, without it their careers and promotions faltered. To feel that ones name was known in such circles was a joy to the Captain's ears. He said

'You are too kind sir'.

The voice immediately indicated his origins as hailing from the West Country. Its vowels conjured up the image of a traditional seafaring man. The Governor broke in.

'Captain Younghusband's vessel is moored across the water in St. Helen's Bay in the Isle of Wight.'

He pushed the map to one side.

'With the information you provided this morning Mr. Peachey we have little time. You seemed clear that the target would affect soldiers but the Royal Navy provides much support and information and I have been seeking advice as to movements, vessels or any other activity in the area that may be of help to us.'

Peachey looked to the Captain.

'We are working blind captain. We know at least two men are in the area and we are told that they may join with others to inflict serious damage.'

'Men to cause an explosion that will occur at a much later date.'

The scepticism in the West County voice filtered through.

'A mystery we acknowledge' Peachey replied.

'To date however, the information received from the agents has been surprising accurate, even though incomplete.'

The captain shrugged his shoulders.

'In all my time in the service to the King, I have been involved with cannon, shot, powder and all forms of ordnance. I have seen with my own eyes when a shot has struck the powder room of a ship. The effect is a terrible one. But the shot must be considered as a fortunate, for the storage is well within the heart of a ship, almost impossible to aim for.'

Younghusband paused and waved his hand generally towards the window. He continued

'Storage on land is even more secure. The powder is stored in a magazine with no naked lights, the light coming through heavy glass panes from passageways that run all round the powder room. Even should someone get past the guards they have to get close enough to set off the powder. To set a fuse for a delay of weeks must be impossible.'

Peachey nodded in agreement.

'We have reviewed this on countless occasions sir and we agree with your feelings on the subject. However it is felt that we must not be found wanting and that every effort must be made to thwart whatever intentions they may have.'

Major Salter moved over and pointed to the map lying on the Governors desk.

'The attack sir is in the Portsmouth area?'

'That is what we are given to understand' Peachey replied.

'Then it could just as well be across the water in Gosport as Portsmouth?'

'I have no reason to doubt that Major. As I say we are at a loss to know the target and hence its whereabouts.'

Captain Younghusband pointed down at the map.

'The main magazine is over here at Gosport. It is away from living areas and the nearest military target is over here at *Blockhouse*.'

Peachey's froze. He felt the hairs on the back of his neck – taut and rising.

'What did you say Captain? What military target?'

Younghusband raised his head and pointed again

'*Blockhouse,* or to give it its full name, *Fort Blockhouse.* It is the battery straight across the water and guards the entrance to the harbour. Everyone always refers to it as *Blockhouse* though.'

Peachey looked at the Governor. Realisation of what he had just heard caused a tremor in his voice.

'Its not a *black house* that we should have been looking for it is *Blockhouse*!'

Having heard "*Blockhouse*" pronounced with the West Country accent by Capt. Younghusband it sounded very similar to "black house". The excitement rose in his voice

'Its obvious now, if one overheard someone speaking in French and they said "*Blockhouse*", the listener would probably hear it as *black house*.'

Younghusband leant forward

'By the saints Peachey, its as plain as day when you say it. As natural a target as any fool would imagine. If Blockhouse was immobilised the harbour could be taken by a strong enough force.'

Younghusband thumped his fist gently in the table.

'Cannon from a ship would bombard the walls of Portsmouth keeping them fully occupied whilst others could keep close to the Gosport side and sail in virtually unscathed.'

The Governor looked round at their faces.

'That is without a doubt the target. How they propose to cause an explosion is still unexplained but we must move swiftly to raise the alarm. Even if we don't know their full intentions, we can foil their bid simply by vigilance and searching for them.'

Captain Younghusband said

'I will get my cutter sent over there at once. The men are not well armed but can search for intruders. The boat is commanded by one of my best Midshipmen. I will see to it at immediately.'

The Governor looked towards Major Salter who was already moving towards the door. Opening it he Salter called out

'Sergeant.'

Footsteps rang out down the passage and short crisp commands were delivered by Salter to the Sergeant who, with an audible 'sir', doubled off to perform his task. Salter returned to his previous position. Looking at the Governor he said

'I have detailed off the Sergeant to take a body of armed men across to *Fort Blockhouse*. They are to inform the duty officer and double the guards around their own Powder and Ammunition Stores. I shall follow.'

Looking at Peachey he said

'If you would like to accompany me sir I will arrange it, but care should be taken as they will certainly be armed.'

'I am most obliged sir' Peachey replied, adding 'I shall need to take my man Fairweather with me and possibly Trevelyan, if he can excuse himself from his current meeting.'

With that he looked at the Governor who nodded and said

'We shall need all the able bodied men we have to ensure their plan is not put into operation. I shall go and address Mr. Trevelyan and request that he join you sir. You say your man is needed. Where is he?'

'He will be waiting in the hall or with the servants' Peachey replied.

The Governor looked out of the window.

'It is getting dark already. You will need to make good speed and arrange for as much light as possible in the Fort.'

As they made for the door. Salter murmured

'I hope to God we're not too late.'

Chapter 24

'Curse the moonlight.'

Courtney glanced up at the eerie glow that was illuminating the road leading to Fort Blockhouse. The Fort, located at the end of the peninsular directly opposite the fortified walls of Portsmouth, had stood firm for hundreds of years. It had proved its worth in the Hundred Years War with France, and strengthened many times since. Its effectiveness in defending the harbour entrance accounted for the fact that the town had never been over-run. It was impressive.

Rousseliere felt intimidated by its solid formidable outline, no doubt enhanced by the moonlight throwing its battlements into relief with the evening sky.

If this were not put out of action the whole plan was in total jeopardy. Its total dominance of the harbour and its approach was without question.

His thoughts encompassed the shortcomings he had found with the lack of trained troops in the area, but a few men, trained in gunnery could still present an insurmountable defence.

The walls and fortifications also meant that even with superior troops invading from the land, gaining entrance was still far from certain. A shiver ran down Rousseliere's back as he imagined the slaughter that would occur to French and Spanish soldiers, were the Fort not immobilised.

Rousseliere agreed with Courtney's cursing of the moon. The advantages of moonlight to guide them, also aided the guards on duty at the entrance. The Fort details came from a hand drawn map. It showed a single entrance; the other gates or doors were locked. That entrance was how they must gain entry.

Rousseliere's military training dictated that this would be the most difficult part. Even the most unwary and bored guards would not be totally asleep. Beyond the gate, the Guardhouse fronted the access road, presenting further potential danger. Once safely inside, the principal features were easily identifiable, and paradoxically, it was easier to move about within the walls than approach the gate without discovery. Of all the time he had been in the country, this was undoubtedly the most precarious.

They approached with caution. It was a good five minutes walk before they settled behind a tree to observe the main gate, having a wide entrance flanked by two pillars. The high retaining wall continued round the perimeter of the Fort. The entrance housed two gates. One was closed, leaving only half the entrance open.

A sentry was on guard outside until the gates were closed for the night, only then opening for an officer or emergency. They watched in silence. Very little happened. The sentry was bored, occasionally pacing up and down and then retiring just inside the entrance to lean against the pillar. Scaling the walls was not an option. Courtney looked unable to do it in normal times, but with the addition of the device now strapped around his neck even less likely.

The Fort was surrounded on three sides by water. They were on the remaining forth side. There was a little land to the base of the walls on the three other sides, before plunging into the sea itself. Entrance had to be via the gate – but how?

Rousseliere knew that when attacking with inferior forces the standard method of levelling the odds was – by diversion.

The question was therefore what diversion? It had to be something that would attract the attention of the guard without him raising an alarm. He looked around and then saw the solution.

Crossing the road he approached the wall near the gate. With the guard leaning back just inside, Rousseliere was shielded by the pillar and therefore unobserved. Lying in a heap were two small barrels, one split open, the other still intact. Numerous other pieces of wood lay nearby.

Picking up the intact barrel, he made a support from the broken wood and propped it up against the wall. It stayed in place - but only just. He then crept back to Courtney.

In hushed tones he explained the plan and instructed him to creep as close to the gate as possible without being observed. The moonlight acted as an aid. The black shadow cast by the wall gave excellent cover. They sidled up as close to the gate as they dared.

Rousseliere then picked up a stone and threw it towards the barrel support. The aim was good but missed and simply bounced harmlessly underneath.

Stepping clear of the wall he threw the second with more force. It fell short but the momentum carried it forward. Striking the wood support - the barrel crashed down. The thud was amplified in the quiet evening air. Jumping up the guard looked and went round the corner to see the cause of the commotion. The moment he turned his back Rousseliere moved forward with Courtney close behind. With only a short distance to travel they were quickly inside the gate.

The Guardhouse had a porch protected by three curved arches with two windows either side. Candlelight flickered through the windows, but of signs of activity there were none. He guessed that the only one out in the cold boredom was the sentry they had seen; the sergeant and other off duty guards were firmly rooted inside.

Moving back into the shadows they cautiously inched further inside until they could round the corner out of sight of the Guardroom. Rousseliere had memorised the map thoroughly before leaving the barn. Experience had taught him that once action was underway there was no opportunity for re-examining of maps or plans.

This turning led down to one of the barrack blocks, located just behind the piggery. He knew his nose would inform him when they reached the proximity of that location.

Opposite, lay the Officers Quarters, and further on, the remaining living quarters. The bulky shape of the magazine and powder store could be seen standing out in stark outline. Peering around in the gloom, the other landmarks now took shape. It was surprisingly large inside, much larger than external viewing lead one to believe. The manpower of the Fort appeared as limited as the other defences he had surveyed.

We shall not be disturbed when gaining our objective he thought.

Sensing Courtney at his side, he pointed to where their target was to be found. Courtney took his arm and indicated that they stoop down.

'I have to prime the device' he said.

Undoing the bag he gently took out the cloth and unwrapped the small barrel shaped object. Taking out the second smaller bundle he passed over a small green bottle also wrapped in cloth.

'Here take this and very carefully remove the cap - here's a knife.'

The stopper was firmly sealed with wax. The knife was the one Courtney had used to slice the rat earlier in the day - *a knife for many applications* Rousseliere thought.

Courtney laid the device on the floor whilst Rousseliere worked away with the knife. Finally the stopper was loosened. Courtney's whisper was harsh

'Give me that - carefully mind you!'

Handling the bottle with the utmost care Courtney gently removed the stopper. Gingerly pouring the contents into the device he promptly resealed it. Tossing the bottle away, he crouched round to face Rousseliere again.

Rousseliere's nose twitched - *it was either Courtney or they were closer to the pigs than expected.*

Rising, Courtney held the device away from his body and whispering in Rousseliere's ear, said

'Its as quiet as the grave in here, we shall not be disturbed.'

Whether there was a saying in French equivalent to *'don't tempt providence'* was unknown, but no sooner had the words left his mouth, the evening's solitude was abruptly shattered.

Raised voices and the clumping of boots from the entrance caused Courtney and Rousseliere to look at each other in amazement. Rousseliere was the first to respond,

'Quickly, we must away from here – up to the top end of the Fort.'

Courtney, holding the device before him needed no second bidding. They dashed around the square hugging what shadows were available. A flight of steps appeared before them. Courtney glanced up; they led up to the battery position facing the sea.

'Up there' he said, 'I will go below along the wall. If anyone comes towards me, distract them by some means.'

With that he moved off. Rousseliere had little option but to climb the stone steps. On reaching the summit he found himself at the battery position. Cannon lined the walls, drawn back from their firing position but roped neatly either side, in precise order. Cannon balls were stacked in pyramid formations; probably 32 pounders he thought, proof of the deadly firepower that could be brought to bear against any enemy approaching the harbour entrance.

Looking further along the wall he gave an involuntary start. Not only was this a line of heavy defence, but it was also being strengthened with the addition of cannon of possibly larger shot. It a flash he knew that his surveys would need to have this piece of unwelcome information added.

The shouting and running of feet was now accompanied by flashes of light. Flares were being lit enabling the soldiers to carry out a more effective search. He moved to the inside edge of the battlement and cautiously peered over. The Guardhouse was now ablaze with light.

An officer was directing operations with two gentlemen standing by. A running soldier passed nearby heading for the soldier's accommodation with another charging up the steps of the Officer's Quarters. There was no doubt that an alarm had been raised.

We have left no trail over here. The diversion with the guard would not raise an alarm; no one else knew they were coming to Fort Blockhouse, so how could a search now be on for them?

Rousseliere's thoughts were confused. The risk to them had increased a hundredfold.

The activity seemed to centre on the Magazine and Powder Room. Soldiers were now taking up position at the entrance and walking around the projecting oval building. A noise to his right made him glance round. A light was coming up the stairs - that was all he could see. The fact that there must be a soldier holding a flare made him instinctively move off to his left.

He stopped dead. Another flare was coming into view at the far end of the battlement. He was trapped!

There was no cover and no other stairs between the two approaching soldiers. They had obviously not seen him since they only approached at normal pace. His planned role was to cause a diversion to let Courtney plant the device. Where Courtney was now, was impossible to gauge.

If he engineered some form of distraction all focus would be on him and he would certainly be taken. It was important to the plan for Courtney to complete the attack, but on the other hand he held vital information as to the defences for a successful result. If Courtney was unable to fulfil his role then it was essential that he himself got back to France.

Instinctively he felt for the information carefully wrapped in its oilskin protective covering within his bag.

He looked about him. What should he do?

Courtney hugged the wall. Where the devil had all these troops appeared from? They were far enough away for him to reach his objective. Thank God the device was already primed. All he had to do was plant it. In a few moments he would have to break cover and move into the open.

Just as he was preparing to move a soldier walked round the corner. As he was not carrying a flare he had not signalled his approach. Courtney froze, standing perfectly still against the wall. The soldier, oblivious of his presence, carried on walking straight towards him.

Courtney slowly slid down the wall and placed the device on the floor. The soldier was no more than ten feet away, looking down the square towards the commotion that had developed. He was almost on a collision course. Courtney unsheathed his knife without a sound. If he remained absolutely still, the man could still walk straight past him but Courtney had decided his course of action.

When the soldier was one pace away, Courtney leaped from the shadows grasping him by the shoulders. His right arm slashed hard across the unsuspecting man's throat.

An agonising gurgle was the only sound, and with a vicious tug, Courtney pulled him to the ground where he lay, motionless. There was just enough light to allow Courtney to see his victim whose head lay unnaturally on one side.

The dead man could hardly be called a soldier for he was no more than a youth of fifteen or sixteen. Age was of no consequence to Courtney who plunged the knife into the heart for safe measure before wiping the blade on the dead man's tunic.

Gathering up the device, he stepped over the body and moved forward to his target.

It had been only a glimpse, but Fairweather thought he had seen someone moving in the shadows. They followed the contour of the wall. Fairweather suddenly stumbled over something.

He jolted back - it was a dead soldier. Blood seeped all around it and Fairweather felt a positive stickiness on his shoes. Then he saw the moving figure up ahead. The man had broken cover and was moving across to a small building standing on its own a few yards away. His pace was not fast and he appeared to be carrying something in front of him.

Without hesitation Fairweather ran towards the figure. His running footsteps announced his pursuit. The figure turned to see Fairweather nearly on him. Courtney was caught unawares. He was near his target and wasn't expecting to be disturbed. The approaching figure was hell bent on attack.   Dropping the device, he felt in his pocket just as Fairweather got to him. Fairweather shot out his hand to grasp him. Courtney struck – his deadly knife plunging into Fairweather who reeled back clutching his wound.

 Courtney yanked the knife out and raised it to strike again.

A single shot! - then silence.

Courtney froze in mid air. His head and body fixed like a statute. Slowly he toppled down remaining motionless on the floor. A single hole in the middle of his forehead, slowly oozed blood.

A second figure holding a pistol walked up behind Fairweather. A telltale wisp of smoke eked from the barrel.

Mr. Percy Trevelyan looked down at the body of Courtney, and tossed the pistol to one side.

Desperate, Rousseliere looked for an escape route – there was none. The approaching figures had not seen him. Suddenly a shot rang out. Both flares stopped in their tracks as their bearers sought the reason. Rousseliere gained a few precious moments.

The construction work to expand the battery was using a beam with block and tackle which was left dangling over the external wall. Moving rapidly he reached the beam. The rope with its attendant shackle was too short to reach the ground but it lessened any drop. It at least gave him a fighting chance.

Grasping the rope with both hands he swung out on the beam but kicking a bucket as he did so. The resulting noise immediately exposed his position. Without looking back he continued sliding down the rope. Friction burnt his hands as he dropped – landing on shingle. This broke his fall but twisted his ankle – pain shooting up his leg.

Two cries rent the air. He could see light becoming brighter as the two soldiers ran towards the beam.

Gritting his teeth against the ankle pain he hobbled around the side of the wall towards the access road. Stumbling and falling he moved on all fours, and made what progress he could over the shingle. There was little space at the bottom of the walls with the sea pounding the shoreline - but there was enough.

Hearing further shouts he paid no attention. His aim - to put as much distance between him and the guards.

The ground under foot stopped crunching as soil mixed with the shingle slightly easing his progress. He could now see the end of the far wall with the road beyond it. Reaching the wall he glanced back – no pursuers.

Of course not. They will take the shorter and easier route through the Fort. Any minute they would be out of the main gate to head him off.

His body heaved with the exertion. Moving forward he thought

No, not to the road itself but down to the shoreline running parallel with the road. Progress will be slower but one is far less visible. The road is built up higher to clear any exceptional high tides.

Now he could hear his pursuers. Shouts and orders carried clearly in the evening air and behind were several flares in the vicinity of the Main Gate.

Struggling on he simply put one step before the other, but bending low to lessen any body outline. The pain in his ankle shot through his body.

He realised that he was making very poor progress. Looking back towards the Fort, he could see soldiers spreading out looking for him.

But more alarming than that, a group was running along the road itself making nearly three times his speed. They were some two hundred yards back and only stopped now and then to check any suspicious object. The road here veered away from the shoreline towards a group of buildings in the distance – some slight relief but not much.

He knew capture was certain death with no allowance being given to his status as a French Officer. Dressed as he was, he would be treated as a spy. His own personal death was not of paramount importance; the vision of France and their ally Spain depending on his reports appeared as a tabloid before his eyes.

Shouts came closer and closer. Looking around for a hiding place he knew it was futile.   As daylight came the searchers would eventually find him.

A light appeared behind him, no more than twenty yards away moving in his direction. Refusing to give up, he knew that even after fighting a spirited defence he would be taken alive.   The fate of Courtney must by now have been sealed, but the success or failure of the mission urged him on.

A few steps more and the soldier with the flare must surely see him. Head down he limped on and then saw something that puzzled him. He couldn't understand why - then he realised.

He knew where he was.   The build-up of the land was for a purpose; it was to accommodate a drain outlet. Of course - the buildings he could see were Haslar Hospital which he remembered were close to Fort Blockhouse.

Looking over his shoulder the light was getting closer. Without hesitation, he turned and waded into the sea.

There it was - the exit of the drain.

The tide was high. Higher than it had ever been when he had used it before. The flare on the beach stopped and he felt exposed. Without a further thought he bent down and moved the end grill and forced himself past.

Total blackness confronted him with the water chest high. Not only high, but moving swiftly. He lifted his bag and held it on his shoulder – the oilskins protecting the plans inside the bag, were not designed for total immersion.

Keep a cool head.

This was the deepest part where the gradient was greatest. If he could navigate this section it would become easier further up.

Suddenly the darkness was transformed into light. The soldier had followed and was shining the flare up the drain. Whilst illuminating the drain, the flare also shone in the soldier's face limiting his effective viewing distance to a few yards. Rousseliere shielded his face.

'No one can get up here, its flooded.'

The voice of the soldier shouting to a colleague was unnaturally booming as it resonated in the drain. Suddenly the light was gone.

Rousseliere trying to maintain his balance and breathing hard felt some relief but *the soldier was right, it was treacherous underfoot and the tide pounded, buffeting one from side to side.*

Pressing painfully on, the water level started to drop a little. His hands were raw from banging and scraping them on the brick lining of the drain, but he was still upright. In utter darkness he could only gauge his progress.

Thank God the entrance for the storeroom is close to the exit.

After a further stumbling and groping there it was - the grill opening he was looking for. Pushing it up he dragged himself upwards, pulled it aside and crawled through.

He collapsed on the floor bettered and exhausted. Slowly his breath and composure returned. He had escaped back to the shelter of the storeroom and the infectious diseases hospital.

How long for though?

The searching troops would probably realise where he had gone and would soon be searching the hospital for him.

Inside Fort Blockhouse the corpse of Courtney now lay bathed in flickering light from several flares held by a group of soldiers. Major Salter was firmly in charge, detailing three men to move the body of the dead Drummer Boy, for that was all he was, whist deploying others to continue the internal search.

Although there was only meant to be two men attacking the Fort, they might have recruited more local support. Salter was taking no chance of anyone else being able to inflict any damage or escape.

'He's dead of course?'

Peachey said looking at the lifeless figure of Courtney. Salter looked at the body then at the speaker,

'Stone dead! - Which is only to be expected with Mr. Trevelyan's firing. Being the best shot of all of us, I asked him to accompany your man to this end knowing that if anyone tried to pass us up here, Mr Trevelyan would pick him off.'

Peachey looked at Trevelyan who turned his mouth down at the edges and slightly shrugged his shoulders as though it was an opinion beyond his control.

The major went to the two men gathered round Fairweather who was still on his back.

'How's this man fairing?'

The Physician replied without looking up.

'He has received a wound in the upper chest Major. Had it been much lower it would have definitely been fatal. His breathing appears stable so his lungs seem intact.'

Peachey stooped and whispered in the physician's ear

'I shall be obliged if you would treat my manservant sir. I shall of course pay all costs.'

'I shall certainly do my very best sir'

Trevelyan who had remained silent since the shooting looked at Major Salter

'How did you know he would come up this end of the Fort?'

'I didn't. It was just a precaution. One well taken if I can be the judge of that, for without your intervention, Mr. Peachey's man would be gone.'

Trevelyan looked puzzled.

'What was he doing up here? I thought the man was to cause an explosion after a few weeks. It's a long way from the magazine'

'I don't think he was heading for the magazine.'

'Then I am at a total loss.'

'I now know what he intended to do but not how it could be done.'

Two soldiers helped Fairweather across the square to the Sick Quarters. He breathed regularly. The wound was narrow due to the thinness of Courtney's blade. It required a second strike to inflict a deadly wound but Trevelyan had prevented that.

Having stemmed the loss of blood and dressing the wound, nature would be required to take its own course. His deep breathing was a distinct encouragement. The physician, widely experienced in military wounds, wiped his hands and said

'That's it for now. His body shows that he's a fit tough character, so I expect a rapid recovery.'

Peachey pressed some money into his hand

'Thank you for your efforts sir.'

He glanced down at the money and said

'I have done no more than any experienced physician sir, but he was fortunate in receiving prompt attention. More fortunate that that poor Drummer Boy.'

The advent of thirty minutes solved the mystery of *The Mistress*. Whilst Major Salter and the onlookers had no knowledge of Courtney's name for the device, its function was now revealed. Major Salter looked at Peachey and Trevelyan

'I myself only realised it at the last minute. As the plan was to kill or maim our troops after a few weeks, we all naturally looked to the magazine. But it wasn't to be an explosion. That's what led us astray.'

'Then what could do such a thing?'

'He was heading away from the magazine and I was puzzled where he was going. Then in a flash it hit me. It was the fresh water well he was after.'

'The well?'

'Yes sir. There is only one in the Fort. If he could poison the water such as it would take effect at the right time it would cause havoc. Everyone uses the same source so it would affect every man jack in the Fort.'

'How can it operate with a delay then?'

Salter indicated the small man holding a cloth in his hands and peering down through small glasses perched on the end of his nose.

'The Doctor here has examined the small barrel the dead man was carrying – be careful not to touch it sir' he added as Peachey moved towards it. Salter continued

'It's an ingenious container. At one end it's filled with acid in a small chamber.'

The doctor pointed to the end of the device with a small glass rod to indicate the section. Salter continued

'The main chamber holds the poison with a small inflated bladder pushing down on its top. The acid will eat away at two thin plates, one between the two chambers and the other to the water in the well. Peachey bent down to examine the barrel more closely. Salter pointed to the end with his sword and said

'They must know how long it takes for the acid to eat through the metal. When that happens it will then allow the poison to move into the acid chamber and for the acid and poison to then leak into the well.'

'What's the bladder for?'

Peachey looking puzzled arched his neck to peer into the vessel. Salter moved his sword to the top.

'I said it was ingenious sir. To allow the poison to easily escape into the well it needs pressure to push it out. Once the holes in the plates are burnt through by the acid, the bladder will push the poison out. But it does more than that. According to the Doctor the barrel is negatively buoyant...'

'Negatively buoyant?' Trevelyan broke in.

'Yes sir, it means it only partially floats. A bit like a submerged log. It doesn't sink right to the bottom but will submerge to a certain depth. In this case, once the acid has created the holes, the bladder pushes the poison out and the barrel will slowly rise in the water as it becomes more buoyant.'

'What good will that do?' Trevelyan said.

'As it rises up, it will allow the poison to mix with the well water far better than just allowing it to seep out. It will then give maximum effect.'

Trevelyan pursed his lips.

'It is a fiendish thing. I suppose they must have tested it many times to find out just how long it takes the acid to burn through the metal to give them the delay they wanted'

'Precisely what the Doctor says.' replied Salter.

He turned to Trevelyan.

'Thanks to Mr. Trevelyan here, he shot the man as he was only yards from his objective. We must extend our thanks again to you sir.'

'A fortuitous shot' he said modestly.

Peachey was staring hard at Trevelyan thinking

How does he do it. He has gained a reputation as a master marksman yet possesses no skill in the art at all. Typically Trevelyan.

Major Salter then turned to both Peachey and Trevelyan

'We can do no more here gentlemen. The Duty Officer has matters in hand. They will send word when they have caught the other who escaped down the wall. He'll not get far. We can then questioned him at our leisure.'

Chapter 25

'You must now be regarded as the finest pistol shot in Christendom sir. Pray enlighten hunting gentlemen such as myself how we can attain your prowess.'

Peachey, eyes a-twinkle, made a mock enquiry to Trevelyan over breakfast.

'The answer my dear Peachey, is not to aim but simply point the pistol in the direction of the target and fire. The more one aims the more error that is introduced.'

Trevelyan was responding to a series of questions regarding his uncanny performance that had now enhanced his reputation and ensconced him as a fine shot, gaining further indebtedness from Salter's regiment. The two men faced each other down for a few seconds before Peachey burst into laughter.

'Your philosophy may be correct my dear sir, but it is not the recommended method. Your results should be considered as a gambler winning the first two high stake games. Beyond that he becomes bankrupt and destitute by playing more.'

Trevelyan's smile matched Peachey's.

'The gods have smiled on me sir and that's a fact. Major Salter gave me the pistol at the Guardhouse as though this was an everyday occurrence. Anyhow, there's one blessing, the Governor must now regard me as a suitable contender for his Ward's hand in marriage. I am a hero no less.'

'Care and avoidance of anything to do with pistols should be your future watchword sir. The Governor is no fool, he will be carried along with everyone else at this stage but do not let yourself be put to the test where your ability can be properly tried.'

'Amen to that' replied Trevelyan.

Sipping his coffee he continued

'Major Salter hasn't produced any news regarding the other man yet then?'

'No, but its only a matter of time before he's caught. There's nowhere for him to go or hide. I look forward to finding out the truth behind all this. I've had sleepless nights I can tell you, but at least we have exonerated my uncle.' Peachey sipped some tea and then continued

'As soon as we have loosened the other agent's tongue I will send a messenger post-haste to him to convey the news.'

Rising from the table and pacing to the window Trevelyan enquired

'What of other agents or collaborators? If they still remain undetected the problem hasn't been totally resolved.' Peachey nodded.

'Faulkner has been unmasked, that's a good one for a start.'

'Hardly active was he?' Trevelyan contended, 'he was really just a contact. I can't see that he was stirring up issues in Portsmouth.' After a pause he continued,

'I grant you we know of none other. On the other hand we do know of someone else mixed up with this to whom some retribution is warranted. I've been thinking about the issue and a possible solution came to mind.'

'Really' Peachey voice contained a mixture of surprise and interest.

'Our Mr. Porter, - do you remember your scholastic work sir, and particularly Palamedes?'

'Only vaguely' replied Peachey whose interest had now been toned down an octave.

'I was thinking about his outcome and how it was brought about.' Peachey frowned attempting to recall the story from the depths of his mind. 'Ah yes it was to do with….' He suddenly broke off and stared at Trevelyan.

'By the saints sir, you can't be thinking …..'

Trevelyan's smile broadened.

'I knew your studies would fair you well one day sir. Yes I am. It would be a fitting end to such a matter.'

Peachey's eyes had widened at such a scheme.

'But how would you arrange such retribution?'

'I think the stable lad here should contact his cousin, the one who climbs like a monkey. A shilling or two for both of them should set us fair. Let me give you the details.'

Percy Trevelyan made his way back to The George from his uncle's house. Silas Trevelyan was always receptive to his visits but there were always two conversations – the one that Percy Trevelyan was giving and the other completely separate one that Silas Trevelyan was answering. *Even now he was unsure if his uncle had appreciated that he was contemplating pursuing a serious relationship with the Governor's Ward, Miss Sophia Gifford.*

His uncle's interest in astronomy was his newfound passion. He was now talking of buying a large telescope to study those far distant objects, along with fellow astronomers in Southsea. Telescopes of the sort Silas Trevelyan was talking about were very expensive but the cost didn't seem to give rise to any concern. Where the money for these kinds of pursuits came from Percy was unclear. The brewing business was successful but not immensely so, according to Silas, which led Percy to wonder where the money came from for such a lavish instrument.

His aunt – bless her, was in raptures regarding his plans for Sophia, but she was equally scatterbrained when it came to details. *Probably a result of living too long with his uncle. A strange household all in all* he thought. His aunt's new companion was well qualified to join them. As Silas had remarked during an earlier visit "*she even has ideas of her own*". That being very true, one that concerned Percy Trevelyan was her desire to travel to the thirteen colonies. The fact that there was extensive fighting and bloodshed gradually spreading throughout the Americas did not appear to register with her to any degree.

Percy knew that matters were deteriorating, with France providing considerable support to the rebels. To travel there at this stage was pure folly. Increasing his stride, he decided to leave these issues for another day. His prime focus now was to dine with the Governor, gain his confidence, and convince the man that he was a worthy suitor to call on his beloved ward.

Arriving at *The George* he didn't enter by the front, but walked around the back to where the aroma of dung and straw mingled with the stale air of ale. The cobbled way lead to the stables. He had to put in motion a task that would resolve an outstanding secondary problem that had concerned Peachey and himself. It was a problem that the Greek solution would satisfy, providing he could get the lad Nathan to use his skills. Knowing the power of ready money he reached into his pocket for some and also felt for the package that was so essential to the plan.

Rounding the corner, he could see the stable lad wielding a pitchfork into a rotting pile of straw. The lad's day was likely to be greatly improved by Trevelyan's visit but someone else's life was to be unexpectedly shattered.

Chapter 26

Sophie was secretly pleased as she looked around the table. The dinner had gone well, cook had prepared delicious soup followed by mutton with a fine assortment of dishes. The wine had been plentiful and the faces of the Governor and Percy Trevelyan were flushed by enthusiastically sampling a variety of them. The two of them had seemed to get on well; that was what delighted her most. She watched as the Governor spoke to Trevelyan,

'I appeared to have misjudged you Mr. Trevelyan. I must confess our earlier meetings had not had much substance to them. I was completely unaware of your accomplishments. Your record over the last few days is second to none. A fact acknowledged by the Regiment.'

'Ah, well I'm afraid that the case has been overstated sir. The happenings have been down to chance rather than military skill.'

The Governor helped himself to another glass of fine Claret, filling Trevelyan's to the brim in the process.

'It matters not sir. Your image is what stays in people's minds. If you are thought to be such, that is how you appear. In your case your reputation now precedes you. Make what you can of it is my advice.'

Trevelyan raised his glass to a silent toast to the Governor. It had bothered him that he was a charlatan, gaining credit through no worthiness of his own. He had now told the Governor to his face that it had been no more than chance. That point had been surprisingly glossed over by the man. A result that thoroughly cheered him.

Sophia felt flushed with the wine, although she had restricted herself to the odd glass. Noting a discreet nod from the Governor she announced that it was time for the ladies to retire and leave the gentlemen with their port.

The gentlemen stood whilst the ladies gathered their accoutrements and filed towards the door. They would further their own discussions on more important matters than military strategies, defence, war with the colonies and other boring topics. Gossip and fashion had much more intrigue than was ever to be found with the men's talk.

Once the ladies had departed the men moved up places so that all now sat in a group near the Governor.

Speaking to Major Salter he enquired

'What of the second man who evaded capture at *Blockhouse* Major?'

'Still at large sir. In fact - vanished. He has little in the way of cover, there being none between *Blockhouse* and the hospital and beyond that it is open ground. The duty officer has men searching the whole area. We shall get him in due course.'

'I am relieved to hear it. I must confess the daring and ingenuity of their plan gives rise to much concern. We must also find who was been helping them.' Turning to Peachey he continued

'Your information was sound sir, and we are in your debt for your astuteness in foiling their work and for the exposure of Faulkner.' He looked round the table from face to face before continuing

'I of course knew Faulkner; he was a worshipper at the Garrison Church having donated money for improvements and adornments. Money which I fear originally came from the French.'

The Rev. Weston coughed and then almost apologetically said

'If I may make so bold sir, he was also a man of business in the town so the money may not be so tainted as you fear.'

'Thank you my dear sir, a consoling comment from the Church is always a blessing. Indeed while we speak, may I say how welcome you are to our assembly. I have not had the pleasure of meeting you socially before and Mr. Peachey has remarked how much of an assistance you have been to him.'

'I don't feel as though my efforts have been particularly praiseworthy sir, in fact I am indebted to both Mr. Peachey and Mr. Trevelyan for their assistance towards me.'

'It was on the matter of assistance that I wished to speak sir. With the events unfolding at this moment in time, we should all remain united. By that I mean that observation and listening can play a very important role in safeguarding the town from similar threats to that encountered at *Blockhouse*.'

Weston hung on every word as the Governor continued

'If you would care to pass back any event, no matter how small sir, I would be most grateful. I have a duty to unearth and smoke out agents and traitors to the cause.'

The Rev. Weston looked somewhat embarrassed,

'I would be happy to do so sir, providing it did not conflict with my calling.'

'Naturally sir. That goes without saying. You have a unique position in society here and come in contact with the widest range of citizens. Believe me sir, we have not smoked all of them yet. I have a mind that there are other agents and traitors within our midst that are working against us. France is not the only enemy we have to face, isn't that so Captain?'

Captain Younghusband nodded, sipped his Port, and looked around the table as though weighing up the reliability of those present, before he said.

'We have intercepted Spanish ships supplying goods and provisions to the rebels in the thirteen colonies. They are working against our interest and I believe that they will show their hand shortly and declare was against us. It is my contention that France and Spain will join together to wage an opportune war. I don't know if London thinks differently to that Mr. Peachey, but by putting two and two together, that is what it looks like to me.'

Peachey nodded his head, and thought, *for all his drink, the captain's reasoning was still sound.* He said

'I believe that to be a good assessment sir.'

Turning to the Governor, Peachey continued

'You have knowledge of other traitors here then sir?'

'I have Mr. Peachey, but establishing the fact is not easy. There is one man, a Scot, who works in the Paymaster's office that I have serious reservations about. That is why any information from whatever source is always useful.'

The Governor, on finishing talking, looked to Rev. Weston as if to make a conclusive point about receiving discreet information. A short lull in the conversation followed, broken when Trevelyan said

'It would seem to me that spies and agents can operate within the same town and be completely unaware of each other - it must depend on who is the paymaster.'

'Quite so Mr. Trevelyan.' The Governor studied his glass as he continued

'Faulkner was an old agent; in fact he was a residue from *Le Secret du Roi*. Louis XV had a labyrinth of such agents, but I don't think it's that active now. I doubt that Faulkner knew about other agents employed by members of the present court of Louis XVI.'

'Or of Spain' added Captain Younghusband.

'Quite so, quite so' murmured the Governor. Rev. Weston then rose from the table.

'Governor, as I explained earlier I have to make my apologies and leave as I have the Bishop coming and we need to be prepared accordingly. I will be pleased to provide any assistance I can to protecting the town from conspirators. I must confess that I didn't realise that the possibility was so widespread, I shall certainly be more vigilant in future.'

The Governor said

'Capital sir, capital. I am indebted to you. We were delighted you could attend and look forward to seeing you more often.'

Weston looked round the table,

'Gentlemen' he said, and to nods and acknowledgements, he took his leave. The men were now reduced to five. After affecting a generous refill of his glass Captain Younghusband said to the Governor

'A useful addition to your informers sir'

'Advisors sir, advisors,' the Governor replied, feigning to correct him, but aware that no one was fooled by the euphemism. Maintaining a slight grin, the Governor added

'It's good that I shall have knowledge from that quarter in future. St Thomas' Church will see more than the troops and selected few that attend the Garrison Church.'

Peachey remarked

'Two places of worship within such a very short distance is unusual sir. The Garrison Church must play second fiddle to the much larger St. Thomas'.

'I would hardly say second fiddle' broke in Major Salter. 'It was good enough for King Charles II to be married in.'

Peachey looked at Salter

'Really sir, I take it you mean when he married the then Catherine de Braganza. Why the Garrison Church? Was it because of the military connection?'

The Governor rejoined the conversation,

'Hardly. It was for two reasons. Firstly because this house and the Garrison Church are one unit and the combination was convenient and secondly, he wanted to keep dry and have a church that had a roof over its head.'

Looking at the puzzled Peachey to his last remark he continued

'Imagine Oliver Cromwell's men being across the water at Gosport.

'Cromwell?'

The Governor nodded.

'Yes. Back in the middle of the last century, Cromwell was attempting to gain full control of the country, Portsmouth, being Royalist, was defending itself, and very effectively I might add.'

'A difficult task for Cromwell I should think.'

'Indeed.' Said the Governor. 'The advantage Portsmouth had was the spire and tower in St. Thomas' church. It formed a masterly observation position to direct fire and deployment against the attackers outside the walls. The Roundheads, tired of this advantage fired at the church and in so doing demolished much of the roof.'

'It was still not repaired for the King's wedding then?' said Peachey.

'Indeed' said the Governor 'it was a long, long time before it was made good again.'

'The Garrison Church is still small for a Royal wedding though' said Peachey.

'It was a simple ceremony in 1662 with few in attendance. The King met his bride to be at the Sally Port when she arrived and they had a civil and church wedding both in the Garrison church and in here.'

He waved his arm around to indicate they were currently in the same room as Charles II had occupied. He continued

'The Garrison Church and house was plenty big enough for his purposes. Documents from the time are still held in the church.'

'An interesting fact' said Peachey. The Governor reached in his pocket and withdrew a small black snuffbox. Tapping it first he offered it around the table, but there were no takers. The sight of the snuffbox prompted Peachey to remark

'The French snuffbox we acquired from those two agents is still not giving up its secret.'

'That's not for the want of perseverance' added Trevelyan.

'From what you told me Mr. Peachey' said the Governor, 'the link or key that you seek seems to be a lost cause now that Faulkner is dead. I would imagine it was simply a means to an introduction.'

'I am rather thinking that myself now sir' replied Peachey. 'A strange means of introduction nevertheless.' Looking around as though assessing if the wine consumption was nearing an end, the Governor said

'Perhaps we should rejoin the ladies soon.'

He whispered in Trevelyan's ear

'I imagine you feature prominently in their conversation.'

Trevelyan glanced around

'One senses ones destiny is being forged. However, it is to my liking, as is my fondness for your Ward sir. That probably counts for much with them.'

'One must wait and see how matters develop over time sir.' The Governor intended to proceed at a modest pace only with his Ward's future, particularly where her opinions veered from one extreme to the other with respect to the gentleman at his side. However he was much impressed with this young man. He had easy conversation, wit and had acquitted himself well over the past few days, albeit that he had modestly played that aspect down.

Peachey remarked

'Governor, this is an interesting house, I imagine it was been built a some while ago.'

The Governor looked around him as though he had not really noticed the house as such before.

'A good residence certainly sir, but not originally designed as such. It was a secular building that was converted to Government House. The origin of the site dates back to 1212 when Peter de Rupibus the Crusader Bishop of Winchester, founded it all.'

Eyes swivelled around the room, following the Governor's story. He rose and selected a framed map behind him.

'See here' pointing to the layout, 'what is now the Garrison Church was originally a Hospice to shelter and aid pilgrims from overseas bound for the Holy Shrines at Canterbury, Chichester and Winchester. The chapel was at one end and the sick and homeless were tended by the Brethren and Sisters. After Henry VIII later destroyed the monasteries and Rectories it became an armoury.'

His finger traced out the area.

'The house and church was subsequently converted from one of the secular buildings.'

Peachy stared at his pointing finger. The Governor noticing his interest said

'That is the actual name of the Garrison Church sir. Of course everybody calls it the Garrison Church but its correct name is - *Domus Dei.*

Chapter 27

The appearance of *Domus Dei* took on a new slant as Peachey, Trevelyan and the trailing Fairweather approached it on a bright if somewhat sharp, crisp morning. Peachey had studied the snuffbox with renewed vigour but nothing the Governor had told them the previous evening made him any the wiser or closer to his quest. Looking at the Garrison Church, or perhaps now calling it by its correct name of *Domus Dei*, his heart hardly rejoiced.

There was nothing to say that the name was related to the snuffbox, but nevertheless there was an air of expectancy.

A Sergeant and a bent figure in black stood by the doorway awaiting their arrival. The Verger, being the doubled figure in black, stepped forward as they approached.

'Good morning gentlemen. I am the Verger and am at your service.'

'Sir' replied Peachey.

'If you would care to inform what you would like to see I shall take you there at once.'

Trevelyan, looking into the man's leathery face said

'You have books and documents relating to the history of *Domus Dei*?'

The verger looked a little puzzled.

'There are some sir.'

'I think we are interested in them to start with. Perhaps you will guide us to where they are stored?'

'What we have sir is in the side room to the chancel. If you follow me we'll go there.'

The sergeant stepped back and kept a respectful distance behind them. His task was simply to be in attendance. Fairweather walked alongside him as the Verger and gentlemen passed through the porch into the long nave. It was an austere church, plain, functional, housing regimented rows of pews for the troops and more elaborate versions at the front for officers and dignitaries. To the right in the corner, was a sturdy font with a delicate carved canopy above.

The canopy was an outstanding piece of work, no doubt bequeathed to the church. It was superior to the standard pews, pulpit and even the lectern that stood like a sentinel like facing down the nave. As they approached the lectern Trevelyan said to Peachey

'Before we examine the books, I suggest we examine the bible. We reasoned that had relevance when we searched in St. Thomas'.

'The bible sir?'

The old man looked up, his body still maintaining a bent posture such that he appeared to be about to fall over. The lectern holding a large edition of the Bible stood alone, seemingly fortified by the power of the word that lay within the pages of its prize. The Verger led Peachey and Trevelyan up the short flight of steps to it. Fairweather remained in the background talking casually with the Sergeant.

The Bible was a magnificent edition. Large, heavily bound with leaves edged with gold, illustrated at the beginning of each chapter by crafted and brightly coloured religious drawings. It lay open at the reading from the last service, its position designated by a thick gold tasselled bookmark. Peachey lifted the two halves of the Bible and closed it, noting how heavy it was to move and adjust. The Verger said,

'This has been here for many a year, I think sometime just after King Charles II was married here.'

'It looks a valuable work' admitted Peachey opening the front cover and examining the inside leaf. There were numerous handwritten inscriptions – made by different hands, with different inks and at different time spans. Nothing was particularly different until halfway down the page he stopped.

A longer insertion proclaimed:

For the redemption
That lies within Domus Dei.
Behold the first of the symbol
And with the key and thrice key
Let it lead you to blessing and reward
To find the true faith.

It was signed with an undecipherable scrawl and dated *September 1747.*

Trevelyan peering over Peachey's shoulder was the first to break the silence.

'It mentions *Domus Dei* and a key' he whispered excitedly. 'That surely must have something to do with the picture on the snuffbox.'

'Well it's a start' replied a thoughtful Peachey.

'What's special about 1747?'

'Nothing in particular springs to mind. However it was shortly after 1745 and the Second Jacobite Rebellion.'

'The redemption that lies within *Domus Dei*? That could possible means something for the person to redeem within *Domus Dei*.'

Peachey nodded

'I certainly don't feel its anything to do with spiritual redemption, but establishing what is the problem. The picture is riddled with symbols I fear, which one is the first?'

'I believe the first to be the crown. The others are keys and a bible.'

'Yes but there's only one. How can it be the first? There must be more than one to be the first.' Trevelyan remained silent for a moment studying the picture on the snuffbox, then said

'Let us consider it another way, what is the symbol?'

'If you are right then it's the crown.'

'Ah but what does the symbol represent?'

'Well a crown represent a ruler, a sovereign, something in the form of a headpiece, it could be many things.'

'Agreed but who would wear a crown?'

Peachey shrugged his shoulders

'A king, a queen, a prince, anyone in royalty.'

'I have a mind that it means a king only. Look at the crown's shape. It is a full crown. A queen's is smaller as is a prince or princess. This is a kings.' Peachey studied the picture again for a full minute.

'You might be correct but what on earth does a king' crown represent?'

'You have just said it ' replied a triumphant Trevelyan 'Kings! Look at the transcription, it says behold the first of the symbol. Replace symbol with Kings and it reads - '

'- first of the Kings' finished Peachey. 'It has a certain logic to it, but what are we supposed to behold with the first of the kings.'

'It may possibly relate to the Stuarts, it says the first of the Kings – it would be James I of England, who was also James VI of Scotland.' Peachey deliberated again for a minute or so.

'1747 has little to do with James I. He reigned well over 100 years before'

'Why would it be need to be 1747, that's only when this was signed.'

'True, it could well be that the date is immaterial,' Peachey admitted 'but the 1745 Rebellion was part funded by the French. I agree though, it has nothing to do with King James I other than he was a Jacobite King. Trevelyan studied the inscription again.

'How would this relate to the 1745 Rebellion? It's a long way South from Scotland.'

'Ah remember they worked their way deep into England. They were around Derby before they broke up and retreated. Had they continued, with the support they were collecting, the chances were high that they would have succeeded. I believe many carried on and moved further South, even to settle here. There was nothing left for them in Scotland.'

Trevelyan nodded.

'Perhaps that's the cause that is mentioned here. It could be the restoration of the Jacobites and King James I is involved in this conundrum. But I have no idea how' he added.

'A clear possibility that. Faulkner was with *Le Secret du Roi* set up by Louis XV, who being Catholic would naturally have supported the Young Pretender in 1745, not only for the faith but also for the defeat of the British.'

They both paused to dwell on that before Peachey continued

'The problem being, Faulkner arrived in Portsmouth well after 1747. That being so, he wouldn't have been able to locate the money without the key - and the key was the snuffbox.'

Each man wrestled with his own thoughts. Trevelyan said

'That might explain how it lay hidden for so long but on the other hand, first of the Kings could be King George I. He was the first of the Hanoverian kings and not even acknowledged as king by the Jacobites. They referred to him as the Elector of Hanover.'

'For that matter it could be the first of the Plantagenet or Norman Kings. The list is endless sir, we must determine a better start than this.'

'Wait! King Charles II was married here, he was the first King after Cromwell at the Restoration.'

Peachey paused then said,

'I grant you King Charles II has some relevance to *Domus Dei*, but I cannot for the life of me see how he can be the first of any Kings. A study of the documents here may be of further help but I fear we are clutching at straws.'

'I am inclined to agree, but I sometimes find if I say the first thing that comes into my head it can lead somewhere.'

'In the past it has lead you into an unhappy engagement with Elizabeth Attwick, so I am not of a mind to subscribe to that argument too much.'

'Ah quite so sir, quite so' acknowledged a humbled Trevelyan.

'We mustn't lose sight of the fact that *Domus Dei* is an important part of this and so is religion so - '

'- The three wise men!' interjected Trevelyan 'they must be the first of the Kings who came from the East and were led to the stable. It must relate to a building of some description so it could be a stable.'

'Why not three crowns then?' murmured Peachey.

'Apart from that minor point it fits doesn't it?'

Stepping back from the lectern, Peachey looked to the Verger who was patiently standing by, but had been out of earshot.

He was carefully studying the two gentlemen who had spent the last few minutes pouring over the inside cover of the Bible. He would have to set this right as soon as they were finished. An ill set Bible would not be tolerated in the Garrison Church. Peachey addressed him.

'Do you know where I would behold the first of the Kings sir?'

'Of course sir.' The answer was so readily given and with no sense of occasion that Peachey and Trevelyan both looked at each other. It was Trevelyan that cut in first

'Then pray be so good as to enlighten us sir.'

The Verger looked faintly surprised and puzzled but stepped up to the lectern. Moving the heavy Bible to one side, he opened it so that it was now spread evenly across the lectern. With a few deft flicks he said

'There we are sir – Kings I'

'Fool that I was' mumbled Peachey. 'The whole theme relates to *Domus Dei* and the bible and here we have been racking our brains when the most obvious solution lay before our eyes.'

'No doubt true sir. A very likely answer but it still leads us nowhere' responded Trevelyan. Peachey gently moved the Verger aside, placed the ornate bookmark to retain the place of Kings I and referred back to the inside cover.

'Assuming we are correct with the first Book of Kings, *the key and thrice key* must be the next line to decode.'

The Verger shrugged his shoulders, he had done as he was bided and turned up the First Book of Kings – *a fact that two well educated gentlemen should have been able to find themselves* he thought *but what else they were talking about he hadn't any clue at all.*

Peachey turned to Trevelyan

'do you recall when we originally studied the snuffbox you said that as there was no key in the box, perhaps the box was the key itself?'

'I do but am none the wiser.'

'You observed that there were six keys painted in the picture?' Trevelyan simply nodded, Peachey continued

'Then number six may be the key. Thrice the key is therefore eighteen. What is six and eighteen?'

'Twenty-four,' was Trevelyan's unhesitating reply, 'but think sir, we are referring to the Bible and the text. Surely it means six and eighteen – Chapter 6, verse eighteen.'

Peachey looked at Trevelyan with widening eyes.

'If correct it's so simple' he breathed.

'It is when you know;' replied a smiling Trevelyan and eagerly added, 'but pray turn up the verse sir.'

Peachey flipped back to the bookmark and hunted forwards to Chapter six. He ran his finger down to verse eighteen and quietly read out the following:

And the cedar of the house within was carved
with knops and open flowers: all was cedar;
there was no stone seen.

The two men looked at each other. The excitement in arriving at a possible solution was now squashed by the complete bafflement of the answer. Trevelyan read it again to himself; slowly forming his lips round each word as he did so. Looking back to Peachey he said

'Knops are knobs. Open flowers carved in cedar? Which wood is cedar here?'

Looking around Peachey could see a variety of woods but which was actually cedar escaped him. He called out

'Fairweather!'

A muffled 'sir' responded and the figure of his man detached himself from the company of the Sergeant. Continuing his internal inspection Peachey turned to Fairweather.

'Is there any cedar wood in here?' Fairweather glanced around

'I wouldn't expect to find much in here sir. Most of it will be oak.' He walked to the pulpit, having checked the lectern itself and moving between the pews ran his hand over the wood as he checked the texture, grain and colour. Shaking his head he moved back into the knave itself and looked around.

No sooner than we appear to be close to a solution it dissolves before our eyes.

There was frustration in Peachey's thoughts.

'There!'

Fairweather's voice rang out. At the back of the church he pointed across to the corner where the font stood. Fairweather's hand pointed to the canopy hanging motionless over the font. It was a lighter shade and enriched with intricate and fine carvings.

'That's cedar sir. Can't see any other though.'

Moving over to the font, all three looked at the carvings. They were darkened with age but still proudly exhibiting the craftsman's skills. Closer examination revealed carvings of several groups of open flowers. Their petals and buds surmounted long slender stems. Protruding slightly above the surface line of the flowers, were three highly carved knobs, or knops as the craftsmen called them.

'Fairweather, gently climb up on the font and see if you can see any stones carved amongst the flowers and knobs.'

Peachey glanced at the Verger whose horrified face indicated that the men the Governor had told him to assist must surely be totally mad. The font was sturdy, made from stone but nevertheless unaccustomed to men clambering up on it. He watched as Fairweather nimbly and gently balanced himself on the edge of the font whilst cautiously raising himself up alongside the canopy. All eyes watched as he ran his hands over the surface, pausing to check for anything that resembled a stone. He shook his head,

'Nothing like a stone at all sir.'

'Wait there' said Peachey and stood as though transfixed staring at the carvings. Finally he said

'Anything strange about the three knobs then?' Fairweather's hands traced the outline of the knops – nothing. Raising his good left hand he grasped the protrusions of each knop and twisted.

'What are you doing that for?' said Peachey.

'Sometimes these carvings are made separately and plugged into the body of the work. The flowers are all carved from the main wood but I don't think the knops are.'

'Ah!' the powerful grip of Fairweather's hand could be seen twisting the centre one from side to side with the turnings increasing with each turn. Suddenly with a pop, the centre pod came free in his hand.

'Is there anything behind or inside?'

Trevelyan's voice was verging on a forced whisper. Fairweather steadied his grip again and his fingers probed the exposed hole left by the knop.

'Its deep in here and………'

Fairweather broke off and slowly withdrew a cloth. It was wrapped around an object extending to about fourteen inches. He handed it down to Peachey, who in turn gently laid it on the floor. The cloth was heavy, and reluctant to unwrap having been left in the same position for many years. Peachey carefully unfolded the cloth to the left and right of the object until it was finally exposed – no one spoke.

A necklace of fine gold with delicate clasps holding deep red ruby stones first took the eye. Further examination showed other jewels gripped in secondary clusters further highlighting the main theme and its blood red glow. Trevelyan murmured

'There was no stone seen. Of course the knop was hiding the jewels or stones, so none were seen.'

'They've been undisturbed for years I'll warrant' said Peachey, 'it is an exquisite piece of work, I wouldn't know how to value it but it would fund many an uprising in the town if it had fallen into the wrong hands.'

'And would fund a return to the Jacobites and what they call the true faith' murmured Trevelyan completing the last line of the inscription. Looking back to Peachey he said

'So when the snuffbox was stolen, the men hadn't yet made use of it.'

'So it would seem. Faulkner almost certainly didn't know exactly where the stones were hidden and needed the snuffbox to tell him.'

'To think he had been coming into the Garrison Church all these years knowing that something was hidden here of tremendous value, must have driven him mad' smiled Trevelyan looking around him.

Peachey added

'Our sneak thief stole the box at the most opportune moment. Without it neither the men nor Faulkner could locate the stones. Our success centres around the simple fact of a chance robbing!'

'Such chances determine history' said Trevelyan.

'Ah, but we have still to catch the other man yet. Without him we cannot be sure the success of their mission was a total failure.'

'True, but without the funding, the important local support will be next to nothing'. Fairweather having replaced the knob back in the font had returned to ground level and stood at a respectful distance away. Turning to him Peachey remarked

'Your knowledge of woods was most useful Fairweather.'

'Happy to have been able to oblige sir' he returned.

The Verger had remained rooted to he spot whilst the revealing of the jewels had taken place, his face fixed in a gaze of stark amazement.

Peachey looked towards the totally bewildered man

'This item is the property of King George and must be taken to his majesty in London. I shall tell the Governor and will also tell him of the great service you provided in the location of the necklace.'

Pleasure of the relief of responsibility of having to explain the taking of the jewels and also of the tribute to his knowledge of the bible, immediately showed by the transformed expression in his face.

'I am pleased to have been of help sir, both to you and of course to the King.'

Images of the scenes in the inns and of his family flashed across the Verger's mind. Scenes where he was cast as a hero and of direct service to the King himself. He could hardly wait to spread the word. Peachey had anticipated the reaction and said

'You will not repeat anything of what you have just witnessed.'

The man's elation evaporated as Peachey continued

'There are enemies of the country who may come and try to locate the item. You must therefore be on your guard and watch for any strangers looking for what we have just found. If you see anyone acting suspiciously then you must inform the Duty Officer himself.'

The Verger simply nodded. Peachey eyed him to emphasise the command, then said

'I shall acquaint the Governor of the position so that a full alert will be maintained. The King himself will be made aware of the happenings here and we must thwart any attempt by our enemies.'

Of this Peachey was certain. It was a wonderful result to have released the snuffbox and bible's secrets, but whilst the other spies might still be at large, they may come searching. It was also prudent to flatter the old Verger in order to ensure this was done. Reaching in his pocket he removed some money that he pressed into the man's hand.

'Take this as a token of the King's appreciation, and remember nothing is to be said.'

Looking at his new found wealth the old man touched his forehead and in the manner of a conspirator said

'My lips are sealed sir.'

Peachey wasn't certain anyone would come, since they had no start point – no snuffbox to even locate *Domus Dei* unless they had been made aware of the fact earlier. Aware that Trevelyan was standing beside him Peachey said

'I have a mind to ask the Governor to keep these jewels and snuffbox in safekeeping and under guard. That way they will be safe, the Governor will be involved with the success which will please him, and as for you good sir, I'm sure it will further enhance you worthiness in his eyes.'

'A skilful move my dear Peachey – every inch a diplomat. As for my reputation I am grateful for all the assistance I can get.'

'In fairness sir, it was your deductions that pointed us in the right direction and enabled the secret to be unearthed.'

Trevelyan shrugged his shoulders in self-depreciation replying

'I am indebted to you for all you have done to help me, particularly against Gadfew – he would surely have killed me had it not been for your intervention.   However what now?'   Glancing around him Peachey replied

'I shall write to me uncle this very morning and get it on the afternoon coach. In fact I am expecting a reply from him regarding my last letter but I can now confirm his information was sound.'

Peachey consider his last remarks with a certain relish then added

'The Court must decide what to do about reinforcing the troop strength here and preparing for an attack.'

'A foregone conclusion I would think' said Trevelyan as they now approached the porch entrance of the church. Peachey shaking his head said

'Far from it. There will be a reluctance to acknowledge my uncle's success in certain quarters if I know the form. A jostling for position before the King, and an unwillingness to acknowledge another man's glory will overshadow all logic.'

'But your uncle was right all along.'

Trevelyan's face showed perplexity and astonishment in equal proportions.

'When did that count for anything at court?'

Breaking from the shelter of the porch Trevelyan involuntarily shivered – whether from the cold or dismayed astonishment was uncertain. They walked on in silence for a few moments, the Verger watching their retreat with a high degree of satisfaction as to his enhanced status and wealth. Breaking the silence Trevelyan said

'For my part I shall see what progress has been made to my own little plan.'

'Ah, the re-enacting of the Palamedes affair' smiled Peachey.

'We agreed it was an admirable solution did we not?'

'Oh indeed we did. It would produce a fitting conclusion to a troublesome affair' Peachey agreed.

'How certain are you that will work?'

'When we return I shall endeavour to establish our position whilst you write to your uncle. Let us meet again when both of us have finished.'

Peachey permitted himself a lean smile

'I await your finding with interest sir.'

Turning around to confront a trailing Fairweather he continued

'Fairweather, contact Major Salter with my compliments and see if there is any news regarding the agent who escaped from the fort.'

'Indeed, at once sir' replied the manservant turning on his heel and heading back towards the Guardhouse.

Peachey then headed to Government House to lodge his newly found prize with the Governor for safekeeping.

Trevelyan, pacing briskly back to *The George,* felt hopeful that the ruse he had set in motion had progressed. This would involve the *killing of two birds with one stone*: a most satisfactory outcome to a devilish problem.

Chapter 28

The aching in his leg had subsided. The food this morning had been welcomed. No-one touched it after it had been to the infectious diseases wards but was fed to the pigs it seemed. The men who were the most ill had no interest in it and there always seemed to be un-issued amounts down the passageway.

The first thing a soldier must do is to assess his position. He had the plans intact. He was still at liberty. Once clear from Portsmouth his chances of returning to France were good. There had been no alarms or searching troops over the last two days – only Courtney was a damper to the positive factors. The most pressing problem was how to get away from Haslar undetected.

Questions however rebounded and reverberated around in his head – the same questions spinning like a child's top, for which he had no answers.

Who had betrayed them?

Betrayed they must have been for all those soldiers to have suddenly appeared at Fort Blockhouse. The worst problem of all was that the suspects were so few.

Courtney was probably dead and had nothing to gain from such a deed. The old man Faulkner was also dead and had no time to tell or warn anyone. This was the greatest enigma.

For all the problems and setbacks he had encountered, the information that he had gleaned was vital for the planned attack.

Had Courtney put The Mistress in place before he was killed or taken?

Of that he couldn't be sure, but he felt in his heart that their carefully laid plan had probably been thwarted.

He stiffened as the storeroom door quietly open. Nell glided in and glanced around.

'That's the last of the bodies taken care of.'

'What have you done with them?'

'Gone to the Paddock sewn up in their hammocks.'
He remembered the Paddock area at the rear from when he surveyed the defences.
 For most it's a lingering death, but many survive.'
Turning she faced Rousseliere.
'That's what you're attempting to do isn't it – survive.'
Her eyes never left his face. A fearful dread spread over him.
She knows. Who else knows? Is escape thwarted?
She sat down opposite.
'You've no need to deny it. I've known all along that matters were not right.'
Rousseliere said nothing. His mind worked quickly. The longer he sat here allowing her to expand her suspicions the worse it was for him. She still continued
'You're trying to escape aren't you?'
He froze. Taking no notice of his silence she continued
'I suspected it from the start.'
He remained silent and she continued
'I only wish that my husband could also escape from his ship and return home where he belongs. I suppose you were pressed like him.'
She thinks I am wanting to get away from the navy!
He looked at her and said
'I have a mind to do that, that's true.'
Putting her hand on the door to ensure it was closed she continued
'Going out by the drain is out of the question. The shore is teeming with Marines. Something to do with *Blockhouse* they say. If you're determined, it will have to be today. I have to take things to Portsmouth and you could accompany me. It is known that I work in the infectious area and no one will bother us, they're too scared of catching a plague or fever.'
'What time do we leave?'
'As soon as I have collected them from the wards.'
He was grateful that she thought he was escaping from his ship and going home to his family.
'Be on your mettle then and be ready for when I return as I can't dally long.'
His voice was quiet but full of conviction.
'I shall be ready'.

This was the start of the return back to France - the most dangerous part.

Once clear of Portsmouth the danger decreased rapidly, with few to bother him and money to pave the way for a swift passage. That was something that Courtney hadn't seen – the money secured in a belt around his waist. It was his last line of defence. Instinctively feeling the slim belt for comfort, he watched as Nell left to attend to her duties. Avoiding any troops that may be looking for him would be eased considerably by her leading the way.

Placing the final items in his bag he moved to the door and listened. After a few moments, voices sounded down the passageway and he cautiously opened the door an inch at a time. A flurry and Nell appeared with a large bundle, large enough to hide behind and a small chequered flag pinned to the front.

A flag to drive fear into any inquisitive soldier he thought for it signified its source as being from the infectious section of the hospital.

Slipping out from the storeroom, he joined her taking the bundle from her. A faint eerie mouldering smell permeated its way from the bundle to his nostrils and he for the first time realised that he might be in danger of contracting some fever or pox from it.

There was no turning back. Lifting his face clear from contact with the bundle but ensuring it obscured his face from any interested party, they set off towards the small gate isolating the infectious wards from the main hospital.

Not a glance, no interest in them, nothing, from the few people passing who were heading about their duties. To them it was a common enough event. Obscured by the bundle he could only see one half of the road and only one set of buildings.

He was aware that they were retracing their steps to the main gate. The entrance was manned with marines with nothing better to do than observe those passing through the gate and to examine wares and bags as the fit took them.

Nell was slightly ahead and called out something he couldn't quite hear to the marines at the gate. They stood in front of her with broad lecherous grins. A glance at the bundle Rousseliere was carrying was enough: they stepped back and resumed their interest in Nell.

He resisted the urge to move quickly and found himself sweating as he moved further away from the gate but seemed to make very little distance. It was like a bad dream where running away from danger had one running on the spot.

Without Nell he had to slow. Turning to look back she was coming at a modest pace with one of the soldiers watching her deliberate swinging gait. As she reached him he moved forward again and they headed down towards the bridge leading across to Gosport again.

The bundle acted like a talisman. Those who knew kept their distance and others followed their example. There were three boatmen plying for hire at the Hard. Rousseliere's money was a sufficient inducement for a passage across the water but he had to sit at the back of the cutter furthest from the oarsmen.

Looking at *Fort Blockhouse*, its imposing and solid presence reminded him of its function and deadly secret that lay behind the dull grey walls. The next time a Frenchman would see those walls was when they were sailing towards them and blasting their way into the harbour.

Hopefully the soldiers who were to land further along the coast towards Southampton would have done their task and neutralised the deathly power the fort possessed by coming overland and overrunning the Gosport Lines. They would offer little or no resistance to the advancing French force as his surveys had shown. A redeeming feature to the plan.

The bumping of the craft landing at the Hard pier broke his reverie. The weather beaten hand, curled bent from years of rowing across the harbour, accepted his money without comment.

He and Nell stepped ashore and walked up the slope to the road in awkward silence. He had decided that he would be walking to the top end of the island. It was only about 5 miles and the road ran alongside the western waterway straight up to Hilsea, where he had first examined the defences when he arrived.

He smiled to himself as he remembered the scant defence that was in place at Hilsea – that information alone was worth the trip.

Nell was the first to speak

'You take care of yourself, do you hear? Get back to your family and keep away from the pressgangs.'

Rousseliere smiled at her.

'I hope your husband returns safely to you and soon enough Nell. If he has had half the luck I have, he will be alright.'

'Amen to that' she whispered. 'God speed.'

With that she picked up the load and walked on.

A strange farewell but no point in dwelling on that, danger is all around.

He looked to the right and the road that led to the trek to Hilsea.

The first pace told him he was taking the first step towards France.

Would he be returning here? Would next time see him dressed in a French Army's Officer's uniform guiding troops towards the targets he had surveyed during his time here?

Slinging the bag over his shoulder he set up a steady pace towards Hilsea.

As his footsteps landed on the road in a regular beat, so a matching step of a line of soldiers beat out a similar sound, as if in unison, in Portsmouth. The soldiers, commanded by the young officer, knew exactly where they were going and whom they had to arrest. That information had come from a source that was totally reliable. They strode purposefully on knowing their target being unaware of their arrival.

Chapter 29

Fairweather was returning to *The George* after seeing his contact. He was aware Henry Peachey had retired to his rooms after arriving back from the Garrison Church to compose a letter to his uncle. This missive Fairweather knew he must get on the afternoon coach to London.

Moving towards the bottom of *King Charles Street*, a line of soldiers approached on the other side of the street. The newly appointed officer was leading with a fixed expression of intent, denoting the seriousness of his duty.

At the rear of five soldiers came the sergeant, a man now known to Fairweather. He was one of the sergeants who had entertained him in their mess at the time Peachey and Trevelyan were being dined by the officers celebrating the outcome of Trevelyan's duel with Gadfew.

The officer, sword in hand, had eyes staring straight ahead; the sergeant however, on catching sight of Fairweather nodded in the direction they were going to indicate that he should follow them. Fairweather stopped, crossed the road, and followed as intimated, although why, he failed to fathom. They continued straight up *St. Thomas's Street*.

The purposeful tread was called to a halt outside a familiar house. He watched as they broke ranks, the officer marching to the front door and unceremoniously banging on it. The troops gathered behind him with the sergeant remaining outside.

When the door opened, the officer forcefully called out

'We have come to search the house in the King's name!'

With no further ado, he barged past the person holding the door open, with three of the soldiers hard on his heels. As they stormed in Fairweather sidled up to the sergeant who produced a broad smile.

'We are about to arrest a French spy' he said with some measure of pride.

'Is it the one who escaped from *Fort Blockhouse?*'

'Nah, this one is a traitor who lives here. I thought you ought to know so you can tell your gentleman Mr. Peachey that we have caught one on our own.'

Fairweather detected a very slight resentment that all the success to date had been through Peachey. This one apparently was not, hence the somewhat smugness of the sergeant's remarks. Sounds of raised voices filtered through onto the street accompanied by banging and a clumping of feet up the stairs. The sergeant said

'Come with me, see the fun, so that you can tell your master what happened.'

They walked to the door, still flung wide open. Fairweather peered inside.

'Whose house is it?' he enquired.

'Mr. Porter, a local businessman and victualer.'

'Ah, we know him' said Fairweather.

'You know him?' The sergeant's voice expressed both disbelief and amazement.

'Yes Mr. Peachey has spoken with him and it was through him that he was mistakenly attacked.'

'Well, we're going to arrest him' said the sergeant attempting to reclaim an element of credit.

Porter's raised voice was plainly heard from the first floor

'This is preposterous, I am no spy. You are clearly in error sir and will regret this. I shall report you to the highest authority.'

'Then perhaps you would care to explain this!'

Waving a letter complete with broken seal in front of him the officer called out

'Sergeant, come and witness this letter which was found in Mr. Porter's chest.'

The sergeant nimbly doubled up the stairs to do as ordered. Fairweather decided to climb the stairs as well, but in his case, slowly and unobtrusively. Porter, full of arrogance said

'Anything in that chest concerns my business dealings and have no concern of yours. Let me see that letter.'

Still retaining a firm grip of the letter the officer held it up for Porter to read. Porter's reddish face changed colour like a chameleon to resemble the whiteness of the paper.

'This is a lie, its nothing to do with me, you cannot possibly have found it there!'

Stepping back the officer said

'Sergeant have your men arrest this man in the name of King George, on a charge of treason. This letter states that the bearer is a French agent and it is sealed with the Great Seal from Versailles.'

'Two men there!'

The sergeant barked out the order and two soldiers on the landing smartly moved either side of the flabbergasted Porter. Grabbing his arms they propelled him forwards and down the stairs. Porter shouted at the top of his voice

'I'm not a traitor.'

'Tell that to the jury' murmured the officer.

Watching them descend the officer made to follow when the sergeant said

'Begging your pardon sir, this is Mr. Peachey's man. I have told him that we were arresting a traitor ourselves here. If you would show him the letter he can report back to Mr. Peachey and tell him what we have discovered.'

Sensing the advantage of such a move the officer re-opened the letter and held it up for Fairweather to view. It was similar to the one they had found in the secret drawer of Faulkner's desk. A large seal was adhered to the back, the writing in French looked similar as before. The officer said

'It is a letter stating that the holder is a French Agent.'

Fairweather stopped in amazement.

The letter was identical in every respect to the one that Faulkner had in the secret compartment of his desk. In fact he felt it was the same letter!

How could it be? Glancing at both of them he said

'Damming proof sir. I'm sure Mr. Peachey and his uncle will be most impressed with the capture of another agent.'

The officer and the sergeant exchanged glances of mutual satisfaction.

'We shall be taking him at once' said the officer folding up the letter and carefully placing it inside his tunic.

'Was there anything else sir' enquired Fairweather looking at the opened drawers of the chest?'

'Only this depravity' said the officer indicating a series of drawings laying scattered on the floor.

The subject of the crude drawings reproduced the image of Bishop in Fairweather's mind, recounting the story of what Porter had done to his own daughter before killing her.

Fairweather followed them downstairs. Something was nagging him. Something very strange was happening here. Mr. Peachey would no doubt clarify the matter quickly but what needed resolving had first to be established. The soldiers filed out the front door with a still protesting Porter. Sensing someone else standing in the room he saw an old stooping man, pen still in his hand as though having been disturbed from his clerical work.

'You are in the employ of Mr. Porter?' Fairweather queried. The man nodded.

'I am - or I was it seems. Last week both Mr. Faulkner and Mr. Porter employed me but now Mr. Faulkner is dead and now Mr. Porter has been arrested as a traitor. I never suspected either.'

'You're not one of them eh?' The old man looked horrified

'I'm an old man eking out my days. I had no idea I swear to you, I just keep the books. Now it looks as though I have no employer any more.'

'I believe you ' said Fairweather 'but perhaps you need to show your co-operation.'

'Of course sir, anything.'

Walking towards the bookkeeper Fairweather gently manoeuvred him back into his room. Ledgers were open on a standing desk with a sturdy tin box on a small shelf below. Glancing at the ledger's neat columns dutifully recording transactions, Fairweather ran his fingers idly down a column.

'You make the payments for Mr. Porter then?'

'When he tells me too' said the old man, watching with curiosity as Fairweather examined his books.

'You haven't paid the widow of the cooper who supplied fifty barrels to him.'

Fairweather's tone had a certain sharpness to it, a fact that wasn't lost on the bookkeeper.

'He told me not to pay' said the man, a querulous waver in his response.

'Why not? The barrels were delivered on time, were sound and fairly priced.'

'He just said I was not to pay sir. I cannot pay anything without his approval.'

'Maybe you are involved'

'Sir, I beg you; I am as true to the King as anyone. I fought for his father. I am not a spy.'

'Then you must prove your worth then.'

'How?'

'That payment needs to be settled to the widow. Porter will not be coming back if I am any judge of things. Find the bill, add a percentage for the delay and her trouble and send the money round this instant. Her late husband supplied the barrels for the use in the Royal Navy, anyone who fails to settle cannot be true to the King and the country.'

Realisation began to dawn on the bookkeeper.

'Are you sure he will not return?'

'French spies or agent will dangle at the end of a rope. Settle now and I will report to my master that you are a true man to the King.'

The man opened the desktop and rummaged around for a moment before bringing out a piece of paper.

'Here it is: the bill for fifty barrels. What percentage do I add?'

'A good ten percent seems a fair figure.'

The old man swallowed hard but said nothing. With great care he entered the transaction in the book. Fairweather looked over the man's shoulder.

'Good, now see to it that the money is sent round this instant.'

'Indeed sir; at once. You will inform your master of my loyalty?'

'Rest assured, I will present a glowing report for you. You will not be troubled by accusations about working for the French.'

'I am in your debt sir. I am much obliged.'

The man's wizened face showed relief all over it, although Fairweather had never actually doubted the man. To see that the widow received her dues from the scheming Porter was pleasure indeed though. He would inform Mr. Peachey as soon as he returned to *The George*.

'I am away to see to my gentleman. Make sure that payment is made without delay.'

'It will be delivered by my own hand sir, this very instant.'

Fairweather nodded and headed for the door, not doubting for a moment that that would be exactly what would happen.

The soldiers escorting Porter had moved out of sight down the road. Fairweather followed their route, but only as far as the *High Street*: his destination being *The George* rather than the Guardhouse. He needed to inform Mr. Peachey quickly of this unexpected development. A development that had a very satisfactory conclusion but there was something very peculiar about all this.

Faulkner was an agent, of that there was no doubt, but the story that had previously emerged about Porter, was that he was blackmailing Faulkner because he was a French agent. This couldn't possibly be true if Porter was an agent himself.

Another thing, that letter was identical to the one in Faulkner's possession, so much so that it could have been the same one! If so, how had it found its way into Porter's desk on the first floor of his house?

The towering presence of St Thomas' Church on his right reminded him of the other strange item of news he had received that morning. The reasons behind these happenings did not make sense. Crossing the High Street to *The George* he was passing round the back when the tall, unmistakeable frame of Percy Trevelyan appeared in the front entrance, cloak slung over one arm and all set to venture out. Seeing Fairweather he called out

'Fairweather'

'Yes Mr. Trevelyan sir'

'What news is there?'

'I was just on my way to see Mr. Peachey this second sir. They have arrested Mr. Porter, the man who killed Bishop's daughter. Not for murder but as a French agent. They found a letter identical to that found in Mr. Faulkner's desk.'

Fairweather waited for an expression of amazement but was surprised that none came.

'Really' said Trevelyan 'that certainly solves a few problems.'

Fairweather was nonplussed. Seeing him floundering, Trevelyan said

'You seem a trifle taken aback by the fact Fairweather.'

'Yes sir, but begging your pardon, it makes no sense.'

Trevelyan paused in the doorway for a moment then said

'Events that should occur sometimes require a little assistance. Do you follow my meaning?'

'Only in a manner sir.'

'Porter is a murderer. You know of one murder, that of Bishop's daughter. I have made sounding myself and there are others. There have been other young girls that have died in the same manner, all at the hands of Porter. You heard me mention the name Palamedes the other day?'

'I was not sure of the name sir'

It is a Greek name, Pal – er – me – dees. He was a Grecians Chief's son sent to force Ulysses to join an expedition to Troy and fight. Ulysses didn't want to go and leave his wife Penelope, so he pretended he was mad. Palamedes unmasked him by putting Ulysses' young son in front of a plough in a field, which would have killed the boy, had Ulysses not at the final moment, confessed to the sham.'

Fairweather listened intently wondering where this was all going, as Trevelyan continued

'Ulysses swore revenge and later forged a letter from the King of Priam, addresses to Palamedes to thank him for becoming a traitor and intending to deliver the Greek army into Trojan hands.'

'I think I am beginning to see the story sir' said Fairweather.

'I think you are too Fairweather. Well to seal the matter, Ulysses had some money concealed in Palamedes' tent as though payment for this traitorous act. It was arranged for this and the letter to be discovered. Palamedes was convicted and stoned to death.'

'A certain end sir'

'Indeed Fairweather.'

'Hence the letter from France appearing in Mr. Porter's chest sir.'

'That might well be the case, particularly if there happens to be at hand a young boy at the Point who is able to climb like a monkey.'

'Up to the first floor of a house with a letter' added Fairweather.

'Yes, I can see you are getting the hang of it Fairweather.'

'So someone arranged all this then sir?'

'Arranged it? Possibly Fairweather but I'm dashed if I know who.'

'Of course not sir - it was only a story anyhow.'

'Precisely Fairweather.'

Fairweather couldn't hide his smile as Trevelyan threw his cloak around his shoulders with an air of innocence that would have convinced the Pope said

'I will let you away to see Mr. Peachey Fairweather. I myself am off to see Miss Sophia Gifford. Kindly mention the fact to Mr. Peachey when you see him.'

'I will indeed sir.'

With a movement of a sapling blowing in the wind, Trevelyan was gone. Fairweather glanced after him then continued round the back in order to make his way to Peachey's room.

The story about that Greek fellow answers many questions. Regarding Porter, can justice be contrived?.

Chapter 30

The Governor's House was scarcely the place for peace and tranquillity. The Governor's head ached and he was beset with problems, none of which he felt were attributable to him. In response to a tap the door, he bellowed

'Come!'

The opening door presented the figure of his Housekeeper. She was the picture of a harassed individual who had just been summoned to the Governor's presence. Wisps of hair hung over her flushed face, under a cap quickly clamped on her head after receiving the summons. With curtsy or bob she said

'You sent for me sir'

'I did indeed Mrs. Pleasants. We appear to be surrounded by calamities and misfortune of the highest order.'

'I think I know what you mean sir, but we are trying our best to accommodate things.'

'Hmm. Miss Sophia has just left me in a state of abject anxiety informing me that matters could not be any worse.'

'Begging your pardon sir but she is overwrought due to the present situation, is there anything that I can do for you?'

'There is indeed Mrs. Pleasants. Overwrought Miss Sophia may be, but the current problem she informs me, is the biggest that has ever befallen mankind.'

Mrs. Pleasants sighed as though anticipating that another problem was to be thrust her way, her head was spinning with the comings and goings but she replied

'Is it a problem that I can be of some assistance with sir?'

The Governor's frown only worsened his aching head, with an exasperated tone said

'Miss Sophia advises me that there is no ribbon to be had in Portsmouth to match her dress!'

Mrs. Pleasants took in the current picture of the Governor. Over the past few weeks she had seen him firm and calm whilst working long hours under the threat of attack to the town. His voice was

always steady with clear unequivocal commands being issued, generating the reassurance that everyone in the town sought.

He was now like a fish out of water. Miss Sophia's forthcoming engagement to Mr. Trevelyan threw up challenges he was completely unused to. For all her own difficulties in ensuring that the dinning and accommodation ran smoothly for the Governor, she permitted herself a small smile.

'It's a trying time for Miss Sophia sir, she wants everything perfect for the engagement and for you in particular.'

'Me?'

'Of course sir. Begging your pardon again sir, I know its not for me to comment but she thinks the world of you and doesn't want anything amiss to let you down.'

'But surely it's Mr. Trevelyan that should be the focus. I myself saw him two days ago who was quite unfazed by the whole thing.'

'This is the time sir when Miss Sophia misses not having a mother, begging your pardon sir. It is the time of her life when all she thinks about is her future wedding day and all the details. She will worry about the small things that matter to her.'

Mrs Pleasants brushed back another wisp of hair as she moved on to the next problem.

'Now as for the ribbon, I saw Miss Louise this morning who has arranged for the exact match to be delivered today. I would respectfully suggest sir that a kindly listening ear is all that Miss Sophia requires from you. I feel sure that Miss Louise will cope very well.'

Placing his fingers to his temples, the Governor eased the throbbing with small circular motions. His features gradually changed, with a humorous smile just in evidence.'

'Thank you Mrs. Pleasants, you are without doubt a balm to a troubled soul.'

She curtsied and left to attend to her mounting tasks.

Pouring himself a glass of port, the Governor sat down to await his visitors and reflected how Percy Trevelyan had asked for his permission to marry Sophia.

The man usually appeared in a relaxed, almost languid manner, but on this occasion was taut, earnest and apprehensive. After some enquiries to his family's and own personal finances for support to his Ward, he had run out of questions. He remembered then saying nothing, rising to pour two glasses of brandy, giving one to Trevelyan and saying

'My full blessing and my own relief. Let us drink to both.'

Trevelyan was instantly transformed back to his usual self, accompanied by a beaming smile. He shifted from one foot to the other as though he were anxious to get away and tell the world.

Over the last few weeks, The Governor had developed a liking for this intelligent and capable man with a sharp ready wit, although many of his capabilities appeared deceptive.

He now awaited both Trevelyan and Peachey.

The door tapped to admit the new young officer assigned to his staff.

'Excuse me sir but Mr. Peachey and Mr. Trevelyan have arrived and wish to know if you are home to them?'

'Of course, of course, show them in.'

'In here sir?'

'In here of course, we can shelter in here without interruptions regarding receptions.'

'Very good sir.'

Trevelyan accompanied by Peachey, who had recently arrived back in Portsmouth from London, entered in apparently good spirits.

'Gentlemen, it is good to see you.'

'Good day to you sir, I hope we find you well?'

'Subject to engagements, plagues and pestilence, I am surviving and expect to survive until Mr. Trevelyan eventually adopts certain domestic responsibilities from me I trust.'

'I shall be honoured to do so' smiled Trevelyan.

Waving his hand in the direction of the port, the Governor said

'Pray refresh yourselves gentlemen. We shall not be disturbed in here. I am anxious to hear the latest news Peachey.'

Trevelyan poured three generous glasses of port, handing one each to Peachey and the Governor. Peachey raised his glass and said

'A toast gentlemen, to successfully defeating our enemies in their attempts at *Fort Blockhouse*, and the foiling the local Frenchies in their quest for funding local support.'

Three glasses were raised and satisfying toasts taken to cement the proposal.

The Governor leant forward,

'So the threat has passed eh Peachey.?' but looking from one to the other continued 'but what of this other agent, the one with the one we killed.'

Peachey's face developed a frown

'We fear he has escaped. How is beyond us. It is suspected that somehow he obtained help from local support that we are not aware of.'

The Governor sipped his port and contemplated these thoughts.

'Vigilance is the watchword. We would be foolish to think that we have a handle on all the local support. There are others we have yet to smoke out I'll be sure.'

Peachey looked from one to the other

'Unfortunately the threat has only been thwarted locally I fear. The main threat from the French and Spanish Armada working with their combined armies still remain. Even now the King has little time for the plan leaving the solution to Lord Sandwich to repel all with the Channel Fleet.'

Two sombre faces looked at him as he continued

'The Royal Navy is in some disarray with the command of the Channel Fleet in question. It would seem Lord Sandwich has much to answer for. But we continue to put our trust in the navy to protect us.'

There was a long pause as each digested this information. Peachey broke the silence to move to brighter topics.

'Of other local issues then Governor, other than the forthcoming engagement of the year, what else has been happening in Portsmouth?'

'Umm, not a lot – oh that fellow Porter, the French spy that you caught, yes well he is to be hung.'

Peachey and Trevelyan exchanged quick looks. Peachey casually replied

'A satisfying outcome and a very deserved one.'

'Quite so, quite so' murmured the Governor.

Trevelyan said

'Well I think that we can look forward to some pleasanter times in future.'

'Now that's worth drinking to' said Peachey and the three glasses were drained to emphasise the point.

The Governor relaxed back into his chair. This was the best he had felt all day. He looked from one to the other.

'A final point Mr. Peachey. The necklace that I safeguarded prior to your taking it to London, was it well received?'

Peachey appeared to adopt a self-satisfied look

'Indeed sir, I was just coming to that. Warm thanks indeed for preventing its use as funding for local insurgents.'

He paused for a moment as both sets of eyes held his.

'The best, and I trust most rewarding of all, is that it has been deemed to treat it the same way as prize money.'

'Prize money?'

Trevelyan's frown showed a degree of puzzlement. Peachey said

'The same procedure as for captured ships sir. The item will be disposed of for the best possible figure and the proceeds divided amongst those involved on a ranking basis.'

The Governor turned to Trevelyan

'For a ship prize, the allocation is one-eighth for a Flag Officer; two-eighths for Captains; one-eighth amongst Lieutenants, Masters and Surgeons; one-eighth between Principal Warrant Officers and Chaplains; one-eighth between Midshipmen and Warrant Officers; and two eighths for the remainder of the crew.'

Turning back to Peachey the Governor said

'How are we to equate with this tradition then sir?'

'On similar, but generous terms sir. Sir Richard will retain one-eighth, we three will retain two-eighths each, and one-eighth divided amongst Fairweather, Rev Weston and those will feel contributed to its recovery.'

'A most generous settlement sir.'

The Governor suddenly felt the morning had been transformed. His headache had disappeared and his income unexpectedly increased.

Trevelyan took a brief pause before saying

'A double pleasure and no mistake sir. Not only spiking the traitor's purpose but, with a necklace of that value, providing no mean settlement to boot. All in all a good day's work.'

Peachey raised his glass again

'I feel another toast coming on gentlemen.'

Three glasses were raised in unison.

The meeting over, Trevelyan headed towards his uncle's house and Peachey pausing outside prior to returning to *The George*, felt a hand gently tapping his shoulder. Turning, he was a little taken aback to see a woman take back her hand over her presumptuous gaining of his attention.

'I do beg your pardon sir, and hope you are not offended by my approaching you, but I wanted to use this opportunity of speaking to you. You will not be aware of me but I am Mrs. Bishop.'

'Mrs. Bishop?'

'Yes sir, the mother of Polly, the little girl that that beast Mr. Porter ill treated and killed.'

Her voice dropped as she mentioned the last part of the sentence.

'Ah Mrs. Bishop. I am truly sorry that I was not immediately aware of who you were. Allow me to express my deepest sympathies with your loss. What may I do for you?'

'Well sir, in view of your kindness in helping my poor husband who so rashly and mistakenly attacked you, and for your endeavours in tracking down that Mr. Porter, I was wondering if you would do us the honour of accepting a small offering. It's nothing grand I fear, but it would mean much to us.'

'A handsome thought Mrs. Bishop but one I couldn't accept as .... '

'It was something made by Polly' she interjected.

From under her arm she produced a small *sampler* – a piece of embroidery evidently done by a child, but nevertheless worked with care. It was simple, with the words

May God Bless this house and
All those who live here
With love and warmth
Polly Bishop (8 years old)

Peachey was aware of the woman's eyes watching his every move. He studied it for a moment, slightly lost for words, then said

'Mrs. Bishop that is very kind of you. It must mean so much to you that I cannot possibly take it from you.'

The woman looked crestfallen

'But sir we want you to have it. It is what little Polly would have wanted; a gift for a fine Gentleman to receive.'

'Mrs. Bishop, I am greatly touched. I shall therefore be honoured to accept it with a slight amendment. That is, I shall have it specially framed with an inscription on the rear signifying that it was presented to me. I would then wish that it were retained for safe keeping for me in your own house.'

The woman looked a little unsure of the proposal.

Peachey continued

'That will enable me to receive it and for you to have a constant reminder of your late daughter. It will also satisfy your daughter's wish to have it presented to a gentleman.'

She immediately nodded several times,

'Of course sir, that would be wonderful.'

'Very well, then its agreed.'

Taking the *sampler* in his hand he looked around for Fairweather.

Catching Peachey's eye Fairweather moved smartly across to his master.

'Fairweather. I wish you to have this sampler framed suitable for fitting in a Gentlemen's residence. Then have it backed such that I may write on it. It will then be handed back to Mrs. Bishop for retention in her family for as long as I so desire.'

'Yes sir, it will be a pleasure if I may say so. Consider it done.'

Looking back at Mrs. Bishop Peachey said

'I think that is a very suitable outcome, and again I thank you for your precious gift.'

'Sir, I don't know what to say, you are a real Gentleman and no mistake.'

'Believe me Mrs. Bishop I was as desirous of the outcome as much as you. Should you need to speak with me again, see Fairweather and he will inform me.'

Glancing at the waiting Fairweather before looking back at Peachey, she replied

'God bless you sir' and bobbed in respect before departing.

Peachey was strangely touched by that event as he strolled back to the main family group. It was undoubtedly a happy and glorious day. He was reminded of their tutor at Oxford who maintained that in order to witness true happiness, one had to experience near despair.

How true – the events in Portsmouth since his first arrival had certainly shown pain, frustration and unhappiness. It was fitting to savour happier times.

He was also conscious that nothing stands still. Whilst the insidious tentacles of the French in the town had been pruned, not all the rot had been discovered – of this he and his uncle were sure.

Was there still another major spy?

Trevelyan was now to be the mainstay of Peachey's uncle's network in Portsmouth. France may well have been hamstrung over recent events in the town but eradication of support was far from assured. Britain with its sapping military efforts in overcoming the rebellion of the Thirteen Colonies was not the mighty force as defender of the realm it once was.

The Romans had lost their influence by spreading themselves too thinly around the world and exposing themselves on the home front. Could Britain be heading in that direction?

All these questions should be answered on another day he thought. The plotting and treachery in Portsmouth would still continue and in future it would be challenged by one Percy Trevelyan.

One Percy Trevelyan he mused to himself again, almost in astonishment at the realisation of the fact.

The same fine September weather settled itself across southern England and France. Rousseliere was welcomed back to France; his surveys proving a stimulus to the military plan. His promotion from Major to Lieutenant Colonel was an acknowledgement of that fact.

He was however staggered to find that the Compte d'Orvilliers had only just sailed and that the Spanish fleet was apparently still not ready. It was ironic that all the danger that both he and Courtney experienced counted for nought, for even if Courtney had managed to impregnate the well, the timing would not have corresponded with the planned invasion of ships and troops.

One factor that he had been reluctant to expose was that the British troops appeared well cared for, the navy even had its own hospital at Haslar. The people in the cities were not overly taxed, with food in plentiful enough supply - a far cry from France. This is something that the King and his advisors must address or who knows what the outcome might be.

The wind also eddied its way through the Sally Port at Portsmouth, across Governor's Green where it gently swirled the ladies' dresses and veils with graceful movements. Two miles from *Domus Dei,* Jeremiah Porter's left leg swung gently. At the same time his right leg also swung gently, neither leg touching the ground. His limp body dangled at the end of a rope hanging from the yardarm.

Jeremiah Porter, child abuser, murderer and blackmailer had met justice.

Whether it was rightful justice being hanged as a French Spy and not for his actual crime was a topic best left for individual thought. Did the end justify the means?

In London, King George III pursued his plan of sending more troops to the rebellious thirteen states in America with scant acknowledgement of the threat to the country from a combined French and Spanish Armada.

The future of Peachey and Trevelyan couldn't readily be forecast at this juncture, but a continuing future certainly lay before them.

www.ingramcontent.com/pod-product-compliance
Lightning Source LLC
Chambersburg PA
CBHW051503030726
47592CB00006B/2070